IR

BOOKS BY SHERRILYN KENYON

SHADOW FALLEN

SHADOW FALLEN

SHERRILYN KENYON

TOR

A TOM DOHERTY ASSOCIATES BOOK
New York

SHADOW FALLEN

Copyright © 2022 by Sherrilyn McQueen

All rights reserved.

A Tor Book
Published by Tom Doherty Associates
120 Broadway
New York, NY 10271

www.tor-forge.com

Tor® is a registered trademark of Macmillan Publishing Group, LLC.

The Library of Congress Cataloging-in-Publication Data is available upon request.

ISBN 978-1-250-77386-9 (hardcover)
ISBN 978-1-250-14451-5 (ebook)

Our books may be purchased in bulk for promotional, educational, or business use. Please contact your local bookseller or the Macmillan Corporate and Premium Sales Department at 1-800-221-7945, extension 5442, or by email at MacmillanSpecialMarkets@macmillan.com.

First Edition: 2022

Printed in the United States of America

0 9 8 7 6 5 4 3 2 1

*For my fans for faithfully standing by me
during the darkest hours of my life.
I cannot express to any of you how much you mean to me
and how much I deeply appreciate that support.*

*For my true friends who made themselves known:
Sheri, Tish, Kim, Carol, Debbie, Sam, Erin, Nancy, Jacs,
Loretta, Ruth, Jordan, Carl, Pam, Shelli, Jim, and Maria.
God bless and keep you, always. I would never have
made it through this hell without you.*

*And for my sons and daughter
who stood strong by my side and for being fearless
in the face of a madman and his minions
as they sought to destroy us.
You are ever my strength and my heart.
Thank you for knowing the truth from the lies.*

*And lastly, to my grand turtle.
You are my newfound joy.
I hope your life is always as precious
and sweet as you are!*

SHADOW
FALLEN

But life had a way of taking him places he never intended to go. And against all sanity, he'd allowed his brother to talk him into this quest for a crown that no one needed.

Indeed, such power came at an unbearable cost. In terms of life and the noose it placed around the victor's neck. William might rule England, but there was never any peace for a man in royal robes.

"Help me, Val." Valteri grimaced at the memory of Will's words and his older brother's pleading eyes when William had come to him at the tourney in Ressons-sur-Matz. *"We're family."*

He'd scoffed at his half brother's sentimentality. *"I'm a bastard by birth and temperament, Will. I've no need of any family, even you. Take your titles and shove them up your arse."*

Unlike his sibling, his parents and grandparents had cast him off at the moment of his birth and judged him cursed, as he'd survived while his older twin brother had been stillborn. Refusing to even look after him, they'd sent him to England so that none of them would ever have to suffer the embarrassment of seeing his despised countenance again.

As if his twin's death had been his fault.

Not one word from any of them for the whole of his life.

Only William had ever laid any claim and then, only when he needed something . . .

It had infuriated him. Had William not been such a high-ranking noble and had they not been standing in France, surrounded by Will's allies, he'd have run him through just for uttering those stupid words.

Brother . . .

But while he was suicidal, he had no desire to be tortured another second before his enemies finally ended his miserable life. He'd suffered more than enough abuse. There was no need to purposefully add more.

Rather than be offended by his hostility, Will had smirked at him. *"You owe me."*

Valteri had scoffed. *"What I owed, I paid back long ago with my sword arm."*

"Then do this for the only thing you seem to love. Money. Win my kingdom for me and I shall reward you with enough coin that you'll never again want for anything. Your reputation is such that I know half the country will surrender the minute they see your banner among my army."

That, too, had galled him.

But his brother was right. Men were terrified of him and money was all Valteri cared about. Unlike people, coin didn't turn against the one who held it. It didn't plot or lie.

Or abandon those who depended on it.

While it could be stolen, given, or taken, it didn't voluntarily leave.

It was the only thing he put his faith in. The only thing on this earth that he could trust.

Aside from his sword arm.

And his horse.

In thirty-three years, those were the only things in his life that had never once betrayed him. Though to be honest, his horse had thrown him a time or two.

But he preferred to think it was due to his own incompetence and not any intentional malice on his horse's part. Otherwise, he'd have to hold a few of his sword breaks in battle against his sword, and that just seemed a bit paranoid, even for him.

Maybe William is finally going to pay you.

"He better damn well do it. And soon." His patience was thin and Will had taken it to a breaking point.

Tossing his blond hair from his eyes, he reached for the tent flap.

William's messenger stood outside, waiting. A frightened man, who paled considerably more when he faced him.

At least this one didn't wet himself. He should be grateful he wouldn't have to traverse a despicable puddle to speak with the runt. They were getting better forewarned about his appearance, he supposed.

Or better trained, at least.

Still disgusted by the lack of backbone, Valteri growled as bitterness burned raw in his gullet. He was used to people's reactions to him—used to the stark terror shimmering in their eyes as if they feared for their immortal souls whenever they met his gaze.

Like he ever had any use for anyone's soul, including his own.

"I pray that, unlike your predecessor who was here two days ago, you've come to tell me my brother sends my pay." His voice was gruff even to his own ears.

One would think his bastard brother would have more important things to occupy himself with, such as torturing other lords and nobles, and taking over this godforsaken country, than harassing him all the time. He still couldn't understand why William had wanted this hellhole to begin with. It was colder than shit and forever gray and dull.

Rained all the bloody damn time.

Personally, he'd be glad to never see it again. Made no sense to him that William would fight tooth and nail to conquer and keep it.

The messenger actually gasped aloud as he glanced up and noted Valteri's mismatched eyes—as did most who first saw them and thought it a mark of the devil.

Which had served Valteri well on the field of battle.

Off the field, not so much.

The youth crossed himself, frantically.

Valteri smirked. "Trust me, your God can't help you. Nor will He save your soul. Or spare your life from me if you continue trying my patience." He made his voice as ominous and evil as possible.

Thankfully, the bastard held his bowels, but he did wet himself after all, which caused Valteri to have to step back two paces.

Panting and nervous, the man gulped audibly. "H-H-His M-M-M . . ."

"Majesty," Valteri finished for him before they both grew old waiting for the man to get his words out.

"Majesty, the king, sends t-t-this for you, m-m-milord." He extended a bound piece of parchment.

It shook so badly, he was surprised the messenger kept his grip.

Well, that's certainly not the gold Will promised me.

Sighing heavily, Valteri took it from his hands before the messenger dropped it in his piss, and broke the seal. Curiosity riding him hard about his brother's lunatic mind, he scanned the contents.

And with every word he read, his mood darkened.

What the hell was this shite? William had given him lordship of Ravenswood Hall, the demesne lands, and all outlying territories?

His brother wanted to reward him for his service *with lands*?

And titles?

Was Will out of his fucking gourd?

By hell's thorny toes, I'll kill the bastard for this! How dare he!

Grinding his teeth, Valteri tightened his grip on the letter. He looked at the messenger, his breathing ragged. "Tell William I'll take care of his rebellion as requested, but I want him to find a permanent castellan for the hall and lands. I have no use for such. He was to pay me in coin, not land, and I expect gold." The last thing he needed or wanted was a bunch of hysterical peasants and others running about, trying to tie him to something and set fire to it again because they thought him possessed.

Fuck that.

The messenger nodded furiously. "Aye, milord. I shall tell him forthwith."

"Do that." Valteri ground his teeth at his brother's lunacy. What was the man thinking? He'd served him well. Given him unquestioning loyalty. Why then would William curse him so?

Make him a lord?

How dare he!

"Bloody bastard," he snarled as he entered the tent, unsure of whom he intended the insult for, himself or William. Especially since it applied to them both from birth and bearing.

Give me lands . . .

He'd like to give his brother a slap to his face.

As if Will didn't know those lands came with an idiot priest and other imbeciles who would decry his godless nature and a birth defect caused by his whoring mother's sins.

Valteri ground his teeth at the bloody memories that tore through him of a childhood no one should suffer. He'd never again be bound to one place.

Bound to any person.

Not for anything or for anyone.

He reached for his sword.

"Who leads this army?"

Valteri whirled at the sound of his dream's voice coming as a whisper in the corner.

No one was there.

Yet it had been real. Not in his mind.

Had it not?

"Mayhap I'm the one going mad, after all." Who could blame him when old memories constantly assaulted him here?

Valteri loosened his hold on the sword and took a deep breath as he tried to put it from his mind. Though it was getting harder and harder to do so.

Ever since he'd landed at Hastings with William, he'd been haunted by the dream of a fair maiden coming for his soul.

Not that he had one. He was sure it'd been kicked out of him long ago by the monks who'd been hell-bent on saving it.

Still, he could feel her, even now, as if she were here beside him.

Grunting at the stupidity, he realized it was more than likely a warning of his imminent demise. Maybe she was the shadow of death finally come to take him from this rotten earth. His portent, as it were.

Good.

Because if it were true, then he would welcome the moment and the peace it brought with open arms.

CHAPTER 1

I curse you for what you've done! For your inability to feel pity or remorse, I curse you to know unfathomable pain. Without mercy! Without cessation! You will suffer as no creature has *ever* suffered!"

Ariel screamed in bitter agony. Those words twisted in her mind like a serpent, twining about her arms and legs, making them heavy. Unbearable. A foreign weight dragged her from the heavens in a violent whirlwind, down toward the mortal plane.

It felt like the hand of a god, tearing her from the skies.

She reached out, trying to stop her fall, but only contacted with rushing air that bathed her body in a strange pelting storm. The savage winds whipped at her hair, her wings, and howled in her ears like vicious hellhounds, ripping the souls of the damned from her side.

What was happening?

None of this made sense. Every part of her ached and pulsed in waves of crashing sensation. She was a Naṣāru—an elite Arel who was born into her position. A resolute warrior whose calling was to stay far from the mortal realm, where their licentiousness could tempt her, except for those brief moments when she was commanded to find dead warriors to return to life so that they could fight in earthly battles that were denied to her species.

Her job was to protect the order of the universe. To defend the primal forces. She was not to know pain.

That was for mortals to bear.

Yet pain ripped down her spine, and took the breath from a body that needed no breath, made a chest heave that should not heave, a stomach churn that had never churned before.

Blackness surrounded her in a swirling funnel. Deprived of her sight and hearing, Ariel reached out with her other senses, trying to find some kind of answer for this. A mixture of odors assailed her—the charred stench of fear, the sulfur of hell, and worse, the bittersweet smell of human flesh.

Before, all these had been muted to her. Now they assaulted her in a pungent bouquet that almost overwhelmed her with a primitive vitality that didn't belong to her world, or understanding.

For good reason. To expose a Naṣāru to such could taint them, and should they turn . . .

There was no power to stop them. They were the fiercest of warriors, who were virtually invincible.

It made them a prize for the dark powers and it was why they were never to venture to this realm.

Suddenly, she slammed against a cold, hard ground, her body throbbing in a way she couldn't fathom.

What had happened to her?

Fury tore through her as she looked about, trying to make sense of it.

The buzzing in her ears gave way to the gentle call of birds frolicking in the forest. But the sound soon dulled until all she could hear was an occasional bird's cry, and the rustle of a breeze through bright late-autumn leaves. Even her heartbeat faded until she could no longer hear it.

Ariel pushed herself up, but quickly fell again, her limbs shaking with unfamiliar heaviness. Her pale hair tumbled around her shoulders, hanging in her face. She tried to breathe through the heavy weight, but her breath caught in the strands suffocating her.

What the hell was this?

Suddenly, a hand snatched back the mass of hair.

Ariel looked up into the face of hatred and she knew the source of her fate. She'd seen this sorceress before. "What have you done to me?" Her throat stung from the use of vocal cords that hadn't existed ten minutes ago.

The old, withered woman glared at her with dark, hate-filled eyes. "You stole from me my most precious possession. I begged you for mercy and still you took my son. 'Tis time you learned what it means to have your heart torn from your breast!"

That unfamiliar rage coursed through her, even more ferociously this time. Never had she known the like. Ariel was a creature of the highest source and they weren't supposed to lose their temper.

To hate.

Yet her body responded to the woman's presence with a burning fury that made her yearn for retaliation. She wanted to hurt her.

More than that, she wanted . . .

What?

She didn't understand the bitter, awful feeling. Nor did she like it.

"Return me to my place!"

The old woman's laugh echoed around her, into the trees of the forest surrounding them. "I cannot undo my spell. Only *you* can."

"What do you mean?" Ariel stared at her in utter disbelief. "I can't stay here." She knew nothing of survival in *their* world.

People *died* here!

A prayer came to her lips, but she knew that wouldn't help. Free will gave all beings sovereignty over their existence, and unless it interfered with matters of life and death, nature, even evil nature, was given its due course.

Damn them all for it!

This wasn't her realm. Her kind couldn't survive in this hideous place where men ate their own.

Even their young.

It was forbidden! Not to mention the fact that she didn't *want* to be here.

Among *them*. Petty creatures like the crone before her, who cared nothing for anyone other than themselves. They lived to sow strife and pain.

Truly, she loathed them all.

Looking up at the clear gray sky above them, Ariel knew she must return to her domain before the taint of mortalness damaged her eternally and left its stink upon her.

Turned her into the pitiless crone before her and made her every bit as cold and unfeeling.

"What must I do?" Ariel asked in desperation.

The smile that curved the crone's lips sent a shiver down her spine. "You must do as I did with my son. You must love with all your heart, then watch what you love most die horribly and in pain. Hold him in your arms while he struggles for life, and cry in misery as you're helpless to stop the angel that comes to steal his soul after he draws that final breath. Only then will you be free."

Are you serious? She was being punished for doing her job?

Ariel shook her head in denial. "I grieve for your loss, but I have no choice about whom I take from this world. I'm given orders that I have to follow."

Whenever a particularly skilled warrior died, the Naşaru were sent after them to recruit them to their ranks as a nekoda. It was a noble calling for her son. But she wasn't allowed to tell that to the crone.

The old woman laughed bitterly. "And now you dance to *my* command." As she walked a small circle around her, dried, fallen leaves dragged crisply under the full ragged hem of her skirt. "I know you don't understand grief. You're not capable of it. But you will, little reaper. *You will!*"

Then she was gone.

Ariel looked around the forest. No trace remained of the woman. If she could dream, she'd blame it on that, but she never slept. Nor did she feel stiff, dry grass beneath her hands, the cool breath of air on her cheeks, nor the heat of the sun on human skin.

Yet she felt those things now, and by that she knew this was real. A true waking nightmare!

"You can't leave me here!" She couldn't be found by her enemies! An Arel alone was a dead one. . . .

On trembling limbs, she pushed herself up.

Lifting her arms above her head, she commanded herself to rise. To fly. What had always come so effortlessly refused to obey her now.

Her golden wings were gone.

I'm mortal. That terrifying thought shot through her mind with a dizzying fright that spun her head and brought tears to her eyes.

How could this be?

She couldn't fall in love. It wasn't possible. That didn't happen to creatures like her. They were never to be so tainted.

"Surrender yourself to the curse. It'll be easier if you do."

Her heart pounding, she spun around at the words and faced a white wolf. Its eyes glowed red.

A demon.

Of course, it would be. What else would stalk her here in this realm?

Those evil little trolls were ever about to tempt and torment those who lived here. But she wasn't so stupid, and she'd never fall for their tricks.

She would never forsake her oath or her station.

"Leave me in peace. I've no use for you."

It moved forward. With each step, its form changed until it became a winged shadow creature. One that smelled as foul as its deeds. Only the glowing red eyes remained the same. "You are no longer in my world. Or yours. You are in *their* world. They will fear you. Beat you. Destroy you. Then where will you be?"

Ariel lifted her chin with a confidence she didn't feel. "If they kill me here, I'll return to where I belong. If I surrender myself to the curse, you'll drag me to your master. I don't belong to your infernal prison, and I refuse to damn myself. You'll *never* own any part of me."

Too many of her kind had fallen to them. She refused to become a member of the Irin. To be marked and hunted by her own brethren while she fought for the dark lords who would abuse her for their own sick amusement.

That wasn't her way. She would never succumb. Not for anything.

His evil laugh rang out. He touched her chin with his icy, chafed fingers. The coldness burned her skin, causing her to flinch. "My master will give me much for the soul of a Naṣāru warrior, especially one who serves Michael. Come, pet, be nice and sacrifice yourself for me. I promise you a cooler spot to bathe in if you surrender now."

She glared at him, her new body trembling in fear and fury over his offer.

Belial.

The name flashed through her mind and she realized some of her powers still remained. But not enough to combat this particular demon, who delighted in mischief and discord, whose evil power was second only to that of Kadar, the king of all evil.

A cold tremor of panic swept through her.

She clenched her shaking hands together, knowing her fear gave him strength.

And that, too, she would never do.

Standing strong, she glared at him. "I deny your call. Leave me and return to your hole where you kneel in servitude."

His eyes flashed, radiating heat and malice. "You will be mine, fair one. And I will gladly serve you to my master." He curled his shadowed form up into a ball and drifted around her head. The rancid odor of burning flesh and sulfur choked her. "How long can you remain true to your cause now that you're corrupted by human flesh and emotion?"

She opened her mouth to deny him, but as soon as she did, the demon encompassed her head, choking her with its stench. The black thickness filled her body.

Ariel fought for breath. Her lungs burning, she fell to her knees.

Still the demon remained inside her, blotting her thoughts, her will.

"You'll be ours, Naṣāru." Belial laughed. "And with you, I will earn my freedom and burn this fucking world to the ground!"

CHAPTER 2

Disgusted that he was still here and had yet to be relieved of his station by his idiot brother, Valteri watched his men training in the list. The sound of clashing steel rang in his ears, making him yearn to leave this place far behind and yield to the familiar call of battle and war.

To what he knew best.

Blood. Gore. Entrails of his enemies on the ground at his feet.

That was home.

Not this rancid country he hated so much.

Battle was his mother. It was the only thing that had ever succored him.

But could he leave?

Nay.

Damn you, Will!

Months had gone by, and he was still trapped here. If he took off without permission, Will would see him hunted down like a dog. And while he was strong, not even he could fight off an entire army without help.

So here he remained.

Because he'd been stupid enough to believe, for one heartbeat, that family mattered.

What he should have remembered was that there was no worse fate for one such as he than domesticity.

No one could cage a wild animal. The beast inside him was salivating for freedom. It was snarling and howling more and more with every dawning sun, until he feared he'd go mad from the rage of being held back from the only comfort he knew.

Even though he'd routed the Saxon rebels as he'd promised his brother, and sent them to London, where they'd met their final fate under the executioner's ax, William still refused to grant him a reprieve.

Now, he wished he'd been the one who'd lost his head.

Instead, Valteri was losing his mind. Bit by bit. Day by day. Especially since there were no rebels left to chase now. No scapegoats to vent his fury.

What few remained hid themselves from his wrath and sword, and for the last few weeks, peace had reigned in the valley of Ravenswood.

Damn it to hell.

Valteri despised peace with everything he had. The extra time it brought—time to think.

To remember a life that had begrudged him every breath he'd ever taken.

As if living, itself, wasn't hell enough. Unlike the men and women around him, he had no purpose in this world.

Other than to make everyone who met him uncomfortable, and to fill their hearts with hatred toward him for doing nothing more than existing.

No one could so much as look at him without cringing or insulting him. With the exception of battle, he was unwelcomed everywhere he went.

Indeed, a leper was treated more humanely. At least with them, they were pitied.

He was demonspawn. Unworthy of anything except their scorn at worst and their avoidance at best.

For God's sake, Will, let me go. He needed to find another war with which to occupy himself so that he had no time for thought, but William steadfastly refused to free him from his duties.

Bloody bastard.

"Milord?"

Valteri turned away from his men to see his squire running toward him. Barely tall enough to reach his shoulder, the dark-haired youth was fair enough in form to make several maids giggle as he passed them. Lucky for him and even luckier for Wace, the boy had no idea the fairer sex found him so appealing.

Yet.

Pity the poor fool the day Wace realized they were watching him with such interest.

All too soon, some lass would no doubt try and trap the boy with her wiles. Then his life would be an even bigger hell than it'd been when Valteri had found him.

Breathless, Wace reached his side. The blush of youthful exuberance covered his cheeks, mottling them to a bright pink that made his blue eyes all the brighter.

Valteri couldn't remember ever feeling that excited about anything.

Not even his first battle.

'Course, he'd been praying the whole time for a fatal blow to end this miserable hell known as life.

Lucky him, he'd not only survived the ordeal, he'd been one of the heroes of the day. Praised for the fact that he'd fought bravely while the others who'd wanted to live had scampered away, trying to save their measly hides.

What irony that.

Sighing, he eyed his huffing squire. "Kitchen on fire?"

Winded, his squire bent over and wheezed. It took several deep breaths before Wace could finally respond. "The men you sent out scouting have returned. They found a woman in a field."

So? 'Twas England. A shepherdess with her flock was as common as the dull, gray sky overhead. No one could pass a field anywhere on this miserable isle they didn't spot a dozen such creatures. Why that would warrant a breathless, galloping squire, he couldn't imagine.

Confused, Valteri scowled. "And a wench causes you to pant at—"

"Nay, milord. 'Tis no wench, but a lady!"

His frown deepened. That *was* a different tale. He couldn't imagine a lady soiling her precious shoes with cow shit. "Where's she from?"

"They know not, milord. Hence why they sent me to fetch you."

What fresh madness was this?

Why bother him with a woman? Even a noble one?

He sighed heavily at the aggravation.

Judas's hairy toes. His men were getting more incompetent every day.

He'd been right. Peace robbed a warrior of all sense.

Irritated by the interruption, Valteri ground his teeth and glared at his squire, who was never afraid of him for some insane reason.

Imbeciles, all. Could they not even take care of a simple lost woman without his direct supervision? Seriously? Were they really *that* afraid of him?

Growling deep in his throat, he headed toward the hall with Wace following after him like a dutiful puppy.

And as he walked, he couldn't help wondering how his brother had ever managed to conquer England with the fools who fought in his army. Surely they could return one simple maid home to her family without disturbing him.

Was that really so much to ask?

After all, dealing with the fairer sex was not something he had much experience with, or tolerance for. Last thing he wanted was to hear her shrieking when she laid eyes upon him. Crossing herself like a frantic nun facing the devil.

Damning him for a birth he cursed as much as they did.

These scurrying wretches he passed on his way to the hall were bad enough, but at least they couldn't look directly at him, as they feared a beating for it, given that they were servants and he their "noble-born" lord.

As if he'd ever done such to them or anyone else. But their cruelty to people like him was enough that they knew what they deserved, so they feared his retaliation now that he was grown and large enough to give back to them what they'd so unkindly given to him when he was a defenseless boy.

Which meant these creatures withheld their insults and scurried like roaches at his approach. And waited until after he'd passed them before they began crossing themselves, and whispering their rumors about his diabolical origins.

Noblewomen were never so kind or restrained.

Nay, they insulted him to his face.

He had yet to meet one he didn't want to murder where she stood. He was certain this one would be no different.

Seething, Valteri pushed open the heavy wooden door of the hall and was met with the sickening odor of baking bread. His lip curling with disgust, he felt his stomach pitch at the stench of it. How he hated manors and castles, and everything they entailed. He'd spent too many years of his life inside places such as this, listening to the echoes of foul rumors that resounded off the whitewashed walls.

He wanted out of this damnable place! He was a warrior, not a lord. And no matter what William thought, he would never be tamed or saddled.

As Valteri approached the group of men gathered in the center of the hall, they shrank back in fear of his approach, reminding him of a group of cringing magpies.

Until he saw the lady, lying in their midst on a bench where the others must have placed her.

His anger dissipated instantly.

For the first time in years, Valteri hesitated. Deep, dark red cloth hugged the woman's voluptuous body, spilling onto the floor like a puddle of blood as the sunlight cut across her features and highlighted them. Her flaxen hair lay atop part of the kirtle, its paleness contrasted by the dress's richness. Never before had he seen a kirtle made in such a shade, nor hair the color of hers. They were so vibrant that they appeared to be living entities all their own.

A golden cross lay in the hollow of her throat, pulsing with each beat of her heart. Its shape glinted in the dying sunlight that still illuminated the room.

His hands suddenly clammy, Valteri wondered at the way his heart raced. He was far from the days of a callow youth, yet that was what he felt like as he stared at her. There was something about her that seemed ethereal. Untouchable. Like the first time he'd been alone with a woman.

He was as nervous now as he'd been for that first paid-for kiss. And that truly infuriated him.

What kind of fool am I?

Granted, it'd been the better part of five years or more since he'd last seen a noblewoman, but still . . . He shouldn't be *this* nervous.

You're just not used to seeing a woman not mired in pig shit and dressed in rags.

Aye, it was nothing more than that.

Wanting to prove it, he reached out and gently turned her face toward him.

The sight of her features struck him like a blow. She was stunning. Flawless. And he knew every line of those high cheekbones and that alabaster skin.

'Twas the face that haunted him from his dreams.

Gasping, he took a step back, releasing her. For once, *he* felt the need to cross himself, and he didn't believe in such stupidity.

How can this be?

Sweat broke out on his forehead. Could he have conjured her? Was this some trick of the light?

A low gasp escaped her lips as her chest rose with a deep breath. His men stepped back in unison, some crossing themselves as if they feared her as much as they feared him.

That finally broke through his mental fog.

Superstitious fools!

Regaining control of himself and forcing away his initial shock, Valteri scoffed at their ridiculousness.

And his own. She was a woman.

Plain and simple.

No more. No less. How she'd infiltrated his dreams, he didn't know, but he refused to believe for one moment that she had any more supernatural power than he did.

Indeed, too many years of people crossing themselves whenever they looked upon him had left him skeptical over the presence of demons and witches. Warlocks and elves, and other such nonsense.

He believed in nothing save his own sword arm.

Had there ever been a God, He'd abandoned him long ago. And so Valteri had chosen to return the favor.

Her long, dark lashes fluttered open, displaying a beautiful pair of deep blue eyes. Aye, the wench was as lovely as any he'd ever seen, and he could imagine how angry her lord must be over her loss. No doubt he was frantically searching everywhere for her.

A frown creased her brow and she sat up, rubbing her forehead as if an ache beat inside her skull. "Where am I?"

His body inflamed by the sound of her rich voice speaking flawless Norman French, Valteri stared at her. How had a Norman lady come to be stranded in the middle of Saxon lands?

And she was no doubt a lady. Her dress and manner could never belong to serf or merchant.

"You are in Ravenswood Hall, milady." He waited for her to look at him and cringe in terror. It was what everyone did the first time they saw his mismatched eyes.

Most recoiled in horror. Some had held their hands up to shield themselves, as if terrified his very gaze upon them would mark them for the devil or cause them to burst into flames.

Others had spat at him. Insulted him and his parents. Truly, he couldn't catalogue all the abuse he'd taken in his life for one accident of birth.

But instead, she turned toward him and met his gaze unflinchingly. "Do I know this place?"

It was his turn to frown. "Do you not know yourself?"

"Aye. I'm Ariel."

"Then why did you ask—"

"But, I can't remember aught else." To his surprise, the terror in her eyes was not directed at him, but at some inner turmoil as she glanced about, then down at the floor. "There was a shadow. . . ." She looked up at him with a sad, vulnerable gaze, and a wave of protectiveness blasted away all the layers of hardness he'd erected around his heart. "A smelly shadow . . ."

Angered over the unexpected sensation, Valteri took another step back, unsure of himself.

Worse? He actually wanted to touch her.

No good could come of *that*. A woman such as this had a lord looking for her, no doubt. She belonged to her husband—was his most valuable property.

Given the curse that had been levied upon him on his birth, he knew better than to lay a single hand to her. There was no telling what her lord would do if he dared such an affront, and while he had no fear of any man, he didn't want to start a war with his brother over some random woman.

He had enough problems in his life. There was no need in adding *that*.

Nay, he had to find her husband and remove her from here posthaste, before any more unfounded rumors began to spread.

"Is this my home? Are you my husband?" she whispered to him.

That unexpected question tore through him like a lance. For a moment, Valteri wished he could answer aye.

And what an odd thing that was. Never in his entire life had he ever wanted an attachment of any sort, especially not to a woman. He couldn't imagine why he'd even think of wanting one now.

"Nay, milady. You were found in a field."

More confused sadness darkened her eyes, and he wondered what memories plagued her.

Not that it mattered. She was no concern of his, and he had to make sure it stayed that way.

Valteri turned, calling to one of the serving women who watched on from the shadows. "Take the lady to my room and attend her needs." He spoke in English so that she could understand him.

The crone nodded and moved to help Ariel rise.

Ariel looked at the woman and her face blanched. Like a cat, she hissed and recoiled from her.

Valteri had no time to process her actions before she scrambled from the bench and grabbed at his waist. Before he could react, she pulled his sword from the sheath at his side and stepped back.

Even more shockingly, she went after the old woman.

No one had ever dared touch him, not even when he was a child. That was startling enough. But what truly floored him was the skill she showed as she lunged at the crone with deadly intent.

He barely disarmed her before she sliced the old woman in twain. "What is wrong with you, milady?"

Her nostrils flaring, she tried to take the sword from his hand. "She means me harm!"

Her entire body shook, and beneath her fury, he saw panicked terror there. She believed what she said.

To his shock, she took his arm in her hands as he continued to hold his sword away from her. "Please, you must listen. She's death!"

He'd never had a woman touch him in such a manner and he found it deeply disturbing.

"Why does she frighten you?" He looked from the top of her pale head to the face of the old crone, who appeared every bit as baffled as he was.

And yet . . .

He wouldn't be so quick to judge. Not after all he'd seen and experienced. Too well, he knew the dual nature of people. How they could be loving and kind to those around them, and then lash out without mercy against innocent children.

Boys like him.

Kindhearted boys like Wace, who'd never done anything except try to please them.

For no reason whatsoever.

It was enough to drive anyone to violence.

Anyone to madness.

There had been a time when he'd been an innocent child who'd wanted nothing more than a mother's love. A boy who had only wanted peace.

All he'd been given was pain and condemnation. Until he'd learned to strike the first blow and protect himself from their cruelty.

Nay, he wouldn't judge this woman. Not until he knew all the facts.

More importantly, all the players.

"I may not remember myself, but I remember *her*! She wants me dead!"

The crone appeared so eerily calm and innocent that it set off his hackles. How could she remain such given the vicious attack that she'd almost suffered? The open hostility of a noblewoman who could order her death for no reason whatsoever?

That told him much, as he'd seen monsters like the crone in his past. Those who preyed on others and then played the innocent victim after they'd pushed their target too far.

"Nay, lord, I prithee for mercy. I would never harm her ladyship." The crone spoke in English, letting him know that somehow she'd learned French enough to understand it, but not respond in it.

Ariel stiffened. "There's nothing wrong with my mind! I can't explain my feelings. But I know she means me harm. I know it!"

"I could *never* harm so fair an angel."

Ariel scowled. "Angel," she whispered. She looked up at him and all the agony in her eyes tore through him. "There's something . . ." Her voice trailed off, and her eyes glazed as if she drifted back into her past.

"It's all right." Valteri resheathed his sword. "I've seen a number of men fall during battle after receiving a blow to the head. Many times they lose their sense for a brief time, but it always returns."

The lady had probably been riding and thrown from her horse. Or mayhap someone had been chasing her. It would explain why she had no escort or mount.

When she fell, she must have hit her head and rattled her brain.

He looked at the crone, his gaze stern. "Until milady remembers herself, I want you to stay away from her."

The crone nodded and withdrew.

Valteri turned to Ariel and held his hand out for her to take it. "Come, milady, I'll show you to your room."

Her warm, soft hand enclosed the emptiness of his palm, soothing his rough calluses. She looked at him as if he were her savior, something no one had ever done before, and it did unimaginable things to him.

Kindness and desire were alien concepts for someone like him. Tenderness even more so.

And that expression on her face . . .

Valteri knew better than to imagine the thoughts that suddenly leapt into his mind. Thoughts of her supple body in his arms while he kissed those perfect lips, and lost himself to her warmth. Aye, those images were raw and they left a biting hunger in his soul that made him crave an ice-cold bath.

It was all kinds of wrong, and he knew it.

He closed his eyes and released her hand as his breathing turned ragged. He had to banish any such thoughts.

She was a decent lady and he was a monster. Whatever he did, he must always remember that.

He belonged on a battlefield. She needed to return to her husband and the comforts of a welcoming home.

Leading Ariel past the raised table, he entered the small foyer and pushed open a door. He stepped back, waiting for her to enter his chambers.

She looked up at him with a shy smile that sent even more blood to his nether regions.

Damn them both for it.

Valteri clenched his teeth. How could he burn so for something he could never have? The monks were right. He was damned and cursed. There was no other reason for her to be here, tempting him like this.

Something, somewhere, surely hated his guts.

Without a word, she walked into his room—because the image of her in his chambers helped the fire in his loins not even a little bit.

She wandered around, touching various items as if she'd never seen such a place before.

How strange . . .

Because he traveled so much, he kept very little for himself. Especially since he was so eager to leave this world, there was no need to collect anything more than the bare necessities he needed to survive. A razor and strop. Comb. An extra buckle. Truly the only thing remarkable about his belongings was the fact that they were so common and so few.

Yet she picked up his buckle to finger it, then placed it back beside his comb before she stared at it curiously.

Where had she come from to be so enthralled over his meager items?

When she stepped to the window, she gave a small squeak. "Oh my!" There was a hint of laughter in her voice. "What are you doing out there?"

Scowling, Valteri moved forward to see what had captured her attention.

Who was she talking to?

Again, he doubted her sanity.

Until she reached outside his window to grab a tiny black mass of recognizable fur that wasn't supposed to be there.

"Come inside, little one," she said softly. "'Tis a chill in the air I'm sure you don't need."

Valteri paused as she turned around with his kitten held tenderly in her arms. He stared in awe of her gentle hands stroking the soft black fur while Cecile nuzzled against her shoulder.

He was ever at a loss with that poor animal that had much more curiosity than sense. To this day, he wasn't sure if the bag he'd found her in on the side of the road was something she'd climbed into by accident, or if someone had put her in it in an effort to kill her.

All he'd known was that she'd been on the brink of starvation and her pitiful cries had touched him as he struggled to bring her here and see her fed and in much better health. He still bore scars on his hand where the terrified thing had clawed him in terror, until she realized that he meant her no harm.

Valteri moved to stand closer to Ariel. Mayhap a little too close given the licentious thoughts in his mind where she was concerned. "Are you not afraid?" Most people shied away from the wee beastie as if it were as cursed as he was.

Ariel looked up at him with a frown. "Afraid of a little kitten? Nay, why should I be?"

He just stared at her. Ever since he'd saved the tiny cockeyed creature, everyone had run from his unorthodox pet in fear and suspicion. Many had called her his familiar and swore that it was proof he was the devil's son.

Ariel kissed the kitten and stroked its ears. "Do you have a name?"

"Cecile."

"What a peculiar name for a cat."

He shrugged. "I've always had a fondness for it." Though why, he couldn't say. "And she doesn't seem to mind it."

Ariel smiled and once more he felt his control wane under the beauty of her features, the happy glint beneath the sapphire hue. When she looked back at him, his stomach wrenched as if someone had struck a fierce blow just below his heart. "And what of you, milord. Do you have a name?"

"Valteri." He waited for the familiar mockery to darken her gaze, given that he was named for a demon lord. One who was known for his ferocity and command of legions of demons. The brothers in the monastery where he'd been tortured as a boy had proclaimed that his namesake had begun every day by eating the entrails of unbaptized infants.

Why his mother had chosen to name him such, he could only imagine.

Her smile widened. "It suits you."

His gut twisted. Her face may not show it, but she did mock him and his cursed looks. Why else would she say such a thing?

With a gasp, she set Cecile on the bed, then took a step forward with her hand raised as if to touch him. "I meant no offense to you, milord."

He moved away from her reach, his lips curled. "You cannot offend me, milady. 'Twould seem fate itself has already done so."

And his bitchtress mother when she'd saddled him with a moniker that was second only to Lucifer's when it came to unholy deeds that were used to frighten small children and make grown men tremble.

His anger raging inside, he turned around and left her, taking care to slam the door behind him to vent some of his fury before he abused a more sentient creature. He was done with this world.

Damn them all.

And damn God above for giving him eyes of two different colors to be feared by everyone who looked upon him.

Ariel stepped forward, then stopped as Cecile meowed. She looked to the kitten. "You think I should leave him alone?"

Cecile cocked her head slightly before she rushed from the bed and collided with the small chest under the window.

Deciding Cecile might be right about Valteri and his mood, Ariel picked the kitten up and helped her find her food bowl.

The poor little creature's eyes were so badly crossed, it couldn't walk straight.

Stroking the kitten's neck, she watched Cecile eat the carefully cubed meat left on the floor. What a pair the two of them made—Cecile couldn't find what she needed any more than Ariel could.

She sighed in complete frustration. Why couldn't she remember anything? She knew her name. How to talk . . . how to do everything except recall her past.

How can I not know who am I?

Where had she come from?

How had she gotten here?

Why was she alone?

Nothing made sense, and honestly, it was terrifying.

The fleeting images that kept passing before her eyes were impossible. She saw hundreds of strange people and places that seemed completely unrelated, and yet how could that be?

Some of them didn't even appear to be of this earth.

"Why do I know how to use a sword?"

She could make no sense of it. Still, she knew deep inside that if she could just find her way back to her memory it would all make sense again. She would know who she was and why she was here.

Why she had such disturbing images and thoughts . . .

After finishing her meal, Cecile set about cleaning herself.

Unable to rest while she was so confused and unsure, Ariel pushed herself up from the floor and walked to the window, where she saw Valteri crossing the yard, dressed in his chain mail and black surcoat emblazoned with a per bar sinister argent and gules and a lion salient or—his coat of arms. The lion and colors seemed highly fitting for such a proud warrior.

Yet he stood out from the other knights around him. And not just because he chose to wear his blond hair long while theirs was sheared to their ears.

It was his air of barely leashed fury that set him apart. That aura that said he was one step away from gutting anyone who came near him. His rage was so potent that it sizzled in the air around him, letting everyone know that he was like a caged beast, ready to attack.

He was ferocious and wild. A creature of absolute beauty, who stood a full head taller than those around him. His features were finely carved as if by a master sculptor. Never had she seen a better-looking man. Nor one who bled such a contradiction of violence and compassion.

She smiled at his confident stride, then looked back at Cecile. A cross-eyed kitten was a peculiar companion for such a fierce warrior. Yet somehow it suited him.

A strange warmth flooded her breast at the mere thought of Valteri. When she'd first opened her eyes and seen his concern, she'd been certain that she belonged to him. That this was her home.

Even now, she had a strange sense of belonging here.

To him.

And she couldn't explain it.

But she definitely understood wanting *him*. He was the most spectacular man she'd ever beheld. His long, white-blond hair reminded her of the brightest snow-covered field.

And his eyes . . .

One the bright green of the deepest sea. The other, the rich brown of ground cinnamon. While they were a bit disconcerting at first, they were so unusual as to be absolutely riveting. Haunting in their complete opposition to one another and each one filled with intelligence and torment.

They reminded her of someone. . . .

Closing her eyes, she struggled to remember who. In the back of her mind was a tiny nugget of a memory.

Of another man.

One who was extremely familiar to her, and Valteri reminded her of this shadow man.

She growled in frustration. The memory was so close and yet so vague. "Why can't I recall this?"

But all she saw was darkness. And a faint tinge of . . .

The sensation was gone.

Ariel sighed wearily. "Who are you?"

Was that man family?

Or foe?

Was he responsible for her being here?

A knock sounded on the door, startling her.

"Enter." Clearing her throat, she quickly pushed those thoughts away.

Slowly, the door opened to reveal a youth around the age of fifteen summers with short dark hair and a beaming smile. He shifted the platter in his arms and kicked the door closed with his foot. "Good day, milady."

She returned his smile. "Good day, my young lord."

As he neared her, the platter tilted dangerously to the left.

With a gasp, Ariel helped him to right it before all the dishes spilled to the floor.

He looked at her with a shy smile, his cheeks as red as the fading sun. Warm honesty, intelligence, and friendship glowed in the bright blue depths of his eyes, and in that instant, she formed a strong liking for the boy.

"Thank you, milady. I appreciate your assistance. It seems I'm ever plagued with clumsiness." He set the platter on the table. "Lord Valteri thought you might be hungry."

Her belly rumbled instantly—as if *it* had ears. "I suppose I am."

He removed the sliced cheese and bread and placed them before her, then quickly poured a goblet of wine. "Name is Wace." He propped the platter against the wall. "Inept squire to Lord Valteri. At least that's what he tells me most days." He winked at her. "If you have any needs—"

"Lord Valteri's squire?" she repeated, interrupting him.

He nodded.

She picked up a piece of cheese as she considered that. "Served him long, have you?"

Suspicion darkened his eyes and he watched her like a mother hare guarding her young from a circling kestrel. "Long enough to know that milord welcomes no questions be asked of a personal nature. Such queries are oft met with a severe tongue-lashing. Which, truth be told, can be worse than an actual beating. Milord is quite the master of harsh witticisms that can cut soul deep."

She sucked her breath in. "My deepest apologies, good squire. I had no idea he'd been so hard on you."

"Oh, not me, milady. He restrains himself for some reason where I'm concerned. He's only a beast if I wake him too early in the morn, and then 'tis never personal. Rather, he grunts and growls like a feral bear coming out of hibernation. But for others . . . His words are like a head injury. . . ."

"How so?"

"Hilarious when they happen to another. Quite painful when you're the recipient."

She wasn't quite sure what to make of that as she chewed her cheese and swallowed it. So, Ariel smiled at the lad to reassure him. "Well, I mean your lord no harm, good Wace. I only wanted to know why his own name bothers him."

"Ah! Then you mustn't have heard of Valterius the Godless." He spoke in a low tone for her alone.

She shook her head. "Should I have?"

Eyes wide, he pulled a chair up next to her and took a seat. Then, he leaned forward on his elbows as if to impart a great secret. "You are definitely one of the few who hasn't. Even when we came to England, it seemed that most everyone we met knew him on sight. Even I was amazed that his reputation had spread so far and wide."

"Why would his fame not inspire your joy? I thought all boys wanted to serve well-known masters."

Deep sadness filled his eyes. "He's a good man, milady." Wace looked around the room as if afraid someone might overhear him. "Behind his back, they whisper horrible, ungodly things about my lord. Things I know to be malicious lies."

"Such as?"

"That he's Lucifer's bastard."

She laughed aloud at the very thought. "Lucifer's bastard, indeed. He doesn't look a thing like him."

A strange light darkened Wace's eyes. He shifted nervously. "You speak as if you know what Lucifer would look like."

Chills crept along Ariel's spine as an image of a beautiful fair-haired man popped into her mind. One who was charming and familiar.

But that was insanity.

So she laughed it off, even though her chills remained. "How could I know such? But my guess would be that he's dark and sinister, with the face of a gargoyle. Nowhere near as beautiful as our lord, Valteri."

And still something inside told her that she was lying.

Wace's humor returned. "Aye, and has pointed ears, no doubt."

"No doubt. And a forked tongue, like a serpent."

"Fangs, too."

That seemed to placate the boy, who remained to keep her company while she ate.

Once she finished, Wace took her to the bower room, where a number of other women were gathered to embroider and sew.

"Milord thought that if you attended your regular duties it might help you to regain your memory."

Ariel scowled as she glanced around the unfamiliar room, and at the women who sat about and gossiped. There was absolutely nothing familiar about it.

At all.

Wace smiled. "I'll leave you to it."

Terrified, she wanted to call him back.

But he shut the door with a solid thud that sounded more like a death knell.

The women paused to look at her in unison.

Ariel swallowed hard as she made her way to a seat.

Still, they continued to stare at her as if she had three heads. It was the most disconcerting thing she'd ever endured.

At least that was what she thought.

Why can't I remember?

She bit back a curse.

"I'm Edyth."

Ariel smiled at the young woman next to her. "Ariel."

That made the woman beam a warm smile back. She handed her a small box.

Scowling, Ariel opened it to find a set of needles like the women were using. She picked one up, but was completely mystified as to how to use it.

She rolled it between her fingers. There was nothing familiar about this at all.

Nothing.

"Are you all right, Ariel?"

"How do you use this?"

Several of the girls laughed at her.

"Do you not know how to sew, silly? Or are you just pretending so that you can put your work off on us?"

Edyth tsked at her. "Don't mock her, Margaret."

Ariel bit her lip as she glanced to Edyth. "Sew what?"

"Whatever you want. Clothes. Tapestries. Repair things."

That only made her frown more. "I don't understand."

With the patience of a saint, Edyth held up the cloth and needle in her hand and showed her how to use it. "You take the needle and thread it."

Ariel gasped as she pricked her finger. "Is it supposed to be so sharp?"

Edyth scowled. "Have you never touched one before?"

She shook her head. "I don't think so."

"You can't be serious!" Margaret gasped.

Another girl snorted. "What is wrong with you?"

Valteri was heading back toward the keep when he heard what sounded like the screams of a thousand furies coming for him.

For a moment, he thought the keep might be on fire.

A number of women ran past him.

"She's insane!"

It wasn't until he sprinted into the building to find Ariel being pulled away by a girl named Edyth that he began to comprehend what had happened.

"You cannot do such a thing, milady!"

"I don't understand why not. Someone needs to teach the beast lessons on behavior."

"Edyth?"

She froze at the sound of his call. Releasing Ariel, she quickly curtsied. "Milord."

"What happened?"

"Your lady walloped Margaret."

He turned at the sound of Wace's voice. "Pardon?"

Wace nodded. "They had an altercation."

Edyth bit her lip. "She punched her like a man, milord. Gave her a blackened eye and everything."

He'd be angry but for the fact that he knew that shrew's tongue and had seen her mock and belittle enough innocent people that he'd had the urge to slap the woman a few times himself.

Lucky for Margaret, he made it his policy to never strike anyone smaller or weaker, and particularly children or women. No matter how vexing or insulting they were.

"Any particular reason for it?"

"She was laughing at the lady for not knowing how to sew."

He scowled at Edyth's words, then met Ariel's unrepentant gaze. "You punched her for laughing at you?"

"Nay, milord. I would never hit anyone for so petty a crime."

"Then why, pray tell?"

Edyth turned red in her face. "Margaret slapped the embroidery from my hands, milord. Then said that an idiot shouldn't teach an incompetent imbecile."

"And you punched her?"

"Nay."

Completely confused, he arched a brow at both of them. "At what point did you hit her?"

"After she insulted Edyth, and Edyth, upset at her words, went for more thread. Her actions startled your kitten, milord. Cecile then skittered out and the wretch kicked her. Hard."

Edyth nodded. "That was when milady socked her one and saved the cat."

"I see." He cleared his throat to cover his amusement. "And the cat? Where is she now?"

Ariel opened the pouch that was attached to her girdle to show him the small black ball that was slumbering inside. "Safe from any harm."

"Margaret, not so much." Edyth giggled under her breath.

Ariel lifted her chin. "I won't apologize for my actions."

"No one has asked that of you."

"Thank you, milord." She cuddled the bag in her arms and headed for her chambers. "If you'll excuse me, I shall put Cecile where no one can harm her and see that she has milk and meat."

Valteri stood in total confusion as he watched her leave them. He had no idea what he should do. No doubt Margaret and her husband would expect some sort of discipline for Ariel's assault.

If she were a man, he'd know how to respond.

What did one do when women fought?

"Milord?"

He turned toward Edyth. "Aye?"

"Please don't harm Lady Ariel for her actions. Margaret was being terribly rude to her."

"Fear not. I have no quarrel with what she's done. I was only trying to think of how to smooth this over with Margaret's husband."

Hesitating, Edyth walked toward him. "If I might speak out of turn, milord?"

"Please. Speak freely."

"Elrich is terrified of you. Should he seek any form of redress, simply scowl and growl, and he'll flee immediately."

He arched a brow at her words. "You think so?"

"Know so. Truth be told I would have done so myself until now."

That stunned him. "And why this sudden courage?"

"Lady Ariel told me you were a fair man, milord. And given her kindness and heart, I trust her judgment." With those words spoken, she rushed off as if embarrassed by her candor.

Or maybe she was scared, after all.

It was hard for him to tell the difference.

Either way, 'twas the longest discussion he'd had with anyone outside of his horse in years.

How strange.

Stranger still was his sudden need to go after Ariel and check on her. He wanted to make sure that she was all right after her ordeal.

He found her in his room, on the floor with Cecile. In spite of her altercation, she seemed fine.

She looked up at him with that innocent gaze that stirred his body more than he liked. "Is something amiss?"

"Nay . . . Aye. You remembered nothing about sewing?"

Sighing wearily, Ariel sat up and shook her head. "Nothing at all." She pushed herself to her feet. "I swear I've never held a needle in my life. I didn't even know what it was called until Edyth told me."

How could that be? What lady wouldn't have been taught to sew?

Even a peasant woman would have those skills.

"Yet you remember using other things?"

She nodded.

"Such as?"

Her gaze skimmed his body in a way that hardened him uncomfortably until she stopped on his sword. *"That."*

He laughed, even though he remained fully alert over the fact that his desire for her made it rather awkward.

She didn't share his amusement, at all.

That sobered him even more than his erection. "You're serious."

"Very much so. I know how to use a sword, a knife, and a shield. Even a staff. Why do you doubt me?"

Valteri gave her a peeved grimace. "Because it's not exactly a skill a father teaches his daughter."

Ariel's gaze turned cocky. "Care to try me?"

Normally, he'd have laughed her off. But for some reason he was curious, especially after her actions against Margaret and the crone.

Just how much skill did she have?

Before he could think better of it, he led her outside to the storage shed where they kept the practice swords his men and their squires used for the training list. Made of wood and padded, they kept the squires from harming each other during their training.

He handed her one. "Show me this skill of which you speak."

Ariel didn't miss the doubt in Valteri's mismatched eyes or his tone. He thought he was humoring her.

But unlike the needle, she knew exactly how to grip a sword.

In fact, this felt comfortable. It was like being at home.

For the first time since waking up, something felt right and natural to her.

She held the sword up to salute him, then lunged.

Grabbing another practice sword, he barely parried her strike.

By her third blow, the smile was gone from his face and he was no longer so cocksure. "You are indeed well trained, milady."

"I told you." She twirled and actually caught a blow to his arm. Had they been using real swords that would have wounded him.

Valteri gasped at the impossible. No one had struck a blow to him in practice or battle in years. "I'm impressed."

She smiled. "Thank you."

And before she could move, he flipped her sword from her hands and disarmed her. "But I can't have you show me up in front of my men."

Laughing, she curtsied to him. "Understood, milord."

To his surprise, he heard applause. He turned his head to see Wace watching them.

"That was incredible, milady! Your skill is unmatched!"

"Thank you, kind Wace."

Growling at his squire, Valteri returned the swords to their holders. "The lady is full of surprises."

"Aye, she is."

If only he could figure out why a noblewoman had been so well trained for war. It made no sense.

But her smile was infectious. "If you'll excuse me, milord? I should like to clean up."

"Of course. Wace? Would you see her back to her room?"

"Aye, milord."

Valteri watched them leave while he tried to solve this latest puzzle.

Just who was this woman and how had she come to fall into his hands? If she had this amount of skill, how much did the man who trained her?

Not that he feared any man. But this was war. Could she have been a spy or assassin sent after him?

That made the most sense. He'd never suspect a woman of such treachery. What better tool for the Saxons to use against their enemies.

One they'd never see coming.

Which meant she was either feigning her memory loss, or it was real and had she not lost her memory, she'd have killed him by now.

That sent a chill over him and finally brought his desire back under control.

What if all this was nothing more than a game she played? People were rotten. No one knew that better than he. To their core center, they conspired and beguiled for selfish reasons, all the while smiling at the face of their victims.

Aye, he'd watch her, and if she held such treachery in her heart, he'd end her. That was the one thing his bitter childhood had taught him. People weren't tools. No one deserved to be used and discarded.

Or abused for entertainment.

As beautiful as she was, he would protect his squire. He would protect his brother.

"A demon I may be, but I am never disloyal."

CHAPTER 3

Ariel had just entered the great hall when she saw a number of men fleeing for their lives, each cursing her lord and protector.

"He's the devil's spawn!"

"Lucifer's own!"

"God save us all!"

They practically tripped over themselves as they ran past her for the door.

Amused and befuddled, she headed in the direction they'd come from, which turned out to be Valteri's chamber office. A large room that was sparsely furnished with uncomfortable, overturned chairs and one large desk where he stood, leaning on it with clenched fists.

But what made her raise a brow was the dagger that was firmly lodged in the door, right at eye level as she entered.

Ariel took a moment to pry the dagger loose. "Bad day or bad aim?"

"Bit of both," he said churlishly. "And unless you wish to be the next unfortunate target of my wrath, you might wish to take heed and run as well."

She set the dagger on the desk, near his hand, and glanced over the stack of papers while he moved to pick up the chairs and right them. "You'll find I'm made of sterner stock. Now that I've seen your precision, I'm not so easily frightened." Wrinkling her nose playfully at him, she skimmed his ledgers. "So what has milord so cross?"

He let out a bearish sigh. "Nothing."

Cocking her head, she noted the letters of complaint that were in three separate stacks. "Are the peasants revolting?"

Valteri scoffed as he righted the last chair and returned to her side. "I wish. *That* I could handle."

"Knocking people about isn't always the answer, milord."

"Says the woman who punched another earlier?"

"I was trying to save your cat."

"And I'm trying to save my sanity."

She glanced about the room where he'd left the chairs, far away from his desk. "Judging from the condition of the furniture upon my arrival, I would say I had much more success with the cat."

Valteri laughed and then froze at the unfamiliar sound. It was the first time in his life he could ever remember doing such a thing.

"So, milord, I ask again, what has you so flustered?"

It galled him to admit his shortcomings to anyone, yet for some reason he'd rather admit them to her than another. "I can't make any sense of these damnable accounts." He handed her the ledger that his steward had been trying to explain before he'd threatened to strangle the bastard.

And meant it.

"These are the rents that are owed that I'm supposed to review, and then I'm supposed to pay taxes on them." He grimaced as she read over the figures. "And before you say anything else, aye, I can read."

She looked up at him with an innocent stare. "Why would I assume otherwise?"

"Because I'm a mercenary."

"And?"

That caught him off guard, as virtually everyone, including his brother, thought him stupid and ill-educated. "I'm demonspawn."

She snorted at that. "What kind of demon wouldn't know how to read?"

"You're not funny."

"Nay, but it's true. Never known a demon yet that was illiterate." Ariel wasn't sure which of them was more shocked by her words.

Valteri or her.

However, the most shocking part for her was the fact that she didn't think it was a joke.

Just like knowing how to use a sword, she had a bad feeling that she had an intimate knowledge of demons as well. That somehow, somewhere, she'd interacted with them.

But that couldn't be.

And such thoughts and words were dangerous. She knew that even though she had no idea how or where she'd acquired that knowledge.

She let out a nervous, fake laugh as she shoved playfully at his arm. "I'm jesting, milord! Just kidding. How would I know the literacy rate among demons? Rather, it just seems to me that they'd have to be fairly literate in order to be so maniacal. Wouldn't you think?"

"Sure." But his tone didn't match that word.

What is wrong with me?

Biting her lip, she looked back down at the ledger and his steward's awkward scribbles. "Um . . . well then . . . what would be the problem?"

"I can't do arithmetic."

That stunned her. She looked up sharply to catch the embarrassment in his mismatched gaze.

"Don't you dare tell anyone!"

"Not a soul, milord. Why would I?"

Valteri let out a sigh of relief. "I mean it, Ariel. It's humiliating enough."

"I would never do something like that. Besides, I should think you could easily do the math."

"How so?"

"Think of it like battle. I'm sure you do the mental calculations every time you step out and see how many men you're facing and how many you have to subtract to win."

"That's different."

She shook her head. "It's the same. Only not as bloody." Taking a piece of paper and his quill, she showed him. "Just think of it like this. You have twenty men here who are coming down the hill." She wrote out the number in sharp, straight scratches. "You have to remove eight to win. How many would be left?"

"A dozen."

"Correct. There's your arithmetic, milord."

"Huh." Valteri stood there, amazed by her. No one had ever been able to simplify it like that before so that he could comprehend those numbers when applied to anything other than battle. How easy she made it seem. "But it's not quite that simple."

"That really is the gist of it." She made marks on the paper. "Think of them as soldiers to add or subtract or multiply for your army, and it'll help you keep your records straight."

Valteri stared at the pages that were slowly beginning to make sense to him as an idea struck. Probably not one of his better ones, but still . . .

Certainly not his worst, by far.

Ariel was a lot more attractive than his surly steward who was terrified of him. Her company far more pleasing.

And she didn't look at him as if he were shite on the bottom of her shoes.

"Would you care to help me do this?"

She gave him a pert stare. "Depends."

"On?"

"Whether or not there will be cutlery involved." Smiling, she held up the dagger and wiggled it impishly between her fingers.

In spite of himself, he laughed again. "Somehow, milady, I doubt that you'll motivate me to such violence."

Indeed, violence was the last thing on his mind as he stood so close to her that he could smell the sweet scent of jasmine coming off her hair.

Rather, the images in his mind were much more tender and inappropriate. Especially with the way the light caught against her pale skin and made it appear so very succulent and tempting.

Assassin she might be, but right then, he'd have gladly allowed her to cut his treacherous heart from his chest.

She set the dagger aside and looked doubtful. "I don't know. It didn't take long for me to try the patience of Margaret, and Wace says that it takes much less to try yours."

He snorted. "Wace would try the patience of Job."

"I doubt that. He seems like a very sweet boy."

"Easy for you to say, milady. You don't bear the scars of his ineptitude. He trips more than he doesn't. Drops anything he attempts to carry, usually right on top of me. And I cannot begin to catalogue the number of times he's forgotten to tighten my saddle properly. If it wasn't for the fact that I know he's just that inattentive, I'd think he was trying to kill me, and I don't think I own a tunic that isn't stained from where he's dropped or spilled something on me. Usually hot and near scalding. Never mind the fact that he loses anything he's charged with tending."

"Then why do you tolerate him as your squire?"

Ariel watched as Valteri grew quiet and sober over her question.

How strange. He'd been jovial as he accounted for Wace's shortcomings and now . . .

Her gaze went to the scar on his hand. A tiny imperfection that made her think of Cecile.

A cockeyed kitten he also protected.

Clarity struck her.

"Because you're afraid another master would abuse him for his shortcomings, aren't you?"

When he spoke, his tone was dry and flat. "The world's full of assholes, milady."

But Valteri wasn't one of them. At least not that she'd seen. He might raise his voice and growl when someone irritated him.

But he'd never raise his fist. Not unless someone else was about to strike the first blow.

Nor was he insulting to others.

Because now that she thought about it, she'd seen Wace drop things on him and he had yet to say a word about it to the boy.

Clearing his throat, he jerked his chin toward his ledgers. "Do we have an accord about the accounting?"

"We do. I shall help you."

"Thank you." Valteri pulled the chair out for her to take a seat.

As she did so, her hair brushed against his knuckles. Valteri had to bite back a curse as his entire body erupted at the innocent contact.

But even worse was the overwhelming desire he had to bury his hand deep in those thick, flaxen tresses and trail his lips over the succulent curve of her neck.

What is wrong with you, man?

He'd gone daft.

Beyond daft. Yet he could barely drag his thoughts away from how much he wanted to carry her off and make love to her for the rest of the day.

She'd scream if you even tried.

That reality jolted him away from his thoughts. As did the truth behind it.

Aye, she would. No woman had ever welcomed him to her bed. Not even those who followed after camps for battle. Even they cringed when he did nothing more than kiss them after he'd paid them for much more.

It was why he'd finally settled on celibacy. There was no need to keep wasting his money on prostitutes when all he ever ended up with was a begrudged kiss. He'd finally decided to save his money and just take care of his physical needs himself.

But the craving he felt for Ariel . . .

It was dangerous and disturbing.

Clearing his throat, he pulled a chair over for himself and handed her the ledger he'd been working with before he'd lost patience with the steward.

"I'm supposed to figure five percent for the tax. How does milady equate that to battle? I lop a hand off each soldier?"

Ariel laughed at his earnest tone. "More like an eye or toenail." She smiled at him. "So, who should we blind first?"

The edges of his mouth lifted as if he wanted to smile and was making an effort not to. "I say the steward. He was a weaselly little bastard."

In spite of her common sense, she was enchanted by the light in his eyes. He was incredibly handsome.

Breathtakingly so.

Her heart pounding, she was tempted to reach out and touch his hand.

Don't you dare! For all you know, you're married!

It was true. She could have a husband and children searching for her.

Yet that didn't feel right. Or seem right. When she'd looked around at the children and others, she had the same detached sensation with them that she'd experienced with the sewing.

As if she'd never been around them before and had no knowledge of them.

However, Valteri's company felt right. Logical.

"Are you sure we've never met?"

He paused to glance at her. "Aye. Why do you ask?"

"I can't explain it, but there's something so familiar about you." Especially his eyes. She felt as if she'd known him in the past. Had stared into those eyes a number of times.

Even the timbre of his voice felt . . .

Comfortable.

Familiar.

Certain mannerisms were so recognizable.

It didn't make sense. And at the same time, the image she had of him wasn't exactly him.

Why can't I see it clearly?

Who was the man he reminded her of? What was her mind trying to tell her? She had a feeling it was extremely important, and yet no matter how hard she tried, she just couldn't bring it into focus.

Of course, it would help if she wasn't so keenly attuned to Valteri. To the rich, heady scent of him and the way his muscled arm brushed against hers. The power of him was enchanting, and the sound of his voice . . .

She could listen to it all day. There was something comforting that drew her toward him against all common sense. She'd never felt like this.

Or have you?

"Are you all right, milady?"

She smiled at him. "Fine."

He inclined his head to her then reached for his goblet.

And sighed heavily at the fact that it was empty.

"Something amiss, milord?"

"My errant squire strikes again." With a wry twist of his lips, he pushed his chair back and stood. "I shall get us more wine while we work."

Ariel attempted to focus on the ledger, but as he walked past her, her gaze was caught by his striking form. Dark and light. The dichotomy wasn't lost on her.

Just as he reached the door, it clattered open and Wace rushed in.

With a platter.

Wine and food poured all over poor Valteri, who stood back with his jaw clenched.

"My lord! I-I-I—"

Valteri held his hand up to silence Wace's sputtering. "It's fine, Wace. I had begun to fear that I might actually make it through the week without wearing something greasy and wet. Now that I'm soiled, I shall be able to put the matter out of my mind." He clapped the boy on his shoulder. "Please see that the lady is served on the table and not her lap while I see about finding something a little less . . ." He grimaced. "Balmy."

And with that, he stepped past the boy to leave them.

Ariel was stunned by his tolerance of something she knew had to be hot and painful.

Wace sighed heavily as he bent down to clean up the mess.

Ariel went to help, but he shooed her away. "Please, milady. I'm embarrassed enough."

"Sorry."

He glanced up with a frown. "Why do you apologize to me?"

She wasn't sure. "I feel awful. For both of you."

Wace shook his head as he cleaned up. "I'd feel better if Lord Valteri would at least yell at me for my clumsiness."

"Why? As fair Cato said, patience is a virtue."

"And cleanliness is next to godliness, but for some reason, I can't seem to master that, either."

She tsked at him. "You're the only one I've ever met who craved violence as punishment."

"Only because I know that I deserve a beating for my ineptitude." He winced. "I try so hard and I swear every time I get near my lord, I do something stupid."

"Ever think it might be because you fear doing something that it makes you nervous?"

He paused to look up at her. "What do you mean?"

"Only that you stopped being clumsy once we talked and met."

"True."

She picked up one of the goblets. "I think it's your fear of having an accident that causes it." She wrinkled her nose. "Except for this one. This one was definitely Lord Valteri's fault."

He laughed. "How I wish it were true. I should have been paying attention when I came through the door." Sighing, Wace took the goblet from her hand. "Thank you, milady."

"For what?"

"Making me feel better. I don't really remember my mother. She died before I learned to walk. But your kindness is what I'd like to think she had."

"I'm sure of it."

With a winsome smile at her, he picked up his platter and quickly took off with a great deal more care.

Ariel frowned at the floor. It was perfect. No sign remained of the mess whatsoever.

Not even a drop.

But the pattern in the floor reminded her of . . .

I'm sorry about your mother.

She scowled as she heard a faint voice in her mind. Deep and resonant.

Ariel wanted to shout in frustration. Why wouldn't it return?

What had happened to her mother?

And where was the rest of her family? Did she have a brother or sister?

"Father." She saw an image of a light-haired man. Fierce. Invincible.

Aye, she had a father.

Ariel cursed as the image vanished before she could figure out his name.

"I'm going to remember. . . ."

She just hoped the return of her memory wasn't something bad. Perhaps there was a reason her mind had flushed it all away. Was it trying to protect her?

How would she know?

With a sigh of her own, she rose, more determined than ever to solve this mystery.

D ays went by as Ariel worked with Valteri, much to the chagrin of his former steward. While the man claimed to detest his lord, he detested and resented her presence even more.

She was everything he wanted to be. Fast. Accurate. And she never tried the patience of Valteri. Yet there was a wall between them and she wasn't sure why. It was as if something about her made him nervous. Ludicrous, to be sure.

Still . . .

Ariel sensed his disquiet as they worked on his latest accounting.

Valteri shook his head. "Is it just me, or does my brother seem to be taxing the air people breathe?"

"How so?"

He gestured at the ledger in her hands. "This is more than just an accounting of his new holdings. I swear, the man is wanting a fee for everything."

His outrage quirked her humor. "Does he not need it to pay his mercenaries?"

She'd meant to tease him. Instead, his humor grew dark. "You resent us?"

"Why should I?"

Valteri's gut tightened at her innocence that suddenly seemed feigned. "We conquered you."

She set her quill aside to cock a brow at him. "You conquered a country, milord. No man has yet conquered me. Nor shall he."

"What of your husband?"

She let out a deep sigh. "I have no memory of such. All I can recall is a faint image of a man I believe to be my father."

"And?" He sensed she was hiding something from him.

Biting her lip, she glanced away. "You'll think me mad."

Nay. He still thought of her as a spy or assassin. "I won't think you mad."

"I see a man who reminds me of you."

That made his gut tighten. Could she have met his unknown father?

To this day, his mother refused to breathe a word of his father's identity.

I swore an oath for secrecy and I will abide by it! Herleva of Falaise was a bold bitch who dropped bastards the way some maids dropped ribbons at tournaments for champions. Her steadfast refusal was why so many believed him the son of the devil.

Why else would she refuse when she'd named the father of all his half siblings?

His personal belief was that his father was so low of birth, she was terrified to let anyone know that she'd screwed a stableman.

Or peasant.

More like a priest. It would explain why he was so cursed.

If he believed in such things.

"Any idea who this man might be?"

Ariel shook her head. "I can only catch a glimpse of him and then he's gone."

"Then how do I remind you of him?"

She let out a small huff. "It's hard to explain. I just . . ." Her eyes were awash with grief.

Maybe I'm wrong. Her plight seemed so genuine. Perhaps she wasn't what he thought.

Don't be stupid. The history of man was written by the hands of the women who'd betrayed them. The hands of friends who'd plunged a dagger in the back the moment someone let down their guard.

All of this could be an act.

What if it isn't?

He didn't dare take that chance. "I hope you remember something soon."

She nodded. "What of you, milord? You never speak of your past. If I didn't know better, I'd think you'd forgotten it."

He laughed bitterly. "I wish," he mumbled under his breath. With a sigh, he did his best to blot the pain of memories he really didn't want—he would give anything to have her memory lapse. "I survived it. There's nothing more to say."

"But what of your parents? Brothers and sisters. I know the king is your brother. Do you have any others?"

He scoffed at the thought. "Not that I claim. Odo came to England with us to conquer this land. Pity that bastard didn't fall into the Channel on our crossing."

Ariel arched a brow at his acrimony. "Why do you hate him so?"

"He's a bishop and an ass. Not even Will really likes him." Valteri took a sip of wine as he remembered some of his brother's insults that had forced Will to separate them before he throttled the little weasel. "As for the others,

I don't really know them at all. Robert is the Count of Mortain. My sister Emma is the Viscountess of Avranches, and Arletta is the Lady de la Ferté-Macé. But as I said, they are strangers to me."

"Do they know you at all?"

"Only by name and reputation. I met Robert one time at a tournament when I knocked him off his horse." He gave her an unrepentant smile. "After that humiliation, he had no use for me, but several choice words. As for my sisters, I wouldn't know them if they were standing in front of me."

"I'm sorry." Ariel felt his pain at their neglect even though he spoke in a deadpan tone.

"I'm not. Given the drama I've suffered by allowing Will into my life, I'm glad to know nothing of theirs."

She laughed. "You're terrible!"

He shrugged nonchalantly. "I only speak the truth."

"And your parents? Where are they?"

"My mother married the Viscount of Conteville, who died a few months back."

She scowled at that. "I'm sorry."

"I appreciate the sentiment, but don't waste it. My mother has been celebrating his death since it happened. I'm told she married him for his title alone, and is now happy to be a widow, especially given that her eldest son has become the king of England."

That made sense, she supposed. "So you stay in contact with her?"

"Nay. She's never so much as visited me since I was whelped from her loins. I only know what Will tells me."

"And your father?"

A sinister darkness came over him. "The devil? I know nothing of him."

She snorted. "Valteri, please. You must know something of your father."

"Only that he dishonored my mother and fled. She refuses to speak a word of him, and I know nothing other than the monastery where I was raised after she dumped me on their less than caring shoulders."

So much pain. She could feel it as if it were her own. "Why didn't you join the order where you were raised?"

His nostrils flared. "Do you know the reason Will locked me here?"

She shook her head.

"His fear that if I ever lay eyes upon that place I'll raze it to the ground and evoke the wrath of God against him."

"Again, I'm so sorry."

"Don't be. I'm the monster they made me, and if I weren't I'd have been skewered long ago. Trust me, milady. The monks did me a service. Had they not raised me with their all-out hatred, I'd have never survived the scorn of everyone else." With those words spoken, he got up and left the room.

Ariel sat there, torn between going after him and knowing that her presence wouldn't soothe him. He was a hard man. But given what little he'd shared with her, she understood why.

Wace had told her that he never spoke to others. She was an exception, and she valued that.

And as every day passed, and she witnessed more of his kindness when he had no reason to give it to anyone, she valued it all the more. Honestly? She liked him a great deal in spite of his prickly nature.

A lily among the thorns.

It was the best way to describe him. Yet with every day that passed, she knew this couldn't last. As Valteri was so quick to point out, there was most likely someone searching for her.

But who?

V alteri paused outside as he saw the sun setting. Strangely beautiful, it reminded him of Ariel. A quiet sheen of color across a dismal landscape. That was her.

Maybe her past is as tragic as yours and that's why she's chosen to not remember.

It was a thought, and would explain much. If he had a chance to forget, even for a day, he'd gladly take it.

And still his doubts and suspicions plagued him. She seemed too sweet to be real.

Too sincere.

Having known no kindness, he wasn't sure what to do with hers. It left him unprepared and unsure.

Every day she was here, he grew more attracted to her.

Don't be stupid. Wife and hearth had never been his destiny. She was a conquered prize, and such creatures were even more dangerous than others.

Let down your guard and you'll have a knife in your back. That had been the only thing in his life that he could trust in. People were treacherous. They were snakes.

And yet he sensed the same vulnerability in her that he'd found in Wace.

Maybe she had been as abused as the lad. Though how anyone could harm so fair a beauty he'd never understand. *The same way they beat down a child.*

Aye. There were soulless assholes aplenty who preyed on any and everyone around them. He'd known more than his share of those animals.

Wincing, he wished he knew the truth of Ariel. Because every day she remained was one more where he was falling under her spell.

If she didn't leave soon, she just might be the death of him.

CHAPTER 4

A week later, Ariel had just finished changing for dinner when the door to her room swung open, without a knock.

Gasping in alarm, she turned to meet Valteri's stern glower. What the devil? He'd never once opened her door without an invitation.

And never had she seen him in this state.

"Something amiss, milord?"

His breathing heavy, he stepped back. "There's a noble ass in the hall who claims to be your brother."

She felt her jaw go slack at that unexpected news and his word choice. Though to be honest, Valteri thought most people to be asses.

He just normally didn't say it out loud.

"My brother?"

"It's what he said."

She stared at him in total confusion. Could it be? Had her family finally found her?

And yet . . .

Something didn't seem right. She still had that strong sense that this was where she belonged.

Her bond to Valteri and the others here had grown stronger every day.

Although that didn't make sense, either.

Still, something felt wrong. There was a hollow feeling in her stomach. A foreboding that she couldn't place told her that whoever waited for her wasn't family.

He was someone else.

Some*thing* else.

Curious about this person and her great sense of foreboding, Ariel followed Valteri into the hall, where a tall, flaxen-haired man stood in the center of the room. He eyed the soldiers around him as if they made him uncomfortable.

The hair at the nape of her neck rose instantly. Every piece of her was on sudden alert. Something about the stranger seemed familiar. . . .

Yet, she couldn't quite place him.

She hesitated.

Suddenly, he turned around and faced her. Her trepidation tripled.

Run! An inner voice shouted at her to seek refuge, as fast as she could go.

This "ass" was evil.

She knew it. Cruelty bled from every pore of his body and it set off every alarm in hers.

An affectionate smile curved his lips. "Dearest Ariel!" He rushed toward her. "Thank the heavens that you're safe. I was so afraid I'd lost you." He grabbed her into a bone-crushing hug.

Ew! Her entire being cringed. It was like hugging a louse.

Pushing against the stranger, she needed to put distance between them.

Trying her best to dig her elbows between them, she grimaced. "Do I know you, sirrah?"

He released her instantly.

With a step back, he gave her a hurt pout. "What game is this, my Ariel? Surely you've had your sport by now. Why, I ought to beat you for straying this far from me, and troubling these good people."

Ariel practically ran toward the one person she knew she could trust— Valteri. "I don't know him!"

Before she could reach the safety of Valteri, the stranger grabbed her by the arm and pulled her to a stop. His rough fingers bit into her flesh, burning her with his cold grasp. "Stop this, this instant!" he growled.

She opened her mouth to speak, but quickly closed it as Valteri stepped forward and removed the steel grip from her elbow.

He placed himself between them. "That'll be enough of that." His tone promised violence if the man didn't back down. "I know not what happened to her, but she no longer remembers herself. Or you, apparently."

The stranger shifted his horrified gaze from Valteri to her. "You truly don't know me?"

"Nay, I do not."

He held his arms out to her, his features a becoming mixture of affection and tolerance. "Ariel, dearest, I'm your brother, Belial."

CHAPTER 5

The name stung Valteri like the acrid bite of an adder. Was this some kind of jest that this man would come in here, and give the name of such a demon to him? As if two supposed Christian mothers would be so cruel to their own spawn?

While his own mother had been sick in the head, he doubted that another would be so cruel.

The demon he'd been named for had commanded the largest infernal force and had been renowned for his merciless battle skills.

Belial . . .

He was the prince of all evil. The right hand of the king of darkness. Indeed, his very name meant wickedness. Outlaw.

Sin.

Among other things.

Surely this bastard mocked him by claiming such a name as his own. If such mockery was his intent, Valteri would beat him within an inch of his *worthless* life.

"Belial?" Valteri arched a skeptical brow.

An arrogant, aggravated look crossed the man's features. 'Twas the same twitchiness he felt whenever someone reacted to his own name. That need to knock some semblance of politeness back into them.

"Aye, *Valteri the Godless.*" Belial emphasized each syllable of his name, the moniker that also stung a lot more than Valteri wanted to acknowledge. "'Twould seem my pagan father had a similar ill sense of humor as your mother to name us both for demons. And you took your name one step further to make a mockery of the Lord above by denying him with such fervor as to have your own brother, and the rest of the world, decry you as such, eh?"

Valteri snorted. "You're misinformed, sir. My epithet was earned by the number of men I've left gutted, on the battlefield and off. Some of them for no other reason than they simply annoyed me by occupying the same room." He made a point to lower his gaze to Belial's abdomen and feet to let him know that he'd be more than willing to add his carcass to that long and impressive list.

But apparently, Belial wasn't one to be intimidated either. Rather, his eyes darkened to a vivid blue as he raked Valteri with a cold glare Valteri might have found amusing in its audacity had his own anger not raged even higher. "Then again, I would think my father must have thought more of me on my arrival to this realm, as he named me for the fiercest of demons."

Valteri laughed. "You think so? Unless the monks who raised me were misinformed, your name means 'worthless.' At least my mother gave me the name of a commander who ruled the battlefield."

His open, rude hostility caused several of those around them to suck their breath in sharply.

Indeed, it was ill manners to insult a guest so. His brother would be the first to berate him over it.

If Will wanted a diplomat, he chose the wrong brother.

Belial curled his lip. "At least I can name my father, milord. Can you?"

That sent the onlookers scurrying for cover.

Ariel let out an audible gasp.

Valteri gripped his sword. The smooth, leather-covered hilt bit into his palm, and he yearned to hear the blade sing an exit from its scabbard and watch as the bastard's head rolled from his shoulders.

It'd been a long time since a man had dared insult him to his face. That reminder of his past, and his despised parentage, did little to curb the roiling heat in his belly, or appease the need in his soul to beat the simpkin before him.

Good thing he'd hurled the first insult in this matter. Otherwise, Belial would be searching the ground for his teeth right about now. However, Valteri wasn't a hypocrite and wouldn't attack when he knew the man was only defending himself.

Touché.

He, of all men, knew the bitter taste of superstition to something neither one of them could control. People were idiots and held to their zealotry with an unreasoning mind.

Belial's laugh rang out. "Come now, don't look as if your strongest wish is to call me to arms. I was only japing with you, man." He clapped Valteri on the back.

His jaw dropping, Valteri stared at him in total shock and disbelief. He'd touched him without an invitation? Were all members of their family deranged?

"Forgive my insults, my lord." Belial turned to face Ariel. He ran a long, thin finger down her cheek and Valteri noted the rigidness of her body, the control she exercised not to cringe in response. "I fear my worry for my sister has overshadowed my common sense." He glanced back toward Valteri. "And manners. I'm sure you can forgive me?"

Not bloody likely. Honestly? He hated this little trollish bitchtress and wanted to run him through.

However, he acknowledged his own part in the name-calling.

Those words sounded sincere enough, even though Valteri still had his doubts. . . . Because something about Belial said that this beast was toying with them all for sport.

Aye, the look from the corner of the man's eye. It reminded him of a cutpurse trying to remain inconspicuous as he carefully watched the soldiers while he wended his way from victim to victim.

There was just something about Belial that was innately sneaky. It set his hackles on edge and left him feeling as if he were in battle, bare-arsed.

Ariel shifted nervously, and looked to him. Her eyes beseeched him for protection.

Valteri stiffened as that familiar look struck a hard chord inside him over the one thing in life he found intolerable—those who preyed on the weak. It was the same helpless, resigned look of dread he'd seen in Wace's eyes when the boy had been a page and under the control of a monster.

Belittled and abused by those around him, Wace had possessed a profound stutter. And when he'd accidentally spilled an entire pitcher of wine in Valteri's lap at a banquet, the fear in his eyes had been palpable.

As had the roar of outrage from his master, who'd ordered the boy whipped. Unwilling to see a child beaten for such an innocent mistake, Valteri had done what he'd once sworn he'd never do.

Taken a squire.

No one would abuse a child, or anyone else, on his watch.

Could Ariel's brother be as abusive as Wace's former lord? That single thought sent a wave of murder through him. If that were indeed the case, he'd never allow her to leave with Belial.

He'd gut the man first.

Forcing a smile to his lips that was supposed to be friendly, but caused the tiny handful of men who'd remained in the room to visibly cringe and step back, Valteri attempted what he'd been told was civility.

So much for that. He knew better than to try and be like the others. Reverting to his normal grimace and glower, he sighed. "Tell me, Lord Belial, from whence do you come? Where are you headed?"

Belial turned his back to Ariel. "Our home lies to the south. We're from Brakenwich Valley. Our father's lands fell to the Norman yoke, and once I realized our cause was lost, I left the battlefield and grabbed Ariel. I thought we'd travel north to our relatives who live in Hexham, where I've been told there aren't as many Normans." Sadness darkened his gaze and he held his arms out like a supplicant at prayer. "Provided, of course, our family there still retains their lands and home."

Such was the result of war. Innocent victims always suffered, even in peace. Indeed, life itself scarred the souls of all who traversed its brutal path.

Valteri had the scars to prove it.

Inside and out.

He shrugged. "I won't apologize for my brother's actions. 'Twas your own people who started this war when they denied him the throne he'd been promised, while supporting a liar against him."

Belial smiled at his words. "Ah, loyalty. That noble mistress who leads so many on a merry chase, straight through the doorways of hell." He let out a small laugh that sent a shiver down Valteri's spine before he spoke in a low tone beneath his breath. "How I love that treacherous bitch. She so facilitates my job."

Had he heard that correctly? "Excuse me?"

"It eases my jaw," Belial spoke louder. "'Tis an old Saxon saying my father used to quote. You know, loyalty makes life easier to live."

That was not what he'd heard. He was quite certain of it, point of fact. But, unwilling to verbally spar anymore with the beast, or shed blood where he ate, he chose to let it go. "Prithee, how is it two English nobles speak French as if they were born to it?"

Belial shrugged. "Our mother. She came from Flanders."

Seemed simple enough, yet when Valteri glanced at Ariel, she had a peculiar expression as she watched her brother warily. Belial scared her, and she was trying hard not to show it. While he respected that about her, he wasn't about to let her leave his protection until he understood what it was about her brother that made her so uneasy. "Well then, we are almost cousins, and as such, I invite you to stay and partake of our hospitality so long as you wish."

Belial cocked a suspicious brow. "Truly? Why would you help *us*, the defeated?"

In spite of his honied tone, there was a direct confrontation in those words. Aye, the look in his pale eyes left no doubt. This was a challenge.

Not that it mattered. Valteri had never backed down a day in his life, and he had no intention of starting now.

His gaze hard, he stepped toward the Saxon noble. "I offer you protection for the sake of your sister. 'Tis obvious she knows naught of suffering. I say we should keep it that way, and as her brother, I would assume you'd agree. For her tender welfare." He raked Belial with a cold glare. "Personally, I care not what you do or where you go. To the devil, if it suits you. But I won't see the lady harmed."

A mocking smile curved Belial's lips. He gave a short laugh. "So be it. For the sake of my sister, we shall stay."

With a misplaced arrogance that told Valteri much about the man, Belial strode from the hall, out into the cool evening, as if he owned the manor.

It was enough to make him want to take his bow and plant an arrow square in that retreating back.

He savored the image. If only it wouldn't have been an act of total cowardice, it would have been beyond temptation.

Ariel moved forward, her eyes filled with gratitude. "I cannot thank you enough for what you've done for me, Valteri."

Then, to his utmost amazement, she raised herself up on her toes and planted a kiss on his cheek and squeezed his arm affectionately.

Shock almost sent him to his knees.

No one had ever shown him such kindness.

Blushing a becoming shade of pink, Ariel excused herself and headed to her chambers.

Alone.

His body on fire, Valteri watched her flee, his cheek still tingling from the warm softness of her lips. He dropped his gaze to the gentle sway of her well-rounded hips, and he clenched his teeth.

Don't even think it. . . .

Yet he couldn't help the image in his mind of her in his bed. Desire shot through him, igniting his blood, his loins. And for one single moment, he allowed himself to think of her in his arms, of her tender voice whispering in his ear while he held her beneath him. 'Twas a dream he'd banished long ago because he'd never thought to meet a woman who would touch him with anything save hatred, scorn, or fear.

And that even after he'd paid her for her services.

Indeed, he was tired of watching a woman cringe in his arms. Of seeing her fight with herself so as not to recoil from him. It'd become so bad that the last time he'd paid for a prostitute, he'd left her before he'd even entered her. Her obvious distaste at being with him had been more than he could tolerate. He'd rather take matters into his own hands than feel as if he were raping a woman he'd bought.

The concept that he'd ever have a woman who actually wanted to be with him had become a unicorn in his mind. Something for fairy tales and campfires. A mythical dream best left for fools and relegated to depths of his past so as never to torment him with what could never be.

But Ariel had pressed her lips to his flesh without any coercion. . . .

She'd smiled at him.

Grinding his teeth, Valteri closed his eyes in an effort to blot out the image. Then he flinched as he remembered the last time someone had dared show her gratitude with a chaste kiss.

Anger simmered in his gut at the memory. Nay, he couldn't allow Ariel to touch him again.

No one must ever touch him. He knew that. The cost was entirely too high.

He would not see her labeled as the devil's whore. He was used to the scorn and ridicule of others. The last thing he wanted was to see her scourged because she dared show him kindness.

Ariel sat at the table on the raised dais, listening to the myriad of conversations that buzzed around her. The last course had been served and still Valteri had made no appearance. She couldn't fathom what kept him away from his dinner.

Then again . . .

Belial sat next to her. He'd remained silent all throughout their meal and she couldn't miss the way he looked about the room at those gathered, as if he were a predator stalking game. Even more sinister, he seemed to delight whenever discord broke out and took a special mental note of it.

Especially at whatever had caused the fight.

His very presence set her on edge and warned her of danger . . . of death, but she couldn't quite say why. Just something about him slithered over her skin like a chill. He seemed friendly enough, yet that feeling persisted until she feared she'd go mad.

As if sensing the same thing about him, people near them began excusing themselves from the tables as if putting as much distance from her brother as they could.

Grateful for the excuse they gave her, Ariel smiled stiffly at her brother. "I should like a walk outside."

He arched his brow with an expression that seemed somehow fake. "Careful, Ariel, the hour grows late and I would grieve should anything happen to you."

Why did she doubt those words?

Because he's lying. She knew it and yet she could think of no reason why.

If only she could remember her past, mayhap then she'd know why her brother bothered her so.

Why she didn't trust him.

Because he's a snake . . .

That was an image she couldn't shake.

"I won't be long." She rose from her bench and quickly did as the others. Put as much space between her and the creepy feeling her brother evoked as she could.

As Ariel pushed open the heavy oak door of the hall, the wood scraped gently against her palms. A chill wind blew against her, freezing her cheeks. She almost turned back toward the dining area, but the last thing she wanted was to face her brother, or anyone else. All she needed was a little time alone, time to think and clear her head without any distractions.

Please let me remember something.

Anything.

She was so tired of not having any sort of tidbit from her past. Of knowing nothing about who or what she was.

How could nothing be there other than faint shadows that taunted her to near madness? It was so unfair.

Clenching her jaw to keep it from chattering, she made her way out into the dark yard. Rushlights had been lit and they provided a modicum of cheerfulness to combat the hidden fears lurking in the dust of her memory that teased her with just a hint of something she couldn't quite recall. As she walked, she heard the sounds of grooms talking to each other in the stable, and various animals settling down to sleep.

With no thought to any particular destination, Ariel followed a worn path around the wooden hall and into a small garden.

An icy rose scent clung to the air while the flowers fought against their inevitable surrender to the approaching winter frost. And yet the beauty of the garden, the out-of-place cheer of the flowers, warmed her. It was strangely pleasant here and reminded her of yet another thing she couldn't recall.

"Milady?"

She jumped at the voice coming out of a darkened corner. Facing the sound, she watched Valteri push himself to his feet and tower over the bush that had blocked her from seeing him. "Milord, what are you doing here?" She closed the distance between them.

He didn't say anything. Instead, he watched her with the steady intentness of a wary fox that had been trapped by a hunting party.

Ariel stopped at the side of the bush, and looked down to the pallet Valteri had made on the cold ground, where a rare leatherbound book lay opened. His intent to sleep out in the cold night obvious, she fought against the sudden pain in her breast over his solitary nature that kept him so distant from everyone.

Cecile slept wrapped in a thick woolen blanket next to a small tallow candle. A wooden platter of cheese, bread, and half-eaten fruit left no doubt that Valteri had taken his meal out here in the cold night.

Alone.

Suspicion filled his mismatched eyes. His was the gaze of an old, tired man. Someone who had known untold suffering throughout their life and who was exhausted from the toll it'd taken. No spark of joy glowed in the hollowed darkness of his soul, and in that moment she knew he sought the welcome relief of death.

That unguarded look haunted her, scared her more than anything else she could imagine. For it was familiar. Somewhere in her past she had been more than acquainted with it.

Had seen it many times.

Why can't I remember?

It was so frustrating to have nothing more than these tiny glimpses that only confused her more.

"Why are you here?" he asked, his voice heavy with need.

"I needed fresh air."

Sudden fire sparked in his eyes. At first, she thought it was anger, but the expression on his face denied that emotion. Rather it was one of longing or hunger.

And that fire called out to her. Drew her closer to him. His gaze drifted over her face as if he committed every line of it to his memory.

Hesitantly, he reached a hand up to touch her cold cheek. The warm calluses of his palm soothed the chill and sent a shiver over her entire body.

Ariel felt an urge to run, and at the same time, she wanted to step closer to him.

There was so much she didn't understand about any of this. So much she needed to understand.

Yet he seemed to be the only thing in her world that made any sense. The only thing that seemed right.

She felt as if she were caught in a maelstrom. Whipped by emotions she didn't understand. As if something was willfully impeding her or pushing her.

None of that made sense.

Any more than her attraction to a man who clearly wanted to be left alone. Why was she so unable to leave him?

You hate your brother.

That wasn't the only reason. There was something more.

And all she could think to ask was the most obvious question. "Why are *you* out here, milord?"

"It's what I'm used to. There's not much comfort in a tournament tent and even less so on a battlefield."

Her heart broke for him. That this was the life he'd chosen for himself because of how others behaved.

The fact that he could still feel anything other than absolute hatred for another was a miracle. Yet there he'd been, protecting his kitten and leaving her with the comfort of his bed. . . .

How could anyone be so kind to a world that had been so harsh?

He made no sense to her.

Valteri struggled with emotions that were so foreign he couldn't even begin to identify them. They were tender and protective.

This wasn't him and he knew it. He hated people. *All* people. Had done so for the whole of his life.

Against his will, the world had turned him into a killing machine. Had made him vicious. People like Ariel's brother who judged him and mocked him.

But there was no mockery in her eyes as she stared up at him tonight. No fear while she stood so close, and that left him feeling weak and vulnerable.

Things he despised because they left him at her mercy. Made him frail.

He should laugh at the thought.

Frail was the last thing he could ever be accused of being. Angry. Hate-filled. Bitter.

That was mother's milk.

Hardened.

Yet she made him feel human again.

Why?

How?

He wanted to hate her for these emotions she awakened.

If only he could.

"Was it not enough you haunted my dreams?"

She frowned at his whispered words.

He captured a strand of her pale hair and rubbed it between his fingers. Her hair was so soft and smelled like frost-covered roses.

"I know not what you mean."

Of course she didn't. He was speaking even more stupidity than the monks who'd once denounced an innocent child as evil.

But should she ever understand the effect she had on him. . . .

Push her away. His mind roared the command. He needed to scare her and drive her as far from him as he could. Make sure that she never ventured near him again.

For her sake as well as my own.

That was the safe thing to do.

The kind thing to do.

It was what he intended. Yet when he moved toward her, his body didn't obey him. Instead, he pulled her closer until she collided with his chest.

The sudden sensation startled them both. She was so much softer than he'd thought. Softer than any woman he could remember.

Her gasp caused her perfect lips to part, and that was his undoing.

Before he could stop himself, he had to know what heaven tasted like. Consequences be damned.

I'm damned already. Let it finally be for something I've done.

Closing his eyes, he lowered his lips to hers and kissed her.

Ariel couldn't move as she tasted Valteri. Her head spun at the contact as she struggled to breathe. Instinctively, she knew this was the first time any man had kissed her.

No one had ever dared. That thought floored her.

She should be offended and yet a part of her she didn't understand wanted and craved this. Ariel wrapped her arms around his broad shoulders, drawing him closer, delighting in the feel of strength and power of his body.

He pulled back slightly, his teeth nipping her lips, then he returned, even more intense than he'd been before. She opened her mouth, welcoming the taste of him, the warmth of his breath. Never in her life could she recall such a heady sensation.

And it caused her to have thoughts so wicked that they left her blushing even more.

Suddenly, he moved away and left her panting.

She opened her eyes to see the fury on his face as he stared at her in disbelief.

His breathing labored, he raked a hand through his long, unbound hair and turned away from her.

"Leave!" he growled.

Why was he so angry?

Ariel opened her mouth to protest, but before a word could escape her lips, he turned around and glowered at her with a face that reminded her of some hell-bound beast.

All that primal violence burned in his glare. She trembled in sudden fear of him and reminded herself that he was a warrior of renowned legend.

And it wasn't for mercy or kindness.

"Woman, as you value your life, take yourself from my presence."

The bitter taste of terror stung her throat.

This was the one man who could very well kill her. Suddenly scared, Ariel fled from the courtyard and back into the safety of the hall.

Valteri watched her flee, guilt gnawing at his conscience. He shouldn't have done that.

The kiss as much as the scare. It wasn't right to take his anger at himself out on her.

Why he'd kissed her, he couldn't imagine. He knew better than to lower his defenses and yield to such base things. And yet she made it so simple to forget all he'd been taught, all he'd suffered.

Damn me for it.

"Ariel." Her name rolled from his lips like the sweetness of wine.

It was as soothing to his tongue as her form was to his eyes. Her taste even more so.

If only he could claim her, but he knew better than to even think such a thought. She reminded him of sunshine and love, of all the things he'd yearned for as a child, all the things he knew as an adult he couldn't have.

Things he didn't deserve.

He was cursed.

From cradle to grave.

The old monks had been right. His life had never been anything more than complete and utter misery. It was why he didn't believe in God.

Why he didn't believe in hell.

Because this life *was* hell, and death would be the sweet release that he craved from it. All he wanted was an eternal sleep where nothing hurt and where he'd never again have to see the face of another person.

Long-forgotten memories surged through him and he remembered the numerous times in his life he'd dreamed of a peaceful haven, of a home with someone who cared for him, someone who saw more than just his physical deformity that marked him as the devil's son.

He was an outsider to this world that had never wanted him in it.

I'm good with that.

Nay, you're not.

Grinding his teeth, he hated that inner voice that called him a liar.

With a growl, he fingered the scar beside his left eye.

"And if thine eye offend thee, pluck it out, and cast it from thee. It is better for thee to enter into life with one eye, rather than having two eyes to be cast into hellfire." The old priest's deranged words echoed through his mind, reminding him of the day they'd almost blinded him for their zealotry.

He'd barely escaped before they gouged out his eye. To this day, he could feel the pain of it.

Not just of their torture.

Of their scorn.

Throwing his head back, he let out a deep-rooted bellow over the injustice of this life that had despised him over his whore of a mother.

Over a father he'd never known.

Neither had wanted him.

And he wanted nothing to do with this world or its people.

He must return to the battlefield. There, he knew himself, his place. There, no reminders existed of his childhood, or the nights he'd lain beaten and forgotten. Unwanted. A useless thing.

On the battlefield, no one dared whisper behind his back or curse him to his face.

Aye, he would send another messenger to William in the morning, and this time, he would demand his brother release him from his duties.

B elial drifted out of the courtyard, giddy with delight. It almost seemed a sin for his plot to go so easily.

He had the upper hand and the stupid bastards still hadn't realized he'd left the playing field.

Or more to the point . . .

Battlefield.

Muffling his laughter, he crossed the yard, past the men who couldn't see him, and left through the gates to venture into the dark forest that waited for his mischief.

Following the guttural chant of the crone, he made his way through the trees to the small fire she'd started in the middle of a clearing. How he loved accomplices. They eased his job considerably, and what was more, he always got two souls for the price of one, or in this particular case, three of them.

In order not to frighten her, and in spite of the fact it greatly diminished his powers, he returned to the form of a human man and approached the crone, who stirred a thick, pungent liquid inside her black cauldron.

"What the hell is that?" He wrinkled his nose in distaste.

She looked up at him with a malevolent smile. "'Tis vengeance. I would have thought you of all things would know its sweet scent."

"Sweet?" He coughed as a stiff breeze blew a whiff of it in his direction. "Smells worse than one of Lucifer's farts."

She shook her head, her eyes glowing from the light of the fire, and from the inner light of her madness. "Were they together?"

Belial backed a goodly distance from the pot and its odor. "Aye. He wants her. But Valteri is a man of fierce control. We'll have to weaken him."

The crone pulled the ladle from the pot and tapped it twice against the side. "What do you think this"—she gestured to the pot—"is for."

Driving away bad neighbors and all sanity by the stench of it.

Belial frowned. "What are you going to do, wave it under their nose until they faint?"

She gave him the nastiest glare he'd ever received and Belial wondered about her sanity to insult him so. "This is my part of the bargain. Yours is to supply the heat to their loins."

"Lust is my specialty." Belial floated up to a low-hanging tree limb where he could watch the crone and her concoction and not be in danger of being gassed by that foul stench. "Have no fear. After the wet dreams I've sent . . . well, I'd hate to be in the physical pain he'll experience come morning."

Belial started to laugh, but another thought struck him. "Come to think of it, I know just a way to make our little Naşāru herself a little less resistant." With a wicked smile, he faded back to shadow. "Trust me, she'll succumb. You can bet your soul on it."

Then again, she already had.

G entle music floated through Ariel's dream. Images of a sweet child-hood spent with her brother and parents accompanied the song, until it woke her.

She jolted upright from the bed.

For a moment, she thought her dream had left her, but with each frantic beating of her heart, she recalled more and more of her dream, her life, until she thought she'd burst with happiness.

She remembered herself!

Ariel was giddy with the thought. She remembered her family and her home! Her servants and pets, lessons and lectures!

With a happy laugh, she threw her blanket off, scooped up her kirtle, and ran to seek Valteri. She couldn't wait to tell him her news.

Pausing briefly in the hall, Ariel looked about, but he wasn't there. She had to find him to tell him.

On trembling legs, she ran out the door and headed for his pallet.

So intent on her quest, she failed to notice the rider rushing from the stable until it was too late to do anything more than scream.

CHAPTER 6

Suddenly, strong arms wrapped around Ariel and pulled her back. Her heart pounded in absolute terror as the rider sped past, narrowly missing her. One instant more and she'd have been crushed beneath the hooves of his rushing horse.

"Dammit, woman, what are you trying to do? Kill yourself? I promise you, there are much less painful ways to die!"

Ariel laughed nervously in relief, grateful Valteri had been there to catch her from her folly. "Thank you!" She placed her hand over his arm that he still had wrapped protectively around her waist.

His grip loosened, but he didn't free her. "You should be more careful," he said, his voice strangely gentle.

To her complete shock, he leaned his cheek against her head for the briefest moment and then must have realized what he'd done, for he shot away from her so quickly that she actually stumbled.

With a stern glower, he swept his gaze over her body. "I trust you weren't hurt?"

Though his tone was sharp, she saw the relief in his bicolored eyes and had to force herself not to smile. To have someone that handsome hold her like that again and be this concerned, she'd gladly hurl herself under a hundred horses. "Just my pride, milord. Nothing else."

He looked away from her as if her gratitude made him uncomfortable. "Pray tell, milady, what was of such great import that you near rushed yourself into death?"

All her fear and uncertainty vanished as her happiness returned. She stepped forward and touched the long blond braid he had draped over his left shoulder. "I wanted to tell *you* first that I remembered myself! My past! All of it!"

He pulled the braid out of her reach and tossed it over his shoulder, his eyes dull and somehow sorrowful. "'Tis glad news, indeed."

Odd, he didn't sound happy.

Rather dismal, point of fact.

"Nay," Ariel said breathlessly, too relieved and giddy to allow him to dampen her joy. She spun in a small circle, arms outstretched. "'Tis incredible!"

Leaning her head back, she watched the sky spiral in a blue and white montage. Her laughter bubbled up through her and she felt as free as the gentle breeze rustling through the bailey. She had a thousand memories of everything! It was the most incredible thing ever!

"Milady, please!" Valteri reached out to stop her dance. "All who watch will think you mad!"

Giggling, she surrendered herself once more to his arms. With one last laugh, she looked up at him, delighting in the feel of his chest against hers. "I care not what they think. I'm too happy to care about their judgment."

A dark, worried shadow leapt into his oddly colored eyes. There was a peculiar panic to him, but for her life she couldn't imagine why he was so concerned.

"Why does my happiness sadden you?"

He swallowed hard. "Because those who claim sanity are the ones who are insane and they will attack like mad dogs if they think for one moment you've lost your reason. Trust me." Releasing her, he stepped away again.

His words were underscored with a palpable anger. He spoke from his own memories and that made her want to soothe the ache inside him.

What had they done to him in the past?

Here she was rejoicing the return of her memories when it was obvious that he wanted to banish his own. The irony of that wasn't lost on her.

"People aren't all evil, Valteri."

He scoffed at her. "That hasn't been my experience." He glanced around the yard. "They're selfish. Cruel. Mean."

"You're not like that."

"Says a woman standing before a man who has butchered hundreds of others."

"In battle."

"Does it matter?"

"You were fighting for your life."

Again, that inward hatred darkened his gaze. "Does it matter?" he repeated.

"My father was a warrior and a gentle man. You can be both." She smiled at him. "Now I know why I've been so drawn to you. You remind me of my father."

His scowl deepened. "You drove him crazy, too?"

She laughed. "All the time. Or so he said. Just as you do." Giddy, she twirled around him once more. "You've no idea of the relief I feel. How much it means to know myself again."

Valteri shook his head as he watched her. It wasn't true. He did know her relief. He'd felt it the day he'd left that fucking monastery. His only regret had been that he'd not razed it to the ground.

But that first smell of air outside its dank, repressive walls . . .

That had been heaven. Even the stench of a blood-and-piss-soaked battlefield had been better.

How he wished he had the courage of the maid before him. She didn't care what others thought. While he liked to pretend he didn't, their scorn still bothered him. Still wounded his soul. Just once, he'd like to know acceptance.

Stupid dream. Yet everyone had that deep-rooted desire.

No wonder she danced with such exuberance now. She knew her place and had her identity back. "I suppose you'll be leaving now with your brother."

She paused to look at him. "Still trying to get rid of me, are you?"

He shrugged. "I should think you'd be tired of my oafish company."

"You're far from an oaf or the boor you think are." She approached him pertly. "I rather like your company."

All the blood rushed to his groin. Damn his body for it. Every day it grew more difficult not to drag her to his bed and find out what it would be like to make love to a woman so passionate and warm. "Careful, milady. When you tilt against a dragon, you could find yourself burned."

Ariel reached out to finger the embroidery on his surcoat. A playful smile curved her lips. "Dragons seldom harm maids. I'm told they sneak them away to their lairs to keep them safe."

Indeed, that was exactly what he wanted to do with her.

And against all common sense, Valteri was just about to reach for her when another rider stormed through the bailey.

"Milord!" He skidded to a halt just before them. "There's been an accident at the castle's construction site!"

His heart skipped a beat as everyone in the bailey came running at the news.

Valteri cursed. "Were any hurt?"

"Aye, milord. I know not how many. They were still digging men out of the rubble as I left to fetch you."

Valteri clenched his teeth. "Wace! My horse!"

Ariel stared at him, amazed at the hostility in his voice, but he betrayed no other sign of fury. How could anyone keep themselves so controlled all the time?

Just like her father. He, too, had possessed a righteous fury that had forever simmered deep inside him.

When he started past her toward his horse, Ariel took his arm. "Let me come with you. I can help."

His taut muscles relaxed beneath her grip, then quickly grew even more rigid and unyielding. She held her breath, certain he'd refuse.

"Very well," he said at last. "Ask one of the women for herbs."

"Thank you." Ariel ran off toward the hall.

At the steps she met the old, withered crone who'd frightened her on her arrival. Uncertainty filled her.

That part of her memory was still missing.

Why do I know you?

This wretch was important for some reason. The crone hated her. She knew it, but why couldn't she remember?

"Here, milady." The old woman extended a faded brown burlap sack to her. "Everything you need is in this."

That expression . . .

Only there had been hatred in her eyes.

Why couldn't she place the woman? She remembered so much of her past, but suddenly she realized great, giant holes still existed. Gaps that left her uneasy and reticent.

In that moment, she felt as if her very life depended on her remembering why this woman was critical to her past.

Her hands cold and trembling, Ariel reached for the bag. "My thanks."

"Ariel!"

She turned at Valteri's urgent shout. Though it should irritate her, it didn't. She more than understood the urgency, and she shouldn't be dawdling while others were in need. Rushing to him, she had to admit that he looked magnificent astride his horse, with the sunlight glinting against his short-sleeved mail hauberk that accentuated every bulge and curve of his well-muscled body. Aye, he was a handsome man. More beguiling than any she'd ever seen.

Unsure if her breathlessness came from her short run or his presence, she quickly mounted the palfrey he had waiting for her.

Valteri barely gave her time enough to situate herself before he kicked his horse into a dead run.

Ariel followed behind, wrestling with her mount. Her mind told her that she'd ridden thousands of times before, but for her life, her body denied it. The reins felt strange in her hands, and she couldn't recall much about controlling the beast.

Nothing about this seemed familiar, in spite of what her mind told her. It was like trying to ram a peg into an unfamiliar hole. No matter how hard she tried, it was all she could do to stay in her saddle. With every stride of the horse, she expected to find herself falling headlong onto the ground.

Terror filled her. And just as she felt herself slipping, she was snatched from her saddle and pulled against a steely wall.

Valteri didn't say a word as he slid back to make room for her in his lap.

Heat stung her cheeks. Not just because she was mortified that he'd been forced to rescue her again, but at the fact that she'd been so incompetent. Why couldn't she do the most basic tasks that others did without thinking?

What is wrong with me?

If she had memories of riding, why didn't she seem to know how to do it?

"Thank you, my lord."

His response was a gruff, noncommittal sound that brought a smile to her lips as his actions forever belied his stern demeanor.

If Valteri the Godless was the beast others thought him to be, he wouldn't bother with the likes of her. He'd have left her behind and without caring whether or not she fell. Instead, he'd saved her dignity and her hide.

There was a lot more to him than others credited. Too bad they couldn't take the time to see what they were missing.

He wasn't just a mindless killer.

And that reality was brought home to her the moment they reached the top of the hill less than a league from the hall, and she saw the horror of what had happened.

Why he'd been in such a rush to get here.

Bile stung her throat at the sight of the mangled men who lay bleeding on the ground, moaning and praying for help and relief. Their pain and misery brought tears to her eyes while Valteri lowered her from his saddle. A wash of terror went through her.

Not from fear.

Nay. Not fear. Because this, *this* was familiar. Why? There was something about their dying that felt as freakishly normal as her holding a sword.

What is wrong with me?

Why would this be normal and riding be alien? That cold slap in the face kept her feet fastened to the spot where she stood.

Leaping from his horse, Valteri rushed toward one of the fallen men and knelt beside him. The older man was covered in blood and gasping for breath. His body was in pieces.

She wanted to say that she'd never seen anyone so badly injured and yet . . .

In her mind, she knew she had.

Where?

How?

Valteri cradled him gently. "Master Dennis, what happened?"

Ariel couldn't see the man's face, but his weak voice drifted to her. "Mortar . . . for the ramparts . . . the rope broke."

She glanced over to the section of wall that had collapsed onto the poor workers. Large chunks of stone lay around the field like the broken hearth of some legendary giant.

"Help me. . . ."

A chill went down her spine at the familiarity of that call.

The frail, agonized voice took her attention from the wall. Ariel scanned the men until she saw a youth of no more than thirteen summers lying on the ground nearby, curled into a ball and crying.

Without a second thought, she rushed to him and knelt by his side. He was just a boy. Blood soaked his pale head from a gash just behind his left ear and a large metal spike protruded from his side.

So much pain in that boyish face. She had seen this before. Had been by someone else's side.

Just like this. It haunted her.

And her heart ached for him. No child deserved to have something like this happen before he had a chance to live. He should be out playing and laughing with friends in the meadows or woods. Not working like a grown man to earn coin for his family.

His pain-filled gaze met hers. "Have you come for me, milady?"

A chill stole up her spine at the familiarity of those words.

She'd heard them before, too.

On the edge of her mind she glimpsed a familiar image, but it vanished before she could make it form fully.

Forcing herself to fight against her rising panic, she took his hand and comforted him. "I've come to help you."

He smiled, his eyes lighting for just a flicker of a heartbeat, then all the glow of life drained slowly from them until she stared into the dullness of death.

He expelled his last breath.

No! Not this child!

Choking on a sob, Ariel dropped his hand and recoiled in horror as a million different images went through her mind. Her breath caught in her throat. She saw people clinging to her in fear and gratitude, the treetops far below her as she . . .

As she—

"Ariel?"

She blinked at Valteri's soft call. Fierce pain ripped through her body, twining around her heart as if it would devour the organ and leave her every bit as dead as the child before her.

How could anything hurt this much? How?

Valteri reached out and wiped away the one tear that had escaped her control and fled down her cheek to chill the skin there.

"Be strong, milady," he said gently. "These men need you."

Men need you. Those words hung like a whisper in the clouds of her mind. Phantom ghosts, taunting her with images she couldn't quite make out.

It was important that she remember. She knew it with every fiber of her being.

"Milady?"

Valteri's voice broke through her haze. He was right, she must help the rest. They were in agony and that was much more important than chasing after the ghosts she couldn't catch. She'd have time to deal with that later.

For now, she needed to focus on the living.

Pushing herself up from the cold ground, Ariel made her way toward the next man who needed urgent care.

With the help of Valteri and several others, she spent the next few hours setting bones and applying poultices. Her stomach churned in painful knots with each beat of her heart until she feared she'd go mad from the stench of blood, and the sight of grisly injuries, some of which she knew were mortal.

She wasn't sure how she knew, but she could tell exactly which of the men would live.

And who was going to die.

Still, she tended them, offering them whatever solace she could.

And while she went through the routine of tending the hopeless, those were the hardest to help, because she knew it was a lie. They were doomed and there was nothing she could do for them, other than try to ease their final hours as best she could.

It hurt so much to watch them die.

Why was *this* so familiar to her?

Over and over, she kept seeing herself walking among the dying. Being aloof.

Why would I not care?

"Here." Valteri stopped her as she reached to bandage another gaping wound. "I'll finish this one. You should take a moment and rest yourself."

In spite of her need to stay and help as many as she could, Ariel nodded and dutifully handed him her poultice.

Honestly, she needed the break. And while he probably did, too, she was feeling a bit selfish and had to take it.

If only for a moment.

Grateful to him, she patted his arm and rose.

Valteri watched her leave, a strange lump tightening his throat at the way she moved. So graceful and elegant even while covered in blood. All through the afternoon, he'd been amazed by her fortitude and control.

By the fact that she hadn't flinched no matter how grisly the injury.

Honestly, he hadn't expected much when she'd first offered to come along. Most noblewomen would have retched and been useless in such a situation.

Too good to get their hands dirty with the blood of common men.

Not Ariel. She hadn't given a single thought to the birth station of anyone she treated.

He'd listened intently to the soft cadence of her voice while she offered comfort and assurances to those who were aching, regardless. She'd eased the men and their loved ones the same effortless way she soothed the pain lurking in the blackness of his own heart, and that mystified him.

How did she always know what words to say?

Conversation had never come easy for him. Words of comfort were even more difficult.

Yet she had no problem speaking to any and everyone. As if they were old friends.

She respected everyone. Never had he met her equal.

And that made him respect her. More than anyone, including his brother.

Until her, nothing had ever lightened his sour mood. And why should it? Life was miserable. Everything about it. From cradle to grave, it was an unending test of who could screw whom the hardest and fastest and get away with it. There was never anyone who could be trusted.

Friend became foe, and foe became lethal.

She'll turn on you, too. Just as everyone else has.

Aye, that was a pathetic fact of life that he mustn't let himself forget.

Clenching his teeth against the burning ache that spread through his gut, Valteri started sewing the wound of the unconscious man. He didn't need the softness of a woman. He was a warrior, fierce and hard, raised by the back of an angry fist. No one had ever comforted him and he had no wish to change his life.

Liar.

Valteri paused at the voice in his head, so crisp and loud it seemed to come from another source than his own mind.

But it wasn't a lie. He could never allow himself to fall victim to anyone. Not for any reason. He'd been there and done that, and had no desire to repeat it. His days of being made a fool or being preyed upon were over. There was nothing worth the risk of it.

In this world, there was only one person who wouldn't betray him.

One person who would never put a knife in his back.

Himself.

People were heartless and they were cold. To protect themselves, mothers would betray their own children. Fathers would cut the throats of their own sons.

He'd seen it too many times.

His own parents had done it to him.

Under no circumstances could he ever allow himself to forget that.

She would sell him out in a heartbeat.

I'm nothing to her.

With three quick stitches, he finished the wound and knotted the thread, then cut it with his dagger.

Needing a break himself, he left the area with the wounded. He scanned the landscape around him, stopping when he saw Ariel sitting on a piece of fallen stone not far away, her expression pensive and pained.

The sight of her beauty there hit him like a fist to the gullet. Worse, it made him harder than hell and sent an image to his mind that the priests would damn him for.

Not that he wasn't already damned. Besides, his mind usually ran on inappropriate thoughts. And the gods knew that Ariel put the most inappropriate thoughts of all time in his mind.

Damn it. Why did he covet her so much when he knew better? His past and his deformity would never allow him the comfort of a wife. Nor could he ever risk passing his deformity on to any child or the stigma he carried to a spouse. Last thing anyone needed was to be called a godless monster because they were in his proximity.

Wounds of the flesh healed. He barely recalled what they'd done to him physically.

It was the insults that never went away. Those harsh words that continued to let blood for years after they were uttered. Words that resonated to the soul. That was what haunted him, no matter what he accomplished.

No matter how strong he grew.

Their words still shredded and gutted him.

Demon they might have accused him when he'd been a boy, but those wretched bastards were far more insidious and demonic than he could ever be.

Unlike them, Ariel was gentleness incarnate. One who deserved so much more than he could ever offer. He had no understanding of love, or kindness of any sort. What could he really give her?

The scorn of people who called him monster and ran at the first sign of his approach?

A cabbage to the head when she wasn't looking?

God knew his brain was rattled enough by such a lobbing, and he wore a helmet. Her tender noggin would never withstand such vicious onslaughts, and he'd gut anyone who dared such an affront to her and tie their innards around their neck for sport.

And that was mild compared to what he'd do to anyone who ever threatened or harmed any child he might one day father.

He flinched at the thought of his child sharing his godforsaken eyes.

Mayhap his enemies were right after all. Demons dreamed of corrupting young innocents, and ever since the moment he'd first laid eyes upon her, he'd had few thoughts save peeling that soft kirtle from her body and making merry with her sweet alabaster skin. Of sinking himself deep inside her until he was lost there for hours on end.

His body ached with the weight of his desire. If he had one moral or decent part left inside him, he'd order both her and her brother from his lands.

Ban them for eternity.

But that was the last thing he wanted to do.

And Valteri scoffed at the very thought of his humanity. Had there ever been any part of him born decent, Brother Jerome had beat it out of him long ago and hung it up on the monastery wall for his amusement. Now, all that was left was a bitter, angry warrior who wanted nothing from this world.

Just a way out as soon as possible.

Sadly, he had yet to meet a man capable of giving him what he wanted most.

Stupid, incompetent bastards. Not a one of them seemed to be able to run him through.

A clap of thunder rent the air, ushering in a sudden, violent wind. He looked up at the sky, amazed at the swiftness of the storm. Dark clouds gathered with an eerie darkness that changed the entire appearance of the landscape.

He hurried to help load the wounded onto wagons to carry them back to their homes in and around the village.

As the last wagon rumbled away, he turned back to the vision who haunted him, waking and sleeping.

Ariel now stood at the edge of the hill, looking out onto the valley below. The winds whipped her dress against her body, plastering the material against her curves so that they outlined each and every bit of her slim posture, leaving little to his imagination. That sight made his mouth water and his body hunger for her even more.

He willed his insatiable lust into submission before it drove him to madness. He must get her back to the hall before the storm drowned them both.

"Ariel," he called.

She ignored him.

Frowning, Valteri made his way to her side.

So much of what she did perplexed him. The way she moved as if all things were new to her, almost childlike, and yet there was nothing childish about her.

He started to touch her arm, then stopped himself. She stared out into nothing, and yet her eyes were focused, not dazed.

"Do you smell it?" Her voice was a faint whisper.

"Smell what?"

"'Tis sweet like a summer garden, yet the bitterness of death and fear contaminate the very vial of life."

His frown deepened at her words. He knew not of what she spoke. "How do you mean?"

She didn't move. "You think me mad."

A chill went down his spine. Could she read his thoughts? "Not mad, milady, just confused." Although, in all honesty, he was beginning to wonder about her sanity.

Or if she was a witch.

You don't believe in that bullshit.

At least he never had before. Yet how else could he explain all this? There was something ethereal about her. Something not quite natural or of this world.

Truth was, he did feel bespelled by her.

Witchcraft was an easy explanation as to why he was captivated by her when no other woman had ever lured him this way.

Don't be an idiot.

He'd always disdained others for those ridiculous thoughts. Only a simpkin believed in such foolery, and he refused to be a hypocrite now.

Demons, fey, and witches. Preposterous fabrications, all to explain the treachery that lived in the hearts of mankind. Better to blame the devil than admit that each man and woman was basically an evil bitch out to smite the very ones they were supposed to love and protect. To admit that instead of being grateful, people were bitter guttersnipes who used those around them for their own personal gain, and then cut the throats of those they called friend, lover, and family as soon as they were done with them.

People were so dishonest that they couldn't even own up to their own nature. They had to invent fey and others just to have an imaginary scapegoat for their cruelty.

It was always someone else's fault. *I'm not beating you because I'm a monster. It's your fault or the devil's that I'm abusing you. I'm doing this for your own good. It's to save your soul for some imaginary god or demon who doesn't give two shits about you, or else I'd have a seizure and die while in the midst of my heartless barbarity.*

He knew that for a fact.

Yet when she looked at him, the torment in her eyes took the very breath from his body and disarmed him completely. She made him want to believe that she wasn't like the rest of the world. That maybe, just maybe she actually had a soul in her body and a heart to back it.

Could this beautiful, innocent kitten turn as rabid as all the others?

Dare he chance it?

She sighed heavily. "I'm so confused. My mind tells me one thing, yet my body says it lies. It's as if the two are enemies waging war against each other and 'tis my soul that serves as prize. Or mayhap my sanity itself."

Valteri wanted—nay, *needed*—to touch her, but he couldn't trust himself to reach out to her. Not when she stood this close to him and he was already this weak.

She was a vicious lure for him. One that made him almost believe there was a devil tempting him to damnation.

What else could explain his reckless disregard of all the lessons he'd learned in his life about the treachery of people.

Do not trust her.

"I know of what milady speaks."

Frustration darkened her brow and she turned back to scan the scenery below. "Nay, this isn't desire. I know the effects of that emotion and it's not as though I don't feel it. I have only to look at you to know *that*."

Those words shocked him to the core of his being. No woman had ever confessed such a thing before. Not even in his dreams.

"Please," she whispered without looking at him. "What troubles me is much more than that. Deeper. My memories tell me that I know things, and have done things that are impossible. Things I can't remember having truly experienced. What I see in my mind can't be right. I know it makes no sense. And I . . ."

She rubbed her hands over her face, her expression one of sheer torture. "Am I deranged?"

His own memories surged. As did a fear that he'd repressed since his boyhood. "Don't ever say that to another soul, Ariel." He growled the words. "Do you understand? People will do unspeakable things to you if they think you mad."

And he didn't want to see her put through the hazards they'd dragged him through.

In spite of every argument that told him to stay as far away from her as he could—to head south to France or even as far as Italy to avoid her and the confusing feelings she awoke inside him—Valteri stepped forward to offer her comfort.

She looked up at him with a guileless frown that tugged at his heart. Aye, this was hell on earth.

For she was all he'd ever wanted.

And everything he could never have.

"But between us, I doubt that anyone is truly sane." If he were, he'd run as far away as he could.

Yet here he stood like a total imbecile.

Rain burst from the dark clouds, unleashing huge drops that pelted them like angry stones.

"Come, milady. Fear no more for your mind. Everything will come to you, given time."

She looked up at him, her eyes trusting and large, and nodded. How did she manage to see him when no one else did? Others stared at him with fear and suspicion.

But never her.

Unused to such trust and tenderness, he felt the last of his resistance fall. It left him naked and vulnerable to her. He hated it. Most of all, he resented the power it gave her over him.

Damn that last shred of humanity that he'd never quite banished. How could it not have been beaten out of him by now? How could there be any-thing left inside his heart other than pure hatred and disdain?

Yet somehow she'd found some shriveled-up part of his decency, and breathed a life into it that he'd have denied three heartbeats ago.

The rain fell harder, pelting him more, but he didn't care.

Suddenly, a bright flash of lightning struck a section of the wall beside them. So close, it barely missed where they stood.

Valteri pulled back in shock, his gaze drawn to the scorched stone that smoldered less than a foot from him.

That had been too close. He needed to get her to safety before the storm turned even more violent.

Or he became more stupid.

Taking her hand, he pulled her toward their horses, then swung her up into the saddle of her palfrey. As soon as he was mounted on his own horse, he reached for her reins so that he could lead her back toward the hall as quickly as possible.

The storm was brutal. If he didn't know better, he'd think the weather had a grudge against him to match that of the rest of the world. It was an all-out onslaught that almost matched the Saxon rebellion he'd been bat-tling these many months past.

Just as he topped the rise that marked the halfway point to the manor, a scream rang out behind him. He turned to see Ariel slipping from her mount.

Valteri tried to catch her, but he wasn't fast enough.

Damn the weight of her heavy woolen dress and cloak that had become soaked in the freezing rain!

'Twas like an anchor about her. Terrified she'd been injured in the fall, he slid down to where she lay on the ground, unmoving.

Her hair hung in her pale face, making her features appear ghostlike and frail.

All the more terrified, he gently brushed away the strands from her cold cheeks. "Ariel!" he shouted over the howling winds and rain, his fear making him unreasonable as he cradled her against him.

Valteri did his best to rub warmth into her skin, but his own hands were every bit as freezing. "Ariel?" he breathed. "Look at me!" Then he gentled his voice. "Please." He hated the sound of that ragged, desperate plea. Almost as much as he hated the ache in his chest from the fear that she might be hurt.

She coughed and opened her eyes. "I can't keep my mount." Her low tone barely reached him through the whipping winds. "'Tis too slippery."

Valteri almost smiled as relief flooded him. Grateful she wasn't harmed, he lifted her in his arms and carried her to his horse.

Ariel gasped at the ease with which Valteri placed her in his saddle and swung up behind her to settle himself there before his arms encircled her in a warm anchor. With a low, deep, guttural command, he took the reins of his horse and hers and spurred them forward.

The fierce power of the horse beneath her, and the man who held her, reverberated through her entire body. They were a united force to be reckoned with and it was obvious that the two of them had been together long enough that they were practically one beast. Which made sense. In battle, their lives depended on each other.

Total trust.

This was probably the only living creature Valteri had ever had that bond with. Everyone else had let him down. She didn't know where that thought came from, but she held no doubt it was true.

He'd been betrayed at every turn.

Starting with his own mother.

So have you.

That inner voice gave her pause. The memories that had come back to her contradicted it. Yet the feeling she had inside verified what she thought.

She'd known betrayal.

But who?

When?

It was so frustrating.

Even more so was the fact that she couldn't stop shivering. She was so cold that it made her teeth chatter.

Valteri looked down at her. "Are you all right?"

She nodded. "'Tis the cold."

He tightened his arms around her, drawing her closer to his hard body. Closing her eyes, she breathed in the scent of sandalwood and rain. Yet as she did so, she saw a peculiar image of him on a battlefield. His armor was stained by blood, his shield scarred from being pounded by men trying their best to kill him.

But what held her attention was the fury and torment that burned deep in his bicolored eyes. There was a madness to his actions as he tore through the other soldiers. One borne by a man who'd been kicked too many times by his life and by others seeking to lay him low.

She could feel his weariness. His disgust.

His need to give as good as he got. To pay them all back for everything that had ever been done to him.

This wasn't about battle or war.

It was pure vengeance.

That was what made others fear him so. His ardent desire to lash out at the world and make it feel his wrath over what had been done to him. To make it pay for the injustice of his birth.

It was raw and biting. Tangible. Never had she seen or felt anything like this.

There's no room in your heart for anything else. You are hatred and blood. That is your curse.

You will never know love or comfort.

Cradle to grave. Like your father. You will be hated.

Gasping, she sat up and almost slipped from his grip. He tightened his hold.

For a mere instant, she saw a clear image of the shadow man who'd been haunting her.

Unlike Valteri, he had dark hair.

But that look of anguished torment and self-hatred . . .

Identical.

Yet the man wasn't old enough to be his father. They appeared roughly the same age. Brothers, maybe?

How could that be? But how else could they be so similar in form and demeanor?

A frown creased his brow as they reached the gates of the hall. She didn't speak. How could she? Ariel wasn't sure what she'd seen or heard. Or even where it'd come from. He'd think her insane if she spoke it.

I am mad.

That was the only rational explanation. Because now she was hearing other voices whispering to her.

Voices that wanted to show her things . . .

Dismounting, Valteri helped her down and quickly carried her up the slick steps, into the main donjon.

No one paid much heed as the servants bustled through the hall, tending their chores. Valteri barked at the first one he neared. "Bring milady a tray to her room!"

She arched a brow at him. He didn't even break his stride. "And you wonder why people fear you so?"

That caused him to return her look in kind. "Feeling cheeky, are you, little mouse?"

"More like a drowned rat."

Growling deep in his throat, he pushed open the door with his shoulder. "Aye, you are." He set her on her feet, grabbed the fur cover from the bed, and wrapped her in it. Though his tone remained gruff, his touch was gentle.

She stepped closer to the fire.

"You need to get out of that kirtle." He opened the small chest beside the bed. "The former lady left several of hers behind when she fled."

She tsked at him. "My mother warned me of men like you, sirrah."

"Pardon?"

"Handsome rogues seeking to get me out of my clothes?"

He actually blushed.

Ariel smiled at something that made him even more handsome—as if such a thing were possible. And that image also reminded her of the other man she'd known.

The one who looked like him.

Clearing his throat, he narrowed his gaze on her. "Careful how you tease, lass. There aren't many men who could resist your beauty. And some would see those words as an invitation."

Suddenly the door opened behind him so that an old crone could shuffle in. She carried two goblets of warm mulled wine.

Valteri glared at her and her timing, which, though convenient, wasn't.

The crone attempted a toothless smile. "Forgive me interruption, lord." She handed him a goblet, then pressed one into Ariel's hand. "But the drink shall do you both some good, methinks." She cast a hooded look to Ariel before she quickly scurried away and shut the door behind her.

Ariel followed the woman with her gaze.

Valteri didn't miss the shadow behind her clear eyes. "She still frightens you?"

She nodded before she drank her wine.

He could well understand that. The old woman was a bit terrifying, as in the type of vision children thought ought to be cooking them up for dinner. Sad to say though, women like her weren't the scariest things in the world. Rather, his nightmares came from frocked friars and bejeweled bishops. Those he'd been told had his best interests at heart.

A pox to the lot of them.

May they all burn in the hell they used to frighten others into subjugating themselves before them. It was the only reason he hoped such a place existed. Surely if it did, their names were engraved upon its walls, with a special place reserved for them and their hypocrisy and lying tongues that stole the innocence of their poor victims.

Disgusted, Valteri downed the spiced wine in one gulp, barely tasting it. And it did nothing to alleviate his chills from his wet clothes or the haunting nightmares of his past.

Not that anything ever did.

Tired and weary of it all, he headed for the door to give Ariel peace so that she could change.

"Valteri?"

He paused at his name on her lips, the sound cutting through him sharper than a dagger. "Aye, lady?"

She crossed the fathomless gulf that divided them with her endless grace and placed her delicate hand on his steel sleeve. "Thank you for listening to my ravings. And for your patience with me."

As if showing her patience was hard for him.

Valteri swallowed, unsure of what to say to that. She stood so close to him that he could smell the sweet rose scent of her hair. She was so beautiful in the firelight. So warm and inviting. How he wanted something clever to say that would make her laugh.

But all he knew how to do was make people cry.

And curse him and his parentage.

"Warm yourself, Ariel. When you're finished with your bath, you can tell me what you remember."

She nodded, then frowned at him. Her eyes clouded as she staggered back. "I feel so strange suddenly."

Valteri barely caught her as she crumpled. Swinging her up into his arms, he carried her toward the bed and laid her against the furs. She appeared so pale and fragile, lying there.

His harsh hand swallowed hers as he rubbed it, trying to warm her cold flesh. "Ariel?" A peculiar bluish tint came to her lips.

That wasn't right.

Terrified she was dying, Valteri rose to get help, but before he could take three steps, his stomach heaved. His vision dimmed. Unable to breathe, he tried to make it to the door.

Until his ears began to ring so loudly he couldn't hear his frantic heartbeat.

As he reached out to steady himself, his knees buckled and sent him crashing to the floor. Valteri tried to force himself to rise.

He couldn't. Instead, he lay there with one cheek to the cold stone, facing the fire.

Cecile ran out from under the bed to sniff at his cheeks. His throat dried to a burning thirst and felt as if it would ignite.

He must get help for Ariel. *Get up, damn you, you worthless bastard! Move!* Closing his eyes, he did his best to summon his strength.

Like everything else in his life, it abandoned him when he needed it most.

Suddenly, Cecile hissed, arching her back. Her tail bushed out. Valteri rolled over to see what had her so distressed. Again, he tried to rise and get help, yet all he could manage was to see a strange shape in the corner. One he'd seen before in his past.

A fleeting memory that was important and one he couldn't remember.

Then everything fell to black.

Akantheus Leucious Forneus had been born for one purpose only—to be a thorn up the arse of his dark father. At least that was what his father had claimed since the day Thorn had cast down his father's battle standard, pissed on it, and declared war on the old bastard.

He'd taken teenage rebellion to a whole new level. And who could blame him? Both of his fathers, natural and step, had ruthlessly used him as a tool in wars he'd wanted no part of, and then turned on him the moment he'd ceased to please them. The moment he'd voiced a single idea not theirs.

Fuck it.

They'd shown him no loyalty or love.

So why should they have expected loyalty from him in return? Their hypocrisy was mind-boggling. At what point in his life was he supposed to have learned such sentimentality as familial respect and bonding when all he'd ever known was bitter betrayal and hatred?

Brutality and vengeance.

Contrary to their stupidity, Thorn had been born with a mind of his own and gifted with enough battle skills to make even the war gods envious. Or more to the point, to make them bow down in defeat to him and his ruthless army.

And so he'd been at war with his father ever since he'd cast off his shackles and refused to do his father's bidding. Had been knee-deep in blood and entrails, and that was fine with him.

He knew no other way.

Not that anything ever changed. He'd been knee-deep in blood and entrails before his rebellion. The only difference now was he protected humanity instead of slaughtering them.

Though some days, he wondered why he bothered. Indeed, there were times when it was hard to tell mankind from the demons who fought for his father.

Like now. The humans among his rank and file were every bit as cruel and cold. Some days, they were even worse.

"Pull back!" he shouted at his men. The demonic army was advancing and he was losing too many.

No need to see any more fall.

Belial was a vicious bitch who lived for the blood and gore. Always had been. And these were dark days for humans.

"Where are our reinforcements?"

Thorn scoffed at the question from his second-in-command. "We've been abandoned."

Hugh turned pale. That was a new look for the seasoned warrior, not that Thorn blamed him. Anyone with common sense would be pissing his armor right now.

"Hellchasers, fall back!" he cried, hoping to save as many as he could.

Damn Belial for this.

Thorn flinched as he saw an entire segment of his right flank go down. *It's what you deserve, you bastard.* Had he not banished his son to Le Terre Derrière le Voile, Cadegan would have been able to rout Belial's forces without so much as a second thought. He was the only knight equal to Thorn's prowess.

Now . . .

Thorn was getting his arse kicked and not liking it in the least. And Cadegan was suffering a fate worse than death because Thorn couldn't bring himself to be merciful enough to kill his own child even for the benefit of mankind.

Damn me for it.

Hugh growled as he fought back another demon. "What has ruptured the balance?"

Killing his own target, Thorn ground his teeth. He didn't have an answer for that. All he knew was that their enemies were growing stronger and they were dwindling in numbers.

Something was feeding Belial and if they didn't discover it soon, it would be too late.

For the first time in centuries, Thorn feared he might actually lose this war.

And his own life in the process.

Dammit! He had to get to the bottom of this and find out what was going on.

Spurring his horse, he rushed up the hill, out of the sight of his men. There was no need in letting a human know what was actually leading them, as they'd never be able to handle it. Nor could he explain it to them.

But when things got this messy, he needed an answer, and he was through playing this shit.

His brethren might be assholes, but he still had a few who weren't totally his enemies.

Glancing back toward the army he led, he made sure none could see him. Then he dismounted from his horse and unfurled his wings.

"Don't any of you bastards shoot me." That would be his luck. Wounded by one of his own who mistook him for the demons they were fighting.

Dodging arrows, he flew over the battlefield and did his best not to focus on his men who lay dead or dying.

Damn Belial for it.

There was no sense in this latest uprising. Malcontent assholes. Those who had no regard for life.

He'd never understood what drove them to such wanton destruction. Even before he'd discovered what and who he was, he'd been at odds with his stepfather, who'd wanted to lay waste to everything he came into contact with.

For pleasure.

Thorn clenched his teeth. He had his whore-mother to thank for those tender feelings.

When she'd summoned Jaden, his real father's broker, forth from the bowels of hell, and bargained for the birth of a son to placate her husband, who was going to kill her if she didn't produce an heir, Jaden had only agreed because he'd known he was consigning Thorn to an eternal battle where his mother's humanity would be at war with his demonic blood.

For that alone, he wanted to kill the primal god who'd made that match.

Jaden thought he was preserving mankind. But the beast inside Thorn was strong, and it became stronger every day.

He lived in fear of the day when that blood would overtake him, and he might become the very monster his father had sought to breed. A demon with no demonic handicap because of his human blood.

An invincible monster that no one could stop.

Like now as he spotted Belial's second-in-command.

Thorn dodged the demon closest to him and swooped in to grab Sorath before he even became aware of his presence. He grabbed him from behind and held his throat with his claws.

"Forneus! You bastard!" Sorath clawed at his arm.

"Tell your bitches to back off."

Sorath motioned the others away from him. "You can kill me, but it won't stop this."

"I know. Where's Belial?"

He laughed until Thorn cut off his ability to make a sound. "Answer or I will kill you."

He was the one being who had that ability, and death for a demon was a very ugly matter.

Sorath sputtered and groaned before Thorn gave him enough oxygen to breathe. "He's chasing a daughter of Michael's."

Thorn laughed at the absurdity. "If he wanted his ass kicked, he should have stayed here."

"Nay. He's found a way to corrupt her. He intends to turn her over to Noir."

And the balance would be broken.

Forever.

With a Naşāru in his hands, his father would destroy the world. There would be no stopping him. "Where is he?"

Sorath laughed. "I'll never tell."

And his army was drawing closer. His time was up. With a growl, Thorn shoved him away and vanished before they captured him.

Shit. A daughter of Michael's in the hands of Belial . . .

How was that even possible?

This was the very thing he'd warned them against and they had all laughed at him for it.

"Demons will never be strong enough."

Bet you wish you'd listened now.

Some days, it didn't pay to get out of bed. This was definitely one of them. Thorn returned to his horse and tucked his wings in.

Sick to his stomach, he looked out over the battlefield. If he didn't find them, this would soon be the entire world of man. Nothing would be left.

The world would be a feeding frenzy.

And everything he'd sacrificed his son to protect would have been in vain.

Fuck me.

He'd send out his scouts to find Belial.

Before it was too late.

CHAPTER 7

Valteri awakened with a start, his throat every bit as tight as it'd been back when chains had held him securely to a church altar while he'd been bound like an animal and tortured for the pleasure of those who were no better than the monster they accused him of being. The Latin words of the priest rang in his ears as if even now the priest was trying to exorcize the devil from him.

Fury raged through his veins as he felt that shame and degradation all over again.

Instinctively, he ran his hand through his hair, searching for the cross that had been branded into the back of his head. Only when he found the jagged scar hidden by his hair did he realize he'd been dreaming a vague memory of days long ago. Though his feelings might feel fresh, the events were buried.

They were a long, long time ago.

How he wished they were only imagined nightmares. But there was no denying what they'd done to the innocent child he'd once been. That young boy had died a horrible death, and been reborn the monster they'd proclaimed him. One who lacked mercy and humanity.

He'd become like them. The worst of all things.

And with that came the sharp, brutal anger that swept over him, and he had a difficult time remembering that he'd ever been so young, so vulnerable.

So unprotected.

How could anyone ever do such a thing to another person? Never mind a child so helpless?

Bastards all!

Valteri took a deep breath to calm himself.

Brother Jerome had died years ago. Not by his hand as it should have been, but he was dead nonetheless. Yet the old bugger was never quite dead enough.

Never was he far from his thoughts or sight.

One piece of monk's robe or sheared head would bring it all back to him. Just as the sound of an a capella chant or the sight of a monastery wall. 'Twas enough to turn him Viking and make him want to burn them all to the ground whenever he passed a monastery.

These nightmares should have faded, along with the passing of the bastard priest, and yet they lurked in the farthest reaches of his mind, waiting for his sleep or some chance encounter before they dared make their presence known. Cowardly memories that always attacked him when he was least expecting it.

Damn them!

Why would they not leave him be? He could battle his memories easily enough while awake, but at night, under the cover of darkness and sleep, they attacked and left him sorely battered. Beleaguered to the end of his reason.

Just as they assaulted him whenever he least expected it. A sight or scent that came out of nowhere.

Valteri growled in frustration.

A sudden soft sigh startled him from his thoughts.

Frowning in confusion, Valteri turned to see the gentle form asleep in his bed.

What the bloody hell?

Horror filled him.

Over and over, memories shredded his soul. Impossible ones that couldn't have happened.

Completely naked, he staggered from the bed as denial screamed out from the farthest reaches of his soul.

Surely he wasn't *that* stupid!

Yet there was no denying what he saw or the images that played out in his head of him and Ariel the night before. Of what they'd done . . .

Of what he'd done to her.

Nay! I wouldn't have slept with an innocent maid! I know better!

His gut contracted violently at the sight of Ariel peacefully resting in his bed. At the sight of the bloodstained sheets wrapped around her pale, bare hips.

There was no denying *that*.

How could I have tainted someone so pure, so giving? What was I thinking? Why was I so selfish?

His mind whirled with images of her soft caresses, her body molding to his. Even now, his loins burned for her and his insides raged like an inferno.

I should have cut off my prick at puberty!

Valteri rubbed at his temples as he damned himself a thousand times over. For one moment of his own reprieve, he'd condemned her to a lifetime of mockery and shame. His very soul screamed against his actions.

How could he have done this?

Was I drunk?

Wanting to beat his own ass, Valteri reached for his breeches and pulled them on. He poured water into a small basin beside the bed, and cursed his foul life before he began washing himself. She'd given him more than anyone and how had he repaid her?

He'd damaged her eternally.

I'm such an ass!

As he splashed his face with water, a new, sudden terror struck him even harder. What if his seed had taken root?

She could have my child. . . .

Valteri clutched at the basin, the edges cutting sharply into his palms as his self-hatred climbed all over him. Why had he not left her when he'd had the chance?

His oath to William or not, he should have fled this godforsaken country.

What is wrong with me? Clenching his teeth, he knew he had only one course of action, and that was even more reprehensible than what he'd already done.

Yet what choice did he have?

Make her a whore or the wife of God's abomination. Either way, she was ruined. No one would ever look at her the same way again or be welcoming to her.

Life as she knew it would never be the same. No one would ever treat her like a lady again.

Even now he could hear Brother Jerome's voice ringing in his ears. *"The angels wept at your birth. In the name of God, we must save your blackened soul."*

Could Jerome have been right after all? Was he really some monster put on this earth for no other purpose than to seek innocent blood?

Ariel's blood.

Growling at his own stupidity over the thought of buying into the monk's insanity, Valteri knocked the basin from the table. Water hit the wall and splashed against his face and chest and still his anger grew.

Ariel awoke with a startled gasp. For a full minute, she couldn't place what had awakened her.

Until she remembered the night before.

Valteri had carried her to bed. . . .

Heat stung her cheeks as she remembered the way she'd broken down and confessed that she was afraid of Belial. That there were still large portions of her memories that were missing.

One minute he'd been comforting her and the next . . .

She still wasn't sure how it'd happened. But there was no denying *this* memory. The heat of his kisses.

The feel of him inside her.

I'm a maiden no more. . . .

She should be horrified. And yet something inside her felt that this wasn't wrong. That she should be tied to Valteri.

It made no logical sense whatsoever. She was the first to admit it.

He was the only solid thing in her life. The only thing she felt that she could rely on.

Depend on.

How could she feel guilt or shame over that?

Yet she could tell by his expression that he felt both. That he stared at her, waiting for her to curse him over something that was as much her fault as his.

She had willingly gone to his bed.

And she'd do it again.

"You startled me." She clutched the blankets to cover her naked body.

Valteri looked away as another wave of desire devoured his will until he couldn't move for fear of what he might do.

Because he knew exactly what he wanted to do again and again with her until they were both sweaty and spent.

"Milady, I . . ." Valteri hesitated.

What could he say? He was cursed and bastard born while she was the noblest of all creatures? That he should never have touched her?

They both knew the truth. No words would rectify what he'd so callously taken, nor would they remove the seed he may have planted. Of all men, he knew the wounds given by people's hostile tongues. The cost of one moment's thoughtless actions because his own father couldn't keep his prick in his breeches.

A lifetime of misery bought for want of one second of restraint.

The thought of so gentle a woman bearing his mother's scars tore through him. How could he put her through an even worse nightmare than what his own mother had endured?

I'm such a selfish ass.

She wrapped the sheet around herself and moved from the bed.

He stood immobile, wanting her comfort, and terrified of what receiving it could cost him.

What it would cost her.

The morning light played against her skin, lighting her hair, and stealing his breath. It surrounded her like a halo. For a moment, he could almost believe in love.

In the goodness of men.

But it was all a lie and he knew it.

People were savage. They didn't care about anyone other than themselves.

Ariel wasn't sure what to say to him. Words seemed so trivial now. Useless, really.

She saw the war inside him that told him to run and the courage that kept his feet nailed to the floor in front of her. How could a man so incredibly strong and noble be afraid of someone as weak as she was?

Yet there was no denying it.

What had they done to him with their cruelty? He was unable to accept even a moment of peace.

A single act of kindness.

"I regret nothing," she whispered.

He winced, then met her gaze with a steeled, stoic glare. "I regret it all."

Those words stung her like a slap across her face.

Ariel started to respond when the door crashed open behind him.

She stepped back with a gasp at the same time Valteri turned toward her brother with a murderous growl.

"Do my eyes deceive me?" Belial arched a brow at them. His gaze went from Valteri to her and back again.

He curled his lips into a sneer. "What hoary game be this? The benefactor demanding his tribute?"

She recoiled again at the insult.

Valteri grabbed him by the throat, then kicked the door closed. "Are you trying to ruin your sister's reputation?"

Belial raked her with a look of utter contempt as he struggled to remove Valteri's hand from his throat. "How could you?"

Ariel lifted her chin against her brother's scathing glare and refused to shirk. "'Tis no concern of yours."

She refused to make any apologies to anyone.

Especially her brother.

Valteri shoved her brother against the wall, his entire body tense. "You will lower your voice," he growled so low that his tone came out like thunder. "And if you ever lay hand to her, I will tear the offending member from your body and beat you with it. Understood?" The sneer on his lips was as unrepentant as she was.

Belial narrowed his gaze. "I demand restitution. You've made a whore of my sister and I will not stand for her to be mocked for your wanton lust."

A shadow darkened Valteri's eyes as he released her brother. He looked at her and she saw all the sadness that burned inside him.

Her chest tightened in fear that he'd abandon her to this scandal.

Instead, he nodded. "I'll have a marriage contract drawn up anon."

Shock poured over her as she looked from Valteri's stoic face to Belial's smug satisfaction. *Don't sound so enthusiastic about it.*

Honestly, she was offended.

A part of her was tempted to tell them both to shove it up their hindquarters, but she knew better than to be so stupid. Once word of this spread . . .

And she was sure her brother would make sure that it did . . .

She'd be ruined. What Valteri offered her was beyond kind and decent.

He was doing the noble thing.

Even if the tone of his voice equated marrying her to the same level as mucking out a pigsty.

Valteri raked her brother with a warning glare. "No one is to know of this morning. I'll not have her shamed for what I've done. Speak one word and so help me, I will rip out your tongue and serve it to you."

Smug satisfaction glowed in Belial's eyes.

And struck a familiar memory.

Only it wasn't of him.

It was a wolf. A white wolf . . .

Why?

Belial straightened his tunic with a pert tug. "I won't have this marriage made in secrecy. For my sister's sake, I want a banquet and full fanfare."

Valteri's jaw tensed. She expected him to resist, or refuse.

But after a momentary pause, he nodded. "I'd have it no other way. She'll be my wife before all."

A malicious smile curled Belial's lips that sent a winter frost against her spine.

"Then her future is now your concern. I charge you take care lest you harm her more than you already have."

Those strange words hung between them. She knew Belial had a hidden meaning, but she couldn't think of what it might be.

There's something you need to remember. . . .

"I'll make sure the priest is notified." Belial laughed before he left them.

Valteri sighed heavily as he faced her. "I didn't ask you before, milady, but I do so now. Do you wish for marriage . . . with me?"

She would laugh at the dread tone except she was sure it would offend him. He was such a contradiction of insecure arrogance.

Of cocksure uncertainty.

When it came to her brother and other men . . . of his place in this world, Valteri never flinched or faltered.

Whenever he drew near her, he was unsure of himself. It was so charming and sweet.

And it sent a wave of tenderness through her. She might not know everything yet, but she trusted him.

"Aye, Lord Valteri. There's no other I would have."

Heated fire sparked in his mismatched gaze. "Then you, milady, are a fool."

His sudden fury surprised her. "I don't understand."

With angry jerks, he pulled his tunic over his head. "You've tied your fate to a man who's damned." He let out a sound of disgust. "I'll send a messenger to my brother to let him know of this. The hall and lands shall be yours to control so long as you finish and maintain the castle I've started. I've a few lands in Normandy that will also be yours."

Was he saying what she heard? Fear took root inside her. "You speak as if you're planning a will."

Turning his back, he retrieved his mail hauberk from the floor. "I won't be staying here much longer. I've other duties abroad."

"And you'll have a wife, here."

"Ariel—"

"Valteri," she shot back, interrupting him. "You cannot run from this. From us. We are tied together now."

Anger darkened his gaze. "Was that your plan last night?"

"What? How could you say that?" Furious, she pushed him toward the door. "Begone with you! You're no better than my brother!"

Valteri was seething as he reached for the door.

Until he heard her whispered words.

"I'm not a whore."

Closing his eyes, he told himself to just keep walking. *Let her hate me.*

But the tears in her voice . . .

Damn it.

He let go and turned back toward her as she pulled her kirtle over her body. "I am well aware of the fact that you are the farthest thing from a whore that has ever existed, lady. Only a woman as noble as you would bring me to the noose of marriage. Believe me, Ariel. I'd sooner be gutted and hanged with my own entrails than do this."

"Then why are you doing it?"

"Because I won't see a lady made a whore because of me. But by marrying me, you will be tainted. I just don't know which will be worse."

"And if the choice is mine?"

He scoffed. "You don't have a choice, and we both know it. This is war, lady. A Saxon maid who takes a Norman into her bed is a traitor to her people. Even if I wasn't devil spawn, they would hate you for what you've done." Dropping his armor, he closed the distance between them and cupped her cheek in his hand. "You've no idea the horrors I've seen. What people will do to each other. They have slit the nostrils of maids for lesser crimes. Scarred their faces."

"Yet you would abandon me?"

With a ragged breath, he shook his head. "Nay. I cannot." Pulling her against his chest, he held her close. "It seems that we're both damned no matter what we do."

Two days later, Ariel glanced about the hall, her heart hanging heavier than the weight of the earth on Atlas's shoulders.

Never had she seen so many dour faces.

True to his promise to Belial, Valteri had drawn up the marriage contract and they had all signed it.

Wace had planned their wedding feast, but no one was festive. Not even the dogs appeared happy as they nosed about for scraps.

The poor musicians kept starting songs, only to stop when no one responded or danced.

They'd have been better off playing a dirge. It certainly would have been more befitting of everyone's somber mood.

"Milord?" Yet again, she tried to take Valteri's mind off the fact that no one approved of their marriage.

He looked up from his trencher, his gaze as empty as the hollow cheers they'd received when they first entered the hall. "Aye, milady?"

She opened her mouth to speak, only to close it as Belial leaned forward with his goblet. "'Twould seem our people have indeed found common ground. Neither Norman nor Saxon has cause for celebrating."

In that moment, she wanted to slap him. Winking as if he knew what she was thinking, Belial stood and motioned for the befuddled musicians to stop. "Good friends, I wish to bless our happy couple with a toast."

"I'll not drink to them," a belligerent voice rang out.

Belial cocked a finely arched brow and slowly lowered his goblet to the table.

In the crowd, she saw a Saxon man struggling against his companions, who were trying to shush him.

"Nay, I'll not be silent." He shoved against them.

Valteri's grip tightened on the knife he held.

Ariel sucked her breath in as she saw a perfect image in her mind of her husband driving that blade straight into the fool's heart.

"This is an evil deed. How can I give my blessing when one of our fairest Saxon maids is sacrificed to a Norman dog. Nay," he sneered, stumbling against the corner of the table. "Not even a Norman dog, but worse. A bastard demon spawned straight from hell! One of—"

"Enough!" Ariel shouted, rising from her seat. "'Tis my husband you address, sirrah, and the only evil I see here this night is that brought by foul rumors and ignorance."

The drunkard looked at her as if she'd slapped him, but she didn't care. She refused to sit by and allow a decent man to be slandered by a fool.

Slowly, Valteri moved his chair back and stood. He scanned the hall and his bland acceptance of the man's words tore at her soul. "Whoever calls this man friend should take him home."

When no one stood to offer aid, Valteri shook his head. With a disgusted sigh, he looked at her, his gaze awash with emotions she couldn't define. How she wished she could make him forget what he'd just heard. And all the other such stupidity that had been hurled at him.

It wasn't right that anyone should be so insulted in his own home.

During his own wedding feast.

And for what? Baseless fears and superstitions?

Over a war their own people had started when they'd failed to hand the throne to his brother as King Edward had promised?

While she despised war and all it entailed, she knew William wouldn't have come here had Harold Godwinson not usurped the throne after Edward's death.

Sadly, Valteri didn't want to be here any more than they wanted him in their lands.

Rather than face them as a heartless conqueror who demanded tribute and blood, Valteri had shown restraint and patience whenever he dealt with them.

Even her own brother . . .

Valteri cleared his throat. "Have no fear of me. I'll not hold his words against him nor will I punish those who help him to his bed. Go in peace." That said, he tucked his knife into his belt and left.

She swept them all with a shaming scowl. "He is your lord, and these are his lands. You would all do well to remember that."

Furious at their behavior, Ariel followed after her husband. She caught up to him just outside the main doors. "Valteri?"

Valteri ground his teeth as he felt her gentle touch on his arm. No one had ever before defended him and he wasn't sure how to respond. "You should go inside before you catch a chill."

She shook her head and he ached to pull her back into their chambers and make love to her for the rest of eternity.

But that was only a dream.

No one would accept their marriage.

Ever.

Everyone's reaction tonight had proven it. If he had an ounce of decency, he'd slit his own throat and allow her to find another husband to stand by her side.

But he wasn't decent.

Ariel tightened her hand on his arm and he allowed her to turn him until he faced her. "Ignore the imbecile. He was drunk. He knew not—"

"He knew."

There was no excuse to be made.

People were assholes.

Thunder clapped over their heads. Though the rain had been a steady drizzle most of the day, the night threatened a volatile storm.

Valteri glanced up at the dark, eerie clouds. "Go inside where 'tis safe."

"I belong with you now."

A bitterness filled his eyes that tightened her throat even more as she feared he'd pull away from her. "Only a fool would want to belong in my cursed life."

Her grip tightened on his arm. "It's not just your life I'm after, Valteri. It's your heart I want most."

Valteri let out a bitter laugh. "Haven't you heard? No heart exists inside me. 'Tis said Lucifer himself ate my heart to ensure I'd never feel love or compassion . . . for anyone."

"Valteri—"

"No more words, Ariel," he interrupted, moving away from her. "I beg you return inside before I taint you further and the others decide there's no difference between us."

She wanted to argue with him more than she'd ever wanted anything, yet she knew he was past listening. This had been rough on him and he needed distance from it.

Tomorrow, she'd work on winning him over.

Tonight . . .

She let out a sigh as she watched him sidestep the puddles, his spine more rigid, unyielding, and unscalable than a distant mountain range.

Wishing she knew how to reach him, she lowered her gaze to the ground. The shimmering depths of the puddles called to her and she moved to stand next to the one just outside the hall's door. The drizzle caused the reflection of the rushlights to distort in their puddles. And as she watched, an image emerged.

"Please spare me! I don't want to die!"

Ariel recoiled at the sharp shriek inside her head. Images tore through her. Demons surging forward. A knight clinging to her in mortal terror as she . . .

As she . . .

"Please!" she cried out, placing her clenched fists over her temples in an effort to recapture the vague memory. "What are you trying to tell me?"

"'Tis late and you should be inside, dear sister."

Ariel whirled around at the sudden voice behind her, her heart hammering in panic. Belial stood a few feet away, his face masked by shadows. For an instant, his eyes appeared red, but as soon as she blinked, they faded into the darkness.

Was that real?

Or imagined?

"Who are you?" she whispered. "Really?"

Pressing his lips into a tight line, he walked a small circle around her, his hands clasped behind his back. "You know me, little sister. We are kin, you and I. I've been in your life for as long as you can remember."

A chill went down her spine at his sinister smile.

He stopped in front of her and tilted her chin until their gazes met. The coldness of his eyes made her flinch. "We *are* brother and sister. Cut from the very same cloth."

Though her mind raged with images of them together as children and adults, her heart denied it all.

It just didn't seem right.

Deep inside her, she knew there was much more to their relationship than just kinship.

He's lying.

She couldn't shake that inner voice or feeling. His presence slithered over her skin and made her cringe.

"Now come inside before you face another storm. One you're not prepared to deal with."

Don't trust him.

Every part of her screamed that out loud. He wasn't what he seemed and his emotions weren't sincere. Yet even so, she had no reason to deny him. So, she allowed Belial to take her hand and lead her back inside.

Hours later, Ariel sat inside her chambers, listening to the raging storm. Each hour that passed, she was certain Valteri would return. Yet each one came and went while she waited, until she knew he had no intention of joining her.

I'm married and alone.

That reality haunted her.

More than that, it made her heart ache. And it gave her just a smidgeon of what Valteri must deal with every single day.

How did he stand it?

People weren't meant to be alone. They needed each other. An image of two parents came to her mind. Yet it left her hollow.

Then she saw a man. . . .

Unbelievably tall, with dark hair. Silvery, swirling eyes and a crooked smile.

That memory filled her with warmth. It felt real, even though she had no idea who he was. He seemed like family.

Not Belial and not the people she kept seeing as her returned memories. "Why can't I figure this out?"

Why had he touched her if he was so opposed to marriage? To being tied down by a single woman?

Nothing made sense.

Cecile stretched beneath her touch. Ariel smiled at the small kitten and continued to stroke Cecile's soft underbelly.

As she lay on the bed, her mind replayed haunting images of the night before. Of Valteri taking her in his arms, his hard body sliding against hers, his hands seeking out the most intimate parts of her body.

Yet something inside didn't quite accept the reality she remembered. Instead of crystal clarity, the images were as blurry as the rushlight in the puddle.

The only real feeling was the need she had to find him and be by his side. To comfort him.

But with that desire came a tiny voice that warned against seeking Valteri and claiming him the way she wanted.

Why? What was wrong with seeking one's husband? She belonged to him and he to her.

Still, the voice persisted.

Ariel shook her head in an effort to clear it. Maybe she was insane.

Go to him.

Startled by the unexpected voice, she glanced to Cecile as if the strange sound could have come from the tiny animal. "I have lost my mind."

Placing her goblet on the bedside table, Ariel snuggled down into the fur-lined covers. She closed her eyes, determined to think no more on the matter. It was late and past time for her to sleep.

Besides, she was exhausted from the strain of all the people sitting in judgment. People who knew nothing of her or Valteri.

She wanted this day ended and a better one to begin.

Those thoughts lulled her to sleep.

"Save him!"

Ariel sat up with a startled gasp. This time, there was no mistaking the voice she'd heard.

It'd been sharp and male. A fierce, commanding sound that urged her to action.

For the first time since she'd awakened and seen Valteri standing over her, Ariel knew what she had to do.

No more. He'd been cast out to the storm for far too long. No one deserved the life that had been forced on him.

She must save him from the destructive path he walked. Show him that he belonged in the world of the living. The two of them had been joined, and so long as breath filled her lungs, she must not give up on him.

On them.

Her heart hammering in uncertain fear of his reaction, she left the bed and dressed, her hands trembling and fumbling with the material. Would Valteri ever welcome her, or would he forever pull away, out of her reach?

Either way, she had no choice other than to try.

As she searched the hall, she ran through her mind all the possible places he could be, and settled on the stable. With the ferocity of the storm, she doubted he'd seek his pallet in the garden.

Nay, he'd be sheltered this night.

If not in her arms, then he'd be with the only creature alive that he fully trusted.

His horse.

Valteri came awake with a start. He glanced about the stable, looking for the cause of his dream, but only his horse, Ganille, met his eager gaze.

Snorting, Ganille pawed at him as if urging him to move over.

"Stop, or I'll feed you bitter vetch."

This time, the snort sounded more like a rude dismissal. Sadly, his horse paid him as much heed as his squire.

I should beat them both.

But he'd never lay an angry hand on anyone or anything unless they struck first. Having been so abused, he'd never carry that forward.

He rolled over, his thoughts turning to Ariel. No doubt she was in his bed.

Alone.

Like him.

Meanwhile, rain pelted against the sides of the stable and a few of the horses nickered and bucked nervously, fighting the ropes that held them inside.

The stench of damp hay and horse shit offended him, causing his nose to twitch in disgust. How he hated stables and the memories they brought.

All the times he'd been mocked.

You're shite, boy. It's all you'll ever be.

No matter how many battles he won or men he defeated, he could never silence those mocking voices. Any more than he could erase the sight of people sneering and jeering at him over a birth defect he loathed as much as they did.

Yet where else would filth like him sleep? He felt no more at home inside the keep than he did here.

In truth, he'd never felt wanted anywhere.

Except in Ariel's bed.

Growling at himself in frustration, Valteri draped his arm over his eyes in an effort to forget it all, and listened to the sounds of distant thunder.

But still his thoughts churned on against his will to quiet them.

Go to her. . . .

I'm not that big of a bastard.

No matter how much he might want to rise from his pallet and seek out his wife, he wouldn't do it.

He'd done her enough harm. She deserved better. Closing his eyes, he forced himself to remember the dour, unaccepting faces of his people. They would forever ridicule his union, and eventually that ridicule would spill onto his precious wife.

He'd be damned before he'd ever cause her that type of pain.

"Well, what a strange place to find a bridal groom."

Fury flared inside him as Valteri shot to his feet. With a sneer on his face, Belial stood at the entrance of the stall, leaning against one post. He set the lantern in his hand down before him. "I would have thought after the eagerness with which you took Ariel's virginity that you'd be on her this night like a wolf to a deer."

"Don't you dare say such to me!" Valteri was disgusted. "She's a lady and my wife, and I'll not have her name bandied about as if she were a trollop."

Belial laughed, a bitter, unholy sound.

There was something insidious about this beast. Deep-rooted and foul.

"'Tis a pity you don't defend yourself with the same vigor."

Valteri arched a brow at the bastard's audacity.

And his stupidity.

Valteri raked him with a less-than-impressed grimace. "I assure you that I can fend for myself well enough."

"Can you now?"

For just the tiny beat of a heart, Valteri swore 'twas Brother Jerome's voice he'd heard.

Not Belial's.

But when he spoke again, the tone and malice were all his and they set fire to Valteri's temper. "I don't see a fierce warrior before me, but rather a scared little boy who allows a drunken fool to mock him before the whole of his people. A little boy who cowers from his own wife. What? Afraid she'll mock you as well? Or are you just incapable of pleasuring her?"

Growling with rage, Valteri charged his tormentor, catching Belial about the waist. They stumbled back against the stable wall.

"So the cat does have claws." Belial let out a sinister laugh. "Come, Valteri the Godless, son of Lucifer, kill me and claim your true right. Even now your wife waits, her loins hungry for your body. Would you deny her your seed?"

Valteri reached for Belial's throat, determined to squeeze the life out of his repugnant body. But as his hands closed around the slender neck, Belial's eyes darkened to a deep, vibrant red.

Shocked by that sight, Valteri let go instinctively, and Belial's eyes immediately turned blue again.

What the hell?

Literally.

Belial broke his grip and moved away. "Nay, you're no coward. You have fought long and hard to get what you want. . . . Or have you?"

Rubbing his neck, he turned to face Valteri. "Tell me, godless one, what do you truly seek?"

Right now, he'd settle for Belial's head on a platter and his lifeless body in a pool at his feet.

Yet . . .

He couldn't get rid of the image he'd seen. Those red, unholy eyes.

Just who or what was he dealing with?

Unsure, Valteri stared at him, giving him due space as he tried to find a logical reason for the trick his eyes had played.

Surely it'd been the flame of the lantern that reflected the red light, or mayhap some trick of his mind.

Aye, that must be it.

I don't believe in demons.

Other than those inner ones that constantly plagued him during silent moments.

Or men who pretended to be good while plotting the foulest of deeds against others for no reason or cause.

And while he might not know what had caused Belial's eyes to shift color, one thing stood certain—he'd be damned long before he confided in the man before him. "What do you care?"

A slow smile curved his lips. "Since you married my sister, I have a vested interest in your future."

With a stupidity that defied belief, he picked the braid off of Valteri's shoulder and dropped it to trail down his back. "I saw the careful instructions written in the marriage contract. How you left all your property to her in the event of your death." He leaned in closer to whisper in Valteri's ear. "Is that what you seek? Is death the dream that haunts your sleep?"

Valteri tensed at hearing his fondest desire put into words. Aye, he longed for death, had done so since the day he'd slid from his mother's womb and not had the good sense to strangle himself with her umbilical cord. Every time he went into battle, he did so hoping someone's blade would at last end his pain.

Belial pulled a dagger from his belt and held it beneath Valteri's chin.

Without flinching, Valteri studied the shining blade. A golden dragon head protruded above Belial's fist.

Raising his gaze, he noted the emptiness of Belial's eyes.

Soulless.

There was no emotion there of any kind. He was as ruthless a killer as Valteri.

One corner of Belial's mouth turned up into a regretful smile. "Nay, I cannot kill you, but you could kill yourself. Tell me why a man who wants nothing more than death has never heeded its call?"

Valteri refused to answer this question. He refused to admit aloud that he had never given up hope that one day his life might change, that mayhap he would someday find a place where he belonged.

A place where no one mocked him.

That in the end, he was just too damn stubborn and stupid to quit.

For that stupid, treacherous hope, he would never end his own life. He would trust in the same cruel fate that had delivered him into such a brutal life to alleviate him of its burden one way or another.

In due time.

Belial smirked. "Do you fear damnation more?"

Valteri's gaze narrowed. "I fear nothing."

"Then here, take my dagger and end all you have suffered."

Knocking Belial's arm aside, Valteri sneered at him. "You think little of your own life to seek me out with your simpkin wit. Begone now before I yield to the desire I have to end *your* life."

The mocking smile did little to ease his anger. Nor did the curt bow. "As you wish, milord."

Then, as quickly as Belial had appeared, he left.

Outside, Belial smiled at the rain that didn't drench him. Nay, the rain, unlike mortal fools, knew better than to evoke his wrath.

How he enjoyed toying with them. 'Twas indeed a shame he couldn't end their pitiful lives. That he could only tempt them to do it for him.

Oh, to have the heady power of life and death. But the actual giving and taking of life belonged solely to other creatures.

A hand touched his shoulder.

He whirled about to face the old crone, Mildred. Lucky her that he recognized her wrinkled face before he'd ripped out her heart.

"Why did you tempt him to die?" she asked in her screechy voice that sent painful stabs all the length of his hated human body. "She must fall in love with him first, and then she must watch as his life drains away. If the Norman dog kills himself before she falls to her desire, you cannot claim her soul and we might have to wait years before she finds another man to love."

Putrid, hot anger ran through him. He'd never liked being questioned. It reminded him of too many nights spent in his master's company. "I know what I'm doing."

"Then explain it to my human wit."

Why could he never once find an intelligent accomplice? One who could understand the nuances of subtle manipulation.

All of mankind was too stupid to live. The sooner his demonic brethren wiped them from this earth, the better for all.

Belial took a deep breath, his head throbbing from the strain of his anger and human form. Soon he'd have to leave and restore his strength. And the dark ones knew he needed every ounce of strength to deal with imbecilic humans.

Facing her, he allowed his full venom to enter his voice, turning it into its true echoing, demonic form. "I knew Valteri would never kill himself. I was merely reminding *him* of that fact."

He smiled, cruelly relishing her fear and his coming triumph. "All these years past, he has lived solely on hope, and now that hope has a name. And *her* name is Ariel. Trust me, crone, she is his undoing."

And both of them were the key to his rise on the other side. . . .

CHAPTER 8

V alteri blew out the lantern, his thoughts drifting between Ariel's innate goodness and her brother's causticity. How could they have come from the same womb?

He frowned as a familiar tightness settled in his gullet. Would he have been so different from his twin brother had his brother lived?

Would his unnamed brother have been cursed with his deformity?

While it was selfish of him, a part of his being that he didn't want to think about was angry that his brother had been spared the misery. At least if his brother had lived, there would have been someone else who would have understood his mindset. His anger at the injustice of his life.

Would they have even been friends?

It was a lot to think about. For all he knew, his brother would have been normal and would have been the first to curse him for casting a shadow on his brother's "normality."

Weary and cold, he leaned his head against the coarse wood of the stall, and allowed his pain to flow freely through him. All his life, he'd wondered how things might have been had either his father or brother been around.

If his mother had actually claimed him.

Valteri preferred to think that they'd have been like William. Definitely reserved and respectful, but not cruel, fearful, or hating.

Closing his eyes, he could still remember the first time he'd seen William. His brother had ridden three weeks to visit the small monastery where their maternal grandfather had abandoned him. Brother Jerome had often described the fear in his grandfather's eyes. *"Fulbert of Falaise begged us to save your soul, boy, and that's what we're going to do!"*

They might have saved his soul, but it came at the expense of Valteri ever believing there could be a god who would turn a blind eye to the cruelty of those who served Him, abusing an innocent child.

How could they really save his soul while they condemned their own?

Ignorant sycophants. How could anyone believe their lies?

Yet Valteri could never truly fault his grandfather for his superstition, any more than he could fault all the poor religious shandys who clung to their beliefs. It seemed ever the plight of the sheep to follow after whatever wolf led them.

Not that William, for all his piety, had ever listened to those evil tales.

Honestly, Valteri still didn't understand why his brother had been different.

Other than the fact that Will had never been anyone's sheep.

To this day, Will hadn't told him why he'd come that day. William had always attributed it to divine providence.

"I was meant to find you, brother."

Whatever it'd been, it'd changed his life, as Will had set him free from that monastery hell and put him under the military tutelage of one of his allies. From that day forward, he'd ceased being the poor possessed child the brothers struggled to exorcize, and had become a determined squire. He'd trained harder than the other boys, knowing he must be the fiercest if he was to ever silence their mockery and scorn.

Even though Lord Hugh had been a bastard who had no more love of him than anyone else, he'd taught Valteri everything he needed to go to war.

Aye, he'd cracked a few skulls, but in the end he'd achieved his long-sought peace. No one dared taunt him to his face.

Not even Hugh.

Until now.

"Valteri?"

He jumped at the gentle voice behind him. How had she come upon him without his hearing her?

"I'm here, milady."

Ariel walked forward into the stable. He felt more than saw her.

The horses immediately quieted as if her presence soothed them as much as it did him. She held her arms outstretched, tentatively searching the area around her, and walked slowly into the darkness where he sat.

The dark shadows where he lived.

Cursing himself for the stupidity, he rose and closed the distance between them. Even more foolish, he took her outstretched hands. Her cold fingers trembled in his and the softness of her skin reminded him of everything he'd ever wanted.

Everything he'd been denied.

"Why have you come?"

"I was worried over you. I kept thinking you'd return, and when you didn't . . . I just had a feeling inside that told me to find you."

He cherished those words. And damned them.

She shivered from the cold, and the wetness of her kirtle that clung to those feminine curves that haunted him, while dreaming and awake.

"You're soaked through," Valteri growled, his hands tightening on hers an instant before he released her.

Ariel reached for where he'd been, but found nothing other than blackness, and she feared he'd left her alone.

Until he returned with a blanket, and draped it over her shoulders. She smiled at his kindness.

"'Twould seem I'm forever drying you off."

She laughed at his gruff tone, and adjusted the blanket, her cheeks warming as she remembered what had happened after the last time he'd chased away the cold.

And at this moment she would happily welcome his touch. Especially the tenderness of his kiss.

Just looking at him, she burned in a way she'd have never thought possible.

"For your kind attention, Lord Gallant, I'd gladly hurl myself into a lake."

He moved away and she sensed her words had upset him.

She closed the gap between them. "I didn't mean to—" She gasped as her foot caught against something, and she stumbled.

Suddenly, strong arms surrounded her as she collided with his hard body. Once more, she remembered the night before. His bold caresses.

Fire danced in her stomach.

Would he ever again seek her out, or would she forever be forced to go to him?

"Thank you," she whispered, reaching up to touch his face.

"Here." His voice was gruff as he lowered her to the straw-lined floor, and took her hand away from his cheek.

When he started to move away, Ariel grabbed his arm and pulled him to sit beside her. "Nay, Valteri. I would have you speak with me, not flee into the darkness like a demon afraid of light."

"And what if I were just that?"

Again, she wished she could see his face. But then, perhaps he found comfort in the shadows that he claimed as home.

Perhaps he needed that in order to confide in her.

Aye, since he couldn't see her, maybe he'd finally open the chains that he kept sealed around his heart and thoughts.

"We both know what you are, milord."

He snorted. "I know what you think me to be and I know truthfully what I am. You, dearest Ariel, delude yourself with a fanciful image of some kind and noble man, who will rescue you from the clutches of your foul brother."

She frowned in confusion. "Is that not what you did?"

"Aye." His gruff voice was full of bitterness. "But in my haste I worsened your situation. Before, you were a treasure any lord would gladly take. Now that you've bound yourself to me, you'll know scorn the likes of which you cannot imagine."

"Like the Saxon in the hall this night?"

He released his breath in a rush, and for a moment she thought he'd leave.

Then he drew a ragged breath. "His words were mild. Your people are defeated and they fear us now. Even drunk, he didn't plow the truly callous field of stinging insults that you'll come to know soon. He knew only too well what crop awaited him, should he sow that discontent and harvest my wrath."

Biting her lip against the sudden swell of sympathetic pain, she thought over the Saxon man and his remarks. If only she could have prevented them from ever being spoken.

But the real question was how many years had Valteri been subjected to such?

A painful knot closed her throat and she drew a deep breath. Would she ever find a way to touch the heart inside him?

More to the point, would she ever be able to show him what she saw? That he not only had one, but held the kind, gentle heart all men should have.

"Come." He held his hand out for her. "I must return you to the hall."

"I'd rather stay with you."

He shook his head. "You cannot, Ariel. You don't belong in my world. It would destroy you."

Ariel started to argue, but was too weary. Valteri was a stubborn man and it would take more than mere words to persuade him to her cause. Perhaps in time she might find a way to reach him, but would he give her that time?

Sighing, she took his hand and allowed him to pull her to her feet.

Tired and weary, she followed him through the stable with only the sound of crunching straw and falling rain breaking the tense silence between them.

He pushed open the door so that they could head back to the hall, and paused. Loud thunder clapped and a new burst of rain broke. Winds howled in her ears.

Cursing, Valteri closed the doors with a loud clatter and moved her back. "We'll have to wait awhile for the rain to slacken."

She smiled, grateful for the weather's intervention.

His silence almost tangible, Valteri led her back to the stall. "Rest yourself. I'll wake you when 'tis time." He moved away.

"Will you not sit with me?"

She felt his reluctance as he took a seat beside her.

Ariel placed her head on his shoulder. He tensed for a moment as if he fought with himself, then he relaxed and draped an arm over her.

Savoring the rich scent of him, the warmth of his body so close to hers, she closed her eyes and wished for the courage it would take to strip his tunic from him and relive her memories of the night before. But should she try, he'd push her away and leave her longing. *I will find a way to reach you, Valteri.*

Somehow.

Before it was too late.

M ilady?"
Ariel came awake with a slow stretch. She opened her eyes to see Wace standing over her. Frowning in confusion, she clutched the blanket to her chin and scanned her chambers. How had she gotten here?

"Where's Lord Valteri?"

Wace grinned. "He left early this morn with several men. He said to tell you he'd return this even."

Wace wagged his brows, the implication of which she knew full well. "He carried you in at first light and warned me to make certain you were left undisturbed."

She returned his smile, but it went no further than her lips. Why had Valteri not awakened her as he'd promised?

Did this mean he'd kept her by his side all night? Even though he constantly protested her presence and sought to leave it?

She shook her head over her baffling husband.

Wace looked past his shoulder, into the hall. "I wouldn't have disturbed you now, milady, but a friar has come and he seeks the lord or lady of the hall."

Ariel scowled at those words. "A friar, you say?"

"Aye."

A sudden thought brought a smile and lifted her spirits. This just might be the chance to ease everyone's fear of Valteri. If she could get the friar on their side, surely the others would see he wasn't a demon.

Throwing back the covers, she rose from bed.

Ariel hesitated as she realized Valteri had left her fully clothed.

Right down to her shoes.

How odd, indeed. They were married now, and even after the passion he'd shown the night they'd been together, he still acted as if he, the fearless, was terrified of touching her.

"Milady, he waits."

Nodding at Wace's insistence, Ariel followed him into the hall. The short, rotund friar immediately stood, his face aghast.

Wondering at the strange reaction, she shortened the distance between them. "Greetings, Brother . . . ?"

"Edred." He nervously brushed his hand over his tonsure. Redness spread over his cheeks and up to the small shaven circle. He cleared his throat and settled a steely gray gaze upon her. "I received a message from a Lord Valteri two days ago asking for someone to come bless graves and administer last rites. I understand some sort of accident took place?"

Of course he did.

Valteri the Godless had asked for a friar to take care of the needs of his people.

But why had Valteri not spoken up when the Saxon criticized him before all for not having done so?

Because he only defends himself on the battlefield and with a sword. He was wise enough to know that words seldom changed anyone's mind. Therefore, he didn't bother to even try them.

No doubt, as a boy, words had only worsened his punishments and criticisms and taught him not to bother.

"I apologize for my delay," the friar continued. "But there was a poor possessed child who needed my aid and I couldn't come any sooner."

"And how was she possessed, good brother?" Belial asked in a mocking tone as he entered the hall behind the friar. He leaned in the doorway, a menacing smile on his lips.

"She was . . ." The friar paused, then frowned. "How did milord know 'twas a girl?"

Belial shook his head. "'Tis the look about you, good brother." He joined them in the hall and wound his arm about her waist. "And the untoward look in your eyes when you addressed my fair sister."

The friar's jaw began to flop like a fish dumped from his water as he realized Belial had just insulted him. His eyes widened and a wave of anger crashed through Ariel.

"Apologize to the friar," she said through clenched teeth. "'Tis no need for you to insult him so."

Belial cast a warning glare to her that sent a frigid shiver of fear down her spine.

Ariel blinked, her mind faltering as another memory surfaced.

"Be nice and sacrifice yourself for me." The words spun through her head, repeating themselves over and over.

Aye, 'twas Belial's voice.

Only he'd looked different then. "Milady?" Brother Edred stepped forward and took her arm.

Ariel glanced from him to Belial, whose brow was lined with . . .

Was it fear?

Yet she couldn't make herself believe Belial would fear anything.

"My sister has had an accident herself." There was no mistaking the caution of Belial's tone. "For days now, she cannot recall herself and is given to spells of dizziness."

"Is milady poss—"

"Nay, Friar, don't say *that*," Belial warned. "Not in this hall. Such words would bring out the fiercest wrath of her husband, who guards her like treasure."

Ariel stared at him. What was he trying to do? Strange, indiscernible whispers shot through her head and a part of her told her if she listened carefully enough, those whispers would answer her questions.

Belial brushed the hair from her cheek and her thoughts stilled. A strange glow hovered in Belial's eyes and one corner of his mouth crooked up. He looked to the friar. "Were I you, Friar, I'd avoid the lady's presence as much as possible."

Brother Edred frowned. "How mean you?"

The slow smile that spread across Belial's face appeared sinister and cold, and a shiver of fear slid to her stomach and clenched it tight. "In due time, brother. But come. I shall show you to the graves and families of the people who need your ministrations."

Ariel watched the two of them leave, and the hazy images of her mind cleared.

Her brother's alliance with the friar didn't bode well. Belial was a wicked man.

Wicked and cold.

Every time he placed a hand upon her, she could feel it in his touch. See it in his eyes.

Over the last few days, he'd made no attempt to speak with anyone other than Valteri or her, and she knew he must have something evil planned to seek the friar now.

But who was he trying to harm?

Part of her urged her to go after them and speak with the friar alone, but another part warned her to stay clear until Valteri's return.

Belial was right about that much. Valteri wouldn't welcome finding her in the presence of clergy. Not with the way he hated them and was forever suspicious of their motives.

Heeding that warning, she returned to her chambers to wash and re-dress.

Valteri reined his horse to a stop. By the looks of his men, he could tell they were ready to return, yet each held his tongue. In fact, as he studied them, he realized not one man among them would even dare meet his gaze.

As soon as he cast a glance at any of them, his subject would avert his eyes.

Bitter amusement filled him. There were some advantages to being well feared. No one dared voice a complaint, but then no one ever approached him for any other purpose either.

He'd never noticed that before. Not until Ariel made him realize just how isolated he'd become. How many nights he'd spent alone without friend, without comfort.

Other than Wace, and even he kept a respectful distance. As his squire, the boy didn't want to overstep his bounds. And Valteri had always been too suspicious of others to even trust his own squire.

That random thought disgusted him.

But Ariel was different. She sought him out even when he wanted to be left alone. Instead of angering him . . .

He welcomed her friendship and presence.

Thirty days. Just thirty short days since he'd first seen her and already she'd ingrained herself into his life.

And he hated himself for that weakness. He knew better than to hold tender thoughts for another, especially a woman.

So why couldn't he block her from his mind?

Valteri winced at the pain in his chest. Never before had the prospect of taking lands appealed to him. Yet to protect and provide for Ariel, he was willing to abide by Will's wishes.

Why was he so devoted to a woman he'd just met?

A maid who'd become his wife.

Why did he feel a need to protect a woman who should be his enemy? He'd conquered her people and had hated every part of this hellhole country.

Yet for her, he was willing to offer her a protection that he'd only ever extended to one other.

A boy who'd been abused like him.

Maybe it was the cruelty of her brother. The fact that he knew what would befall her if he left her to her own means.

With his lands and blood alliance to William, she'd never again be homeless. Never know the fear of hunger or cold.

That would extend to whatever seed he might have planted within her.

Should Valteri fall in battle, William would make sure that she'd have her choosing of any lord who met her fancy, as she'd be among the richest widows in Christendom. He could secure a promise from his brother that Ariel would have her choice and that neither her brother nor his would ever override her pick of spouse.

Aye, that would be the best for all of them.

Ignoring the part of him that screamed out he should hold on to her with everything he had, Valteri wheeled his horse about. "If there were bandits stealing from the crofters, 'twould appear they've fled."

As expected, none of his men replied.

"Let us return."

At least that finally restored their glee. They were as eager to part with his company as he was with theirs.

Valteri kicked his horse toward the hall.

As he raced, a sudden dread filled him. He couldn't wait to be with his wife, and that feeling made him sick to his stomach.

I must never touch her again.

No matter how much she tempted him. If they were lucky enough that she had yet to conceive, he couldn't tempt any more ill fate.

Gah, I'm afraid of a tiny maid. . . .

He shook his head at the irony. He'd stood in battle against the best England had to offer without flinching. No scratch had ever marred him.

Now a simple Saxon maid had brought him to his knees. Made him afraid to even return home.

You have to leave her. You know that.

Men only respected warriors, and only as a feared warrior could he keep their lying, gossiping tongues still. With his absence, Ariel's goodness would win over the people.

In time, they'd forget and forgive her ill-begotten marriage. Provided they didn't have to look at his cursed form day in and day out.

No matter what, he must leave Ravenswood. In spite of how much his soul argued against it, he knew it was the only choice he had.

The only real hope Ariel had.

One word against his lady, and he'd gladly take the fool's tongue for it.

If he stayed, it would only be a matter of time before he was forced to murder someone.

Don't be stupid. . . .

By the time he returned, Valteri had convinced himself he'd be far better off without Ariel. Setting his mind on the actions he must take, he rode into the bailey.

Children danced about in a frenzied haste, kicking up their feet and more dust than a herd of uncontrolled stallions. Laughter rang out as well as cheers and songs.

What was this?

They hadn't played in the yard since he'd come here with his army.

Valteri pulled his horse to a stop. Amazed by the sight, he stared at them in disbelief. Not since they'd landed in England had he heard the merriment of children.

Only their screams and curses.

Their prayers for the death of him and his Norman brethren.

Suddenly, the group of dancers broke apart and out of their center Ariel rose to her feet with one child held on her hip, clutching at her braid. His heart stopped. Never in all his life had he beheld a woman more beautiful, more stunning. The sunlight laced through her hair like finely woven gold. Splotches of pink darkened her cheeks, and she smiled the very smile that must make every angel in heaven weep with envy.

His body hardened to the point of pain. He struggled to breathe against the sensation. Once more he reminded himself why a life with her could never be. Why he must never go to her for comfort or release.

But damn it, he really didn't want to listen to reason right now.

She set the child aside and they joined hands with the others and circled round in a dance. Her voice rang out above the others, more enchanting than any he'd heard before. "If ever a man deserves salvation, because of a grievous separation. Thee shall rightly be that man. For never a turtle in the loss of her companion was at any time more cast down than thee."

Ariel smiled at the child to her right and drew a deep breath before continuing her song. "Everyone mourns for his land and country when he parts from friends of his heart, but there is no farewell, whatever anyone may say, so miserable as that of a lover and his sweetheart."

Her sweet soprano melody and words echoed around him, taunting him, consoling him, whispering to his blackened soul, to his craven heart. Savoring each fragile tone, he closed his eyes.

Aye, she was a woman to make any man proud. So why must he, her husband, turn her away?

Because she could never truly be his.

"Fate, you cruel bastard!" he snarled under his breath as he dismounted.

His belly roiling with heated anger, he tossed his reins to a waiting groom.

Pulling off his gloves and helm, he started toward the hall.

"Valteri!"

He closed his eyes in an effort to banish the joy her voice brought. He didn't want to hear his name on her sweet lips. It served no other purpose than to weaken his resolve.

She ran and grabbed him by the arm, her eyes shining with happiness.

Valteri stared at her, his heart pounding, his body leaping to life.

She was his.

And he knew he could never really have her.

Damn him for it!

Because at this moment, nothing would please him more than to pin her against the nearest wall of the closest darkened alcove and have his way with her.

To let her sweet, delicate hands chase away every hated part of his past until there was nothing left but the two of them.

"Come, milord, you must join us!"

He frowned. "Join you?"

"Aye!" she said with a laugh, pulling him by the arm toward the children.

Valteri shook his head, horror filling him. "Nay, milady. I cannot. I'll frighten them."

She hesitated for only a moment before taking his gloves and placing them inside his helm, which she set on the ground. "Pash! Frighten them indeed."

Leading him by the hand, she laughed and stopped before the children. "We have another dancer."

Was she insane?

The horror of his past assailed him. No one ever allowed him to play with children. Not even when he'd been one.

Mothers had snatched them up or aside and spat at him the moment they saw his eyes.

Valteri glanced around at the faces and noted their immediate fear and reservation. "Ariel, please."

A sharp frown drew her brows together as she noted their reactions as well. She released him and put her hands on her hips. She cast each of them a chiding grimace. "Don't tell me *all* of you are afraid?"

No one spoke, but he could tell by the terror in their eyes that each and every one of them would rather face Lucifer, himself, than touch him. Valteri started to move away, but a small girl stepped forward.

"I'm not afraid." She smiled up at him. "If milady says not to be afraid, then I have no fear."

Before he could move, the little girl reached out and grasped his thumb with her tiny hand. Her touch was as light as a breath of air, yet it sent a wave of pain crashing through him that nearly toppled him.

Valteri stared at her elfin face and the shining dark locks that surrounded her rose-hued cheeks.

"Come, Lord Doubt." Ariel took his other hand. "We have a dance!"

Still unsure of himself, Valteri allowed them to lead him in their game. He felt like the greatest of all fools as he stumbled through the steps. Never in his life had he danced, and the intricate moves escaped his clumsy feet.

Ariel laughed, then broke from the circle. Taking him by the hands, she leaned back and twirled about with him.

Valteri stared in awe as the rest of the world spiraled in a dizzying blur around them. Only her beautiful face and the joy of her smile was in focus.

And it enchanted him more than he wanted to admit.

Mesmerized by her, he struggled to breathe. Instinctively, he pulled her toward him.

She stumbled in her dance steps and lurched forward with a gasp.

Valteri grabbed her before she fell, but his effort to save her unbalanced him as well. Entwined, they tumbled to the ground.

Her laughter, joined by the children's, rang in his ears. Ariel lay upon his chest. Her hair that had come free of its braid spilled across his face like a bounty of satin.

He inhaled the warm, sweet scent. Closing his eyes, he allowed himself for a moment to pretend they could have a lifetime of moments like this. That he could look forward to years of such enjoyment and laughter.

She squirmed on top of him until she sat by his side, looking down. Her eyes sparkled like the finest sapphires to ever grace the earth. His body hardened even more.

At this rate, his lust might very well kill him.

But he'd shamed her once with his hated carnal desires. He refused to do so again.

She reeled her hair in and smiled the very smile that melted his wretched heart. "My thanks, Valteri. The ground appears far too solid, and I'm most grateful not to learn for myself what bruises it yields."

And before he could move, she leaned forward and kissed his lips. Though it was chaste and brief, it set a thousand flames flickering in his belly. His desire trampling his reason, Valteri pushed himself up and captured her in his arms then pulled her back for another, more satisfying kiss.

She gasped, then surrendered herself to him as the children made sounds of their displeasure.

"He's kissing her! Bleh!"

"Why grown-ups have to do that?"

"It's so gross!"

Ignoring them, Valteri drank of her warm, sweet lips that tasted finer than all the wines of Normandy. Nothing would give him greater pleasure than to spend eternity in her arms.

Finally, he felt a light tugging on his surcoat. "Milord, milady, the friar comes," the little girl said, before erupting into giggles.

Ariel pulled away, her cheeks a delectable shade of pink. She gave him a shy smile as she stared at him, her eyes filled with warmth and love.

He'd never thought to receive such a look.

"Lord Valteri?"

That unfamiliar voice pulled him away from his desire to embarrass them both.

Blinking in an effort to divert his thoughts, Valteri pushed himself to his feet. He held a hand out for Ariel and assisted her before he turned to face the friar.

The moment he saw the shriveled little man with his tonsure and brown robes, he had to force his lip not to curl. But nothing could stop the flood of hatred that flowed through him.

He'd spent too many years with so-called brothers of God, who used their title to further their own corrupt ends. Even though he tried, he just couldn't muster any kindness toward any of them.

If not for his people and their beliefs, he'd banish all such creatures from his lands.

With that thought, he forced himself to be civil and not run the friar through. "Brother Edred, I presume."

No doubt this was the same cowardly friar who, upon the arrival of Valteri's army, had run from his hut.

Instead of helping the people who depended on him, he'd made sure to protect his own ass.

They always did.

The little man smiled as he drew closer. "Aye. I've come as you . . ." His voice broke off as he looked up and met Valteri's gaze.

The look of terror was one Valteri had become more than accustomed to.

"Holy Mother of God!" Edred clutched at the wooden cross about his neck. "'Tis true, Normans are the sons of Lucifer!"

Fighting back the urge to slap that look off the monk's face, Valteri retrieved his helm and gloves from the ground. He approached the friar. "If we are the devil's own, then I'd wager that the Saxons are his whore. After all, 'twas your faithless King Harold who took holy vows to support my brother. And no sooner had Edward died than your Harold seized the throne with more lies and treachery." He raked the friar with a glare. "We are here under papal authority and with my brother, Bishop Odo, leading part of our army. So 'twould seem we represent your God, not your Satan, and that He, Himself, endorses our endeavors."

Ignoring the man's gaping, indignant stare, Valteri headed for the hall. So much for his useless daydreams of acceptance. The people of Ravenswood would always demand the presence of clergy, and as long as clergy remained, so, too, would rumors of his birth.

Damn Will for dragging him into this.

Valteri swung open the door with such force that it bounced off the far wall. His fury simmered deep in his gullet.

Even now, he could feel the sting of the brand as it sizzled against his skull, hear the words of Brother Jerome echoing around him. A child no older than five, he'd screamed and cried for them to stop. Had fought against the chains holding him until he had permanently scarred his wrists.

Over and over, he'd stated his innocence.

Over and over, they'd condemned him, taking pleasure in the pain they'd heaped on an innocent child.

So be it.

He'd much rather be associated with the devil than a god who could allow such misery to be given in His name. At least the devil was honest about his treachery. He didn't hide behind so-called works of charity that masked horrors far worse than any hell.

And yet all he had to do was look at Ariel and he could almost believe in God. Her goodness and beauty had to come from some truly divine source.

Valteri gripped his helm in his hand, and struggled against the urge to throw it into the wall. He must calm himself. The past was just that, the past. The future was all that mattered now.

What future?

Valteri paused, all his fury wilting beneath a bitter, stinging wave of regret and despair. He knew he couldn't stay and pretend the past had never happened, that people would leave him and Ariel in peace.

Sooner or later, they'd all turn on him.

His only hope would be to take her away and live in isolation. To give up everything he'd ever known.

Ever fought for.

He closed his eyes, trying to imagine her on a farm, her back bowed by years of hard work, her gentle hands scarred and chafed.

Nay, he could no more subject her to that kind of life than he could end his own misery. She was a noble lady and she deserved all the privileges and wealth that title granted her.

Sighing in regret, he knew what must be done. Once William released him from his vows, he would seek another war.

CHAPTER 9

Valteri splashed icy water on his face and scrubbed at the grime plastered there by his hard ride. No doubt dancing with Ariel and the children had added even more dirt, not to mention his rather pleasant fall with Ariel.

He smiled at the memory, until his anger surfaced.

Why had the friar chosen *that* moment to show himself? It'd been the first time in Valteri's life that he'd truly enjoyed himself. That he'd forgotten who and what he was.

He never should have paid the Saxon peasant to find the odious brother and return him to his post.

As if sensing his ill-begotten mood, Cecile yowled and jumped from his washstand. Miscalculating the distance, she hit the edge and fell back against the floor.

"Here, now." He scooped her up and placed her where she'd attempted to land. "Did you hurt yourself?"

She purred under his hand and gently nuzzled his fingers, her pink tongue roughly stroking his scarred knuckles.

Until Ariel, Cecile had been the only creature to show him love.

Stop your maudlin.

He was a harsh man who knew naught of comfort or gentle words. That was his lot, and he'd long ago accepted that fate.

All of his anger fled and he found the part of himself that accepted the life he'd been given. There was no need for his anger, not really. He had people's respect and fear—what man could ask for more than that?

A soft knock startled him from his thoughts. Pulling his hand away from Cecile's soft fur, he reached for his tunic and donned it. "Enter."

To his utter amazement, Ariel walked in behind five of the children from the yard. He frowned at them, wondering what could bring them to his room.

"Kyra has something she would like to say to you." Mischief glowed deep in Ariel's eyes.

The little girl who'd taken his hand stepped forward, her arms held behind her back. She bit her lip as if trying to keep her face straight, but the corners turned up until she was forced to smile brightly.

"Say it, Kyra," one of the boys urged.

Her face turned pensive and her eyes began to tear as if something greatly distressed her. A pain coiled in his stomach. Why was Ariel forcing this poor, frightened child to confront *him,* a man who obviously terrified her?

"I don't remember what I'm supposed to say," she whimpered.

Valteri stared at her in disbelief. Could it be she truly wasn't scared of him?

The boy rolled his eyes and huffed. "The dance, silly!"

She looked back at the boy, her tears vanishing. She wiped the tip of her nose with the back of her hand, then smiled again. "Oh, that's right!" She raised herself up on her tiptoes, her smile returning. "We wanted to thank milord for joining us. And we . . . we . . ."

"Would like him to join us again," the boy supplied for her in a highly vexed voice.

She nodded her head. "That's it! We want milord to join us again." Her chest swelling in obvious pride, she ran back to the boy, and Valteri noted the flower garland she clutched behind her back.

"Kyra! You forgot something." The boy pushed her back toward him.

Her mouth formed a small O. Turning around, she ran back to him, holding the garland in front of her. "We made this for you, milord, so you'll have one like us the next time you dance." She handed him the garland.

Valteri took it, his hand trembling slightly from the weight of some emotion he couldn't name. The carefully plucked flowers and greenery chafed the calluses on his palm, and soothed the calluses of his heart.

Nothing had ever touched him so deeply. The thought and time they'd spent on the gift, a gift designed solely for him, made the garland the most precious item he'd ever owned.

The little girl leaned forward, cupped one hand beside her mouth, and whispered in a loud voice, "Creswyn said he wouldn't be afraid of you next time. He said if I—"

"Kyra!" the boy barked. "'Tis late, we must get home."

"All right," she said with a huff. Facing Valteri once more, she tugged on his tunic until he bent down to her level. To Valteri's utter astonishment, she gave him a light kiss on his cheek.

In spite of everything he'd ever learned, ever been taught, Valteri smiled, his throat far too tight for him to speak. Never in his life had he thought a child would dare come near him, let alone touch him. And here on this day, this one brave child had twice reached out.

He swallowed against the painful lump in his throat, and tried to squelch the hope that flared inside him.

Nay, he knew better than to trust others to follow the child's example. He'd learned long ago not to trust in such things.

With a cry of outrage, her brother rushed forward and took her by the arm. Instead of the usual caustic comments, her brother shook his head. "Kyra, you're not supposed to kiss a lord!"

Valteri cleared his throat and ruffled her hair. "'Tis fine. I take no offense."

Creswyn looked up at him, his youthful eyes relieved. "Thank you, milord. She's a wayward child. I know not what we shall do with her." His wistful voice was far too old for his years. A tone he must have heard countless times from his parents.

Valteri plucked a flower from his garland and handed it to Kyra. "Treasure her. Always."

She smiled, sniffed the flower, then skipped from the room.

Ariel closed the door behind the children, her heart lighter than a fairy's feather. She turned back to face Valteri, who stared in awe at the garland in his hand. He reminded her of a child clutching its most precious toy.

Smiling at the image, she crossed the room and touched his arm. Hard muscles flexed beneath her palm. "Milord has a most handsome smile. You should practice it more often."

He took her hand and studied her palm. "I've never had a reason to smile. Not until you."

Giddiness rushed over her. Ariel clasped his hand in hers and reached her left hand up to cup his cheek. Loose tendrils of his hair slid between her fingers in a wicked, sensual way that added chills to her body.

He closed his eyes and held her hand against his cheek as if savoring her touch as much as she savored his. "Milady, why have you come?"

Those familiar words shot through her. Ariel recoiled from him, her mind whirling. She stared at the floor, where an image of a battlefield seemed painted against the stones.

Screams echoed, men clutched at her.

She whirled around, trying to remove their cloying, clutching fingers that pulled at her hair, her dress.

"Leave me!" she shouted, pushing at her kirtle, where their grips held fast.

"Ariel?"

Suddenly, the images vanished.

Blinking, she looked up into the concerned frown of her husband. "'Twas horrible," she whispered. "Why do they haunt me?"

"Who haunts you?"

"The people." Terrified, Ariel shook her head, trying to make sense of it all. "I see them. Hear them. *Feel* them. Why won't they leave me alone?" She drew a ragged breath. "'Tis as if they want to hurt me and I know not why."

"It's all right, Ariel. I'm here. No one will harm you so long as you live. I shall see to that."

Ariel wanted to believe that. Yet the light in his eyes belied his words. "You want to leave me. Who will protect me when you're gone?"

A shadow passed across his eyes and she could see her words had struck a part of him.

She crossed the floor to stand before the window. Still, the images lurked in her mind like a violent whisper from the past. "I must be mad," she whispered, her anger faltering. "There can be no other explanation for what I see."

He grabbed her by the shoulders and turned her to face him. Fury sparked in his eyes, making them cold, unreadable. "You are not mad, milady!" His tone was bitter and angry. "You must never say that to anyone. Do you hear me!"

"Why?" she asked, stiffening her spine to stand against him. "'Tis the truth."

"'Tis a lie. I've spent many a day next to those who are mad. Believe me when I say that you are far more sane than any person I've ever met."

Shock poured over her. "What do you mean you've known those who are mad?"

He backed away from her and clenched and unclenched his fists as his breathing turned ragged. When he spoke, she could barely hear him. "As a child, I lived in a small commune of monks and friars. For Sunday mass, the local villagers would bring in those they deemed mad. The brothers would tie us to the altar where we could receive God's benediction." He sneered that last word, then turned to face her. "Having known them, I am most certain milady is quite sane. The ones who were really mad were the bastards who tortured us."

Pain sliced her heart at the thought of him being treated in such a manner. "They tied you to the altar?"

"Aye." Though his eyes were blank and his tone hollow, she knew those events had bred the ferocity of him.

"Were you not afraid?"

"I was terrified every fucking minute."

Images of him as a defenseless child filled her. How could anyone do such a thing to a small child? She could barely comprehend it. "Oh, Valteri, I'm so sorry."

He moved away from the soothing touch she offered. "Don't be. It was a long time ago." Rubbing his left hand over his right shoulder, he put more distance between them. "At times it no longer even seems like it was really me. Rather, that it happened to someone else. Someone I never really knew." When he looked back at her, anger and hatred fired his gaze. "'Tis the past, and the past is best left behind."

A knock sounded on the door a moment before Wace stuck his annoying little head in. "Milord, milady, the steward bade me tell you that all are awaiting your presence to sup."

Wishing she had more time to explore the matter while her husband seemed willing to talk about it, Ariel nodded. "We'll be right out."

Wace shut the door.

She turned back toward Valteri, and from the expression on his face she could tell he had no intention of joining his people, or furthering their conversation.

Save him, the voice repeated in her head.

"Valteri, you should join us."

"I'd rather die."

His stubbornness sparked her anger. How could she save him when he persisted with his isolated ways? "Do you intend to spend the whole of your life in exile from living?"

A strange light darkened his eyes. "I do indeed. It's worked well for me so far."

"Has it?" She narrowed her gaze on him. "If you don't give people a chance to know you, then they shall never see past the rumors."

His obstinate, mocking snort made her long to toss something at his head. "Should I go out there, the rumors will only worsen."

"How do you figure?"

"Don't. I know. Experience has tutored me well."

Ariel let out an exasperated breath. How could he be so stubborn? She approached him, but he refused to look at her. "Fine. Stay here as long as you wish. But if you truly had put your past to rest, then you wouldn't continue to isolate yourself from the world. Your past still haunts you, Lord Valteri, and until you face it and conquer it, it will never cease tormenting you."

That said, she left the room.

Valteri stood in the center of the room, her words echoing in his ears. He wanted to deny them, but deep down, he knew she'd spoken truly.

Aye, his past dogged his steps like a hungry wolf waiting to devour any tender part of him it could touch.

Damn it all! Why couldn't she just leave him in peace? All he wanted was for the entire world to just forget him. In the past, that had seemed simple. No one ever sought him out. Wace did as he was told and left him to his own. Why couldn't Ariel do the same?

Just because she had some peculiar notion that she could somehow make everyone forget who and what he was, didn't mean she could. If he'd learned anything in his life, it was that people rejected him. So he'd learned to reject them first.

All the years past had tutored him well on what would happen should he join in a common meal.

The whispers. The stares.

He was never part of them. Never really welcome.

Was she insane? He'd been rejected by those who were his allies, and here she thought to make him welcomed among the people he'd murdered in battle for his brother.

Hers was an impossible quest.

A bitter pain cramped his stomach. So be it. 'Twas time his bride also learned what he'd known for the whole of his life.

No one wanted him.

They never would.

Ariel looked up as Valteri entered the room. A smile curved her lips. Aye, she had won this battle, with any luck she might take the war.

Valteri sat beside her at the long table, his face drawn and strained.

"You could at least appear to look forward to the meal," she whispered.

He scoffed as he reached for his goblet and motioned Wace to bring him wine. "Trust me, Ariel, smiling frightens them even more."

"Pash." She wrinkled her nose at him, then passed the bread over so that he could have a piece.

He shook his head at her and she knew the words in his mind as if he'd spoken them aloud. He thought her every bit as stubborn as he was. She smiled at the thought. Perhaps she was, but then he needed that for his own good.

Someone needed to stand up to him.

Once the servers had finished bringing in the meal, the friar motioned for all to bow their heads for prayer. Out of the corners of her eyes, Ariel noted Valteri kept his head up, his stare focused on the far wall.

The friar's words rang out, faltering only when he noticed Valteri's actions as well.

Edred finished his prayer then looked to Valteri. "Milord doesn't join the prayer?"

Valteri's jaw tensed. "I do not force my beliefs on you, brother. I pray you give me the same courtesy."

Ariel kicked him beneath the table.

He gave her a hostile glare that stole her breath. She opened her mouth to speak, but before she could, the steward stepped forward.

"Milord, there are travelers at the gate who wish a night's lodgings and food."

"Bring them inside."

The steward hesitated as if he wanted to say something more. Finally, he leaned and whispered in Valteri's ear.

Ariel frowned, wishing she knew what passed between them.

"It matters not. Bring them in and seat them as noble guests."

A surprised look crossed the steward's face, but he said nothing more and hastened to do Valteri's bidding.

Despite a need to ask about the matter, Ariel held her silence, knowing she'd find out soon enough what had caused the steward's upset.

After a few minutes, the steward returned, leading three men, the oldest of which appeared no more than one and a half score of years. Their long hair and beards told her they were Saxons and their proud bearing and clothes bespoke their nobility.

Stiffly, they approached the table. Their reluctance obvious, their gazes narrowed almost in unison as they noted Valteri's eyes.

The eldest member of their party bowed stiffly. "We thank you for your hospitality."

Ariel held her breath at the obvious slight. 'Twas indeed rude to beg hospitality and not at least acknowledge Valteri's lordship.

No doubt Valteri had noticed as well, but he gave no indication of the Saxon's omission. Instead, he nodded slightly, and the steward sat them at the end of the raised table.

Belial leaned forward to rest his chin in his palm, and Ariel wondered at the mischievous look in his eyes as he scanned the newcomers.

Brother Edred engaged the men in English. Ariel returned to her food, noting Valteri's tenseness, which set her own hands trembling.

She managed a few bites before Belial's voice rang out. "Now that we have a friar in residence, 'twould seem fitting that we have my sister's union blessed by him."

Ariel choked on her food, aghast at her brother's audacity, especially after Valteri's earlier declaration.

"What say you, Lord Valteri? Should we not have a wedding mass?"

Why was Belial deliberately provoking him?

Valteri took a drink of wine, then turned to face both Belial and Edred, who had paused his conversation with the Saxons and now sat poised expectantly. "'Twas my understanding the church thinks marriage too sinful to bother with. I believe the official writ says it is a secular matter best left for secular courts."

Edred nodded. "That has long been held true, but the last council held that all unions should be blessed."

"Then bless my wife and leave me in peace."

Outrage hardened the friar's gaze. "Why does milord refuse a divine benediction? Is there something about our Heavenly Father that frightens you?"

"Nothing about your God could ever frighten me. Save your comforts and words for those who believe. I have no use for such."

"Blasphemer!" Edred shrieked, coming to his feet. "Heretic!"

Valteri stood up and towered over the much smaller man.

Edred stepped back into the chair beside him, his eyes wide and filled with fear.

Ariel held her breath, uncertain what to do.

Valteri's lip curled as he raked a glare over the friar. "You forget your place, brother. If your God is not offended by the unseemly cowards who represent Him, then I doubt my few words will incur His wrath."

"Milord, please." Ariel took Valteri's arm. "I beseech you to hold your tongue."

A tic started in his jaw. "Do not defend this lecherous oaf to me, milady. I know his kith and kind far better than you. And I *beseech* you to avoid his presence lest you soon learn what true horrors lie beneath his robes." He raked a sneer over Edred. "There's not a one of them I'd ever put at my back, including my brother, the bishop. They're all faithless liars and hypocrites."

Heat stung her cheeks, his double meaning more than clear. Before she could reply, he left the hall.

Lifting the hem of her kirtle, Ariel ran after him. "Valteri!" She caught up to him just outside the door. "I cannot believe what you just did. What you said! Are you trying to make them hate you?"

In spite of the darkness, she detected his angry glare.

Even so, she refused to let the matter die. "You speak of men rejecting you when 'twas you who provoked Brother Edred."

"I provoked Edred?" His tone was laden with disbelief. "He was the one to hurl insults, not I."

"You knew what his reaction would be when you refused to bow your head."

His nostrils flared. "I will not be the hypocrite he is and bow my head in respect to a deity I have a difficult time believing in." He shook his head. "Really, Ariel. Do you know why William won't let me leave England?"

"Nay."

"Because he knows that of all his brothers, I'm the only one who won't come at his back."

That gave her pause. "But I heard that Bishop Odo rallied the troops for him."

"Aye. And Odo hedged his bets with Harold Godwinson in the event

Will fell. He played both sides, and Will knows it. Even now, Will suspects him of treachery, along with the others. It's why he won't let me leave. He wants me close in case either Odo or Rob decide to make a play for his throne."

Her stomach lurched at the thought. But then, she understood. She couldn't trust her own brother, either.

And she didn't have a throne to protect.

"William is lucky to have you."

Valteri scoffed. "Will is a fool to want something best left alone. But that is neither here nor there. Tell me, lady. What kind of god creates a race where brother is constantly slaughtering brother? Yet that is what He's done from the beginning when Cain rose against Abel."

Ariel wanted to deny it, but he was right. "You shouldn't say such things, Valteri. How can you not have any faith?"

Valteri took her hand and flattened her palm against his chest. "I feel my heart beat. I feel the wind against my cheeks. For the whole of my life I have listened to creatures such as Edred tell me that I am not human. That I am God's abomination. They have cursed me, beat me, and called me monster, all in your God's name. If I believe in your God, then I must believe the words they say about me. Why else would an omniscient, omnipotent God allow me to suffer in His name at the hands of His servants?"

Those words and the emotion in them tore through her.

He was right. She couldn't deny the truth he spoke or the reason behind it.

"We are all given free will to choose good and decency or succumb to darkness. All of us are called upon for different paths, and I don't know why you have been given yours."

Valteri took her by the arms, his touch strangely gentle. "Forgive me, milady, but I cannot believe in what you say. If I accept your belief, then I must accept what the priests have told me about myself, and I refuse to believe Lucifer is my father."

He released her and headed for the stable.

Ariel watched him go, her heart thumping heavily against her breast. No wonder he'd isolated himself from everyone. She could barely conceive the loneliness, pain, and despair such isolation must cause.

The human soul had never been created for such a journey. 'Twas a wonder Valteri had lasted so long.

"Milady?"

She turned to see Wace standing in the doorway. "Aye?"

"The people are anxious. The steward wishes for your return so that they may be soothed."

Ariel stepped toward him. She studied the youth, his face pensive and drawn. "Tell me, Wace. How long have you traveled with Valteri?"

A frown drew his brows together. "Almost four years now, milady. Why?"

She sighed and glanced back at the stable as Valteri left it astride his charger. Without looking in their direction, he galloped through the bailey and out the gate. "Has he always been as he is now?"

His frown deepened. "I know not what you mean."

"Has he always avoided being with people?"

"Aye. Truth, this is one of the few times we have stayed in a manor for more than a day or so. Normally we travel from battle to battle, or tourney to tourney, seldom ever sleeping indoors."

"Has he ever spoken to you about why he chooses to live such a way?"

"Nay. He seldom speaks to me other than to give me my duties."

Her heart aching, Ariel moved to return inside, but Wace caught her arm.

"Please don't judge him harshly, Lady Ariel. I know the types of things servants and men whisper about him, but I swear on my own soul that they're all lies. Lord Valteri may not be godly, but he's far from a sinister demon. In all the time I've served him, he's never once raised his voice or his hand to me. But many times my former master led me to mass while bruises darkened my flesh from the blows he'd personally delivered. Lord Valteri is a good man, undeserving of such criticisms."

She patted his arm. "'Tis honorable the way you stand by your lord, but have no fear. You need not defend him to me. Like you, I know he's not the monster others think. You may rest easy on that account."

Wace nodded and returned inside.

Holding the door, Ariel stared in the direction Valteri had ridden.

She must find the loose rivet in that armor he kept around his heart, and remove it before it was too late. And something inside told her that her time was almost expired.

He was dead set on a fatal quest.

And it was near the end.

CHAPTER 10

A chill wind stole up Ariel's spine as she stood on the battlements looking out over the dark valley. The sentry moved past her, but said nothing. She knew he must think her mad the way she'd stood here since supper broke apart. Yet that didn't concern her. It was her husband's absence that continued to plague her thoughts most.

Though she could scarcely see more than a few feet from the gate and her body shook from the cold, she couldn't leave her post. She needed to watch for him. Something inside kept her feet still, her gaze locked onto the eerie forest below. If she listened carefully, the rustling wind would fade and she could almost swear she heard Valteri riding over the land, searching for the comfort he needed.

"Milady?"

Ariel turned, expecting to see the sentry. Instead, it was the eldest Saxon nobleman. A frown lined her brow. Whatever could he want with her?

"Greetings, milord. What brings you away from the fire?"

"Like you, I couldn't sleep. I thought a walk might calm my troubled thoughts." His gaze drifted to the sentry several feet away and he whispered, "'Tis most difficult to rest in the home of my enemies."

Were it not for the humble look in his eyes, she would suspect him of mischief. But as she watched him, she saw a man reserved, not one out to make more trouble. "You have no enemies here."

A shadow darkened his gaze to a deep, almost unreadable hue. "Nay, milady, you are not, but your husband most definitely is."

She opened her mouth to speak, but he raised his hand to silence her.

"I meant no offense. In truth, you remind me too much of my own sweet Wenda for me to offend you."

She detected the softness in his voice as he spoke the woman's name. "Wenda is your wife?"

"Was," he corrected, his voice strained, and his eyes as sad as if his grief still lay fresh within his heart. "I fear she died two years past while birthing our first child."

Sympathetic pain coursed through Ariel and she reached out to touch his arm. "My condolences."

He nodded, looking away from her. "It was hard at first, but I have long since come to terms with her departure."

Rubbing her arms against the chill, Ariel noted the catch in his voice. It was identical to the one in Valteri's when he'd spoken nearly the same words earlier that night.

Did all men speak denials against the pain in their souls even though it was obvious that they burned there like fires?

Did the denial help?

Nay, not likely. Men seemed to forever state the opposite of what they needed. What they yearned for most.

The Saxon took her by the arm and led her farther away from the sentry. "Milady, there's a personal matter of which I'd like to speak."

Instantly suspicious, she looked at him, confused by his words and what question he'd dare broach. "You ask after a personal matter when I don't even know your name?"

He smiled, yet it did nothing to allay her fears. "Forgive my oversight. I'm called Ethbert."

"And I'm Ariel."

"Aye, milady. I asked after your name several hours ago."

She stiffened her spine in apprehension. What would cause him to ask after her? "Why?"

"I . . ." His voice trailed off and he looked away. After several minutes, he drew a deep breath. "At first I thought you Norman, what with the way you spoke their language, but a short while ago your brother explained to me what had happened. How the Norman forced you to take his hand."

More suspicion mixed with her fear, narrowing her sight. She could well imagine what stories her brother might tell. "And what did my brother say?"

"That the Norman demanded you marry him. That he gave you no choice."

Fury blotted her thoughts. "'Tis a lie!"

He furrowed his brow and stepped away from her, his gaze wary. "What?"

"Aye, you heard me." She ground her teeth over Belial's treachery. "Lord Valteri, unlike my brother, asked me whether or not I agreed to the union. I accepted Valteri of my own free will."

Still, skepticism shone deep in Ethbert's eyes and he laughed bitterly. "Do any of us have a choice anymore where our lives are concerned? Since Harold fell, I doubt any of us can choose aught without Norman consent."

The hostile fury in his voice surprised her. A deep foreboding started in her soul and begged her to listen. "I hear rebellion in your tone."

He looked at her in startled alarm. "Nay. I have accepted my country's defeat."

"Then why have you left your home?"

He shrugged and braced his arms against the wooden battlement before him, his gaze focused into the dark distance. "We're traveling through, on our way to see if our sister survived the invasion. Ill rumors have passed to us of her abasement and we wish to see for ourselves what has become of her."

Her anger failing, Ariel nodded her head. "Then I shall pray for her safety."

"My thanks, and I shall pray for yours."

"Why? I'm not in any danger."

He shook his head, but didn't look at her. When he spoke, his tone was grave. "Methinks you are in far greater danger than you know."

Belial knocked the crone away from him, his anger burning deep inside. Brittle leaves rustled beneath his feet as he walked a circle around the clearing, his thoughts churning over her disclosure. "How could you have been so foolish!"

Rising from the heap where she'd landed, Mildred wiped the blood from her lip and narrowed her eyes. "'Twill work, I assure you."

"But why?" he insisted between clenched teeth, his hot, angry breath forming a cloud. "Why would you make the Saxon swoon for her when 'twill serve no purpose other than to turn Valteri away from here?"

"Nay, 'twill raise his jealousy!"

Belial seized her again and drew back his arm. Before he slapped her, he stopped himself. No need to abuse her further. The damage of her stupidity had been wrought. All he could do now was try and salvage as much as he could.

Why can I never have an intelligent accomplice? Just once!

He wiped his hand over his chin, trying desperately to think of something. But he was weary, too weary to think clearly.

Valteri refused to stay by Ariel's side long enough to consummate their union, and so long as he chose to ride about the countryside, Ariel would remain chaste and pure.

Dammit! How he hated self-control.

"Just you wait," the crone began again. "When Lord Valteri sees his beloved in the arms of another—"

"Arms of another?" Belial spat, his fury pitching in his demon's belly. "Ariel will never allow such. And even should she, Valteri will no doubt leave. He'll look upon the Saxon as a worthy replacement for himself."

Belial sighed, forcing himself to calm so that he could focus his thoughts. "You're so stupid!"

He needed a better class of minion.

And he needed one fast.

*   *   *

Thorn pulled up short as he entered his tent and found the last thing his shitty day needed.

A confab of Arelim waiting on him. They were the guardians of humanity. Those assigned with making sure the demons didn't overrun or overstep and wreak even more havoc than normal on the unsuspecting weak.

And not just any Arelim. The head bastards of them.

Michael, Gabriel, and Sraosha. It was enough to make his ulcer have a baby, given that he usually only saw them when they were at the end of his sword, trying to kill him.

Even though they were supposed to be on the same team.

These days.

Back when he served his father, they were fatal enemies. Somehow the bastards had missed the memo that he'd switched sides and they were now supposed to be playing nice with each other.

Thorn inclined his head to them. "Assholes, to what do I owe this displeasure?"

Michael bristled before he grimaced at his companions. "Told you we were wasting our time."

Gabriel held his hand up to silence him. Unlike the fair and ever perfect Michael, he was dark in skin tone and eyes. Even with no hair, he was still every bit as beautiful as one would expect from the winged guard. "We have a situation."

"I figured as much since I didn't think you were here to invite me for tea and biscuits. Not to mention the battlefield I just left where we are getting our asses handed to us by our enemies." Thorn set his helm down on his chest and reached for his particular "mead" to pour himself a flagon. "I would offer you a drink, but I don't think any of you have a stomach for my vintage."

Sraosha curled his lip. "We don't need a demon!" He moved to leave.

Gabriel grabbed his arm. "Today, we do." He pierced both his companions with a hostile glare. "In case you missed our earlier discussion and as you just noted, Belial is kicking our asses. To track a demon of his level, we need a demon of his level. Our Necrodemians are worthless."

Thorn snorted. "So glad to hear you admit that."

"Don't get cocky. Your Hellchasers won't be any better."

"Depends on the Hellchaser." Thorn winked at Gabriel. "I assure you I have some that can bring that bastard down. Myself included."

Never mind the fact that he had a grudge against Belial that was a long time coming.

Thorn took another swig. "So what's Baby Belial doing to make *you* crazy? I thought I was the only one he was picking on lately."

Michael finally relaxed. "I wish. He's captured one of my lieutenants."

Thorn arched a brow. "How's that possible?"

"We've no idea. Her name is Ariel and we can't find her. No one knows where she is or what happened to her."

"Thought you were omniscient."

Michael sneered. "Don't make me hit you."

Yet Thorn so loved tormenting him. This was what he lived for.

"Anyway," Gabriel said, drawing his attention back toward him. "We need you to find her and return her to us."

No small feat there. "Well, you're in luck. I was about to go hunting anyway. It dawned on me that my favorite menace wasn't here. Which had me wondering why his troops were attacking so vehemently."

Gabriel frowned. "I don't understand."

Thorn let out a weary sigh. "Hence why you get your asses kicked all the time. Called distraction, buddy. Vicious little war tactic. Keep your enemy's eye on one thing while you go off and do something else. It wasn't until a couple of days ago that I caught on to what the dipshit was doing."

Normally, he wasn't so slow on the uptake.

But things had been a bit hectic lately.

Because of what Belial had been doing to keep him distracted.

"We don't play games with people."

Thorn choked on his drink. Yeah, right. "The fact that you can tell that lie with a straight face offends me." And that was the basic difference between their sides. With his former ilk, they made no bones about the fact that they were evil and couldn't be trusted.

With Michael and crew, they lied and promised utter faithfulness and honor.

Until they stabbed you in the back while smiling in your face.

But then that was the thing about betrayal. It could only come from people you trusted. Those you didn't expect it from.

Good news, he never trusted anyone. His childhood had tutored him well on just what traitorous, lying bastards everyone could be.

Even his own mother.

He pitied the rest of the fools who had yet to learn the lessons his youth had taught him.

"So you want me to find your soldier. Return her to you and banish Belial back to his hole."

"Exactly."

He nodded at Gabriel. "An Arel . . . I'm thinking that's worth at least twenty pardons."

Michael gaped. "Twenty? Are you mad?"

"No. Quite happy, point of fact. I have you three in my office, begging me for a favor. That always makes my day. Now, I have the ability to strong-arm you for new additions to *my* army. That makes me even more deliriously Panglossian."

Sraosha made a sound of supreme disgust. "This was a waste of time." He started to leave.

Gabriel stopped him. "We need him."

Sraosha and Michael growled low in their throats.

Thorn smiled. He loved whenever he had them over a barrel.

Gabriel scowled. "Why are you so dedicated to helping the damned escape the sentences they've earned?"

"Because unlike you pricks, I understand the difference between those who are born rotten and those who made mistakes because they were fucked over by creatures like you who ensured that their only choices in life were bad and awful. Just because someone was betrayed into committing acts they didn't want to do, I don't think that they should be eternally damned for it."

Or, in his case, because they'd been betrayed at birth by forces conspiring against an infant.

"Rather than pat myself on the back for some imagined goodness I was supposedly born with and never earned, I'd rather actually go out and do some good for others." Thorn cleared his throat. "So do we have an accord?"

Gabriel nodded. "But I have the right to veto five of your choices."

Thorn bristled, but knew that if he didn't give in, they'd refuse the bargain entirely.

Saving a single Arel from Belial would be worth pulling twenty souls out of their respective hells. Too many had been damned for wrong reasons. He was all about redemption and giving others a second chance.

People like him.

So far, he'd only been wrong a handful of times. Most of the souls he'd bargained for had done him proud.

The few who hadn't . . .

He paid dearly for those mistakes.

So had they.

By his hands.

"Agreed." He held his arm out to Gabriel.

With a grimace, Gabriel shook his hand. "Find her. Quickly."

Valteri paused at the castle's site. Darkness lay across the stones and half-built walls, turning their shapes into ghastly, evil beasts that could frighten even the stoutest of hearts.

That was what people thought when they glanced upon his own likeness, even in the full light of day.

Against his will, Ariel's words drifted through his mind, and he flinched at the truth. Perhaps he did provoke some of those fears by his words and deeds. But then it'd always been easier to allow people their beliefs than to try and make them see past his deformity and into his human soul.

As a child, he'd reached out to the brothers and they'd recoiled in horror.

Or backhanded him for the affront.

As a squire, his lord had shied away from him just as the monks had done. Indeed, if not for William's direct orders, no lord would ever have accepted him as a squire.

"You're a freak, boy! Be glad I owe the duke a favor, else I'd throw you to the wolves for fun."

Even now he could hear his brother's men arguing over who would take him, and Will's voice ringing out in an order for his best knight, Hugh, to take him.

Hugh had quickly made certain Valteri knew better than to approach him on any matter. And when Hugh had bothered to train him in war, Valteri's lessons had been hard, brutal, and malicious.

Since the moment of Valteri's knighting, Will had urged him to take lands and a wife. And each time he'd turned aside Will's offers.

How happy his brother must have been when he received news of his union, but Valteri knew he could never have the happy marriage Will shared with Maude.

Nay, no matter how much his fetid heart cried for him to stay, he must leave.

Even though part of him longed to believe that Ariel, Will, and the children wouldn't be the only ones to accept him, he knew better.

Life didn't work that way.

If wishes were horses, even beggars would ride.

This one afternoon in no way made up for his lifetime of hell.

Will was king and no one would dare mock him, but Ariel and the children could easily turn into Edna. To this day, he was haunted by the kind old woman who'd once taken mercy on him and who had been branded a witch and driven from her home. But not before they'd thrown everything from rocks to rotten vegetables at her. Burned down her cottage and slaughtered her animals.

Last he'd heard, she'd starved to death during the winter months, while she'd been forced to beg.

Just like her, they would be abused and tormented for their charity toward him, and he had no desire to see them hurt because of him.

Not when he could prevent it.

Despite the denial of his soul, Valteri knew what he must do. In a few hours, once dawn arose, he'd summon Wace and make his way toward London.

There, he'd make certain William gave him his release. Then he'd return to battle.

It was what must be done.

Wheeling his horse about, Valteri headed for the manor.

Out of nowhere, something streaked before his destrier. Ganille reared, kicking in fright and bucking as Valteri jerked the reins to avoid the unknown object. Whatever it was, it jarred his senses while he struggled with his mount.

His horse refused his commands.

An unfamiliar stench filled Valteri's nostrils, choking him. Ganille shot up the hill and again the streak appeared.

It hit the ground in front of them.

"Whoa!" Valteri pulled the reins.

Shrieking, the horse reared against the partially finished wall, penning Valteri between his backbone and the damp stone. He cursed as the rough masonry tore through his tunic. Pain engulfed him, but still he held his seat.

Then suddenly, the reins broke from his hands and Valteri found himself on the ground beneath the thrashing hooves. Instinctively, he put his arm up to shield his face. Sharp hooves struck the bone of his forearm, numbing the full length of his arm until he could scarce lift it.

Lowering his head, he tried to get away, but Ganille followed as if he were an enemy in battle, kicking and bucking. A thousand pains racked his body from each and every strike of those biting hooves.

Barely able to breathe, he finally succeeded in pulling himself away from the frightened horse.

Aching in pain, Valteri lay to the side of the wall as agony tore through him. Damn, it hurt.

Dampness covered his right temple and cheek. Without checking, he knew it for blood. Aye, the salty taste left no doubt.

He needed to get back to the manor before he passed out. Last thing he needed was to be unconscious out here, exposed to the elements and wildlife.

Exposed to enemies who wanted him dead.

When he attempted to rise, his sight dimmed even more and he fell back to his knees.

He drew a ragged, pain-filled breath. He'd never make it back in this condition.

Out of the hazy corner of his gaze, he saw a white wolf approaching.

His body burning with agony, he pushed himself up and stumbled toward his horse.

He reached for his sword that was strapped to his saddle, but Ganille bolted at his approach before he could unsheathe it.

Too tired to resist, he fell to the ground where he was sure the wolf would end his useless life. At last Ariel would be spared his presence and the mockery of his people. Mayhap it would be best for him to die like this.

Closing his eyes, he waited for the wolf to rip out his throat.

Ariel woke up with a start. A haunting howl echoed in her ears from some faraway wolf that stalked the night. One that seemed oddly familiar.

A sudden image appeared in her mind. She recoiled in horror. Somehow, she sensed Valteri's pain. Heard his short, raspy breaths as he struggled for consciousness.

He was hurt, she knew it. She didn't know how, yet she couldn't deny the part of her that heard him whisper her name, the part of him that reached out like a desperate soul from the grave.

Throwing back the covers, she bolted from the bed. In seconds, she donned her clothes and rushed into the hall, seeking Wace where he slept against the far wall.

"Wace," she whispered, gently shaking him awake.

He yawned widely before opening his eyes to stare at her in disbelief. "Milady?"

"Aye." She pulled his blanket from him, and glanced to the other people sleeping nearby—which reminded her to keep her tone low. "We must hurry."

"Hurry?"

"Aye," she repeated, trying to stifle the agitation in her voice. "Your lord needs you!"

He glanced about the hall like a drunkard seeking his ale. "Is he here?"

Seriously? Why would she be waking the boy if Valteri were here?

Biting back her irritation and sarcasm, she handed him his tunic. "Nay. You must help me go to him."

Frowning, he stifled another yawn as he shrugged on his tunic. "What do you mean, go to him?"

Ariel gathered his shoes from the floor and urged him to take them. "He's injured and we have to help him."

"He's injured?" That chased the sleepiness from the boy. He grabbed his shoes and donned them. "Where is he?"

"The castle site." She scowled as soon as she spoke. How did she know that?

Yet she was most certain she would find him there.

Wace paused in tying his breeches and stared up at her as if he doubted her sanity. "What do you mean he's—"

"Enough questions! We must hurry."

Though she could barely see his face in the dark shadows, Ariel had the distinct feeling he wanted to argue further, but he held his tongue.

Soon they were headed across the yard, and finally into the stable.

Without a word, he began saddling their horses.

Once he finished, Ariel started to mount, but his hand on her arm stopped her. "'Tis unsafe, milady. Many outlaws and rebels travel by night. I think I should—"

"Nay, Wace. We shall be fine. I know it."

He bit his lip and for a moment she feared he would naysay her plea. "All right, milady, but if any harm should befall you, Lord Valteri will feed my hide to the dogs." He helped her mount.

"Lord Valteri will be too grateful for your help to be overly harsh."

"So say you. But I've seen him skewer men for far lesser grievances. Such as burning his toast. I'm pretty sure you mean more to him than toast."

She laughed.

"Which is why I wish you'd stay behind. If something happens to you, milady, I'll be skewered for sure." He mounted his horse and they were off.

Breathing deeply, Ariel clung to her saddle and tried to ignore the cold wind that whipped against her cheeks and settled in her bones where it chilled her very soul.

Once again, she struggled with something her mind told her she should know how to do and yet it felt foreign and strange to her.

I won't lose my saddle. Not now!

Valteri would be all right. The images of wolves in her mind were just the devil's playthings. And yet she could feel a wolf's warm breath on her neck, smell its putrid scent as if it stood over her even now.

Eternity seemed to have passed before they topped the hill where the castle's construction site stood. Anxious and frightened, Ariel scanned the area for any trace of her husband, but only the vacant, isolated stones greeted her eager gaze.

"No one's here, milady." Wace urged his horse closer to hers.

"Nay, I know . . ." Ariel paused, listening carefully.

Once more she heard a faint groan.

"Over there!" She leapt from her horse and ran toward the sound. Rounding the stone wall, she hesitated.

Valteri lay on his side, facing the woods. Even in the darkness, she could see the blood that soaked his clothing, feel his pain as if it pounded through her own body.

Ariel choked back a sob. "Valteri?" She rushed to him and knelt by his side.

He made no move. No more sound.

Was she too late? Her heart pounded in fear as she gently pulled him onto his back. His eyes were half-open and his chest lay so very still.

Terrified, she wiped the blood off his icy cheeks. "Milord, please!" she begged, her throat so tight that she could scarce draw breath.

"Ariel?" he whispered in such a low tone that she barely heard him.

Relief shot through her. Grateful beyond measure, she gave a small, nervous laugh. "Aye, milord. I'm here."

Wace knelt beside her, his face grim. "We shall need a litter or cart to move him."

She'd known Valteri would be hurt, but never once had she considered that *he,* her fierce, untouchable warrior, would need assistance to return. "I'll wait here while you go for help."

"But milady—"

"I'll be fine until your return."

As Wace opened his mouth, Ariel shook her head to silence him. "Please, no more arguments. You must hurry. I know not how much longer he can last."

Reluctance shone deep in his eyes, but Wace said nothing more.

As he mounted and rode away, she tore strips of cloth from her under-kirtle to bind Valteri's wounds.

Ariel stanched the flow of blood as best she could, but she feared her efforts wouldn't be enough. With each frantic beat of her heart, it seemed his breath fell shallower and shallower.

"You should have gone in his place," Valteri whispered.

"You shouldn't speak." She gently brushed his hair from his cheek. "You must save your strength. Besides, I'd have fallen without my brave knight to pull me astride his horse."

Valteri reached his hand up to take hers, his grip so weak it stole her breath. He placed her hand over his heart and she felt the soft, feather-like beating beneath her fist.

Warm, sticky blood clung to her skin, but she refused to draw her hand away in spite of the panic inside her that urged her to run from the pain she felt.

Nay, she must be strong for him. No matter how much her fear spoke otherwise, she must give him her own strength.

He swallowed and jerked her hand as if a wave of pain shot through him. How he could stand the number of injuries he had and not cry out, she couldn't fathom. Indeed, she wanted to cry for him, but she knew he wouldn't welcome her tears, and that alone kept her eyes dry.

With her free hand, she stroked his pale, cool cheek and traced the stubble lining his jaw.

Valteri closed his eyes and panic gripped her heart, stilling it instantly. "Valteri?"

He opened his eyes and looked at her.

Ariel drew a deep breath. "I thought you—"

"I shall live through this, Ariel." He gave her hand a tight, reassuring squeeze. "The injuries are not as bad as the blood makes it appear."

She returned his tight squeeze, praying he was right. "I shall hold you to that, and if you speak falsely, I shall never forgive you."

The intensity of his stare made her tremble.

You must watch him die!

Ariel flinched at the raw, angry voice that shot through her head. Chills spread across her body and she tried to grasp the fleeting memory. Yet it vanished into the depths of her mind like an errant child fleeing at its parent's approach.

She must remember!

Even her very soul screamed at her to recall the words.

Who had said them to her . . .

Why?

"Ariel?"

Her thoughts scattered at the sound of his voice. "Aye?"

He cleared his throat and gripped her hand. "I know not why you're here, but I'm glad you came."

Holding him close, she smiled, her throat tight with joy and fear.

As she started to respond, she heard the sound of horses approaching.

It was too soon for Wace to be returning.

Valteri ground his teeth and started to rise.

"Nay, milord!" She pushed him back to the ground, then rose.

The riders came closer.

Closer still.

Her heart pounded as she tried to see into the darkness.

It wasn't until the first rider was almost on top of her that she realized why it'd been so hard to see him. He was dressed all in black. Even his armor, helm, and chain mail were black.

As was his horse.

The knight beside him was in a dark burgundy surcoat over equally black armor.

They seemed even larger than Valteri on his. Deadlier.

Never had she seen anything more intimidating.

How could they fear her lord when these men rode the earth? Surely they were the devil incarnate. . . .

Her heart pounded so fiercely that she wasn't sure how it remained in her chest.

She did her best not to let her fear show, but she had the distinct feeling that they knew anyway. Just as an animal could sense fear. She had no doubt that they could, too. That they somehow fed on it.

Soundlessly, the one all in black held his hand up and clenched his fist tight.

"Damn, Leucious, speak to the poor girl before you make her wet herself. I know you're an arse, but still."

The horse stomped and snorted as if indignant on his rider's behalf while his master turned toward the knight in burgundy. Though she couldn't see his face, she was sure he was smirking at his companion.

And before he could speak, a third rider came over the hill at a breakneck pace.

Only this one, she unfortunately knew.

Belial.

He reined his horse to a hard stop just in front of the two newcomers. Something the poor animal resented so much that it caused him to rear.

Which made the black horse prance and start forward. Luckily, the one called Leucious was skilled enough to hold him in check. But as the men faced each other, there was a tension between them that was palpable.

And it sent a chill over her.

Belial let out an evil, sinister laugh. "Well, well. To what do I owe the honor of *this*?"

The black knight unsheathed his sword and pointed it straight at Belial's throat. "I think you know."

Finally, she saw more of the second knight. His burgundy surcoat held the strangest crest. A white bird that was wrapped within a thorny, gray S. Oddly enough, his destrier matched the same color gray, as if it'd been done apurpose.

"Hand her over and we'll make this painless."

Belial laughed at the second knight's request. "There's only one problem with that, my brothers. If you take our sister home, her husband is going to object to it."

CHAPTER 11

Ariel sat down as Belial's words rang in her ears. Instinctively, she reached for Valteri's hand.

"Are they your brothers?"

She glanced at her husband and shrugged. "I know not." And she didn't. For her life, she had no memory of either man.

A foul curse rang out from the black knight as the second one dismounted. "What have you done, Belial?"

Belial held his hands up in surrender. "Nothing. I had no part in this."

"Why don't I believe that?" Leucious's tone was filled with disgust.

The burgundy knight scoffed. "Probably because you hate that bastard almost as much as I do. And trust him even less."

"Hey!" Belial dismounted and headed for the burgundy knight. "A little harsh, Shadow. You could try and play nice."

"With you? Sod off." The one called Shadow removed his helm.

Ariel actually gasped as she saw his exceptionally handsome features. Steel-blue eyes were set in a perfectly formed face. A face that she recalled, and yet couldn't place it to any specific memory.

Somehow, she knew she knew him. She just didn't know how they'd met, or when.

He gave her a kind smile. "Ariel?"

The moment he touched her arm, she saw an image of them as children.

They were playing.

Laughing.

They were friends and she felt it with every part of her being.

Relieved to finally remember something, she gasped, then smiled. "I know you."

He inclined his head to her. "Aye. Of course you do."

"You got into trouble for me." Her mind whirled with the first real memory that she recalled. "You were a boy, and I wasn't supposed to be . . . somewhere. I-I can't remember where. But you took the blame for me."

"My father's study. You wanted to see his armor, and you broke his buckle."

She fingered the scar that ran just under his jawline. "You were beaten terribly for it."

He snorted. "I was beaten terribly for everything. Including breathing." His gaze went from her to Valteri and narrowed. "Leucious? Get over here."

"Can I kill Belial first?"

"Don't tease me." Shadow moved Ariel aside before he went to Valteri and knelt beside him. "I can see why she was drawn to him."

Leucious removed his helm to reveal a pair of frigid green eyes that were incredibly clear. Like Shadow, he was unbelievably handsome, with a full day's growth of dark brown whiskers.

He didn't say a word until he stood next to his brother.

Then he cursed foully. "Belial!"

"I did nothing."

Confused by all of them, Ariel was desperate to know what had them so upset. "What is it?"

Shadow looked up at Leucious. "He's bleeding badly. We need to get him back to his . . . whatever."

Ariel finally heard the sound of a wagon. "That should be his squire returning with a ride for him."

Valteri stared at Shadow. "Do I know you?"

He shook his head. "Nay. We've never met. Believe me, if we had, you'd remember it."

As soon as Wace and the others were there, Leucious and Shadow carried him to the wagon and placed him gently on it.

Ariel climbed into the back to ride with Valteri. "Will you ride with me?"

Shadow blinked in shock at her unexpected invitation. He glanced over at Leucious. "Is it safe to leave you two alone?"

Leucious sneered at Belial. "Probably not."

"Good, then. I'll ride with the lady. See to my horse, will you?" He climbed into the wagon and settled down beside her.

In spite of her worry and the seriousness of the situation, she had to stifle a laugh. "Are you really my brother?"

He frowned at her. "You can't remember anything, can you?"

"Nay."

"That's so strange."

"You've no idea."

Shadow crawled closer to Valteri. "And you? How did you meet Ariel?"

"She was found in a field and brought into my manor by my men."

"And what? Belial just showed up?"

Valteri nodded. "Aye."

"Huh . . ." Shadow bit his lip as if he were pondering the matter. "And your father, Lord Valteri? Who might *he* be?"

Torment filled his eyes. "My mother never named him. Why do you ask?"

A strange feeling went through her as she watched Shadow study her husband. "Do you know his father?"

That got Valteri's attention.

And caused Shadow to grimace at her. "I have a suspicion."

She looked at him expectantly.

"Don't give me that look. I could be wrong. I'd hate to name him and then look like an idiot. Not like I don't do that enough already. Besides, I give you the name . . . you call him 'Father,' and I turn out to be wrong, he'll attempt to kick my ass, I'll beat his, and it'll just be a whole bloody war I can do without."

"And if you're right?" Ariel asked.

Shadow sighed. "Not sure it'll do either of them any favors. The gods know, having a father never did me any good." He met her gaze. "You either, punkin. It's why you're in this mess."

"I don't understand."

"The day you get your memory back, you will." His ominous tone sent a chill down her spine.

"Who's her father?"

He let out an evil laugh. "Even if I told you, you wouldn't believe me."

"And who are you?"

He laughed again at Valteri's question. "A mercenary bastard." He spread his hand out and Valteri instantly fell unconscious.

Ariel gasped at his gesture and her husband's response to it. "Did you do that?"

Blinking innocently, Shadow scowled. "Do what?"

"Cause my husband to pass out?"

"How could I do such a thing?"

"That's not an answer."

"Isn't it?"

Suspicion crawled over her skin. "You're toying with me."

"Nay, little one. I'm not Belial. Believe me when I say that I'm on your side in this matter. Though most cannot, *you* can trust me."

"I don't understand."

Shadow gave her a lopsided grin. "Neither do I. At least not until we beat some answers out of Belial, which I relish the thought of doing. For now, lay your worries aside. Leucious and I are here to ensure nothing ill befalls you or your lord."

She wasn't sure why she trusted him, but she did.

Maybe because his was the one, true memory she felt and he seemed remarkably calm and kind, in spite of his words.

Nodding, she let out a relieved breath and settled down beside Valteri.

Yet in the back of her mind lay an uneasy feeling.

This wasn't going to be as easy as Shadow made it sound. She knew it. There was something insidious about their family.

And she needed to know what.

B elial scrambled from Thorn, but Thorn wouldn't let him get far. "What did you do?"

"I told you, I did nothing."

"Fine. I'll get Michael here and you can explain to him how it is that you allowed his daughter to marry a mortal."

Belial went cold at the threat. "You do it and I'll summon *your* father."

Thorn laughed. "You want me to? Been awhile since I saw old Daddy-kins. If you're trying to threaten me, it won't work. Remember that we're the same flesh, he and I. You have failed him. I just piss him off."

He paled with the knowledge.

"That's right, bobbin. You, he would gut. Me . . ." Thorn shrugged. "I just get lectured. He's still hoping to charm me back into his fold." Which was why Michael and his ilk refused to trust him. They were terrified that one day he would cave in and return to his father's loving embrace.

Kadar was the king of all evil. The lightless void that made the dark so terrifying.

And he'd rather die than ever play nice with that bastard.

Not that they made it easy on him with the vim they showed where he was concerned. Honestly, he wasn't sure why he continued to fight for their cause. Even though he was evil incarnate, his father was much kinder to him, most days.

But then, he knew.

Damn *her* for it. Women were the curse of them all, and the woman he'd given his own heart to had done a fine number on him.

And that made him want to rip the wings off Belial.

The demon put up his hands to shield himself. "She's been cursed. Not by me. By a witch. And there's nothing we can do. Ariel's trapped here until the curse is met."

"Well, that fucking reeks!"

Belial straightened and shrugged. "Only if you're Ariel."

He glowered at him. "And so, what? You thought if you corrupted her while she was human, you could hand over her soul to your masters?"

Belial nodded.

Thorn rolled his eyes. "My father would have laughed at you for the offer."

"Nay, he would not!"

He snorted. "I negotiate with the bastard constantly. Do you really think that I don't know what he'll take and when he'll say to piss off?"

"The soul of an Arel—"

"Is common. He has an entire army of them."

"She's a daughter of Michael."

Thorn narrowed his gaze on the demon. "Which you knew before I told you?"

Belial took a step back. "I . . . I . . ."

He tsked. "Dangerous game you're playing. Have you any idea what Michael would do?"

Belial snorted. "She's not his only bastard."

"No, but she's one of his favorites." Her mother had been a particularly strong nekoda who'd died fighting against one of their worse demonic enemies. . . .

Ambrose Malachai.

And still Belial refused to see the stupidity of his actions. "It wouldn't be our first battle."

"Could be your last."

Belial scoffed. "You seriously overestimate his abilities."

"You seriously underestimate them."

"Are you telling me that you're afraid of Michael?"

"Hardly. Rather, I have a healthy respect for his skills. As should you."

With a derisive snort, Belial stepped away. "You forget the number I command."

"I forget nothing. Ever. But you'd do well to remember what happened the last time my father's army rose up against the Kalosum." The Army of Light was a powerful force that had put his father's army down and left him imprisoned with his sister, Azura, while his other sister, Braith, had "vanished."

Belial sneered. "He was betrayed!"

"So he says." Thorn wasn't so sure. His aunt Braith was ever one of great surprises and he'd never quite figured out if she'd betrayed his father or was betrayed by him before she'd left. "And what of Valteri?"

Belial scowled in confusion. "What of him?"

"Do you think it wise to toy with him?"

"What's a human going to do?"

Thorn froze as he realized Belial's full stupidity. He had no idea what he was dealing with.

Who he was dealing with.

Interesting, given how obvious it was.

"Again, I wouldn't underestimate anyone in this scenario."

Belial blustered. "That's why you're where you are, and I'm—"

"Enslaved," Thorn reminded him. "I live freely. No one holds my leash.

And while you may command a few demons because my father allows you to, I lead the entire army of Maziqim."

"Only because they're traitors!"

"Nay. They were loyal . . . to me." A gift from his father, which Kadar had regretted since the day he'd unleashed them into Thorn's command. For all his father's gifts, he'd never seen that one coming.

Still, Belial refused to back down. "You can't interfere with her free will."

"Neither can you. You can only tempt."

"Then we're at a stalemate."

Not exactly. Thorn held a much bigger piece to this puzzle. He just had to figure out how to play it.

And when.

CHAPTER 12

Bright yellow flames coiled around Valteri's legs. He flinched at the blistering heat that scorched his flesh. As he struggled against the ropes that bound him securely to a stake, he realized that they weren't true flames, but rather the desperate, vicious arms of demons holding him there.

He fought against them as hard as he could, yet their grip never wavered, never lessened.

Even hotter than the fire, their breath singed his cheeks and burned his lungs. He struggled to free himself from their grip, but it was useless.

The demons were relentless.

They wrapped their arms about his chest and neck, clawing at him. Pulling him down through the hot coals and into a stifling cavern. Raw sulfur glistened on the walls, the stench of it clinging to his nostrils.

Screams and howls filled his ears. He heard thousands of souls crying out for mercy. And even more laughing at their misery.

All his youth, Valteri had listened to the priests and monks warn others about the cries of the damned.

Those warnings paled in comparison to the reality surrounding him. Nothing on earth was equal to the soul-chilling anguish those screams betrayed.

"Valteri?"

His heart pounding, he turned toward the soft, soothing voice that reached out to him through the heat and misery.

Ariel floated above a bloodred sea.

The pale gossamer dress barely concealed her luscious curves. Her white hair blew around her shoulders, brushing against his face and bare chest in a tender caress that stole the air from his lungs.

His body burned anew as he hungered for her in a way he'd never hungered for any woman.

He tried to reach for her, but his arms refused to obey. She floated toward him, a light, gentle smile curving her lips. Hands softer than down touched his face and slid over his stubbled cheek.

Valteri closed his eyes against the power of that touch, and he stood helpless before her. Pleasure the likes of which he'd never known coursed through him.

He needed her more than he'd ever needed anything. He knew that now, yet he no longer felt the desire to curse his weakness. Nay, he wanted to shout with relief and release.

Still, he couldn't move.

Feather-like lips touched his. Drawing her closer, he held on to her for the sake of his soul. He deepened their kiss so that he drank of all her kindness until everything else faded away. All the horrifying sounds and pungent smells.

It all was gone.

He knew nothing more than the feel of the woman before him.

Then suddenly, his arms were empty.

She was gone.

"Valteri!"

He opened his eyes to see a group of Saxons pulling her away from him. Pain racked his body.

"You'll not have her!" The old Saxon lord ran down into another cavern, while he dragged her behind him.

Ariel shrieked and tried to pull away, but the Saxon held fast to her.

An overwhelming emptiness consumed Valteri. Fury blinded him. No one would take his Ariel! He'd rather die than live another moment without her by his side.

He ran after them, intent on killing the bastard.

But more demons ran between them, separating them.

Gold wings sprang out of Ariel's back and an ethereal glow highlighted her entire body.

Suddenly, that glow blinded all of them.

"She doesn't belong here."

The creatures around him hissed those words.

"But *you* do!"

Valteri scowled at them. "Get away from me!" He tried to knock them away. "Ariel!"

She ignored his call.

Furious, he tried to get her attention. But instead he came face-to-face with a man with eyes like his.

One brown and one green.

Stunned and confused, he stared at the stranger. Yet there was something eerily familiar about him. With long dark hair, the man was even in height with him. "Who are you?"

Al-Baraka. The demons whispered the name that meant "broker."

Katadykari—the damned.

"We are all demon born."

Valteri turned to find an orange-fleshed demon behind him. But this one wasn't attacking.

"But it's up to you whether or not you're damned." With those words, Al-Baraka turned and unsheathed his sword so that he could help to fight off the demons after Valteri. "Go! Never come here again!"

Flames burst all around as the orange demon kicked him.

"Valteri?"

Out of nowhere, gentle hands stroked his cheek with a warm softness he could scarcely comprehend.

Opening his eyes, he stared up into the tender blue gaze of his wife.

His wife. He swallowed at the thought. For once the title didn't fill him with dread. Nay, it was more like a caress.

A slow smile spread across her lips and her eyes softened even more, bringing a raging fire to his loins. Though a thousand aches pounded through his body, not even they could detract from the need he felt for her.

"Good evening, milord," she whispered, rising from his bed with a gentle grace.

Valteri reached for her arm. He didn't want her to leave. Not after his nightmare.

He'd almost lost her to demons.

"Are you all right?"

He nodded, not quite trusting his voice. Reluctantly, he forced himself to let go.

Smiling, she rose and went to pour a cup of wine, then brought it to him. He stared at her graceful movements and had to squelch the urge to pull her into his arms.

As much as he wanted to claim her, he was too ill for such at the moment.

That thought summoned an image of people taunting her, but he banished it.

He wasn't a coward. He'd never been one.

Last night, he'd almost died and left her.

How stupid he'd been to think that would be the answer. But this world was filled with all kinds of monsters.

She needed protection, and how could he leave her to anyone else to protect?

Never again would he allow his fears to rule him.

He had fought for a brother he barely tolerated.

Fought for coin he didn't care about.

Only a fool would refuse to fight for the woman who'd claimed his heart.

He knew that now.

No one would keep them apart.

Not even him or his stupidity.

And he'd crack the bones of the first person to ever bring the blush of shame to her cheeks. If he had to kill every person in this valley to keep her safe, then by hell he'd gladly do it.

She helped him up and tilted the cup to his lips.

The warm, spicy wine sated his thirst, but did nothing to appease the hunger in his loins.

No sooner had she removed the cup from his lips than he gently took her hand and pulled her close.

Closer still until he could kiss her sweet, parted lips and breathe in the rich, heady scent of her rose bath oil. She smiled against his lips. Delight shot through his entire body. His wife would never deny him. Never cringe at his touch.

Not his precious Ariel.

After a moment, she pulled away and gave a short laugh. "Milord, you must be careful lest you pull the stitches from your side."

Valteri followed her gaze to his bare ribs, and saw the neat, even stitches that closed a wound. The thought of Eve being created from Adam's rib came to his mind, and he grimaced. Though he was every bit as cursed as Adam, he could only hope that his mate would never be forced to bear the brunt of his own sin.

"How long have I slept?"

"Through the day and well into the night."

He frowned. "A full day?"

"Aye." She pulled a wooden platter of food from the chest and brought it over to him. "You have raged with a fever since mid-morning."

Then it truly had all been a dream.

Yet it'd seemed so real. So *very* real.

Valteri took a slice of cheese from the platter and carefully ate the sharp tangy bit. His head pounded needles of pain that darkened his sight, and as he wiped at his damp forehead, he noted the healing wounds there as well.

"How are you feeling?" Ariel refilled his cup.

He marveled at her beauty and the fact that she'd come to him when he had needed her most. "Like my horse trampled upon me."

Her sweet laugh rang in his ears. "I do believe the correct way of riding is on a horse's back, not under his belly."

Her eyes twinkled as she sat next to him. "Care to tell me what happened?"

Valteri swallowed his food, his mind focusing on the night before. He remembered the streak and the wolf, but everything else was jumbled. "Something frightened my steed and he threw me."

She cocked a finely arched brow. "Threw *you*, milord?"

Her teasing voice lightened his heart and he rubbed his hand over her arm, delighting in the feel of her soft dress, a dress that hid even softer skin that he longed to sample with his lips. "Aye, milady. And I'm most 'shamed to admit that 'twas not the first time I have fallen from the saddle."

She tilted her head, her demure smile lighting coals in his belly. "But surely the first time since your childhood?"

Her light mood was infectious and he reached out to finger her cheek. "Most certainly."

She laughed and touched his hand, sending another wave of heat through him. Ariel glanced to his forehead and her smile faded.

"Ariel?" he asked, concerned over the sudden absence of her mirth.

A smile returned to her lips, but its hollowness did nothing to alleviate his worry. She shook her head and pulled his hand from her cheek. "'Tis nothing. Just a passing thought."

He set his food aside and took her cold, trembling hand in both of his. "What is it?"

She moved away from him to stand before the open window. The confusion and pain on her face brought an ache to his own chest. Valteri longed for a way to soothe her, but was uncertain what to do.

Her silence rang in his ears. Had she already been mocked by his people? Did she regret ever having signed the agreement for marriage?

A thousand such thoughts raced through his mind as he waited impatiently for her answer.

She drew a deep breath, but still refused to face him. "Before you awoke, you spoke of demons and . . ." She paused, her frown darkening. Shaking her head, she drew another deep breath. "Forget it. 'Tis foolishness."

"What is foolish?"

Ariel took a step forward and stood at the foot of his bed. "When I found you, I heard a voice whisper that I must watch you die."

A chill crept along his spine. "Watch me die?"

Her distress reached out to him and he longed to soothe her fear. "Well, maybe not *you*." Her voice was barely more than a whisper. "But it said 'watch *him* die.' The voice sounded so evil, so cold that I wondered if it might be the devil himself whispering it to me."

Valteri held his hand out to her, his chest tight. "Ariel, come to me."

She walked forward and took his hand, her own like ice inside his palm.

"'Twas nothing more than your fear speaking. There are no demons who stalk this earth, seeking victims. Our greatest enemy is ourselves. You've said it yourself. People often choose the rod that beats them."

Her gaze lightened and a smile curved her lips. "I told you 'twas foolish."

"There's nothing about you foolish. Other than wanting to spend time in my boorish company." He pulled her into his arms and held her against his chest. "You were worried, 'tis more than understandable and more than appreciated."

Ariel nodded, but inside, she found it hard to believe him. No matter how many times she'd told herself the words meant nothing, a tiny voice in her heart kept reminding her of them and telling her to listen well, as that could very well be a real memory.

What if it was?

Just as that voice that kept urging her to run?

But how could she? All she wanted was to stay with her lord, bear his children, and grow old by his side.

His warm breath fell against her cheek, his muscled chest was strong against her side. Aye, this was what she wanted, all she'd ever want.

Should she leave, she knew she'd never again feel safe or happy.

For now, her only real memories consisted of him and the one she had of her brother, Shadow.

He leaned his head back into his pillows and tensed as if another wave of pain cut through him. Guilty that she clung to him when he needed his rest, Ariel rose and retrieved his platter from the floor. Placing it on the table, she felt his gaze upon her like a tender touch that caressed her heart.

She turned around to see his gentle eyes and the adoration that shone brightly in his unique gaze. At this moment, she wondered how she could ever fear he might not want her, and yet his words about leaving echoed in her mind like a quiet thief sent to steal her safety, her happiness. She offered him a smile, but couldn't quite shake her fears.

"Where are your brothers?"

Ariel cringed over a query she'd been dreading. "Well . . . that's an interesting question."

"How so?"

"Last I saw, they were fighting to see which of them would have the honor of beating Belial."

He cocked a smile at her. "I knew I liked them for a reason."

She tsked at him.

Valteri pulled her back into his arms. She smiled as a wave of happiness rushed through her.

He might not say he wanted her, but his actions spoke loudly enough. She laid her head on his chest, careful not to tug any of the stitches, and closed her eyes. His heart thumped beneath her cheek, delighting her with its healthy song.

As she lay there in soothing silence, it surprised her that he didn't try to leave and take his bed elsewhere, as he had done since their marriage. Though his wounds must surely plague him, they were not so severe that he couldn't leave should he choose to do so. Indeed, his current wounds were slight compared to the deep, horrifying scars that lined his back and wrists. Scars that had stolen her breath when she'd first seen them.

"Milord?" she whispered.

"Aye?"

"Where all did you go last evening?"

He stroked her hair, his hand pausing for a moment on her cheek as he played with stray strands that tingled against her face. "I needed time to think, time to plan."

She sensed his sadness almost as much as if it beat inside her own heart. "You're still planning to leave?"

When he didn't speak, she looked up at him. By the sadness hovering in his eyes, she knew exactly what he'd been planning.

And that thought tore through her with waves of resounding pain that crashed against her heart until she feared they would tear the organ asunder.

Emptiness filled her and she tried to imagine living without him, but all she could see were years of circular misery stretching out before her. Years of longing for someone who refused to stay. "When are you leaving?"

He winced. "Damn me for it. I can't."

Shock riveted her. "What?"

He let out a disgusted breath. "I won't leave you unprotected."

Tears filled her eyes. But before she could say or do anything, a knock sounded on the door.

Wace pushed the door open. His gaze lightened as he noted his lord's improved condition. "I brought fresh wine and food." He placed the tray next to the platter on the table before the fire then approached the bed with a reluctance that brought an ache to Ariel's chest.

She gave a quick squeeze on his right shoulder to offer him courage and nodded for him to speak.

Even though Wace kept his spine straight, she could feel the tremors that shook him. Had she known the inadvertent terror she'd cause the poor lad, she'd have never insisted on his help.

The youth cleared his throat and bravely lifted his chin as if he faced the worst horror imaginable. "I didn't mean to leave milady unattended to seek help for you, milord. I pray that you can forgive me."

Though Valteri's face and tone were stern, she saw the twinkle in his eyes. "Aye, she could have been harmed, boy."

Wace gulped and nodded. "I know, milord."

Valteri met her gaze. It was her fault, she knew. She only hoped Valteri would continue to hold to the gentle scolding in his gaze and not turn toward anything more sinister.

He looked back at his squire. "But then my dearest lady is rather impossible to argue against. I have a feeling that had you not returned to seek help as she asked, the three of us would still be up on that hill trying to decide who should go and who should stay."

A smile broke across Wace's lips. "Then you're not angry at me?"

Valteri shook his head. "Nay, I owe you my life, lad. How could I fault such noble actions? Besides, I have yet to ever win an argument with her, either."

Wace smiled.

"But," Valteri said, and immediately Wace's expression sobered. "In the future I would have you seek others when dealing with milady's requests. Though you should always obey her, I would not have her harmed, no matter what argument she may give. I trust her safety to you, and I'd be much sorrowed to have that bond of trust broken."

"Aye, milord." Wace clapped his fist to his shoulder and gave a sharp bow.

She wanted to say something to ease the sting of Valteri's words, but any argument she gave would undermine his authority. Pressing her lips together, she forced herself to silence.

"May I take my leave, milord?"

Valteri nodded.

With one last curt bow, Wace made a quick exit.

Even so, she noticed the lightness of his step. The boy was happy again. Like her.

Ariel shook her head and smiled. Well, maybe the chastisement hadn't been so terribly bad after all.

No doubt his dread of the encounter had been far worse than the actual experience.

She turned back toward Valteri and saw the paleness of his cheeks.

He was tired and needed his rest. The voice she'd heard meant nothing. He wouldn't perish from his wounds.

Here, he was safe, and in little time he'd heal and be just as he was. Only better, because now she was going to make him grateful that he'd decided to stay.

As she moved away, he stopped her. "I would have you join me."

Ariel nodded. Returning the platter to the table, she doused the candle, removed her kirtle, and joined him in the bed.

He wrapped his strong arms about her, drawing her closer to his warm, fevered body. She trembled at the foreign sensation of his heat against her bare flesh. Not since the night he'd taken her innocence had he held her in such a manner, and she found the reality far better than her weak memory.

Indeed, she burned from the desire his touch wrought. She longed to roll over and bring his body back into hers, to ease the throbbing ache inside her to have him. Her stomach pitched and tightened from the weight of her desire, but she reminded herself that she must remain still. His wounds were far too fresh for him to carry out her fondest desire.

"Ariel?"

"Aye?"

"Why do you weep?"

"I'm merely happy to have you home and in one piece." Grateful that he was giving them a chance.

He rolled her onto her back and kissed away the dampness on her cheeks. "I would never have you shed a single tear on my behalf," he whispered, his voice bringing a flood of joy to her breast. "I would never willingly cause you pain."

His lips covered hers and she reveled in the taste of warrior, the taste of wine on his tongue. Chills shot the length of her.

Valteri slid his body against hers and she moaned from the pleasure of his weight. It seemed like an eternity since he'd held her. She ran her hand over the strange circular scar on his chest that seemed so out of place with the others. . . .

As if one of the monks had used a branding iron on him. She wanted to ask about it, but knew that the memory of that wound would only give him pain.

He nipped at her throat with his teeth and pulled back with a groan. "Would that my body belonged to me this night." He let out a wistful sigh. "Methinks I should see that horse gelded for his actions."

She laughed at his words. "There's always the morrow, Valteri. Take heart. I have no plans to leave."

And now, neither did he.

Yet even so, she had a bad feeling that something evil was coming for both of them.

CHAPTER 13

As days went by, Ariel marveled at the quick recovery Valteri made.

And since the arrival of Thorn and Shadow, Belial had been strangely silent and absent. Pleading illness, he'd seldom come near her. Something that made her ecstatic.

For that alone, she worshiped her two new brothers.

Yet the two of them kept a respectful distance from her that she didn't quite understand.

Now, she sat outside in the small garden, trying to mend a tear in one of Valteri's tunics.

How did the others make this look so easy?

Her mind told her that she'd done this a million times, and yet she couldn't get any of the stitches right.

Not to mention, she'd much prefer being with her husband and listening to his rich, deep voice than the rustling leaves that surrounded her.

But he was a creature forever in motion. She was lucky that he'd given her several days to coddle him. According to Wace, that was a precious gift he'd never allowed another.

Then, two days ago, he'd started pleading with her to allow him to leave his bed and go about his routines.

To her eternal regret, she'd finally judged him well enough.

Provided he didn't stress himself overmuch.

"Aye, it sounds like an omen."

Ariel frowned at Brother Edred's voice drifting through the shrubbery. She started to call out and let him know she could overhear him, when his next words caused her to freeze where she sat.

"The Norman is the devil's own, without a doubt. Since first I saw him, I've wondered at his hair. Never before have I witnessed a Norman wearing hair in such a peculiar fashion. I wonder at what marks he seeks to conceal."

"The beast's mark, I'd wager," Ethbert sneered with a hostile venom that sent a wave of anger through her.

Their voices faded for a moment before the friar spoke up again. "I, too, have seen visions of hell where the very demons bowed down before him, paying homage to their overlord."

"But what of the lady?"

She stiffened at Ethbert's question and the evil mischief they brewed.

"Like blessed Mary Magdalene, her heart is pure, but she follows the corrupt path of the flesh. I fear his evil beauty bewitched her so that she cannot see her husband for what he really is. A demon among men."

A demon, indeed!

Ariel threw the tunic aside, rage burning raw in her throat. What could be more evil than a gossiping tongue?

For these six things doth the Lord hate. Yea, seven are an abomination unto him. A proud look, a lying tongue, and hands that shed innocent blood, a heart that deviseth wicked imaginations, feet that be swift in running to mischief, a false witness that speaketh lies, and he that soweth discord among brethren.

Obviously, the friar needed to spend more time reading the Bible and less time sowing discord and lies.

No wonder Valteri felt the way he did toward Edred and his ilk.

Rising to her feet, she intended to give them both a lesson they wouldn't soon forget.

"Ariel!"

Before she could take another step, Valteri rounded the corner of the pathway and headed straight for her.

Her anger melted at the joy in his eyes. A blush stained his cheeks and he was still breathing heavy from his ride.

"Valteri!" She tried to sound stern, but failed terribly. No matter how much she might want to castigate him for straining his wounds, his obvious happiness prevented her from saying anything that might dampen his mood. "You shouldn't tax your strength."

He came to rest beside her and seized her hands in his, bringing them to his lips, where he kissed first her right, then her left. Chills spread over her body at the gesture and the warmth of his touch against her flesh.

He offered her a hesitant smile and all thoughts of chastisement vanished. "I know I promised, but I couldn't wait to return."

Those words made her heart soar.

She cocked a playful brow, but couldn't prevent one corner of her mouth from lifting in humor. "Well, you seemed eager enough to leave me this morn."

His gaze turned serious and he tightened his grip on her hands. "I apologize for that, but I had business most pressing."

Her humor faded beneath the sudden turn of his own mood. What business had pressed him to leave her side so early?

Had he changed his mind, after all? Was he going to leave her?

She swallowed against the stinging lump in her throat. Was this the good-bye she'd been dreading—nay, fearing—for so long?

"Business most pressing?" Her voice cracked from the weight of her fear and pain.

"Aye." His dual-colored eyes twinkled. "While you were tending me yestereve, I realized I'd forgotten to take care of something rather important."

She frowned in confusion. Had his fever and delusions returned? "Which is?"

He pulled at the pouch dangling from his girdle. Opening it, he retrieved a small wooden box and handed it to her.

Ariel stared in amazement at the silver-inlaid box. It was exquisite.

He must have traveled as far as the town eight leagues away to purchase it. But why would he make such a journey?

"Open it," he urged.

She flipped the catch with her thumbnail and opened the box. A startled gasp left her lips and joy beat deep inside her. Nestled on a bed of rare silk lay a gold ring encrusted with tiny, sparkling emeralds.

Tears filled her eyes as she looked from her small treasure to her much larger one. "A pledge ring?"

He nodded, his gaze warm and loving. "I realized last eve that you were without one, and I'd not have anyone doubt that you are mine."

Ariel pressed her trembling lips together and pulled the ring from its container. The jewels winked at her as if they knew some jest that had escaped her notice. Never had she expected such a gift!

Valteri took the ring from her shaking fingers, kissed it, then placed it on her right thumb. He looked up at her, a small, timid smile on his lips. "Like your presence in my life, Ariel, it fits."

She closed her eyes, savoring his words. But still the doubt lingered beneath her happiness, quelling it until she could stand no more.

"Does this mean you really intend to stay?"

He looked away from her and she tensed, afraid to hear his response. For several terrifying minutes he stared at the small postern gate surrounded by vines. Emotions crossed his features and she struggled to name them, but they passed so quickly across his face that she dared not try.

His grip tightened on her hands and he sighed. "Of course I intend to stay."

Crying out in relief, she threw her arms about his shoulders and held him tightly. The strength of his chest against hers stole her breath and caused her heart to pound.

Suddenly, his lips claimed hers.

His rich, masculine scent filled her head and she trembled. Aye, this was what she'd wanted. All she'd ever want.

Her body burned for his touch and she ran her hands over his back, delighting in the dips and curves of his muscles. He entwined his hand in her hair and cupped the nape of her neck, tingling her scalp.

The very next thing she knew, Valteri swung her up in his arms.

She gasped in alarm. "You're going to hurt yourself!"

"Nay, and even if I do, I don't care." He carried her through the hall and to their chambers.

With a gentleness she could barely fathom, he laid her against the bed.

Ariel trembled at the force of her desire. At last she'd have her fondest wish.

Valteri stared at her like a starving man eyeing a king's feast. The raw hunger in his eyes sent waves of desire through her. She wanted him to devour her, and she longed to taste the rich, salty ripples of his muscles until she'd had her fill. But part of her heart told her that she'd never be sated with him.

Nay, she'd always want him, always yearn for his touch.

Licking her lips, she offered him a hesitant smile. "Come, my lord Valteri," she whispered, pulling him back into her arms. "I have waited for you."

Valteri closed his eyes at her words, savoring each and every syllable.

Even if he was damning both of them to an eternity of rumors and hostility, he couldn't stop himself from seizing this one moment, this one woman. He needed her, and the only way he could let her go would be to cut his own heart from his chest.

Nay, he could never leave. If there was a God above, then this must be His way of making amends for all he'd suffered. And if this was his reward, Valteri decided it'd been worth each and every torment ever delivered, and he would gladly relive all of it for this one moment in her arms.

She wrapped herself about him and he shivered from the tenderness. He tasted her silken lips, her neck, where he inhaled her divine rose scent. His lips tingled from the saltiness of her skin and he drank of it deeply. This was the only nourishment he needed, the nourishment he'd starved for the whole of his life.

Heated fire replaced the coldness in his heart. Every color and scent seemed amplified and more vibrant to him, as if he'd opened his eyes for the very first time. As if he had been reborn.

Her hesitant touches echoed through his soul, crashing through every single barrier he'd placed around himself to keep from being harmed.

Now he stood before her like a naked babe on the edge of a cliff.

And just like that child, he wanted to cry out in desperation. Never had he felt so exposed, so very vulnerable, and indeed he knew one word of rejection from her would destroy him.

She pulled his tunic from him, her hands eagerly exploring each dip and curve of his flesh. Valteri closed his eyes, his body burning.

"Do your wounds still plague you?" She ran her fingers over the stitches in his side.

Valteri shook his head, his throat tight. In truth all his wounds both past and present seemed completely healed because of her.

She gave him peace.

"All I feel is you, Ariel, and you could never bring me pain."

Those words made her blush. Her head reeled with the masculine scent of him, the gentle pressure of his strong hands roaming over her flesh. Everywhere he touched, hot chills rose up.

Ariel brushed her lips over the hard stubble of his neck, delighting in the salty taste of his skin. His throaty moan reverberated under her lips and thrilled her more than all the glorious mornings of the world.

"I need you," he whispered against her cheek.

Ariel pulled him closer. "I will always be here for you."

She shivered as he pulled her kirtle from her, and heat stole up her cheeks. Even though she'd already given herself to him, she was embarrassed for him to see her. Before it'd been dark, but in the full light of the day, she lay completely exposed, completely vulnerable to his gaze, his touch.

His eyes burned with an intensity that stole her breath as he moved again and retook her lips.

Valteri nibbled a path to her throat, and nipped at her tender flesh. Sharp, pulsing fires burned inside him. It seemed as if the first time with her had never been.

Not a callow, untried youth, he still found himself shaking from expectation. Nervous almost beyond endurance.

Her lips brushed the flesh just below his ear and he shook from the boiling desire that pitched inside him.

"Come to me, milord," she whispered, her husky voice urging him further.

He separated her thighs.

Ariel shivered in expectation as she reveled at the sensation of him lying against the length of her. She held her breath, afraid he would yet change his mind and send her away.

Or worse, that he'd leave her again.

And that thought made her fear that he would one day leave. That would kill her.

Valteri was her life, her breath.

His body heat reached out to her and she raised her hips to him. With a groan, he buried his face in her neck and slid inside her.

All of a sudden, a horrible, body-wrenching pain tore through her pleasure. It seemed as if she were being halved in twain. Her stomach lurched and burned and Ariel gasped from the agony.

"Ariel?" Valteri's voice sounded so far away that she longed to ask him where he'd gone.

Yet her head spun as if *she* had fallen into a well or some other deep hole.

Strange lights and images spiraled around her, stealing her breath. A hundred foreign voices spoke simultaneously, some accusing, some in pity.

From somewhere far away, she heard weeping and lamentations. Her chest tight, she tried to focus her thoughts, but like someone falling from a steep cliff, she couldn't find anything solid to grasp.

Suddenly, the images stopped.

Brutal pain exploded inside her body. Out of nowhere, her memories returned with rich, sharp clarity.

All of them.

"Dear gods!" she cried, shoving against Valteri.

His gaze confused, he held her against him. "Milady, what is it?"

Milady.

That single word hovered in her mind like a nightmare, an unbelievable terror that paralyzed her.

Over and over, the veil in her mind was shattered. All the images that had been foggy became crystal clear.

They all made sense.

Shadow. Belial.

The man with eyes identical to Valteri's . . .

Shite . . .

"Nay!" She moved away from him to cover herself with the fur-lined blankets. Ariel cowered against the edge of the bed, too horrified to think. "What have I done?"

Valteri looked at her as if she'd struck him and he slowly moved from the bed and retrieved his breeches. The pain in his eyes told her that he thought her rejection was of him.

With a trembling breath, Ariel stiffened her spine against the terrible, unbelievable truth she must deliver to him.

"'Tis not you, Valteri," she assured him.

She glanced up, but couldn't bring herself to face the misery that burned in his eyes.

Why? she wanted to scream. Why had this happened?

That horrid wretch of a witch!

Mildred and her cruel stupidity. So wrapped up in her own misery, she failed to look past it and see what her quest for vengeance could or would mean for others.

For the entire world.

"I have damned us both."

And damned more than that.

A frown lined his brow as he moved around the bed to touch her, and though he appeared calm, she could sense the roiling anger inside him. "How so?"

Ariel closed her eyes in an effort to banish the warmth of his hand against her bare shoulder, the comfort he offered.

Comfort she must shun. And shunning Valteri was the last thing she wanted to do.

How was she to tell him what she now knew about herself and the others?

He'd never believe her words. In truth, she found it impossible to believe and she knew it for reality.

Belial had played her well.

They all had.

But that one demon had surely earned his place in Azmodea for his treachery.

"Milady, what has caused you such distress?"

Her heart pounding, Ariel considered several ways to broach the matter with him, but nothing seemed right.

How could she tell him that she was something he didn't even believe in?

That both of them had been nothing more than the pawns in a game they hadn't even known they were playing?

"You will think me insane."

He brushed her hair away from her shoulder. "I will never think that of you."

She shook her head, refusing his reassurance. She must maintain distance between them.

For his sake and for her own.

This wasn't about carnal knowledge. She was the daughter of Michael and he . . .

He had no idea who his father was, but she did.

Holy gods, what had Belial done?

Had Kadar brought them together to toy with them all? Just how sick a game was this?

Valteri gently took her chin in his hand and forced her to look at him. "Talk to me."

Ariel bit her lip. He would lose his mind at the truth. She could only imagine the rage.

Provided he ever accepted the truth.

Even now, anger sizzled in his gaze, scorching her with its intensity. His jaw twitched. "What vexes you, milady? Tell me."

In his mismatched eyes she saw his fear that she'd rejected him.

She couldn't allow him to believe she'd spurned him when he was her very life.

Don't do it.

Keep silent.

She knew not to say anything and yet before she could stop herself, the truth tumbled from her lips: "I'm an Arel, Valteri."

He scowled at her. "A what?"

Groaning in exasperation, she struggled to find the right words to make him understand. "There are powers here that I know you don't want to believe in. That you've refused to acknowledge. But they're real and a war is raging that has nothing to do with your brother, William. I'm a part of that fight. A warrior, just like you."

His scowl matched her own. "How so?"

Ariel didn't even know where to begin. If she had her powers, she could show him and that would make this so much easier. And with that, she realized that she still had parts of her memory missing.

Parts she didn't quite understand.

But one thing she did know. . . .

"I swear to you that I'm speaking the truth. I was born from the powers of light, and the darkest powers have brought us together in an attempt to weaken my father and take you captive."

Valteri looked away, his heart strangely blank. It was as if his body didn't know how to react to her words and so decided to feel nothing.

"Well . . . my luck still holds, eh? I finally found a wife and it turned out she's insane."

She glared at him. "I'm not deranged! I know you don't believe me, but you must!"

Valteri just stared at her. Not even the urge to curse came to him. Maybe he'd already died of his wounds.

Surely that alone could explain this strange surreal defeat that echoed through his body, whispering through his soul.

"Very well, milady. You're an angel. Where are your wings?"

Ariel cringed at his question. "I said I was an Arel." But a vicious side of her really wanted her wings to sprout out and make him eat those words. "In my true form, I actually do have wings. However, I was cursed to be human, and so it seems that my ability to spring them out has been taken from me."

"What of your brothers?" His gaze darkened. "Are they Arels, too?"

Ariel bit her lip. How in the name of anything holy did she begin to answer that loaded question?

"The plural's 'Arelim.' And they're not exactly my brothers."

He arched a brow. "How so?"

Ariel shifted her grip on the cover she held. How could she even begin to explain this one? "Well, Thorn and Shadow are sort of like my brothers. Though they're not very well trusted among my kind. Thorn more so than Shadow. In fact, he has a lot in common with you, on that point."

"And Belial?"

Ariel hesitated as she feared Valteri's reaction.

But lying just wasn't in her nature. It never had been.

"In truth, he's the demon, not you."

His expression turned droll and irritated. "How so?"

She took a step back. "As you so often say about yourself, he was demon-spawn. Born of demons. His only purpose is to damn others and wreak havoc. Only in his case, it's true."

Chapter 14

Ariel braced herself for more of Valteri's mockery as trepidation filled her. Should she have told him that?

Maybe it would have been better for him to continue to deny the truth.

If Belial found out that Valteri knew the truth of him, what would he do? He was a cold-blooded bastard.

Ruthless.

He'd destroyed so many people. And for what?

His own gain? To make his overlords happy? She'd never understood what had made Kadar and Azura want to harm mankind. Prey on them.

From the beginning of time, they'd seen humans as the ultimate vermin.

Same with their servants, who'd always been set on the utter destruction of everyone and everything.

There was no kindness in any of them. All they wanted was to take over the world and ruin the lives of anyone who got in their way.

Her mind reeling with all the damage Belial had wrought throughout the centuries, she reached for her kirtle and donned it.

Silence hung between them like a thick pall.

Valteri turned away from her, and the betrayed expression on his face hit her like a fist to her heart. To think she'd been so worried about his leaving.

As if physical distance was the worst thing that could separate them.

What actually separated them was far more than just his brutal past, far more than what could be eased by a few tender words. They were two different beings entirely. Nothing could traverse the chasm between them.

He wasn't demonspawn.

Valteri was the son of an ancient, primal power. One who'd done his best to ensure the survival of mankind.

A creature who'd enslaved himself to the king of all darkness and the queen of shadows to ensure that the greatest evil facing man would remain in chains and unable to break the world.

His father was a hero.

Jaden must have had some reason for fathering him. He didn't do anything haphazardly. Especially not when it concerned humanity.

But to leave his son in this world unprotected . . .

Utter madness.

The last time a primal power had done that with a son, Kadar had taken the boy in to be his guardian in Azmodea—the hell realm where Kadar was trapped. While Seth wasn't the son of Jaden, he was the son of the god Razar, and almost as powerful. And a potent force for Kadar and Azura to use in their war against Ariel's father and the forces of light.

If Kadar could enslave Valteri the same way he'd done Seth . . .

A shiver went down her spine.

The combination of those two half-human warriors, along with the Adarian Malachai, who held dominion over all the demons . . .

Even without the powers of their missing sister, Braith, Kadar and Azura could use the Malachai to break free of their prison and overrun the world. And they would rain down hell upon it.

That was why Thorn and Shadow were here.

Why they had stayed.

The fate of the world was in their hands and if they failed. . . .

Everyone was doomed.

Surely, Jaden had known the repercussions of leaving a son in this realm without him or another to watch over the boy. Why would Jaden have been so careless and cold?

Was he no longer on their side?

That thought was even more chilling. Had all these centuries of serving evil finally turned Jaden?

If that was the case, then Valteri was in even more danger than he knew.

He'd been tortured by humans over a lie when the truth wasn't much better. He could very well be a pawn to a father who might be willing to sacrifice him for his own freedom. . . .

Surely, Jaden wouldn't be that cold.

Would he?

But what else made sense?

Why would he have fathered a son with a human when he knew better? After the horrible fate that had befallen his other sons and grandson?

All of them had been sacrificed in this war.

Wincing, she didn't know what to say to Valteri now.

Not if her suspicions were correct. Either his father was a selfish ass who wanted to sacrifice him.

Or he was so thoughtless that he hadn't cared what happened to his son.

All she knew was that she ached to soothe some of the pain that bled from every part of him, but his rigid spine made him seem unreachable.

Formidable.

Just like his father.

And just like his father, his enemies wouldn't rest until they saw him in chains.

S hadow paused as soon as he saw Ariel entering the donjon. With a polite excuse, he extricated himself from the extremely attractive serving wench who'd been offering herself to him.

If only he'd had a little more time.

And if Thorn didn't have such a nasty habit of taking pleasure in interrupting his pleasure.

Rotten bastard.

"There a problem, pet?"

Ariel's ball-shriveling expression answered that affirmatively.

"I see you have your memory back."

She nodded. "Is there any way to restore my powers?"

"'Fraid not, punkin." He jerked his chin toward Mildred the Crone, who was watching them while she cleaned. "She put one hell of a whammy on you. I could fry her for you, though. Return the favor, if you'd like."

"Don't tempt me. You're almost as bad as Belial."

He scoffed. "I'm worse than Belial. You should remember that, if you have your memory."

She returned her gaze to him. He had his long hair pulled back into a sharp ponytail. It made his face all the more alluring. More masculine, as the beauty of his hair didn't compete with the perfection of his chiseled features. "Nay, Shadow. You're more ruthless to those deserving, but you still have a soul and a heart. The two things that Belial lost a long time ago. I might not have my powers at present, but I've seen you when I did, and you can't hide the truth from me."

He looked away sheepishly. "Don't say that shit out loud. Someone might hear you."

That was his worst fear. For his enemies to know that he wasn't the cold-blooded bastard they thought him.

And he had a lot of enemies. Too many, in fact. They never left him in peace.

Her heart ached for him. "I will keep your secret." Rising on her tiptoes, she kissed his whiskered cheek. Then, she whispered in his ear, "You know that Valteri is the son of Jaden."

"Aye," he breathed.

"Does Jaden know?"

He glanced around the room before he answered. "No. According to my agents, he only knows about Caleb and Xev."

Xevikan Daraxerxes was a terrifying demonic beast. Shadow's half brother through their mother, Azura, he served as the right hand of the Malachai demon. In fact, he was Adarian Malachai's Šarru-Dara, or Blood King, who fed power to the Malachai so that he'd be able to destroy the world should Azura and Kadar ever break out of their prison and unleash the Malachai so that they could rule the world again as its dark gods.

And why was Xev enslaved to the Malachai? Because he'd betrayed his own mother by fighting for Ariel's side during the Primus Bellum—the first war of the gods. Rather than serve the dark gods, Xev had changed sides to fight for his wife, who was a warrior, like Ariel, for the Arelim army.

The same was true for Caleb Malphas. Because he'd fallen in love with a human and switched sides to protect humanity, he'd been punished, too.

At the end of the war, Jaden had turned his back on them and refused to help them escape their unjust convictions.

No one knew why.

Xev and Caleb had done what was right and decent. And they were spending eternity being tortured for it.

Just like Shadow.

"I can't let Valteri share his brothers' fates."

"Nor I. I'm sick of the gods and so is Thorn. Watching them play these games with the innocent."

"Then how do we fix this?"

Shadow snorted. "That's always the rub, dearest. Damned if I know."

V alteri narrowed his gaze as he scanned the letter from William. His grip tight, he again read William's dispensation of all the Ravenswood lands and titles to him.

I should be grateful.

An image of Ariel drifted through his mind, her arms open, her lips curved up into a warm, welcoming smile. Even now, he could hear her laughter as she danced around him.

For the first time in his life, he could imagine himself with someone. See himself growing old with a woman by his side.

Even more terrifying, he could imagine children.

His children.

Valteri shook his head, disgusted by the mere thought. He should know better than to even consider such a fantasy.

It's not for me. I'm a warrior. Through and through.

He didn't need anyone.

Damn sure didn't need children. Wace was aggravation enough.

And yet . . .

Cursing himself for loving a woman who was obviously insane, he crumpled the parchment into his fist. Why hadn't he listened to himself and left England right after William's coronation?

If he had any sense, he'd defy his brother and go now.

Your wife needs you.

Valteri flinched at the voice in his head. Whatever was he going to do? She was mad and he was a fool.

Mad.

That one word chased itself through his thoughts like a silent phantom seeking blood. He'd had plenty of experience dealing with the deranged.

His brother being the most recent one.

Damn the loons of his youth.

The last thing he wanted now was a return to having to walk the eggshells of his past, where every word had to be measured with care.

For that was the thing about insanity.

It only grew and became stronger. In time, she'd become a stranger. Not the lady who'd won his heart, but someone he'd never recognize.

And what would she be like once her reasoning fled? Would she be violent like the others who'd attacked him for no reason, or one of the poor souls who curled up like a tiny kitten afraid to move?

And what then?

Would her brothers cast her to the likes of Edred for exorcism, or worse? He flinched as he saw himself as a boy being tortured by them.

Damn them all! They were the monsters in this world. Not the imagined demons they claimed they were after.

Valteri closed his eyes against the pain in his chest. He wanted to leave and yet he couldn't make himself give up on her. Of all the things in his life, she alone was worth saving, worth protecting.

Damn you, William, for getting me into this.

Hours later, Valteri came out of the stable just in time to see Ariel heading for the hall.

"Milady?" he called.

She continued on her way without pausing.

Frowning, Valteri started to walk away, but stopped after two steps.

Was she avoiding him? It wasn't like her to ignore him so.

Concerned that something might be wrong, he hastened after her. "Ariel?"

She hesitated. Panic flickered in her gaze a moment before she lifted the hem of her gown and sped forward.

What was that?

More concerned than ever, Valteri quickened his pace, and finally caught her as she entered the hall. "Ariel? Did you not hear my call?"

She looked up at him with an amused stare. "Aye, I heard you. But I needed to come in here before you stopped me."

"To what purpose?"

She opened the door wider and smiled so that he could see a large feast had been prepared. "A celebration for you."

He scowled at her. "Pardon?"

"Wace told me that you'd been declared the lord of these lands. I thought a celebration was in order. Come, Valteri, Lord of Ravenswood."

He hesitated. "Milady, please. Do you not remember what happened the last time we attempted such a thing?"

Thorn and Shadow came up behind him.

"That was before I was here, brother." Thorn clapped him on the shoulder. "I dare anyone to say a word now."

"As do I. 'Less they wish to feast on their own entrails." Shadow winked at him. "I say we drink, feast, and wench!"

"Shadow!" Ariel chided.

"Well, not Val. He has you. But I can wench aplenty."

Thorn snorted. "How are you not diseased?"

"Who says I'm not?" Shadow raked him with a frown. "I just hope it's terminal. Let me out of this life. I'm done with it."

She was aghast. "You're awful!"

Shadow grinned at her. "Incorrigible from my first breath to my last." And with that, he went off in search of wine.

Thorn headed off after him.

Valteri shook his head. "Those two are so strange."

"Indeed, they are."

"Yet I like them and can't figure out why."

With a sigh, she nodded. "I know. I feel the same."

He laughed. "But they're your brothers. You should like them."

She arched a brow at his comment.

"My brothers are different. They're asses. Giant ones, point of fact."

"As can be mine. Much of the time." Taking his arm, she led him toward the table that was set with all the foods Wace had told her were Valteri's favorites.

Ariel debated if she should try again to tell him the truth.

That they weren't her brothers.

They were more akin to his.

He won't believe you.

Besides, he was happy, and that was such a rare thing for him that she didn't want anything to taint it.

But as she moved to take her seat, she caught the eye of the old crone. The hatred there chilled her to her soul.

Mildred was brewing evil. She could feel it. It crawled over her skin like a living, breathing creature.

"You will hold what you love in your arms and you will watch as he dies."

Those words echoed in her ears. She remembered her curse. The old woman intended to kill Valteri.

To punish her.

Ariel winced as she remembered everything. The warrior she'd escorted from the battlefield—Mildred's son—who had been honored to join ranks with her brethren.

And his mother's wrath over something that Ariel had had no part in. Her role had been minor. All she'd done was escort him from where he'd fallen to those who offered him a chance to live again. To do what he'd wanted to do with his afterlife.

For that, she was being punished.

And so would Valteri.

It wasn't right.

In that moment, her stomach cramped. By marrying him, she'd condemned him.

Belial had been right.

She wasn't just a psychopomp. This time, she was the hand of death, and she'd stupidly dealt it to an innocent man.

Valteri felt the darkness from Ariel as he reached for his wine. "Is something amiss?"

She smiled and shook her head. "All's well."

Lifting her hand, he placed a kiss to her palm, amazed by her and the feast she'd made for him. No one had ever been so kind or thoughtful. And he couldn't believe his good fortune.

How had someone so special fallen into his life?

That thought brought back his dream to him. The notion that with the good came an even greater evil.

Happiness never lasted. At least not for him.

Night invariably followed the day.

Was this only a setup for something far more foul? At no time in his life had he ever been allowed to take a breath and just enjoy one moment of his existence. Every heartbeat had been an endurance.

Surely this was no different.

What evil would follow? What cost would he have to pay for daring to enjoy this time with her?

But then, he knew.

You are cursed.

He'd been told that every day of his life. By everyone around him. No peace. No quarter.

His dream had been a warning, and he knew in his heart that fate would tear them apart.

Sooner rather than later, he would lose her.

And there would be nothing he could do.

CHAPTER 15

Belial lay against the prickly, sweet hay, his body aching in twisting, heated agony. At this moment, he didn't even possess enough strength to change into his true form and leave this desolate world.

Not that he cared.

Not after the secret he'd just learned . . .

Those roving little bastards thought themselves so smart. And here he'd thought they'd come to protect Ariel.

He would laugh if he were able.

Valteri the Godless was in fact Valteri fitzJaden. . . .

Bloody figured.

His plan had cost him much, but it'd been well worth the price of staying in this wretched human body for so long.

To get the soul of Jaden's son, he'd gladly do it all again. There was no telling what Kadar and Azura would give him for this. He could only imagine the reward. . . .

A giddy rush surged through him. Now, all he had to do was plan Valteri's death.

With the curse fulfilled, he'd escort that bastard straight to his master's throne.

His smile widened. How simple. He'd chain them both to Kadar Noir's throne.

And reap his eternal reward.

Out of nowhere, an image of Seth went through his mind. What they'd done to the boy when he'd first been brought into Azmodea.

Against his will, he flinched at the memory.

That child had been brutalized.

For a second, he felt guilty for what he was doing to another innocent. But neither Ariel nor Valteri were as young as Seth had been. Unlike Rezar's son, they were trained warriors who'd taken their fair share of lives.

They wouldn't hesitate to kill *him*.

No one had ever taken pity or mercy where he was concerned. Not even his own mother. From his first breath, she'd saddled him with a name that meant "worthless," and that was how she and everyone else had treated him. How everyone looked at him.

But if he returned home with the son of Jaden he would be worthless no longer. And they'd finally have to give him his due.

People were weak and petty. Mindless guppies following wherever their group swam. The few he'd known with their own minds usually fell to his temptation in no time.

Nay, there was nothing about human beings that couldn't be corrupted— given the right inducement.

Arelim were just the same. And he had even less use for them.

They held themselves far above him and everyone else. As if they were somehow better. Smarter. When they were all cut from the same chaotic goo.

The same vengeful gods.

Taking a deep breath, he steeled his will for the coming deaths. He would have no pity for either of them. Better they suffer than him.

He'd had enough for a million lifetimes.

"There you are!"

Belial looked up at Brother Edred, who stood at the stall's opening, leaning against a wooden post. Worry filled the old man's gray eyes and for an instant, Belial feared Edred might be able to detect his real appearance.

"Greetings, Friar. What brings you to the stable?"

"I have a matter I'd like to discuss with you."

Belial hesitated. Normally, the man's presence would be of no consequence to him, but he wasn't in his usual fighting shape. Given his weakness, he wasn't sure if he could keep his human cover intact.

And if it failed before the friar . . .

That could be awkward.

While the little bastard wasn't exactly godly anymore, the friar still bore enough divine benediction to weaken him further. And even from his current distance, he was causing Belial's belly to burn and twist, his head to throb and ache.

The friar stepped forward.

Sweat trickled down Belial's face, making his cheek itch. "Brother Edred," he said quickly, stopping the friar before he came too close. "I beg you stand back before my illness taints you as well."

"Illness, you say?"

"Aye. Could be plague."

Eyes wide, the friar returned to the opening of the stall and darted his gaze over Belial's body. "A jest?"

Not really. He'd like to unleash it all over them, but he knew better than to say that out loud. "Of course. 'Tis just a cold. But still, I'd hate for you to catch it."

Instead of making the friar happy, those words only seemed to darken his mood. "Mayhap 'tis the evilness that resides in this hall that taints you more."

Now this was interesting, given that *he* was the evil in the hall. He couldn't wait to hear what idiocy the friar came up with. "What's that?"

Edred stroked the wooden cross that dangled about his neck and cast his gaze around as if seeking something or someone. "Can you not feel it? 'Tis like a serpent crawling in the bowels of the earth beneath our feet, waiting for just the right moment before it burrows its way up and bites our ankles when we least expect it. Since first I came here, I have felt Lucifer's presence."

How quaint of them to think Lucifer was the scariest thing in their little universe to fear. He would laugh in the man's face, except for the fact that the little ape wouldn't get the joke. "Lucifer's presence, you say?"

"Aye, and Lord Valteri is his servant."

Belial had to bite his tongue to stifle the laughter. What a pitiful fool. He couldn't resist toying with him. "Aye, indeed. Lord Valteri is surely damned, and can no doubt benefit from your grace. What do you intend to do?"

"First, I must make your lady sister understand the beast that she has married. Mayhap I'm not too late to save her precious soul."

If only he knew.

The bald little man was too late to save even his own. *That,* the Lucifer he feared would one day lay claim to, and no one would stop him or the demon he sent for it. The little backbiting hypocrite deserved it and more. Belial wished he would be there to see the little monk's face once he realized that all his investment of thumping his Bible and dutifully making his prayers was wasted because his heart was blacker than that of any of the pretend demons he lectured about.

That his tongue and deeds damned him more than all his "faithful" prayers could undo.

How could the little bastard not read his own holy book?

Whoever says he is in the light and hates his brother is still in darkness.

For there are many who are insubordinate, empty talkers and deceivers. They must be silenced, since they are upsetting whole families by teaching for shameful gain what they ought not to teach. One of the Cretans, a prophet of their own, said, "Cretans are always liars, evil beasts, lazy gluttons." This testimony is true. Therefore rebuke them sharply, that they may be sound in the faith, not devoting themselves to myths and the commands of people who turn away from the truth. To the pure, all things are pure, but to the defiled and unbelieving, nothing is pure; but both their minds and their consciences are defiled. They profess to know God, but they deny him by their works. They are detestable, disobedient, unfit for any good work.

Here the friar stood, breaking every one of the commandments he was supposed to protect. Every covenant he was charged with keeping. Proud, while spreading lies about his own innocent overlord and scheming against that innocent man and inciting others to attack him for no reason.

Trying to get him, a demon, to help him convince Valteri's own wife to turn against him so that they could kill that innocent man.

And for what?

The friar's fear?

His personal gain and vanity?

Others would look to the friar as a legend and authority. See him as something more than the pathetic little maggot he actually was.

Honestly, Belial admired Valteri, though he'd never admit to that out loud. In spite of how hard others had kicked him down and spit on him, he'd risen above them all to become a true noble man. He'd let nothing and no one hold him back.

While they laughed in his face and had deliberately sabotaged his armor and given him substandard equipment to use in battle, he'd outfought them all.

Proven himself, time and again, to be the better warrior.

Now this little weasel was here, like all the others, plotting against him to lay him low.

Just like me.

That dose of reality stung hard.

And still the friar prattled on. "Will you help me, my lord, to expose the vileness inside him? Then the fair lady would have no choice other than to believe us."

His stomach churning as his conscience continued to flog him, Belial sighed. "And how would you expose him?"

The friar pulled a vial out from a pouch he had attached to his rope belt.

Belial had to keep from laughing as he saw the holy water that would have absolutely no affect whatsoever on Valteri.

"A drop or two of this upon his skin and all will know of his true origins."

Oh, to have that amount of faith in his own stupidity.

"And if your water has no effect on him?"

Edred's brows shot up in shock and he crossed himself. "Could he be so powerful?"

"He could be . . . something."

"Then I shall pray on it!" The friar scampered off.

Belial slid to the floor as sweat rolled down his cheek.

"You're weak."

He cringed at the sound of Shadow's voice coming to him out of the darkness that bastard called home. The shadows he'd been named for. "What do you want?"

"The head of my father delivered to me on a platter. My mother's heart in my fist. Peace for all mankind . . . but I'd settle for you to just piss off."

Belial scoffed at his old enemy. "We all want something. I'd settle for *your* heart in my fist." He grimaced as another wave of pain tore through him.

Shadow stepped into the light so that Belial could see the arrogant wanker. Dressed in a burgundy surcoat and chain mail that seemed so out of place on such a heartless creature.

At least when it wasn't covered in blood and entrails.

Those eerie gray eyes were piercing with their intelligence. "Why don't you head home? Why put yourself through this torment?"

With a shaky breath, Belial cut a menacing glare toward him. "You know why."

"I do, but it won't work. See, you keep thinking that you can buy good-will from creatures who have none. They're morally bankrupt and selfish. Doesn't matter how much you give when they think they deserve. That's an ever-sliding scale where you lose. I learned that a long, long time ago." Shadow moved forward and squatted down beside him. "They'll never be grateful because they think whatever you do for them is their due, and they'll always demand more. Until they use you up completely, and you're nothing but a shattered, hollowed-out husk they leave behind. They *will* suck you dry, my brother. Sadly, they're the real vampires. Not those made-up nightmares that mankind fears."

Damn him for the truth he spoke. "I would slap you if I had the strength."

He laughed. "I know you would." Shadow reached out and brushed the hair back from his forehead. "You look like shite, brother. Want me to take you home so that you can rest?"

Belial knocked his hand away. "Why would you help me?"

"Because I was you, once. Angry. Pissed off and pissed on. Hating everyone and everything. Some days, I still am you. I know that irrational fury that drives you to lash out at the world and especially those who hate you for things you can't help. For the things you are and aren't. Those who really hate you for what you've bled to accomplish because they think it was given to you, while you know the scars you carry for having earned it. But hating them won't bring you any more solace than sitting here and wallowing in your misery. So get up off your arse, demon. No one gives a fuck if you live or die."

"Then why bother?"

"Pure spite. If nothing else, every breath you draw infuriates every enemy you have who begrudges you for the fact you're not dead. That alone has kept me going through many a winter's storm."

Belial laughed, hating the fact that he was beginning to like this bastard. "Truth?"

He pulled the sleeves back on his tunic to show the deep scars where he'd once sliced his own wrist. "Is now. I almost ended my life once, and then decided I wasn't about to give them the satisfaction of knowing they'd driven all hope from me. If nothing else, I'll steal that victory from them."

"I'm so tired of being kicked, Shadow."

He laughed bitterly. "We all are. Some days we're the boot and some days we're the arse. Personally, I prefer being the boot, but I have to say that many times I've been the arse that deserved the boot. And today, you have definitely deserved my foot up yours."

Taking Shadow's hand, he allowed him to pull him to his feet. "I still have to give Kadar a soul."

Shadow shook his head. "Think long and hard about what you're doing. You never know the enemies you make when you're trying to make a friend."

Those sage words sent a chill over him.

And true to his promise, Shadow took him back to Azmodea so that he could leave his human body and renew his strength.

Yet unlike him, Shadow's appearance didn't change. He was still as human here as he'd been in their realm. "I thought you were a demon, too."

"I am."

"Then why haven't you changed forms?"

Shadow released him and stepped away. His lips quirked in an evil smile. "I'm a lot more powerful than you know. And not at all what you think. Why do you think they call me the prince of Shadows?" And with a wink, he vanished.

Shadow left Belial and headed down the dark, smelly hallway toward the small cell where he knew his target would be waiting. The sounds of the damned and tortured echoed off the midnight walls around him that oozed a red, sticky mixture that'd always reminded him of blood.

How Thorn could stand living in this hell realm, he'd never understand. While his own fortress home was much nicer than this, it was still gloomy as shit.

And far too close to their parents for his comfort. What the hell was wrong with his cousin that he'd choose to live here?

But then that was a long and frightening list.

"Shadow?"

He drew up short as he heard his uncle's voice. And here he'd thought to surprise him.

Should have known better.

Jaden would have smelled him coming. Felt his powers. After all, they drew them from the same place.

He entered the room where Jaden rested. "Hello, Uncle. How are you?"

By the expression on his face, it was obvious that Jaden wasn't on vacation. In fact, he looked as if an enema might do him some good.

Or a long night of a heavy drinking binge.

Sitting in a chair with a book, Jaden scowled at him. "Perturbed by your presence. You should know better."

"And yet I never do better. Bad genes, they tell me. Comes from your side of the family."

"Indeed." Jaden brushed his hand over a nasty bruise on his cheek. "Come to see your mother?"

"Is she on fire? Beheaded?"

"No."

"Then why would I bother?"

Jaden laughed. "You're such a surly little bastard."

"And you're a huge motherfucker. What do you eat? Fertilizer?" It'd always bothered him that his family stood head and shoulders over him. Jaden had a full seven inches, which irritated him to the core of his soul. Especially given that both his parents were tall as shit.

Jaden turned a page. "Must have been your anger and misspent youth that stunted your growth."

"More like the venom I sucked from my mother's tit."

Closing his book, Jaden shook his head. With the same pair of mismatched eyes that he'd gifted to Valteri, he watched him. "You're in a bad mood, even for you. Something in particular wrenched your testicle and drove you here?"

"Manner of speaking. I wanted to ask you a peculiar question."

That got his attention. He quirked a brow in an expression almost identical to one of Valteri's. "This I can't wait to hear."

"Do you know how many children you have?"

"What game are you about?"

Shadow saw his eyes flickering in the darkness of the small room. A warning that in spite of his captivity, Jaden's god powers were kicking in. "Not a game. Just curious if you know."

"I have two sons. As you're well aware."

Shadow nodded. So Jaden had no clue about Valteri.

Interesting.

"And if you were to have any more?"

"Are you offering me your services?"

He gave the older god a dry glare. "Answer the question, you bastard. If you were to have a child out there. Would you know?"

"Of course."

Yet there was a light in his eyes that undermined the confidence in Jaden's tone. "Unless . . ."

Jaden scratched his chin thoughtfully. After a moment, he spoke again. "It's not really possible."

"What?"

"If a child were born without powers or if they were bound for some reason. Then I'd have no way of knowing."

"Why would anyone do that?"

Jaden shrugged. "Why would anyone want *my* child?"

He had a point. Especially given the fate of his last two. Shadow shuddered. Yeah, being Jaden's kid wasn't a blessing. Bad things always seemed to befall them.

"For argument's sake. If you did have another child out there. What would you do?"

"Depends. If I liked the kid, I'd protect it. Should the child prove to be a danger to the world . . ."

"You'd destroy it."

Jaden's mismatched gaze turned dark. "I'm not my sister. I would never risk or condemn the world for my child."

Funny, Jaden was speaking to the wrong audience. Shadow was on Apollymi's side in this matter. The concept of a mother who would sacrifice the world to save her son . . .

He'd kill to have a mother so loyal.

Or anyone who wouldn't stab him in the back. For that matter, he'd take a friend who wouldn't trip him if they were being chased.

Damn, his life really was pathetic.

"If you're expecting a hero cookie from me for your devotion to this sick world . . . don't. I'm all out."

Jaden snorted. "Interesting to hear *you* say that."

That dig hit home, as they both knew the sin he'd committed that stung him to this day. "Fuck you, Jaden."

"Don't flatter yourself. You're not my type. I prefer my women to be more demure."

"And I prefer mine to have a conscience and a heart." And with that, Shadow left before he started a war that neither of them could afford right now.

But it was tempting. Damn Jaden and his mouth.

One day, he hoped someone gave that god what he deserved. More than that, he hoped it was him who did it.

For now . . .

Shadow had much to consider.

Were Valteri's powers bound? That was an interesting question. Was the boy blessed enough to have been born human or had someone or something else intervened?

And if they had intervened, why?

The why was the disturbing thing. Because no one did that lightly.

Shadow flinched as he remembered when the Dark-Hunter Acheron's powers had been unbound. It'd almost ended the world. Of course, a lot of that had to do with Shadow's aunt Apollymi, Acheron's mother. The goddess had been furious and intent on ending the world for what mankind had done to her son.

Still . . .

It'd taken Acheron years to learn to use and control his god powers. Some of them, he still had trouble with.

How would Valteri respond if his were suddenly unleashed?

Well, there was one way to find out.

CHAPTER 16

Ariel stared out the window, her gaze following Valteri across the yard. She closed her eyes, savoring the image of his proud, handsome bearing, his hair loose and falling gently over his shoulders. He really was edible.

The mere sight of him made her body burn as she imagined him again standing on the edge of the cliff, reaching to comfort her.

Of him naked in her bed, holding her close . . .

She clenched her teeth and cursed her weak human body. Why had that old bitch damned her to this?

Even now, that demanding need for him tore through her and robbed her of all sense. Made her not care about the consequences of staying with him.

How did humans stand this insatiable hunger? No wonder they risked life and limb, even eternal damnation, for a taste of each other's flesh.

Opening her eyes, she shook her head and begged for strength.

As she stared up, she noted the intricate lines of the wooden rafters above her head. Strange to see their beauty there and how men had crafted them to protect themselves.

Never before had she needed shelter from storms or the cold. Such things were unknown in her world.

While they had buildings made of stone or gold, they weren't needed for protection. They were there simply for convenience.

And though she'd always been "happy," she'd never known the type of joy that filled her whenever she thought of Valteri.

If only she belonged here.

And Valteri . . .

Son of Jaden. How would her husband react if he ever learned the truth of his father? Where would he belong, then?

On earth?

Or with the other gods?

Guardians forbid that he ever reside with his father. Kadar and Azura would use him against his father, and there was no telling how they'd abuse him for their sick entertainment.

It was enough to make her lose her mind. And that wasn't even counting the small matter of the old crone who wanted her dead.

But only after she watched Valteri die.

Ariel clenched her teeth against the bitter wave of resounding pain that reminded her she couldn't escape the horrors of this world without a price that was too dear to pay.

The death of Valteri.

How could she break an unbreakable curse? Once such a thing was unleashed, it had to play out.

Why?

Those were the rules. She'd be yet another tragedy for poor Valteri.

Nay, she corrected, she'd be his last trial, and he was the first lesson for her.

A lesson on how to love. How to cry.

Damn them all for it.

What good could come of the newfound feelings inside her when they would only cause her heartbreak for all eternity?

One single tear slid down her cheek. Could she find some way to protect him, to keep him safe from all of them and their sick machinations?

A knock sounded on the door.

Ariel wiped the tear from her cheek and cleared her throat. "Enter," she called, expecting Wace, but instead Mildred walked in.

Anger and hatred stung her breast, but as quickly as it appeared, it died. She couldn't really hate the woman for what she'd done. Not after being in their world and sampling the raw intensity of their emotions, especially that of true human love. She well understood the woman's motivations.

Her need to strike out.

But she'd never understand how Mildred could punish innocent people in her hatred.

What was wrong with her?

The crone moved forward with a tray laden with covered dishes. "Lord Valteri bade me set a table for the two of you to sup here this even." She placed the tray on the small, round table that rested before the fire.

Ariel watched her slow, methodical movements as she prepared the table for their meal.

The woman appeared serene and completely at ease with her treachery.

Mystified by her cruelty, Ariel couldn't understand the crone's peace of mind.

"How could you?" she asked suddenly, needing an answer as to why the woman had betrayed them.

Mildred paused and looked up. "Bring you food, milady?"

"Damn an innocent man? Valteri had no part in anything. How could you curse him when he's done nothing to you?"

The lines around her old eyes crinkling even more, she gave a malevolent laugh and continued pulling rounded covers off the food.

"Innocent? I dare you to try and convince the good Saxon people around you of his innocence. He and his kind have robbed our lands and stolen our dignity. Killed indiscriminately. And for what? Power? Land? To *rule* us? How is that innocent, I ask you?"

Ariel shook her head in denial and took a step toward her, determined to make her see reason. "He's committed no more crimes than any other man in his position. Your own son was a warrior. Do you think he never killed anyone in battle?"

Snorting a denial, the crone lifted her empty tray before her like a shield and backed away. Her gaze heated by hatred, she raked a sneering glare over Ariel. "One more Norman dead and damned doesn't concern me. Women struggle for months to give them life and what do they do with it? They use it to kill and destroy. To ruin us all! Damn them, and all men, I say."

A shiver rushed through her body. How could anyone be so cruel? "Even your son?"

Her eyes changed. Deep, dark sadness and grief swam in the crone's aged gaze and a wave of pity and empathy filled Ariel's heart.

"Nay." Mildred's voice cracked. "My son was the finest of any born. Unlike the other callous fools of this world, only goodness beat in his breast. He would have been a great man had he been given the chance to live." The fire returned to her eyes. "And *you* took him!"

The accusation stung her. Ariel hadn't understood the woman when first they met, but now she knew only too well what love felt like.

"I took a warrior who fell in battle."

"Nay!" The platter shook in her furious grip. "He was healing. Just as I was about to cure him, you came in and stole my precious James from me! You murdered him!"

Aghast, Ariel stared at the woman. How could the crone believe something so ludicrous? "I had no part in his death. At all. He died of his battle wounds."

"Nay!" she cried, dropping the platter and covering her ears. "You lie!"

"You know me better than that." Ariel reached out a comforting hand, but Mildred recoiled from her touch. "I speak the truth. You've damned me for something I didn't do. But it doesn't matter what killed him. 'Twas his time to leave and naught could have saved—"

"Nay. I"—she pounded her breast with her fist to emphasize her words—"was his only hope. I could have saved him had you not stolen him away."

Ariel shook her head. "I swear to you that neither of us could have done aught to save or kill him. Your son's time had ended. But if it gives you any solace, he's happy now. He has meaning in what he's doing."

Her ancient lips quivered and tears filled her hollow eyes. "He was happy here with me. If he'd had a choice, he would have stayed."

Ariel sighed heavily. "His time here had ended. And he made his choice on where he wanted to be."

She shook her head in denial. Moving across the room, she eyed Ariel like a feral beast wanting to rip her heart from her breast and feast upon it. "I'll have your soul damned for what you did!"

Ariel prayed for the right words to make her see reason. Before it was too late.

"Don't forget that your own soul will be lost through this deal. You sold yours for a useless curse against two innocent beings. If you step back now, it won't be too late to reclaim your bargain. But if you don't . . . you will lose. Everything. Will your vengeance be worth an eternity of torment?"

The woman pursed her lips.

Ariel moved closer, hoping that she was finally getting through to her.

Instead, Mildred bolted.

The door slammed shut behind the old woman.

Damn it!

Why couldn't she make her see reason?

Where did this leave her? Pain coiled around her heart. Once a curse had been posed, nothing could remove it, except its fulfillment.

But could she prevent it? If she left Valteri and isolated herself away from any other mortal, maybe she could stop the curse.

All she had to do was never care about anyone. If no one died, it would be averted. Simple.

She could do that. Right?

"Ariel?"

She started at the voice behind her. When she turned around, her heart stilled. There before her stood her senior Arel Raziel.

Though he'd always been handsome, he'd never been more beautiful to her than he was at this instant, standing in a ray of sunlight, his alabaster wings glistening. His golden eyes glowed as he watched her, a sad smile hovering over his perfect lips. "Raziel?"

"Aye. I felt your turmoil. And had to come."

Ariel crossed the room and drew him into a tight hug. Joy and relief coursed through her body. "I'm glad you're here!"

Raziel squeezed her tight then pulled back, where he stared into her eyes with an earnest look that stole her happiness. "Thorn has apprised us of your situation. But there's naught we can do. Even now, I risk much by coming to you."

"Seriously?" She was aghast that no one would help her in this.

"Aye." Sighing, he tucked his wings down and shook his head, his face grim. "You know that we're not supposed to interfere with the course of human events."

"This isn't human! Curses are beyond their ken."

"The crone made her choice and so you were transformed."

She wanted to throttle him over his nonchalant tone. Over the fact that . . .

He was as unfeeling about her plight as Mildred had accused her of being with her son's life.

Dear God, now she understood the old woman's frustration and hatred.

It reeked. And as with Mildred, she wanted to strike out and make him feel the weight of her pain. To understand what it was he was putting her through and asking her to suffer.

But she knew that was impossible.

"What am I to do?"

Raziel looked away and shrugged. "You must fulfill the curse."

Anger and agony choked her. "Is there no other way?"

"None. And now that you've lain with a man . . . you knew the consequences. You made your choice."

And none of them would have any mercy on her.

A chill ran down her spine. Fear pounded in her heart and she dreaded the next question she must ask. "Am I damned for what I will do to him?"

"You know I cannot answer that. I don't make those judgments. But if I were you, I wouldn't count on any leniency."

The knot in her throat tightened as she thought of her husband. "And what of Valteri? What will happen to him?"

That vacant stare was really beginning to piss her off. "Do you truly need my answer?"

Nay. What she needed was his compassion.

A modicum of mercy.

He and the others already knew the circumstances of Valteri's life. What would happen if he fell into Kadar's hands.

Yet not even those events, in all their horror, would be enough to save his soul or his life. "Then there's no hope?"

He tsked at her. "There's always hope."

"But—"

The door opened and Raziel burst into a thousand shimmering fragments.

"Ariel?"

She blinked, her heart thumping, her eyelids as heavy as if she'd awakened from a sound sleep. As she stared into Valteri's confused eyes, Raziel's visit almost seemed like a vague dream.

Had Raziel really been here?

Or had she imagined it?

Valteri looked at her with a sharp frown. "You're pale. Are you all right?" Gently, he took her by the arm and led her toward the bed.

"Aye," she whispered. "'Twas a passing moment of dizziness." She hated being dishonest with him, but the last thing he'd want to hear was that she'd been visited by an Arel in his home.

Suspicion hovered in his eyes as if he doubted her excuse. "Then I'm glad I decided we should take our meal alone tonight."

Ariel smiled, but the insincerity of the gesture blistered her conscience. She couldn't stand not telling him the complete truth, but after the last time . . .

She didn't want to make him angry again.

"I'd like that very much. However . . ." She glanced at the food. "We need Wace to bring us our supper."

"Excuse me?"

"I fear this may be tainted."

His scowl deepened. "How so?"

"Just trust me, Valteri. I wouldn't advise eating it."

"Oh."

She knew that he assumed someone may have spit in it. Her fear was that Mildred might have added poison as a special seasoning.

If his lesser fear would clear their meal, she wouldn't argue.

Without a word, he opened the door and called for Wace to come clear their dishes and bring new ones.

But as the boy obeyed him, a newfound agony consumed her as she thought over what she must do. She'd have to leave him. If he was to have any hope whatsoever of living, she couldn't stay here.

Sooner or later, Mildred would kill him.

Therefore, she'd savor these last few hours and be grateful for them. Maybe that would be enough to ease the ache of a human lifetime spent alone.

Then again, what if she wasn't human? What if she was still immortal?

Horror filled her. The crone had put her in a human body. But what if she still didn't age?

What if she were damned to this form until she found someone else to love?

There was a nightmare she hadn't even contemplated.

Dear gods, no!

Because in her heart, she knew that she'd never love anyone else. Not like this.

No other man could ever equal Valteri. Biting her lip, she watched as he doffed his mail and set about washing the grime and sweat from his face and chest. A myriad of scars crossed his back, attesting to the brutality of his life. Yet he never spoke a word about it. Never complained or whined.

He endured. How many could do that with such grace and dignity?

Without hatred filling every bit of their hearts?

He was unique and kind. No one else would ever win her heart with the ease that he did.

Looking away, she longed for a way to take each and every deep, brutal mark away and to erase the memory he no doubt carried from the moments he'd received them.

Moments he'd never let steal his kindness or his humanity.

Even now, she wanted nothing more than the courage to bridge the distance between them and touch those rippling muscles of his back, to slide her fingers over the ridged planes of his stomach.

Every nerve in her body danced with desire, and a heated throb pounded in her blood, demanding she yield to its call.

How could she even think about leaving him?

Her unique gem?

He needed her, and though it pained her to admit it, she knew she needed his smile. His touch. It almost seemed worth the price of her soul to stay with him and make the most of the time they had together.

But that time would bring an even higher price.

His life.

She shivered. Nay, that price was far too dear.

Nothing was worth that. She could never be so selfish.

Rising from the bed, she retrieved a tunic for him from the chest by the window. He wiped his hands on a towel and his features softened as he took the tunic from her hands. "My thanks." His rich voice stung her with regrets.

Ariel offered him a smile as Wace finished replacing their meal, hoping he couldn't read the thoughts in her mind. Or see the sadness in her eyes.

He shrugged his tunic on and she clenched her fingers into a fist to keep them from reaching out for his comfort.

If she left him, he might yet survive this ill-begotten curse. But if she stayed and he died, then she would be every bit as much to blame as Belial and the crone.

She could never do that to someone who'd suffered as much as he had.

To someone she loved so dearly.

Desperate for another solution, Ariel touched his cheek, savoring the rough whiskers that scraped against her palm. He closed his eyes and she ached to make him believe the truth of their existence.

Too bad she didn't have a way to expose Belial's demonic form. If Valteri could see what he really looked like, then they'd know him for what he was.

Not only Valteri, but Belial's pawns would recoil in horror of his true, hideous appearance and either forsake or fight him.

But as a beautiful man, his beauty deceived them. It weakened their resolve, and they listened to him. That was the worst part about his kind. They used their looks to make others more vulnerable to their guile.

Once they were sucked in, it was almost impossible to get them out from the demon's glamour.

Many would kill themselves rather than admit they'd been duped. The weak-minded were such easy prey. And so hard to save.

She'd never been able to get them free.

Thorn and others of his ilk had some success, but not always.

Those who want to be deceived will always be deceived.

And when he had called unto him his twelve disciples, he gave them power against unclean spirits, to cast them out, and to heal all manner of sickness and all manner of disease. Heal the sick, cleanse the lepers, raise the dead, cast out devils. Freely ye have received, freely give. Provide neither gold, nor silver, nor brass in your purses, nor scrip for your journey, neither two coats, neither shoes, nor yet staves. For the workman is worthy of his meat. And into whatsoever city or town ye shall enter, inquire who in it is worthy, and there abide till ye go thence. And when ye come into a house, salute it. And if the house be worthy, let your peace come upon it, but if it be not worthy, let your peace return to you. And whosoever shall not receive you, nor hear your words, when ye depart out of that house or city, shake off the dust of your feet.

Not everyone could ever be saved.

That was what broke her heart.

But she could save Valteri. And she was going to.

No matter what it took.

Valteri held a chair out for her. "Come, milady."

Ariel sat down, reveling in the close proximity of his body while he adjusted her chair. His warm, rich scent invaded her head and she breathed it in deeply. She'd miss that the most. That, and the feel of his arms wrapped about her.

Swallowing, she reminded herself why it had to be.

Valteri filled their cups, his fingers brushing against hers as he placed her goblet near her sliced trencher.

"Thank you, milord," she whispered, but the tightness of her throat made the words painful to utter.

Valteri took his seat and for the first time, she allowed herself to look fully at his face. Instead of the usual tenderness in his gaze, she noted a tenseness, a guarded barrier that shielded his emotions from her.

She frowned in confusion and reached for her knife. "Does something vex you?"

He sliced the roasted venison Wace had brought for them, and placed a large portion on her trencher. Glancing up at her, he shook his head. "Nay, why should it?"

Her frown deepened at the faint sarcasm underlying his words. For a moment she wondered if she imagined it, but as he set about filling her trencher with lamprey and apples, she saw the tightness of his grip, the tautness of his jaw.

"Have I done something to offend you?"

Cocking an eyebrow, he sat back in his chair and studied her with an unreadable stare that set her hands trembling. "Why would you think that?"

The look you're giving me? She barely bit back that sarcasm as she held no doubt it wouldn't endear him to her at all.

Instead, she shook her head and looked back at her food. Something was amiss, but Valteri made it obvious that he had no wish to discuss it.

Irritated, Ariel drew a trembling breath and concentrated on her supper. They ate their meal in awkward silence.

Valteri repeatedly downed his goblet of wine only to refill his cup. She frowned as he again filled the goblet to the brim and ignored his food.

Though redness laced his eyes, he didn't act drunk, but heaven knew he had consumed more than enough wine to intoxicate three or four normal men.

Trying her best not to pay his strange mood any heed, she ate slowly but didn't really taste her food. Indeed, everything she tried tasted like unseasoned porridge.

At last he looked up at her with a grave frown that made her wish he would again ignore her presence. "Tell me, Ariel, why did you marry me?"

What an odd question.

She swallowed her bite of food and considered why he'd asked her such a thing.

Taking a deep breath, she considered how best to answer. Was he afraid that she had regrets?

Did he?

The only regret resting in her heart came from their differences.

Didn't it?

And without hesitation the answer entered her mind. "I wanted to."

He swallowed his food and took another drink of wine. "Why? Why would you bind yourself to a hated stranger, a man not of your kind? One who conquered your people?"

His words startled her. Lowering her knife, she leveled her gaze with his. "You are a noble man, Valteri. You follow your conscience. That makes you my kind."

He snorted a denial. "What conscience is that? The same one that took your virtue?"

Then, he leaned forward against the table, his gaze piercing her with its probing intensity. "Come to think of it, I didn't take your virtue that first night, did I?"

Her heart stilled at his implication. A shiver of foreboding darted up her spine and she tightened her grip on her knife. "What do you mean?"

"I've given much thought to you this day. Things that had escaped my notice found their way to my mind and at last I know what to call you."

Ariel tensed at the seriousness of his voice, the emptiness of his eyes. "And what is that, milord?"

"Witch."

CHAPTER 17

Shock poured through Ariel at his unexpected declaration. "We've already explored this." She carefully directed her attention back to her roasted venison and away from Valteri's searing glare.

"Aye, and I wish to know why you lied to me."

Setting her knife aside, Ariel swallowed in fear and uncertainty. What could she say?

"As you've said repeatedly yourself, sir, I'm not a witch."

He didn't respond to that.

Her heart thumped against her breastbone and she averted her gaze from his probing eyes, eyes that told her exactly what her husband sought out of fate. Valteri longed for death too much and she had the most wretched fear in her stomach that he would try and fight against the curse, daring it to take him. And that was one battle her fierce warrior could never win.

"Aren't you?"

"I know not what you mean."

Uncomfortable with the turn in their conversation and terrified of any more difficult questions, Ariel moved to leave the table, but he captured her arm. His grip tight about her wrist, Valteri pulled her back into her chair.

"Please, answer me, Ariel. Have you bewitched me?"

The heat and anguish in his eyes, in his touch scorched her. She ached for his pain, wanting the words or spell to undo the curse and to keep him safe for all eternity.

If only there were some way . . .

"You're drunk, Valteri."

"You're avoiding the question."

She ground her teeth. "I didn't lie, milord. Nor did I bespell you. I've tried repeatedly to tell you the truth. You're the one who denies it."

Ariel clenched her fists, anguish flowing through her. Why had she ever told him what she really was? Why hadn't she seen this coming? She should never have pressed the issue.

Rather, she should have just told him she was insane and left it at that.

A soft draft brushed against her, raising chills upon her arms. She tried to invent some tale to explain her earlier words, but nothing came.

Too used to honesty, she had little experience with deceit. That expertise belonged to Belial and his ilk.

Suddenly an idea came to her. Aye, she'd use Valteri's own logic against him. "What of my brother then, milord? If I'm a witch, what would that make him?"

The confidence in his gaze faltered, then his eyes sparked fire. "He *is* a demon, isn't he?"

Oh, *that* he would believe.

Damn her luck! And damn him for being able to see the truth of Belial while he was drunk.

"And what of Thorn and Shadow?"

"Demons, too, I'd wager."

"So now you believe in them?"

"Why not? What the hell? Demons. Angels. Let's believe in the whole giddy crew, shall we?"

"You need to go to bed, Valteri."

He scoffed as he released her. "What I need, sleep won't repair." A tic started in his jaw. "Tell me the truth, Ariel. What are they? Men, demons. Or just another asshole sent to torment me?"

Ariel chewed her lip, trying to decide what to say. What should she tell him?

Tell him the truth. She flinched at the voice that sounded so much like Raziel's, she wasn't sure he wasn't in the room with them.

Dare she trust that voice?

At this point, she wasn't sure which side was even lying or using her anymore.

"If I were to say yea? What then would be your reaction?"

The fire faded from his eyes. Pushing his chair back from the table, he slowly stood. "I want the truth."

"Would you accept it?"

A knot tightened her throat as she watched him pace the area between their table and bed.

"I'm not human, am I?"

That question caught her completely off guard. "Pardon?"

He paused beside the fire to pin her with a look so tormented and raw that it left her breathless from the pain. "The scars on my body aren't from battle. I've never once been harmed from another's sword. Whenever I fight . . . something unholy possesses me. Don't think that I'm unaware of it."

A peculiar, faraway look entered his eyes. "I never wanted to believe the bastard monks who told me that I was hellborn or hellbound, but with every battle I've had to wonder how it is that I'm never scathed. Others fall all around me, and while I seek to die, I'm never harmed."

Agony filled his gaze. "It never made sense to me. How the monks could scar me so easily with their whips. But no mortal weapon made of steel could ever pierce my flesh."

Her heart wrenched at the bitter agony in his whispered tone. "Valteri, it's not what you think."

"Isn't it? How else do you explain all this?"

"You're not a demon."

"Then what am I?"

She went to him and took his hand into hers. "You're not a demon. You're not the same as Belial."

He scowled at her.

"Those whips can harm you because they're not weapons, per se. You were born of a god . . . and while you can be harmed by things that aren't considered a weapon, you can't be killed by any of them. Only a weapon forged by a god, made in the halls of gods, can end your life."

He laughed at her explanation. "Do you think me insane to believe that?"

"How else do you explain it? Or the fact that you heal faster than most? It's why you weren't killed when your horse stomped you . . . how he was able to injure you. As for Belial, he's a demon and he's here to claim both our souls. If you were demon-born, he wouldn't have to do that. Your soul would already belong to his master."

For once, Valteri listened to her. "And why are you here?"

"When someone dies, there are a lot of . . . things that want their soul, for a lot of reasons. There are many who do what I do—escort the souls of warriors. We try to ensure that every soul is protected as it travels from this realm to the next. Unfortunately, we're not always successful. Whenever a soul is lost in transit, it's a blow to the universe, for the light of that soul goes out for all eternity. Our job is to protect those lights as best we can."

She gestured at the door. "When I came for the soul of a young man who'd died in battle, his mother couldn't accept his fate. She traded her own soul for the powers to rip me from my world into this one and trap me here to punish me for doing what I'd been ordered to do."

He was taking the news much better this time than he'd done before. Of course, it probably helped that he was drunk and would probably forget it all.

"The crone you fear?"

She nodded. "Belial was here when she first cursed me. This is a sick game for him."

Ariel swallowed. "While Lucifer is to be feared, there are far worse things in the universe than him. Belial serves a dark lord called Kadar, or Noir. He's an ancient god who wants to reign over the world as he did long ago."

Valteri listened quietly as she explained things he wanted to deny.

Yet how could he?

As he'd said, he'd spent his whole adulthood baffled by the fact that he'd rushed headlong into battle and never been harmed. Even when he should have been. Somehow, he always knew when to counter and strike.

His gifts were unholy.

Even when swords had grazed him, they'd left no mark.

It was why he'd denounced the god that the monks had told him had cursed him from birth. Because he didn't feel evil. The last thing he'd wanted to be was damned for something he couldn't help.

But her words gave him hope for the first time in his life that there might be another explanation for his "gifts."

For his birth defect.

"Why does this Kadar want you?"

"Because of a war that was fought long ago. The Primus Bellum. The gods of light and dark tore this world apart in their feud. Belial and Shadow are veterans from that war. As were my father and yours."

He gasped at her words.

"It's true. I wasn't born then, but they were. Others of my kind, Arelim, fought for the Kalosum, the light army. Anytime they can claim one of us and turn us to the dark to become an Irin, they call it a victory. In my case, because my father's one of the Naṣāru—a leader of the Arelim—they deem it an even greater victory if they can claim me."

Ironically, that explained much.

She placed a fragile hand on his forearm. "*You*, Valteri, aren't the son of a demon. You're the son of someone a lot more powerful. Your father fought against Kadar and his army. He was part of the Kalosum. One of their key members. Your eyes aren't a deformity. They mark you as Jaden's son. He is extremely powerful, and if Kadar ever laid hands to you . . . there's no telling what he might do."

Scowling, he stared down into her blue eyes, praying that she was insane, but only clarity stared up at him.

"You and Thorn should be bitter enemies. His father and yours are mortal opponents. But he turned his back on Kadar and has been on our side for centuries now. There's nothing evil about you. Only how you've been treated."

She walked herself into his arms and held him close. "And there's the bitterest irony of all. Thorn was raised as a beloved son while his destiny was to serve his father and tear this world apart. You, who were born to be a sword for honor and good, were only shown the worst of those you protect. For that, I am eternally sorry."

He held her close as bitter memories surged through him. What hurt most was that in all his life, there was not one single good memory there.

Not one.

His life had been nothing save loneliness and anguish. Every day laden with the deepest desire that it would be his last.

Now . . .

He didn't know what to think. About any of this.

"How do I know you're not lying to me?"

She laughed in his arms. "Some things you just have to take on faith."

He scoffed at that word that he despised more than any other. "You ask a man for faith when all he's known is betrayal. It's impossible."

"The fact that I'm with you in this realm should be impossible. Yet here we are."

Aye.

Closing his eyes, he kept looking for a hole in her story. Something he could use to argue against her reason. But sadly, it all made too much sense.

"I won't let Belial harm you, Ariel."

She leaned back to look up at him. "I'm not the one you should fear for. If you believe nothing else from me, Valteri, believe this. Should you fall into their hands, all you have suffered in the past will seem like a dream to what is to come. They will do things to you that are beyond comprehension. And not even you will be able to fight them. But more than that, they will use your powers and strength to harm this world, and that, neither of us can allow."

"I have no powers."

She gently unlaced his tunic to show an old scar on his chest where he'd been branded. One she'd touched so many times, and now that she had her memories restored, she knew exactly what it was.

Why and how it'd been given to him.

The only question was who had branded him and when.

"Nay, love. Your powers were bound by this seal. But one day . . . something will unlock them. God help us all when that day comes."

CHAPTER 18

Valteri shook his head in denial. "That's not a seal."

Ariel let out a bitter laugh. "Aye, love. It is."

He staggered back as he stared down at it.

"Do you remember when it was given to you?"

He shook his head as he tried to remember. "Nay. It's always been there." His head spun at what she was telling him. "Does this mean that my twin would have shared my powers?"

"Aye."

"Then how did he die?"

"I know not. 'Tis possible the binding spell was done before you were born or upon your arrival in this world and that could have killed him."

Valteri sat down as he tried to come to terms with the story she told.

If he dared to believe it.

The things she spoke of . . .

They were unnatural.

Yet they made sense.

Running his hand through his hair, he grappled with her disclosure.

"Are you all right?"

"I need air."

Ariel watched as Valteri left the room. She started to go after him, but in spite of all the drink he'd imbibed, he seemed rather stable on his feet.

He'll be fine.

Besides, she had preparations she needed to finish.

You have to do this.

More and more, she felt as if time was running out for them.

Hours later, Ariel crept silently through the hall, making sure everyone was asleep. She pressed her lips together, afraid that each trembling breath rattling in her chest might awaken a nearby sleeper.

This was her only chance to save Valteri. She must leave him behind, no matter how much her heart ached for him. No matter how much she yearned to remain by his side.

If she stayed, he'd die.

A man spoke in his sleep.

Ariel froze, her heart hammering in her ears. He turned on his side and began a steady snore. Releasing a quiet sigh of relief, she tiptoed toward the door.

How she wished Valteri had sought their chambers to sleep after he'd left to think about what she'd told him. But after hours of waiting, she'd given up hope of his return.

All Ariel could do now was pray he wasn't sleeping in the stable.

She pushed open the hall's door, flinching as a tiny squeak echoed, a squeak that sounded louder than thunder to her anxious ears. A nearby woman spoke in her sleep, but no one awoke enough to question her. Taking a deep breath for courage, she wedged herself out the door, then closed it tight.

Frigid winds whipped against her cheeks, numbing them before she'd taken no more than a few steps. An early, light snow fell against her face and hair. Ariel drew her fur-lined cloak tighter, trying to banish the cold from her body.

With any luck, the snow would cover her tracks and Valteri would never find her.

Pain swelled inside her breast, but she forced herself not to think on it. She must do this.

For both their sakes.

She entered the stable, then paused.

Damn her luck! Valteri lay just inside the first stall. In spite of her sense that told her to grab a horse and leave, she moved closer to him.

Through a crack in the planking, a rushlight shone, illuminating his handsome face.

Now that she knew who he was, she saw just how much he favored his father. They were almost identical. Same angle of brow. Same perfectly sculpted features.

The only difference was that Jaden had dark hair, and an aura of intolerance even thicker than Valteri's.

Other than that, they could pass for twins.

But what tugged at her heart was how very vulnerable, so very lovable he looked while he slept.

Her body burned for him, for one last touch of his flesh against hers, but it could never be.

Closing her eyes, she savored the memory of his kiss.

If only she could stay with him, be his wife like a normal mortal woman, she'd gladly pay the price of her own soul.

But how long until the curse worked its treachery and she damned him forever?

A day? A week?

Every moment she spent near him, she jeopardized *his* soul.

His eternity.

And the fate of the entire world.

I could never be so selfish.

Noir would torture him unmercifully in Azmodea. Use him to breach the barrier into this world.

I have to stop them.

Holding that thought inside her heart, she forced her feet away from him and moved to take a horse. A gentle mare called to her as she neared the last stall.

"You'll not harm me, will you?" she whispered.

The brown mare stared at her with gentle eyes.

Ariel smiled before reaching for a bridle. "You'll have to help me," she whispered in the lowest of tones, holding the bit to the animal's teeth like she'd seen Wace and the groom do. "I'm not sure how this needs be done."

The mare took it in her mouth.

Ariel stroked the mare's nose, grateful she understood her, and worked the leather straps into their correct positions around the mare's head.

With a wishful sigh, she glanced to the saddles, but decided against it. She doubted she could lift one, and even if she did, she had no idea of how to fasten it.

No need to risk an injury to herself or the horse, or waking Valteri with that.

Instead, she took a blanket from the wooden post, draped it over the mare's spine, and led the animal out into the cold, lonely night.

Though she ached to look back at Valteri, she knew better than to try. A single glance in his direction could very well destroy her will to leave him.

Mounting the horse, she kicked her into a gallop.

Ariel expected the sentries to stop her at the gate, but instead they waved her through.

They were more interested in keeping people out than keeping them in.

Grateful for that, she rode for leagues before she slowed the mare's pace. The horse snorted, and pranced as if suddenly skittish from some foreign scent. Soothing her with her touch, Ariel looked about to see what had her horse so upset.

"Leaving so soon?"

Demon stench filled her head and she struggled not to gag. "Go away!"

Belial laughed, then materialized in front of her. "Why would I listen to you?"

"Because you're too weak to be out here."

"Am I?"

That sent a shiver over her as she realized that he was stronger now.

How?

Belial started near the horse, but because his powers were renewed, the animal backed up, leery of what it smelled from him.

He smiled wickedly at her. "So what did you tell Valteri?"

"That I was mad." While she didn't believe in lying, she knew better than to tell this bastard the truth.

"Did he believe you?"

She shrugged with a nonchalance she didn't feel, especially since she was lying. "Of course he did."

"Aye, but he's not like the others. Is he? He's not so easy to deceive."

By Thorn's hairy toes, he knew. She could sense it with everything she had.

But on the off chance he didn't, she decided to try and brazen it out. "You're right. He denies his god. Therefore, he cannot believe in what we are. To do so would force him to believe in a god he cannot accept. Because if he accepted that his god lives then it would mean that his god had forsaken him and left Valteri to suffer. You of all things know he will never accept or believe that."

Belial laughed. "Aye, and I need both your souls for Noir. So I cannot let you leave! You're my key to his deliverance."

No sooner had the words left his lips, than the mare bolted.

Ariel struggled with her terrified mount, holding tightly to the reins. Keeping her head low, she prayed.

Limbs and shrubs tore at her hair, her body, beating her until she throbbed with pain.

Forest animals scattered out of their way before they were trampled. They traveled on through the darkness and Ariel tried to see what obstacles lay before them, but the mare continued her furious run at a pace that prevented her from seeing anything.

She tightened her grip.

Out of nowhere, a large shadow appeared, its demon's teeth snarling.

The mare shrieked then reared.

Ariel fell from the mare's back and landed in the snow. A fierce pain filled her head before everything went black.

Rough hands shook Valteri awake. Cursing and knowing his squire would never be so stupid, he reached for the culprit's throat, angered that anyone would awaken him in such a manner.

"Release me!" Belial snarled.

Out of sheer unexpected shock over the sound of the demonic thunder,

Valteri let go. Had he doubted Ariel's words before, that removed the last of it.

Nothing human could have made that infernal sound.

Now he knew exactly what he was dealing with. "Why are you here?"

"Ariel's gone."

His anger evaporated under a fierce wave of suspicion, as Valteri immediately suspected Belial of treachery. "What do you mean she's gone?"

Belial's face was a paragon of innocence, but he knew better. Only something foul would cause Ariel to leave the safety of their keep.

The demon had some part in this, he had no doubt, and if she were hurt because of Belial, then the demon would know what true hell was.

"I went to check on my sister," Belial said innocently, lighting a small lantern close to Valteri's side.

Valteri shielded his eyes against the sudden glare.

Belial hung it from a peg and handed Valteri his mail hauberk. "Since her newest outbreak of madness, I've been worried over her. I wanted to see if she still believed herself some otherworld creature, and when I entered her room, she was gone."

Bullshit.

Worry and anger tore through Valteri as he shrugged his hauberk on. Where could she have gone, and why?

Worse, had this bastard done something with her to get back at him?

What was it that Ariel had told him last night? He was supposed to kill himself?

Was that Belial's plan? Harm her? And in doing so think that he was so weak he'd harm himself in response?

Nay. He was prone to homicide, not suicide.

Scrambling to his feet, Valteri glanced about the stable. Though the horses were a bit unsettled, he had little trouble locating the one that was missing.

"Dammit!" he snarled. Had Ariel really left the safety of the hall on her own?

Why would she do something so stupid?

Because you're too repugnant for her to bother with. Valteri flinched at the involuntary doubts that were never far from his mind.

But he quickly squelched his own stupidity. She didn't see that part of him. It was why he loved her.

Love . . .

That single word made him flinch. Damn his heart for the weakness. For the betrayal.

If he could, he'd rip it out of his chest and stab it himself.

How dare it make him care for someone who could only bring him pain. He knew that as surely as he breathed air.

People were treacherous and disloyal. They plotted and they schemed. He knew that better than anyone.

Yet in spite of it all, he loved her, and for that he would be damned.

I'm the greatest fool ever born.

But more than that, he was Ariel's fool.

"We must find her!" Belial insisted.

Valteri curled his lip at the demon, wanting to put him through the wall of the stable. He didn't dare pursue her with that bastard on his heels. He needed to get rid of him first.

"Why should we seek her if, as you say, she left of her own accord?"

Belial's jaw went slack. "But what if her mind has fled her again? Even now she could be lying in that storm, close to death."

Now it was his turn to gape. "Storm, what storm?"

Belial threw open the stable door.

Oh dear God! Valteri swallowed at the swirling snowflakes that cascaded so thickly around that the air outside appeared as a solid white wall. Howling winds whipped the large snowflakes into a brutal dance until he could scarce see three inches before him.

What in the name of God and all his saints had she been thinking?

Ariel would never be able to survive such a storm. She wasn't used to this world or its harshness. He had to find her.

Before they did.

Or before she died.

CHAPTER 19

While Valteri saddled his horse, Belial gathered food and supplies. "I'll wake the others."

"I'll wait for you," he lied to the oaf. "Get Wace and your brothers. Have them meet me here while I saddle their horses."

With a nod of his head, Belial left him.

Valteri waited until Belial had vanished into the storm and was gone for a few minutes.

Once he was certain Belial couldn't see him through the bitter snowstorm, he mounted his destrier, his saddle tilting slightly as he adjusted himself and his sword.

"I know, boy." He stroked his horse's mane, feeling guilty that he asked this of his old friend. "We've been through worse, you and I, and I need you to do this for me. I promise, I wouldn't take you out there if it wasn't important."

His horse snorted and pawed as if he was still resentful. Not that he blamed him.

Drawing his cowl over his head, he looked back at the keep to ensure that there was no sign of Belial or anyone else.

"You better not have caused this, demon." Because if he'd put her in harm's way, and if she were harmed over it, there'd be true hell to pay.

Valteri would rip his insidious form to pieces. His lady had best be hale and hearty when he found her.

Kicking his horse into a run, he sped across the bailey and out the gate.

Damn, it was a cold, miserable night. Valteri double-cursed the weather that forced him to slow his horse's gait lest it harm Ganille. Ganille's hooves slid on the frozen soil until he feared both of them would fall, and the last thing he wanted was to risk an injury to the only real friend he'd ever known.

"It's all right," he assured his horse. "Take your time. Be careful."

Worse than the ice, swirling flakes continued to obscure his vision.

His cheeks burning from the cold, Valteri ground his teeth in aggravation.

How far could Ariel have gone in this?

When had she started out?

Because it was so thick, the snow would have obscured her tracks in a matter of minutes.

"How can I ever find you?"

You do have powers. . . .

Ariel's voice from earlier that night whispered to him. Instinctively, he placed his hand to the scar where he'd been branded.

While he couldn't remember that one, he remembered the brand that was hidden beneath his hair. Even now, he could see the old monk's twisted, hate-filled countenance as he'd snarled the Latin words at him that he hadn't understood.

"Let Saint Benedict bind this demon's powers! Keep them inside him so that he cannot harm another!" Then more words had followed, only they hadn't sounded like Latin to him. They'd seemed to be from another language.

But the pain of the brand on his skull had been such that Valteri couldn't really comprehend any of it.

Only the sound of laughter ringing in his ears had overridden his pain and the smell of his burning flesh.

He couldn't even remember now what he'd done to cause them to attack him so. Why they'd felt the need to drag him to the altar and assault him.

Of course, back then, those attacks had been so commonplace that they ran together in his memory. One huge amalgamate nightmare.

Had it been a similar moment when his so-called powers had been bound?

He looked up at the sky and blinked as tears froze against his eyelashes. Lost, and terrified of losing the only good thing he'd ever had, he did what he'd never done before.

Valteri prayed. "If that's true . . . please, God, give me what I need to find her. Please, don't let her die because of this." He choked on his fear. "Because of me. Let me have what was unfairly taken."

Ganille shifted.

And nothing changed.

The storm continued to howl and he had no idea which way to go. For that matter, he wasn't even sure which way he'd come.

They were both going to die of exposure out here.

Few humans possessed enough survival skills to live through a night like this.

He doubted if Ariel would even think to find shelter before the cold overtook her.

His heart shattered as he saw images in his mind. Ariel laughing with the children. Of her reaching for him with desire glowing deep in her eyes.

The sweetest taste of her lips on his. Her hands roaming freely over his naked body.

No other woman had ever wanted him.

No one. Period. Had ever touched him with a kind hand.

Not even his own mother.

And the truth was, Valteri couldn't imagine a life without Ariel anymore. Of returning to the empty isolation he'd known since his birth.

Losing her would be like losing a limb.

Nay, it would be like losing the heart that beat inside his chest.

"Please, help me," he whispered. That, too, was something he'd never done as a man.

He'd stopped asking for help as a boy when his pleas had fallen on the deaf ears of his tormentors who'd had no compassion or mercy for him.

No one cared.

The world was cruel and it was merciless.

You are nothing to anyone.

Bastard born. Your own parents wouldn't claim you.

Only Ariel had ever cared. Only she had ever seen anything more than a worthless piece of shit.

I can't fail her.

Suddenly, a foreign warmth spread through his body. One the likes of which he'd never felt before. It started in the center of his gut and radiated outward, toward his fingers and toes.

Throwing his head back and closing his eyes, he let out his war cry. His breath billowed around his head in a thick cloud.

Breathless, he felt so peculiar. And when he straightened in the saddle and opened his eyes again, he could see.

Not like before. This was different.

He still saw the blizzard, yet he could see through it, too. Just as clearly as if it were a sunny day.

No longer did he feel the cold. This was how he felt in battle. That serene calm where he was aware of everything and nothing. Where he heard the universe and yet he was disconnected from his own body.

Valteri would never forget the first time he'd felt this way. Not long after his knighting, his lord had thrown him into war.

"Die with dignity, you bastard! You better not run!"

Why should he? There was no one who would have welcomed him home. So Valteri had gripped the leather straps of his shield and the hilt of his sword. Not even on a horse, as his lord hadn't deemed him worthy of one.

He'd run toward the enemy, hoping to find peace at the end of a lance someone would run through him.

Instead, he'd seen everything as it'd come for him while he fought. Every arrow. Every sword.

Deftly and without thought, his body had moved of its own accord.

He'd been a puppet to some higher force. His mind had turned completely off and it was as if something else had controlled him.

When he became aware again, the battle was over.

He'd stood among the slain, covered in blood, but completely unharmed.

Only then had he felt the weight of his armor, or heard the moans of the dying. Felt his own thirst or smelled the putrid stenches of war.

They had simultaneously hailed him a monster and a hero. And while no one wanted him as friend, they definitely didn't want him as a foe.

That inhuman power and sensory disconnect was what he felt now.

He urged Ganille forward, guiding his skittish horse through the snow. Somehow he knew where the road was. He saw it so clearly.

Instinctively, he knew where to go, and in no time, he found a small brown palfrey whose reins were ensnared on the side of the road in a bramble bush. She shrieked and tugged at the lines.

Cold winds bit into his flesh and his joints were stiff from riding as he dismounted.

"Easy now," he breathed, approaching the panicked horse with care.

Moving slowly so as not to further alarm the mare, he gently patted her side until she calmed. Then, he took her bridle and untangled her reins. Scratches marred her flesh as he rubbed his gloved hand over her flanks, noting the blood seeping there and over her bare back.

What the hell had happened?

As he eased the mare back, he saw a damp red saddle blanket on the ground that was embroidered with his dragon.

This was definitely from his stable. He hadn't mistaken the horse.

"Ariel!" he called, hoping she was somewhere nearby.

Only the howling winds answered his call. No doubt, his voice had been lost to them.

Tying the mare's reins to his destrier, Valteri searched the area on foot, calling for his wife, his heart lodged painfully in his hoarse, sore throat.

Where could she be? Had the palfrey thrown and trampled her like it'd done the blanket?

All too well, he remembered what it felt like to be stomped by his own horse.

Could Ariel survive such an attack? Unlike him, she was tiny and frail. Unused to being brutalized.

Valteri closed his eyes, hoping she was all right. He couldn't bear the thought of her as otherwise. Then, he felt a strange pull. Something inside knew where to go.

Listening to it, he headed straight toward a large tree.

Vaguely, he saw a small lump lying in front of it.

He rushed forward and knelt down to find her there.

"Ariel?" he gasped, pulling her over, and into his arms.

Her face was a ghostly white and a large bruise swelled against her right cheek.

Terror consumed him. She lay too quiet. Her body was too cold.

"My lady?" His voice trembled with the weight of his fear and panic as he gingerly pulled the strands of pale hair free from her cheek. "Please, Ariel, speak to me!"

Her eyes fluttered open and the dazed look gradually sharpened. "Valteri?"

Relief washed over him. His heart hammering in gratitude, he lifted her in his arms and cradled her close to his chest so that he could press his cheek to hers. "Don't speak. I must find us shelter."

Nodding, she draped a finely shaped arm over his shoulders and snuggled her head against his neck. In spite of the freezing temperature, desire and tenderness crashed through him, almost crippling him with their sharp waves.

Nay, he could never let her leave him, not as long as breath filled his lungs.

Valteri pulled her cloak tighter around her and stumbled back to their horses, but with every step he took, he heard her wince from pain. "It'll be all right, Ariel. Just a little further."

He must find somewhere close by to check her injuries before she succumbed to them, or worse, before their journey maimed her.

As carefully as he could, he mounted his horse with her and rode back the way he'd come. Another blast of wind and snow struck them, causing his horse to rear. Ganille snorted, pawing at the air.

"Whoa, boy!" he ordered, but the horse barely settled. More wind howled and Ganille panicked, running through the forest.

Valteri struggled for control of his horse and to maintain his tenuous hold on Ariel. For several minutes, he could do nothing more than remain in his saddle as they crashed through the snow and high foliage.

Suddenly, the snow thinned, and there before them stood a small, dark hut with a thatched roof. Ganille shook his head and quieted, pawing softly at the snow.

Valteri blinked at the little cottage. Unsure if he should believe his sight or luck, he turned Ganille toward it and reined to a stop in front of the door.

Throwing his leg over the saddle's pommel, he held Ariel tightly and slid to the ground, trying to jar her as little as possible.

He took a great deal of care as he approached the hut, waiting for an angry Saxon to rush out and attack him. That was what they normally did whenever they saw a knight approaching.

But no light or sound appeared.

Was it deserted?

"Hello?" Supporting Ariel against his chest with one arm, he knocked on the door. It swung open, its leather hinges creaking as a gust of wind caught it and sent it slamming into the interior wall.

Valteri entered, then paused to scan inside. Definitely empty. Whoever had owned the small cottage had left it years before. Cobwebs hung like palls over a few meager pieces of rough wooden furniture, and a musty, sour stench clung to the damp air.

Curling his lip, he made his way to the small cot that sat against the far wall.

With the toe of his boot, he tested the leather straps that crisscrossed the ancient frame. It appeared sound enough, but he couldn't quite banish his misgivings.

Still not fully convinced it would hold even her light weight, he carefully lowered Ariel to the cot, ready to catch her if it gave way.

When it didn't collapse beneath her, he sighed in relief and touched her cheek.

She looked up at him, her gaze awash with relief, pain, and exhaustion.

"Rest here while I make you a fire and tend the horses."

Nodding, she closed her eyes and placed her bare hand over his glove. "Thank you for coming for me."

His chest tightened. Did she think he could ever leave her in such danger? "Did you doubt me?"

"Nay," she whispered. "But a part of me hoped you wouldn't find me. I don't want to be your death, Valteri."

Misery and happiness both raked his heart. *I'm a sick bastard.*

Wanting to kiss and strangle her, he doffed his heavy cloak and placed it over her.

She remained still, her damp, pale hair fanning out around her. He longed to run his hand through the silken mass, but her words hung in his heart like an anchor stone.

Clenching his teeth, he turned away.

As quickly as he could, Valteri returned to the horses and unsaddled Ganille. Though the barn had seen better days, it still remained intact enough to offer shelter for the horses. He draped his saddlebags over his shoulder and retrieved an old, rusty ax from the barn's wall.

It took a while to find wood dry enough to use, and to locate the small piece of flint still resting in the aged ashes of the last fire the dilapidated hut had seen. As he set about making a fire in the center of the room, he sensed Ariel's gaze upon him.

Glancing over his shoulder, he saw her blue eyes open and focused on his movements.

Unable to discern the emotions flickering in her gaze, he continued striking the flint until he had a decent fire started. Winds howled outside, pounding the hut with a force that made him wonder how it continued to stand the abuse without collapsing. But then, he of all men should know how hearty even the frailest of things could be.

Rising from his task, he turned to face her. "How do you feel?"

"Cold," she said, her teeth chattering.

Valteri crossed the room to stand above her. In spite of the sympathy inside him, his anger mounted over her foolishness. "As well you should. What did you mean leaving on a night such as this?"

"To keep you safe."

How could he argue that?

Sighing in frustration, Valteri picked her up and carried her closer to the fire. Though she said nothing, he noted the rigidness of her body, as if she wanted him far away from her. Careful to keep the cloaks between her and the filthy floor, he set her beside the saddlebags.

When he reached to lift the hem of her kirtle, she grabbed his hand. "What are you doing?"

His throat tight, Valteri sat back and removed his gloves from his hands. Ignoring her question, he touched her left thigh. She gasped in pain and her entire body jerked.

"I need to check your injuries, Ariel. I heard you wincing as I carried you, and every time your hip touched against my body you trembled."

"Oh." She ran her hands over her arms as if to banish a chill. "And it should be noted that the weather was not so bad when I started my journey. How was I to know that it'd turn this ferocious?"

He shook his head at her as he slowly inspected her for injuries. "Still . . . you should have stayed."

"And let you die? How could I do that?" Ariel drew a deep breath and met his gaze. "I had no choice."

"No choice?" he asked with a sharp frown. "You always have choices, milady."

"And I seek only to protect you."

He knelt beside her and cupped her chin in his warm hand. Against her will, he forced her to look up at him. "I can protect myself."

Tears of frustration filled her eyes at his unreasonableness. "How can you ask me to sit by and watch you die in my arms?"

One corner of his mouth lifted into a charming grin. "There's no other place I'd rather die."

Outraged by his teasing at something so serious, she glared at him. "How can you be glib? 'Tis no jest."

"I've never been more serious." His tone said otherwise.

And though she longed to deny it, the sincerity of his gaze told her that he spoke the truth. "I don't take your life or your soul so lightly, and neither should you. I wish you were more heedful of my warning. This is not a jest, Valteri."

He sat by her side. The firelight played in his hair, flickering shadows across the handsome planes of his face. "You shouldn't have fled because you feared for me. Death is what happens to us all, is it not? Was that not your very job before you came here?"

"Aye." Reaching out, she brushed a strand of hair from his icy, red cheek. "But you, milord, should have an entire lifetime to live. You shouldn't die so young just because of a curse that has nothing to do with you. Not to mention that if they lay hands to you, they could use your powers to free the Malachai demon onto this world."

Fire burned in his eyes. It scorched her with its intensity, melting her will. "Curses have followed me the whole of my life. What do I care for one more? And what do I care what happens to a world that has never done me any favors?"

She buried her hand in the top of his braid at the nape of his neck and pulled him close. "Those other curses weren't for your death."

"Trust me, they were. Many have cursed me to die. In this life and the next. Eternally, and to be damned to hell and beyond." He stroked her back, his touch warming her far more than the fire. "Given all that hatred, what do I care if I pass through this life as soon as possible?"

"*I* care."

His grip tightened around her waist. "As an Arel or as my wife?"

"As your wife!" How he could doubt her feelings for him?

He scoffed and pulled away. "But can you really be my wife? Can Arelim take human vows?"

A chill went over her. There was something she hadn't considered.

Could she? While she'd known a number of Arelim who'd slept with mortals and had children with them, she'd never known any who'd married them.

Until her.

"You're not exactly human."

And that sent another fear through her.

Neither was Apollymi. The goddess of destruction had fallen in love with a Sephiroth warrior. While they weren't Arelim, they were close kin to them.

That relationship had been so frowned upon by the higher powers that it had led to the Primus Bellum.

Consumed with a newfound terror, she bolted from the cot. "What have I done?"

Could loving Valteri cause another such war?

"Ariel?"

She couldn't even speak of the horror. His father was Jaden, brother to Apollymi. If the gods had feared the power of Apollymi's child mixed with a Sephiroth, would they not fear the powers of her child mixed with Valteri's?

Nay, Apollymi was a dark goddess. Sephirii were warriors of light. It was the mixture of those two contrasting powers that had bred the Malachai race of demons. Creatures so powerful and dark that they were virtually unstoppable.

She and Valteri wouldn't have that same mixture. They were both creatures of light. It was why he was still good in spite of the hate that had been delivered to him.

Surely, their relationship would be allowed. Just like her mother and her father's.

Right?

Do you want to find out?

Dare you find out?

His gaze darkened and the sudden suspicion in his eyes stung her. "What?"

"I know not, Valteri. I never felt this way before. In the past my senses were dull. 'Tis only now that I see true colors, smell true scents."

"And what do you feel?"

"I . . ." Ariel paused.

She couldn't say it out loud. Would the curse work immediately if she did? Over and over, she saw him falling dead before her, and she knew she could never utter the words lodged in her throat.

I love you.

So, she sighed instead. "What of you? Why do you want me to stay so badly?"

Valteri shook his head and rose. His emotions were so entangled that he didn't know how to answer so simple a question. Part of him would die for her, and another part wanted to curse her existence and all that she stood for.

Fate was indeed a cruel bastard.

"What can I say, Ariel? When I look at you, I see a promise for a future and that terrifies me. Because the one thing I've learned in this life is that the worst betrayal always comes when you learn that the one you'd take a sword for is the one holding the hilt."

"I would never betray you."

"So said Judas."

"I thought you didn't believe."

Valteri scoffed. "I believe in all traitors."

And that broke her heart. "And what if I promised you that I would never, ever betray you?"

"That would require the greatest act of all faith on my part."

"Would you not give me that?"

"I don't know if I can."

And how could she ask it of him when the truth was that she no longer even knew what her own true nature was.

Aye, she'd been born an Arel, but she'd been tainted by this mortal flesh. Had lived as a mortal being. Like the Atlantean god, Acheron, who'd been cursed to live a mortal life, it would leave a scar on her.

Forever.

She would never again be the same.

Any more than Valteri was.

Half god. Half human.

Like Acheron.

He wasn't what he would have been had Jaden claimed him.

By being together these last few weeks, they had changed each other.

In numerous ways. She now understood emotions and felt for others. He was no longer alone. He craved her company.

She could no longer imagine a world without him.

What are we going to do?

Wishing she had the right answers, she traced the embroidery on his cloak. "I remember flying. The air fluttering against my cheeks, but that air never felt as it does now."

She let out a heartfelt sigh. "Am I Arel or human? There are times when I feel myself going mad from the strain of trying to decide."

Ariel raised her right leg and encircled it with her arms. With one cheek pressed against her knee, she looked up at him.

Valteri swallowed hard as he watched the shadows play across her sad countenance.

Rubbing his jaw, he wanted to ease the ache in her eyes, but for his life, he could think of nothing. "But even if you are human for now, what of the morrow? Do you know when you will again retake your true form?"

"Nay. The crone never told me that part."

Would she be transformed as soon as he died, or would she live out a normal human life?

"Then you're more human than you know."

She frowned as if confused by his words. "How do you mean?"

Sighing, Valteri returned to sit beside her, but he didn't look at her. Instead, he studied the fire. "None of us ever know how long or how short a time we have. Most people spend the whole of their brief lives afraid of death. It's the one true demon that stalks men. The one demon they can fight for a time, but in the end we all must fall beneath its brutal fist."

"Except for you. You court him."

He nodded. "But the filthy little bastard has always eluded me." He tossed a stray piece of wood into the fire and sighed. "At least you have one advantage over us—you know for certain what awaits you in death."

She shook her head. "So you say. But if Belial has his way, he'll drag me off to Azmodea and trap me there."

"Can he do that?"

Ariel scowled as she considered it. "I'm not really sure. I've never been there. Only heard the stories of its misery. Mostly from creatures like Shadow and Thorn, who speak of the pain and torture. It's supposed to be a dark, tormented place that's filled with the awful entities who live to prey on others. There are places to hide, but if they find you, they will attack without cessation."

"So it's like here, then."

She rolled her eyes at his sarcasm. "Only worse."

"Doesn't sound like it to me."

She lifted her head to stare at him. "You don't understand, Valteri. There's no one there to help you."

"And that would be different from this world, how?"

Ariel opened her mouth to argue with him and then realized that from what he'd experienced in his life there was no difference. Her gaze dropped to the scars on his body.

Not from war.

From cruelty.

"Sorry. I forgot."

He sighed wearily. "Human or demon, makes no never mind to me. They are both out to use and abuse anyone who gets in their way."

She wished she could tell him differently. But the truth was that she hadn't seen much better behavior herself. "Thorn and Shadow came to help us. For no reason."

"Have they?"

"They haven't hurt."

He snorted then sighed as he threw another piece of wood into the fire. "I don't know, Ariel. I just keep thinking . . ."

She gave him time to continue, but when he seemed to have forgotten, she prodded him. "What?"

"If there is a God, why has He punished me for things I couldn't help, and damned you for events you couldn't prevent?"

"That wasn't God. It was a vengeful woman who was lost in her own grief, and a self-serving demon out for his own advancement. They had nothing to do with God."

"Why hasn't He stopped them?"

"Because of our free will. As much as it hurts, it's our gift and our curse. To interfere with it would take it away from us."

He pierced her with a harsh stare. "It didn't feel like free will when I was a child, chained and beaten."

She pulled his head down so that she could kiss his lips. "I know. We can't control our obstacles or what others think or may do. But we are all the masters of our own end. Of the choices we, ourselves, make."

Valteri grimaced. "You say that, and yet I recall a story Brother Jerome used to tell of the pharaoh who was born to be damned. Was that really his choice?"

"Of course it was. All the pharaoh had to do was free the Hebrews and even he would have been saved. Instead, it was his own stubbornness that damned him. His pride that cost him his life."

A strange look crossed his face and she struggled to name it.

"What?" she asked.

He looked away, his body more rigid than the sword strapped to his hip.

Ariel reached out and touched his shoulder. The muscles beneath her fingertips were taut with strain. "Please tell me what haunts you?"

His jaw twitched. "Just an old memory."

"Will you not share it?"

Valteri stared at her and the pain on his face reached deep inside her and touched her heart, making it pound. "I was told that my father, after seeing me for the first time, was so stricken with grief over my deformity that he cursed my mother and abandoned us." His low tone was bitter and harsh, laden with the full weight of his anger and hatred for his father. "They said that he never came back or spoke to my mother again. Because of me."

Tears filled her eyes and she bit her lip to keep from crying out at the injustice. How could anyone believe such a thing?

"You know that's not true, right? Shadow told me that your father knew nothing of your birth."

Valteri looked away. "Everyone told me that my father never returned because he went on a pilgrimage to atone for the sin of fathering me, and was ambushed and slaughtered by the Saracens outside of Jerusalem. The monks claimed that the Saracens carried out God's punishment. And while the brothers blamed me for my father's death, I always blamed his pride for refusing a less than perfect son."

Her heart ached for him.

So much pain. So much unnecessary sadness. "They lied to you in order to hurt you."

He shook his head. "How can I believe that I have a choice when my own father, a god, is being held in captivity? How can I have a choice when even he doesn't?"

He had a point, but still . . .

"Jaden gave up his freedom to protect others. He made his choice." Ariel traced the line of his jaw, his whiskers prickling her fingertip, sending coils of pleasure through her. He sat so close she could feel his heat, even stronger than that of the fire. "I wish I could make you believe," she whispered, noting the chills that rose on his neck.

When he looked at her, her breath faltered at the tenderness in his eyes. "When I'm near you, I can almost believe in anything."

Before she could move, he leaned forward and captured her lips.

Ariel growled with pleasure. She ran her hands over his back, pulling him closer to her.

Though she knew she should push him away for both their sakes, she couldn't bring herself to do so.

Not right now, when she needed this comfort.

Valteri nipped at her lips, drawing them between his teeth and gently scraping them. She shuddered, her body exploding with a demanding need.

He laid her back against the floor and she went willingly, delighting in the feel of his weight pinning her down. Ariel closed her eyes, savoring the raw, earthly vitality of his touch, his body.

Never had she imagined anything feeling so wonderful. Not even the freedom of flight could compare to the warm, heady sensation of his kisses.

He left her mouth, and buried his lips in her neck. Ariel arched against him, her body sizzling in response to his touch. She wanted him. Heaven help her for she couldn't find it within her to push him away.

She might not truly belong in his world, but she was his wife. And a wife belonged to her husband.

Nay, she'd never hurt him.

Never betray him.

Tonight she'd try not to think of what might happen on the morrow. Of what they might do to them.

To the world.

For now, she needed his touch as much as he needed hers.

Valteri inhaled her rich rose scent, his head reeling as if he were still intoxicated. He knew he should leave her. If he had any decency within him, he'd rise from her body and sleep outside with the horses.

But no matter how much his mind argued, his heart wouldn't listen. His limbs refused to obey.

He promised himself that if she gave any indication of fear or gainsay, he'd release her. But she continued to hold him close, her tender hands running the length of his spine, sending wave after wave of pleasure coursing through his veins.

No one had ever accepted or welcomed him the way she did. And nothing had ever felt better than her luscious curves that molded against him, pressing against his chest, his hips. His body burned for her.

She encircled his shoulders with her arms.

Valteri looked into her eyes and his breath faltered at the gentle need that hovered in the rich blue hue.

She smiled up at him. "For this night, I would have you as husband."

Ariel watched the emotions play across his face—disbelief, longing, and finally happiness. He returned to her lips, his breath sweeter than any wine. She pulled at his tunic, wanting to feel the strength of his chest against her palms.

The fire played across his face, displaying the raw hunger in his mismatched eyes. She trembled, unable to believe that he desired her so much.

Reaching up, she took his braid and slowly undid it until his hair cascaded over her. Its ends tickled her neck and face. As she had longed to do so many times, she ran her hands through the silken strands.

Valteri closed his eyes and turned his face to gently nip at her arm. Ariel sucked her breath in between her teeth, her breasts tingling. No man could compare to her warrior. He alone stood most honorable, most noble, and she vowed to let no harm befall him.

Somehow, some way, she was going to find a way to save him.

Even if she had to fight Noir herself.

Whatever it took. They would not take him because of her. She wouldn't allow it.

He reached for the hem of her kirtle and she shivered as the cold air contacted with her naked skin. Her breasts tightened in response. Heat stole up her cheeks and she tried to cover herself from his gaze.

"Nay, Ariel," he whispered, running his finger down the center of her bare chest. "You have naught to be embarrassed about."

Ariel swallowed, still uncomfortable. But as he dipped his head to her breast and took it into his mouth, she forgot her nudity. All she could think of was the passion coiling in her stomach, the all-consuming pleasure running the length of her body. His hair spilled across her breasts, her stomach, tickling her, inflaming her senses.

She cradled his head as he suckled, his tongue sending a thousand quivers to her belly. His hands roamed over her flesh, but when he touched her left thigh, she gasped as pain slashed through her pleasure.

Valteri pulled back with a frown. How could he have forgotten her injuries? He ran his hand over her thigh and grimaced at her wound. The whole length of her thigh and hip was red and bruised.

As gently as he could, he probed that injury. Finally he deduced no bones had been broken. "You should have reminded me," he whispered, his voice hoarse with guilt that he'd been so neglectful.

She touched his chin, turning his face until he met her gaze. "It didn't hurt until a second ago."

He found her humor terribly misplaced. "And now?"

"The only ache I feel is the emptiness in my arms. Come, Lord Norman, I need you to banish that emptiness."

Valteri stared in disbelief of her words. Before he could stop himself, he pulled her against him. Her hands danced over his naked chest, exploring him. He closed his eyes, savoring each delectable touch.

Lying on his back, he pulled her atop him.

Ariel gasped at her position. His leather breeches felt strange beneath her bare buttocks and a demanding throb pounded. He ran his hands up, over her chest, cupping her breasts. Her head swimming with pleasure, she arched against him.

Did all humans feel this way when they coupled? For some reason, she doubted it. Nay, what existed between them was something more than lust, something more than special.

Valteri reached up and buried his hand in her hair, pulling her forward until her lips touched his. She gasped as her breasts brushed against his hard chest.

His warm strength surrounded her, chasing away all the chills brought by the drafts in the old hut.

Ariel closed her eyes, wishing she could stay with him like this for all eternity. Oh, if only she could remain human and they could break the curse. She would never ask for more than Valteri's love, his touch.

Pain flickered in her breast at the thought of how temporary this moment was.

How fragile life could be.

Ariel trembled at the truth, but pushed it out of her mind. She might not have been born to it, yet she felt as if this was her home and Valteri was her destined mate.

Curse be damned.

Suddenly, he rolled her over. Ariel bit her lip as he fumbled with his breeches. Expectation flooded her heart and set it pounding even as heat crept up her face.

He pulled his breeches from him and she feasted on the sight of his bare body. Never had she seen anything so glorious.

Hesitant and somewhat afraid, she reached to gently touch him. She traced the trail of curls that tapered away from his belly. He drew a sharp breath and she smiled at her power over him.

Valteri closed his eyes, savoring her questing touch. Never before had a woman been so bold, so eager for him. What was it about his precious Arel that made her reach out when others refused?

But would she leave him?

Fear tore through him and he vowed to never let her go. So what if he died on the morrow? At least he would die having known happiness. No matter how brief. And if he had to die, then nothing would please him more than to draw his last breath while staring into her eyes.

Her hand cupped him and he gasped. Unable to stand any more, he pulled her hand away.

She looked up into his eyes and he shivered at the innocence, the love that shone so brightly. Would she still have that look when the sun broke them apart?

If there was a God, then he prayed that he died before he did anything to make her look at him with hatred.

Never let me break her heart.

As if sensing his thoughts, she ran her hand over the scar on his chest. She fingered his brand and a frown darted across her brow. "I can assure you that the ones who did this are damned for giving such pain to an innocent child. No one preys on the innocent without it exacting a foul price."

Taking her hand, he brought it to his lips and nibbled her fingertips. Fire danced in her belly, tingling her body. "For your gentle touch, milady, I would gladly suffer through it all again."

Warmth flooded her body and she pulled him against her chest. She held him tight, wishing she could have stopped the torture he'd received.

All of a sudden, he covered her with his body and her thoughts scattered. Ariel trembled against the pitching fire coursing through her veins.

He kissed her deeply, separating her legs with his knees. Her head swam from the pressure of his lips, the taste of his mouth, and she reached up to hold him close. He braced his arms on either side of her, cradling her head in his hands. Warmth flooded her at the tenderness of his touch.

And then he slid inside her. Ariel tensed at the sudden fullness. His hips resting against hers, Valteri began to nibble the flesh behind her ears.

Chills and unbelievable pleasure spread through her, tightening her stomach, her loins. She threw her head back with a throaty moan. Never had she felt anything like the quivering pleasure pulsing through her. She gripped his shoulders, raising her hips to draw him deeper inside.

This was what she wanted. This feeling of belonging and of being needed.

At her invitation, he began to slowly rock his hips. Ariel bit her lip at the strange dance. With each gentle stroke, her body burned more.

Valteri closed his eyes against the elation bursting inside him. Not even his dreams could compare to the reality of what he experienced. Her swollen breasts rubbed against him, urging him faster. She ran her hands down his spine and over his buttocks, and he trembled from the force of her touch.

If he died right now, he knew he'd have no regrets over his damnation. The feel of her beneath him was well worth the price of hell, and then some.

Ariel quivered as he buried his face in her neck. His breath echoed in her ears and his soft moans delighted her. This was her husband and she vowed to fight for him.

For eternity if she had to.

As he moved against her hips, a strange pulsing warmth grew. She arched her hips, pulling him in deeper, marveling at the bittersweet pleasure. He moved faster and the throbbing grew until she feared she would die from it. Then, just as she could stand no more, her body burst.

Ariel moaned, her entire body shaking. Never, never had she experienced anything similar. Her heart pounding, she wondered if she had died. Surely that alone could explain the falling sensation.

But then Valteri's arms tightened about her and he, too, convulsed. He groaned softly then collapsed against her, holding her so tightly that she almost cried out in pain.

"Am I still alive?"

He laughed in her ear. His hold loosening, he leaned up and kissed her gently on her lips. "Aye, love. The curse has yet to find us."

Though his tone was light, she found no humor in his words. But even so, she couldn't bring herself to dampen the wonderment of what they'd done by castigating him. "Is it always like that?"

Valteri shook his head. "Nay. 'Tis never so sweet as it was this night."

Warmth spread through her and she swept his hair up over his shoulder. His arms braced on either side of her, he stared down at her with an intense look that stole her breath and left her even weaker. She traced the stubble on his jaw and offered him a smile. "I'm glad that I've given you what no other has."

She just hated that the price for it might be his very life.

Valteri lay in the still quietness, listening to the winds howl and the fire crackle. Ariel's hair spread out over his chest, its silken ends soothing his skin. He'd give anything to stay like this for all eternity.

But what of the morrow?

Was there any way to spare her from the curse?

"Valteri?"

He started at her gentle voice intruding on his thoughts. "I thought you were asleep."

"I had a wonderful dream." She turned in his arms until she stared up into his eyes. The brightness of her gaze warmed him. "You and I were drifting in a glorious ray of light so bright that we couldn't see each other, but I could feel you. Your breath was my breath. Your lungs, my lungs."

"My heart, your heart?"

She smiled up at him. "Aye."

"But what happens when the night comes and ends the sunlight?"

She frowned and playfully hit him on the shoulder. "Ever the doubter, aren't you?"

Valteri brushed her hair back from her face. "My life has taught me to be wary."

Sadness replaced her happy gleam.

A twinge of guilt tweaked his conscience that he'd stolen her happiness, but he couldn't force himself to be so optimistic.

Especially not in this.

His life had ever been a study of kicks to the crotch and slaps in the face.

Just when he thought life would be good, something always came around to jerk him off his feet. Never once had he been spared any ridicule or shame.

Why would that change now?

After all, he was cursed.

She'd said it herself.

And by the weight of her sigh, he'd say that she'd come to the same conclusion. "So how did you find me in the storm, anyway?"

Valteri wondered what had made her ask that question. "Belial told me that you were gone and I set out after you."

"Belial?" She tensed in his arms.

"Aye."

"'Tis his fault that I fell from my horse. He tripped her during the storm." A scowl knitted her brows. "What mischief is he planning now?"

A chill of foreboding raced over him. The hairs on the back of his neck stood upright. How much power did the demon truly possess?

"Is he among us?"

Ariel shook her head and settled back in his arms. "Nay, I can tell when he approaches. 'Tis a stirring in the air, and the stench of brimstone chokes me."

Valteri held her close, his heart thumping heavily. "Do you know his limitations?"

She ran her hand down his ribs, drawing small circles in a tender caress that seared him. Her breath fell across his chest, raising chills. "When he's in human form, his powers are limited. He can only beguile and tempt. 'Tis his demon's form that's so dangerous. Then he can infiltrate the mind or possess a body."

Again foreboding seized him. "Infiltrate the mind?"

"Aye. He can manipulate memories, or steal them as he did with me. He's also a master of dreams, using them to weaken his victim's resolve."

Valteri fell quiet as he remembered the nightmares he'd had. Could Belial have been the cause of them?

I should have kicked his ass in those. . . .

"What of Thorn and Shadow? What are their powers?"

Ariel paused as she considered them. "Thorn, I'm not so sure about. Like you, he's a powerful warrior, but beyond that, he doesn't let anyone know what his full range of powers are. No doubt, he fears anyone knowing his limitations."

"And Shadow?"

"His are insidious."

"How so?"

She lifted her hand up to show her shadow. "It looks so harmless, doesn't?"

"Aye."

"It's not." She locked gazes with Valteri. "Our shadows know our sins. They are the keepers of the darkest part of our souls. It's where we relegate the things we're not supposed to think. The us we're not supposed to be."

He scowled at her words. "How do you mean?"

"Shadow can walk among their world. Where our deepest darkest parts live a life of their own. He can find out anyone's secret. Learn all about someone and spy on anyone. It's why they call him the prince of Shadows and his mother, the queen of all shadows. She has the same powers."

"That's terrifying."

"Aye, but the most terrifying is that they can separate us from our shadows and use them against us."

He gaped at her disclosure. "I'm still not quite sure what you mean."

"You spoke of your twin, but we all have one from the moment we're born." Again, she lifted her hand and waved at the shadow on the wall. "Think of it like a good twin and a bad one. Shadow can release the bad twin and allow it to become a separate being from us."

"Why?"

"Because our darkness can defeat anyone. It can overcome us and force us to do things we'd never do otherwise. Shadow's world is truly the most terrifying. He grew up among the darkest, scariest parts of everyone."

"Then how can you trust him?"

"He's never done me harm." She smiled at Valteri. "In many ways, he reminds me of you."

He scoffed. "And Belial?"

Ariel clenched her teeth. "His powers are weak compared to theirs. But the one thing I'm certain of, he wants my soul more than he's ever wanted anything. There's no telling what he'll do to secure it."

"Then he'd best beware."

"How so?"

"I would do anything to protect it." Valteri touched her cheek. "I won't see you harmed. I don't care how strong he thinks he is, I assure you, he's no match for me."

Horror swam in her gaze. "And that, milord, is my worst fear. You going after him."

Morning came, but it brought no joy to Ariel's heart. Though she was more than grateful Valteri had saved her and that they'd shared the night, she feared what would follow.

What new nightmares were lurking for them.

The voice inside her heart urged her to flee, but where would she go?

Especially now that she knew for a fact he'd follow her.

Valteri entered the hut, his cheeks mottled by his exercise. "I've saddled Ganille." He stretched his hands out to the fire and she admired the strength and beauty of them.

"Tell me, Ariel . . ." He drew her attention away from his hands, hands she remembered seeking out her most intimate parts and thrilling her, back to his face. "Where's your saddle?"

Heat stole up her cheeks from both his question and her brazen thoughts. "I didn't take one."

He cocked an eyebrow. Lowering his hands, he turned toward her. "No saddlebags either?"

She shook her head.

"How did you plan to survive your journey?"

Ariel rubbed the chills from her arms and sighed. "Forgive me, milord, but I've never had to plan such things before. 'Tis only recently that I've had to worry over being hungry"—she gestured to the walls surrounding them—"or needing shelter."

He crossed his arms over his chest and gave her a piercing glare. "Then I suggest you never again try and leave."

Though his words should have made her angry, they didn't. He was right. Though she might be well-versed with a sword, she stunk at planning an escape.

He held his hand out toward her. "Come, we should make our way back while the weather's pleasant."

Ariel pushed herself up, but pain ripped down her leg. She sat back down immediately.

Valteri rushed forward, a stern frown on his face. "Are you all right?"

"Nay." She hissed in pain. "'Tis the bruise. I fear it won't allow me to walk."

Without a word, he scooped her up in his arms and carried her to the horses.

Ariel savored the feel of his arms around her even though she knew she shouldn't. She damned that curse. But for that, she could stay with him forever.

Valteri placed her atop his horse, then mounted behind her. He pulled her back against his chest and wrapped his arms about her waist. Snuggling her head under his chin, she listened to the deep throb of his heart, grateful for its healthy, steady beat. He touched her cheek, his grip tender.

She expected him to say something, but instead he seized the reins and kicked his horse forward.

Ariel closed her eyes and tried to focus only on the moment, not on the coming future and what it might bring.

But it was hard when she was worried about everything.

Around midday, they stopped for a brief meal. Valteri found them a comfortable, dry spot and spread his cloak on the ground. He set her upon it, then pulled the saddlebags from his horse and set about preparing a light snack.

Before he could finish setting everything out, Belial and a group of Valteri's men joined them.

Ariel met Belial's amused gaze. No doubt the evil demon had guessed what had transpired between them the night before.

Indeed, the bastard had probably planned on it.

So be it. As long as she remained in human form, she was Valteri's wife and she had no intention of denying her husband what comfort she could.

What of his life?

She flinched at Belial's voice inside her head.

The bastard was still strong. She'd have to remember that and take more precautions.

"Ariel!" Belial cried, feigning concern. "I'm so grateful to find you safe. You had me terribly worried."

"Like a pimple in your nether regions, I'm sure." She returned his smile.

His men let out nervous laughs while Belial glared at her.

Even Valteri laughed.

She tsked. "Forgive me, brother. I didn't mean to cause you worry."

Still glaring, Belial kicked his horse over to her. "I trust you weren't harmed?"

She had to crane her neck to look up at him, and she had the distinct impression that he enjoyed making her strain. "I'm fine. All things considered."

He dismounted, knelt beside her, and whispered just for her ears. "I suggest you not try and escape again."

"Don't threaten me, demon." She made sure Valteri's men couldn't hear. "I *know* the extent of your powers."

His smile sent a chill over her. "I hope for your sake that's true, but what if you're wrong?"

Belial's words were meant to shake her confidence, her resolve, and to provoke the fear he needed to feed from.

It didn't work.

She wasn't afraid of him. Rather, she wanted to punch him. Right in the throat.

"Ariel?"

She turned to see her husband approaching as if he sensed something was wrong.

Valteri held himself rigid; no part of him betrayed that he knew the truth about Belial. Pride swelled inside her, and with it hope.

They might beat this bastard yet.

"Is your brother overly chastising you? Would you like me to beat his ass for you?"

Belial arched a brow at that, but held his tongue.

"We're fine, my husband."

"Then come." Valteri led Belial's skittish horse toward him. "Let's return."

Though the journey back was uneventful, it wore against her nerves.

Even without speaking, she could feel Belial's malevolent intent, his treacherous gaze seeking her out and noting the way she held on to her husband.

If only she possessed the powers to see inside Belial's mind as easily as he seemed to be able to read hers.

It wasn't fair, but then what was?

In little time, yet not soon enough, they rode into the bailey, where Shadow and Thorn waited.

The children broke from their play and ran to greet them, with rosy cheeks and bright smiles. Her heart warming at the sight, Ariel waved to them.

Edyth paused next to Ganille and smiled. "We made snow angels, milady! Would you like to see them?"

Ariel returned her smile, but before she could answer, Valteri spoke up. "Milady is injured, good Edyth. It may be awhile before she can see your angels."

Edyth's face puckered into a worried frown. "Will you be all right, milady?"

"Aye. It's not serious."

"Come on, Edyth!" a small boy cried. "We've got Creswyn pinned down."

Ariel stifled her laugh as Edyth eagerly ran to join the other children.

Valteri dismounted, then helped her down, his arms a perfect cradle for her body.

Ariel wrapped her arms around him, noting the darkening of his eyes as he stared at her lips.

Smiling, she wished they were alone so that she could yield to the part of her that longed for his kiss.

His grip tightening, he carried her through the hall to their chambers and placed her on her bed. He pulled her cloak from her shoulders and folded it.

A strange look crossed his face as he watched her. "At least I have no worries about you running away. Not until your leg heals."

Ariel swallowed at his tone. "Aye, but I would give everything I have, if *you* would."

He placed her cloak back in the small chest then turned toward her. "I refuse to run. You know that."

"You're a fool."

"Only for you."

And with that, he left the room.

Ariel wanted to strangle her stubborn husband. How in the name of anything could she save a man who didn't want to be saved?

"I will find a way."

But as the crone came in with a snide, knowing smile, she knew that her time was coming due. And that any moment was about to be Valteri's last.

Mildred would see to it.

And if she didn't, Belial would.

CHAPTER 20

Ariel greeted every dawn with fear and anxiety. Would this be the day they killed Valteri to punish her?

Would she have to hold him and watch him die?

Because she dared to love him?

It was as if Belial and Mildred intentionally dragged the days out, to make sure they maximized her torture.

And each day, she tried a new way to break the curse. With Shadow's help, she researched everything she could, but there were no answers.

Not even their shadows had a clue how to undo it without the crone's help or intervention.

"Only the crone can rescind her curse. I'm sorry." Shadow at least was sympathetic. "If you want, I could kill her for you. That might help."

His solution was becoming much more appealing as the days went by.

More snow had fallen the night before, blanketing the land in a pure white cover that made her wonder how evil could rest so comfortably around them and not at least be touched by the innocent beauty of this world.

Then again, evil had always been without conscience. Never caring how much harm it did to those around it.

She sat outside watching the children make their snow angels while she sipped a cup of warm cider. Their laughter rang in her ears and brought a smile to her face.

Why couldn't everyone be so happy over something so simple? That was the biggest tragedy of becoming an adult. That moment when life buried the joys of laughter gained from a simple run or from the sensation of warm sunlight on one's cheeks.

The joy found in capturing a sunbeam in the palm of your hand.

No one should lose their appreciation so soon.

And Ariel had so enjoyed these last few weeks. Valteri always stood near, ready to assist her. She'd taught him to play chess, while he'd taught her much about human feelings and desires. But their time together only made her greedier for his presence.

Greedier for a lifetime spent by his side.

"Milady?"

She turned at the old gnarled voice to find Mildred approaching.

"I beg your forgiveness for disturbing you. . . ."

Ariel stared at her and though she ought to hate the woman, only pity filled her. "What do you need, Mildred?"

"I . . ." The crone glanced away. "I know I have no right to ask, but I seek your charity."

Seriously? She had some nerve. "My charity?"

"Aye. I need you to forgive me for what I've done."

Her jaw went slack. How could she even ask such a thing?

Had the withered creature fallen and hit her head?

Mildred sank to her knees in front of her. "Last night . . . my Peter came to me."

Even more confused, she tried to make sense of what she was saying. "Your son?"

"Aye." Tears filled her eyes. "Though he no longer looked the same, I knew it was him. He told me of his new role and how happy he was to be fighting against those out to harm us all. That I should rejoice for what he'd chosen to do. He bade me seek forgiveness so that I would no longer be damned for what I've done."

Was this some trick of Belial's?

Baffled, she tried to make sense of it.

Until she saw Thorn stepping out of the shadows behind the woman. The intensity of his green eyes told her who was behind Mildred's strange turnabout.

Aye, he'd have the ability to arrange such a "meeting."

That was what Shadow had meant yesterday when he'd told her that he had one more trick he wanted to try.

"'Twas my grief and pain that caused me to seek vengeance against you, milady. What I did was wrong. I see that now. I don't want to be damned for it. Can you forgive me?"

Ariel's chest tightened. True sorrow and regret mingled in the crone's eyes. She meant what she said.

How could she deny this woman what she asked?

Indeed, forgiveness seemed a small request.

Ariel smiled sadly. "Aye, Mildred, I forgive you."

And even as she said the words, she meant them. Unfortunately, she'd learned all too well these weeks past why Mildred had cursed her.

What it would mean to lose someone she loved.

Fear flickered in the old woman's eyes as she desperately held on to Ariel's hands. "Is it too late for me to save my soul?"

Biting her lip, she looked over the woman's head to Thorn and arched a questioning brow. If anyone would know, he would. Bargaining for such souls was what he did.

She'll be fine. His voice was loud and clear in her head. *As long as she stays clear of Belial.*

Ariel inclined her head to him, before she met the woman's gaze. "Aye, but heed my words. Curse no others. Stay away from Belial and all his ilk in the future."

Mildred nodded, her eyes wide and fearful. "Anything else?"

"Free me from my curse."

Scowling, she hesitated. "I don't know if I can."

Shadow and Thorn drew closer.

"How was your pact set?" Thorn asked.

"I promised to serve Belial, and do as he said."

Ariel let out a relieved breath. Well, at least it was a standard deal. "Did you set your pact in writing?"

Nothing could break a signed agreement, especially one signed with blood.

"Nay, milady. I know not how to write. I took a verbal oath to give him my soul upon my death, and then he cut my hand and drank of my blood."

How stupid are you?

But she stopped herself from saying *that* out loud. She would never understand how humans could be so vengeful and shortsighted.

At least now they knew what they were dealing with. It would be a little tricky, but far from impossible. "Did Belial specify when your death would take place?"

"When the curse is fulfilled."

Ariel growled low in her throat. It seemed everything hinged upon Valteri's death. But if they could free Mildred, then maybe they could break the curse, too. "Can we get her free?"

Thorn let out a slow, thoughtful breath. "Maybe."

Ariel smiled at her. "See. There's always hope." Raziel's words echoed in her head and she chose to believe them.

"Thank you, milady!" Mildred kissed the hem of Ariel's kirtle.

Ariel pulled her dress away from her. "Please, no need in doing that."

The old woman smiled gratefully.

Ariel cupped the woman's cheek in her hand. "But remember that you must take care. Belial won't take kindly to losing you. He will try and claim you. If all else fails, should you die before we break this curse, if he shows up to claim your soul, then you must invoke the name of Azriel or Adidiron. One of them will come to your aid and take you to your son."

"Azriel or Adidiron. I won't forget."

Shadow snorted disdainfully.

Ignoring him, Ariel smiled, wishing they'd help her, too. But she knew her friends would never turn their backs on this woman.

She touched Mildred's hand and the old woman's eyes turned gentle. "I should never have blamed you, milady. You're truly kind."

And with that, she rose and scampered off.

Shadow came forward with a sneer twisting his lips. "You just had to give her my father's name, didn't you?"

"Sorry. But he's the one most likely to kick Belial's ass over this."

Shadow scoffed. "Pity he'd never help his own sons."

Thorn passed an irritated smirk at him. "Don't expect sympathy here. Want to trade fathers?"

"Want to trade mothers?"

"Fuck. No. You keep that rabid bitch far away from me."

They both turned to stare at her.

"What?" she asked innocently.

Shadow shook his head. "At least your sperm donor and mother were neglectful. Sad when that's the choice we envy."

It was indeed, and said it all about their respective childhoods and what had led them both to being who and what they were.

A breeze blew an odor toward Ariel and she stiffened, recognizing the stench.

No sooner had it infiltrated her nostrils than Belial appeared, walking from beside the manor as if he were on a leisurely stroll about the bailey.

As soon as he saw them gathered, he headed straight for them.

"Well, well. A confab of my least favorite people. To what do I owe this displeasure?"

Shadow grinned widely. "We're planning your boot party. Would you prefer being kicked in the head or the crotch?"

Thorn laughed.

Belial, not so much. "Aren't you bored yet? Why are you still here?"

"Mostly to irritate you. My favorite pastime."

Thorn shrugged. "Free alcohol. Besides, I have nothing better to do, apparently."

Wrinkling his nose, Shadow stepped forward and raked Belial with a flirtatious once-over. "Not to mention, I just love the way your ass jiggles when you walk. Shake it, baby. You give me a hard-on for days."

Belial curled his lips in distaste. "You're a sick fuck."

"Not what I've been told. They actually cling to my groin for more. Just ask. The list of recommendations in that department is quite impressive."

"He's right." Thorn laughed. "If he ever visits me, I can't get good help for weeks. It takes them that long before they can walk straight again. His stamina is the stuff of legends."

Looking sick to his stomach, Belial scurried away.

Ariel laughed. "I'm not sure if I should be scared or impressed that the two of you were able to scare away a high-ranking demon with so little effort."

Shadow winked. "Bit of both."

Thorn scoffed at him. "Neither, actually. It's easy to scare something when you know what gets under their skin. Belial's too stupid to not flaunt his aversions. It's why he never wants to be on my father's bad side. His torture would be tremendous."

He looked at Shadow. "As would yours."

"How so?"

"Keep you celibate and sober for a day. I think you'd spontaneously combust."

Shadow considered that. "Let's not put that to a test. You could be right."

Ignoring their banter, she turned her thoughts back to Mildred. They were halfway home now.

"What of the curse?" she asked them. "Can we break it now?"

Thorn sighed. "That's still the crux, isn't it?"

Ariel gestured in the direction Mildred had gone. "If she doesn't want vengeance anymore—"

"It doesn't change the fact that she made a blood pact with Belial and he still wants you."

Shadow snorted. "More to the point, he wants Valteri."

She cringed inwardly. "So, what do we do?"

Shrugging, Shadow gave her a wicked smirk. "Kill the bitch. Problem solved."

Ariel screwed her face up at his solution. "Shadow! We can't do that! She's asked for forgiveness!"

Again, he shrugged. "No, you, daughter of two Arelim, are a good guy and can't do that." He turned his gray gaze to Thorn. "The son of the king of all darkness would normally not have a problem with it, either, but his blood is corrupted by a human mother who long regretted her bargain and now, he wants to be a good guy, too, and won't kill an innocent. Dumbass that he is. I, on the other hand, am the spawn of the queen of all shadows, and an Arel father who isn't exactly known for following rules and who has no feelings or sympathy for anyone. That gives me a predilection for a certain moral ambiguity that the two of you, and most others, lack. I've got no problem gutting her for this reason, or any other. So I say kill her and be done with it."

She rolled her eyes.

"I'll remind you of that expression when you regret not listening to me. After all, the simplest solution is usually the right one."

Thorn snorted. "And as I recall, shedding needless blood was what got all of us into this, wasn't it?"

"Which is why shedding blood is what will get us out of it."

"Would you two stop?" Ariel pressed her hand to her temple to alleviate the ache that was beginning. "We can't kill someone who just asked for forgiveness."

Thorn struck Shadow in the center of his chest. "Yeah, you insensitive ass."

"Better that than a dumbass."

She ignored his quip. "Should we tell Jaden of this? Ask for his help?"

They laughed at her question, then sobered when they realized she was serious.

"Would he not help?" she asked.

Shadow shook his head. "Not bloody likely."

Thorn sighed in frustration. "Sadly, I'm with Shadow on this. Jaden doesn't normally involve himself unless he has something to gain from it. However . . ."

His hesitation gave her hope. "However, what?"

He grabbed Shadow by his hauberk. "Let us see about something. Arel, keep your wings crossed. We'll be back."

She watched them step back into the shadows so that no one could see them and vanish.

As they did so, her anger rose. "Beware, Belial. I will finish this." She wasn't a useless pawn.

For centuries, she'd fought against him and his ilk. While she didn't have the experience Thorn did when it came to blood curses, she wasn't without her own knowledge and resources.

And Belial was about to see just how much of her own father she had in her blood.

CHAPTER 21

Ariel sat in the library of the chapel, waiting for word from Thorn and Shadow as she tried to find a way to break the curse.

So far, everything she found had corroborated what Thorn and Shadow had said.

The only way out was to kill Mildred.

Damn it. There had to be another solution. Something that didn't involve killing the invoker and offering up their heart in place of the victim.

"Why would anyone cast a blood curse?" she mumbled under her breath.

The shuffling of feet intruded on her thoughts.

She glanced over her shoulder to see Brother Edred approaching. He crossed himself before the altar then rushed over to kneel by her side.

"What are you doing, Lady Ariel? Are you seeking forgiveness for some sin?"

Turning the page in the manuscript she was reading to something innocuous before he saw the subject matter at hand, Ariel glanced at him. "Nay, brother. I have no public confession that needs be made."

Rather, she was looking for information on Belial.

A frown furrowed his brow as he ran his gaze over her body as if searching for something. "Then what has kept milady here for all these hours?"

She lifted an inquisitive brow, amazed by his confession that he'd been spying on her while she read. She started to take him to task, but all of a sudden an idea formed in her mind.

Aye, even with his sins, Brother Edred could prove a worthy ally.

"You know, good brother, there is a demon in our midst."

"Ah, child! Finally!" He patted her clenched hands. "At last you've seen the truth of your husband's nature."

Ariel removed her hands from his grasp. "Not my husband, brother, but another man. One far more evil than you can dream. . . ."

He scowled. "What makes you think 'tis someone else?"

She leaned in close as if to whisper a terrible secret. "I've seen the signs . . . curdled milk whenever he is nigh. And the smell of sulfur."

His eyes widened. "You're certain it's not from your husband?"

"Aye. Most certain. It only happens whenever Lord Valteri is away. That's how I know 'tis another."

Edred produced a small vial from his robes. "Take this, lady. It's holy water. Should evil approach you, sling this in its direction and it will scatter it away."

If only it was that simple.

"Thank you, kind brother."

He blessed her before moving away.

Ariel watched him leave. Oh, to be so stupid.

How he lived with himself, she couldn't imagine.

With any luck, he'd stop pestering and plotting against Valteri and detect Belial of his own accord.

She didn't dare make that accusation herself, for fear the friar would accuse her of communing with demons.

Too many times, she'd been charged with escorting the legal victims who'd fallen prey to the more barbaric nature of men like him. Victims who'd been wrongfully accused by ignorance and fear.

Or worse, pure malice and malfeasance.

By those who wanted to use others and get them out of the way. She'd never understand the cruelty of people. Those who believed lies for no reason.

Those who wanted to spread poison for the sake of harming the innocent. They lied to make themselves look important or to steal what they weren't entitled to.

People like Edred were what she feared even more than Belial. Because they, unlike the demon, couldn't be reasoned with. Nor were they brave enough to attack on their own. They were insidious and unfeeling. Pretending to be friendly while plotting and lying behind the backs of those they called friends.

Like the dogs they were, they would come in giant packs to rip others to shreds.

Without mercy or compassion.

Those were the ones who'd preyed upon her husband when he'd been a helpless boy, and she refused to let them persecute him for another minute.

"I will keep you safe, Valteri."

From all the demons out to get him.

Human and otherwise.

She had no idea how. But somehow, she'd find a way.

There had to be some way to break the curse and find a bloodless solution for all of them.

CHAPTER 22

Belial hovered in the shadows of the stable, his body translucent as he floated around the rafters. At last he could again convert to his demonic form on his own. He threw his head back and laughed, reveling in his growing power.

A flash of brown caught his eye.

Drifting to the top of the stable so that he could peer more closely out the crack between the chinks, he spied Edred crossing the yard. The fat little friar cast a furtive glance around as if seeking someone, or mayhap avoiding someone.

Belial frowned, an uneasy twinge settling in his belly. Something was amiss.

"What are you up to . . ."

He lowered himself to the floor, returned to his human body, and nonchalantly made his way outside.

"Lord Belial!" the friar called.

Stifling his smile, Belial walked over to him. "Greetings, brother. What duties have you this day?"

The friar seized his arm and quickly pulled him off to the small garden beside the hall. He scanned the garden like a fearful mouse looking for a cat.

Belial longed to claw the tight grip from his elbow, but he tolerated it, knowing that eventually he'd find out what had the little man so distraught.

"I've just spoken with your sister." Edred kept his tone low.

Belial cocked his brow in expectation. Could the fat little mouse have fondled the wrong piece of cheese? "Did you now?"

"Aye, milord." His eyes grew large and round in fear. "And she spoke of demons among us!"

Belial gave him a patient, chiding smile. "Of course. Lord Valteri—"

"Nay. She said 'twas another. That we must be vigilant!"

"Another?" He gasped, feigning fright as he leaned nearer. "Did she name the beast?"

Edred shook his head, his gaze wistful. He wrung his pudgy hands. "I'd give aught if she had, but alas, she said only that she'd seen signs."

Belial tsked. "Oh dear."

"Indeed."

He patted the man's arm.

So Ariel was learning to play subterfuge. Damn her. She was good at it, too. She had the friar won over.

Who'd have thought?

He had to stifle a smile at her resourcefulness. Clever little Arel. He'd have to watch her more closely. Ariel was learning his job and ways a little faster than she should have. No doubt Shadow and Thorn were tutoring her.

Bastards!

He admired a quick learner and worthy adversary. But even so, she could not outthink him, and her little ploy with the friar could certainly be turned against her.

"'Twould appear Lord Valteri is gathering his minions. Unleashing more unholy terror here."

The friar crossed himself, his entire body trembling.

Belial breathed in the sweet bouquet of the man's fear, nourishing his starved soul on it.

"Do you really think demons are gathering among us?"

"Aye," Belial said gravely. "I know they are for a fact. We must expose Valteri. Fetch the Saxon nobles. Together we may yet outsmart the devil's mind and his mistress."

V alteri left the hall, but before he took three steps outside, Brother Edred ran up to him and slung water in his face.

Irritated, he cursed, wiping at his chin.

Glaring at the small, little man, he fought his urge to beat him. "What is the matter with you?"

"Forgive me, milord . . . I-I-I didn't see your approach. I beg you humbly for forgiveness." The friar stepped back.

Still wanting to thrash him, Valteri narrowed his eyes. From what he'd seen, it'd been no accident.

Rather, deliberate.

And irritating.

The friar had intentionally doused him.

With a sinister growl, Valteri pushed the man aside. "Pay attention where you walk. You could have hurt someone, mayhap even yourself."

Drying his face, he continued on toward the stable.

B elial pulled Ethbert down behind the large shrub as Valteri walked by with a furious countenance. "See! I told you."

Ethbert clenched his teeth. Aye, Belial had been right. Valteri possessed such power that not even the friar's holy water had blemished his evil flesh.

He'd walked away as if nothing had happened.

Over and over, he remembered his dream of hell, of the demons bowing down before Valteri as their evil overlord.

Hatred seeped through his veins. If only Harold had survived, then these beasts would not be feasting on his good, Saxon people.

Brother Edred joined them, his wise old eyes troubled. "Whatever are we to do?"

Ethbert ignored the question and excused himself. He might not be able to defeat the devil, but maybe he could save Ariel.

While the Norman beast may have brought her back here against her will, with any luck he might be able to thwart this evil and free her once and for all.

E nter," Ariel called.

She looked up from her tangled and mangled sewing to see Ethbert entering her chambers. Frowning at the Saxon's presence, she couldn't imagine what he might want with her.

Not since he'd first come to their hall had he sought her out. "Milord, what brings you here?"

He moved to her side then paused as he caught sight of Cecile. With a stern frown, he watched the cat's weaving path as she made her way across the floor.

A strange look crossed his face, and if Ariel didn't know better, she'd swear the small kitten frightened him. His jaw twitched as if he longed to say something.

She waited for several heartbeats. When it looked as if he might continue his silence, Ariel gave him a patient smile. "Is something troubling you?"

He looked back at her, and she struggled to read him, but his emotions eluded her. "My brothers and I intend to leave within the hour, milady."

She looked back at her sewing and took a careful stitch that still was a terrible one. "Then I bid you godspeed and safety."

He knelt before her and took the needle from her hands. Staring up into her eyes, he reminded her of a supplicant seeking divine aid. "Dearest lady, if you wish, we can take you with us."

Stunned, Ariel stared at him. Why would he say such a thing? "Pardon?"

He took a deep breath and touched her knee. "I know you ran away and that the Norman brought you back. If you still wish to flee him, we can take you. I assure you this time he'll never find you."

Was he insane?

"I have no wish to leave."

He took her hands into his.

Startled by his touch, Ariel stiffened.

"Please, milady. Let me help you."

Just as she opened her mouth to reply, a loud crash sounded from outside.

A gasp lodging in her throat, she tossed the tunic aside and ran to see what had happened.

As she entered the hall, she stopped, her heart pounding ever more.

Valteri lay in the center of the floor, a large, broken chandelier by his side. Wace stood over him, staring up at the ceiling.

A group of servants stood nearby, none moving. 'Twas as if they were too scared to breathe.

Crying out in fear, Ariel rushed to her husband. "Milord, are you all right?"

"It almost crushed him!" Wace said before Valteri could answer her question. "Never before have I seen such." He gulped at her. "It just fell. For no reason."

Ariel scanned the splintered wood and twisted iron that littered the area around Valteri. Wace was right. Another inch, and Valteri would have died instantly.

"Please forgive us, milord!" The servant closest to him wrung his hands in nervousness. "The rope slipped from poor Aldred's hands while we were trying to replace the candles. 'Twas an accident, I swear it! We meant you no harm!"

Valteri pushed himself up and rubbed debris from his tunic. For a moment, suspicion darkened his eyes, but as he looked from the old man before him to the younger men, Aldred, who was huddled by the wall, terrified Valteri would beat them for the accident, that suspicion lifted and he relaxed. "Fear not. No damage done."

"No damage!" Ariel gasped. "You could have died."

As soon as she said the words, she realized what had happened.

The curse.

How could she have been so foolish as to not think of it immediately?

All these last weeks, it'd only remained dormant, lulling them into a false sense of security, waiting for a chance to catch them unawares.

Waiting until it would do the most harm.

Cold rushed over her body, dimming her sight.

She backed away from Valteri as Mildred's hate-filled words echoed through her head. *You must watch him die.*

Today, she almost had.

Thorn and Shadow were right. There was no way to break a blood curse!

Realizing what was going to happen, she turned around and ran from the hall.

Returning to her chambers, Ariel scanned the room as full-blown panic took root. Her chest burned and her breath came in short, sharp gasps. She felt as though she'd pass out, or die herself.

This was real.

Death was coming.

She was going to lose Valteri.

One of her kin would be here to claim him and there would be nothing she could do to stop it.

"Nay," she whispered. He couldn't die. Not when it would be her fault.

How could she have thought for one moment that she might stave the curse and free them?

"Ariel?"

She turned at Valteri's voice. He pulled her into his arms and she shivered.

"It was just an accident. Nothing more."

"It was the curse," she whispered, afraid the next moment might rob the strength from his arms, the breath from his lungs.

An image of the young Saxon boy dying in front of her crept into her mind and she stiffened. Tears gathered in her eyes. She didn't want to see Valteri like that. To watch his life drain out, his vibrant mismatched eyes turn dull.

Valteri shook his head. "If it was the curse, then I'd be lying dead." He stepped away from her and held his arms out. "Do I look like a phantom?"

She shook her head, her tears spilling down her cheeks. "'Tis the curse, I say."

Valteri wiped her tears from her face, his warm hand only making her fear grow. He stared at her with wonderment and she saw the pain lurking in the odd-colored depths. "No tears, Ariel. I'm still here." He kissed them from her cheeks.

She nodded and he pulled her back into his arms. He held her for several minutes. Each one seemed suspended in time and she savored every beat of his heart.

But this wouldn't last.

It couldn't.

She was a threat to him and she knew it.

Heaven help her, but she had to leave him.

A knock sounded on the door an instant before Wace opened it. "Forgive me, milord, milady . . ." He bowed his head, his cheeks flushing. "I was—"

"I know, Wace." Valteri sighed. "Wait by the horses."

Wace nodded and left them alone.

He rubbed his hands down her arms. "No more frets, Ariel. All shall be fine. You'll see."

She nodded, her throat too tight for her to speak. With a heavy heart, she watched him strap his sword to his hips.

Never had she hated a sword and what it stood for more.

Ariel followed him through the hall and out into the yard. He swung up onto his saddle, and she admired the handsome form he made there as he placed his helm on his head.

She'd never see him again. That thought ravaged her heart, her soul.

I have to do this.

There's no choice.

And this time there was no coming back.

For his sake.

So, she committed every line of his body and face to her memory. That memory would be her only comfort in years to come. That and the knowledge that he was safe from her curse.

Safe from Kadar's slavery.

It didn't matter to her that she'd spend hollow, empty years wishing for a man she knew she could never have. Aching for a love she'd once known. She couldn't risk causing him harm. Not over this.

It was the right thing to do.

Yet it was so hard.

Lifting the reins, Valteri gave her one last, tender look.

Ariel waved at him and forced herself to smile. *I'm no better than Edred and all the other hypocrites.*

The heated look in his eyes stole her breath as he kicked his horse and sped out the gate.

Damn me for hurting him, too.

She clenched her hand into a fist and lowered it to her side. "Take care, my precious Norman," she whispered.

Closing her eyes, Ariel wished the rota had fallen on her. At least then her misery would be over.

Her heart weary and pained, she turned around and saw Ethbert standing with his brothers.

She approached them with a determined stride, knowing this must be done.

"Have you changed your mind, lady?"

No. The last thing she wanted was to leave.

But sometimes fate forces us to do things we don't want to do. Life takes us down paths we don't want to walk.

Not for ourselves, but for those we love.

To protect them.

For the first time, she understood what love really meant. Why Thorn and Shadow were so bitter.

How odd that she'd once judged them over something she thought she knew and yet she'd had no idea what it really meant.

Sacrifice wasn't just a word. It was an emotion so strong that it ached to the very core of her soul.

It meant choosing to do what was better for someone else than what was better for yourself. Choosing their life and happiness over your own.

A lesson she, a creature of light, had learned from those born in darkness.

"Aye." She was amazed by the steadiness of her tone. *Don't do this.* Her heart and soul begged her to stay.

But that would be selfish.

She couldn't ask Valteri to pay for her love.

Only her absence could keep him safe.

"I shall go with you."

CHAPTER 23

Valteri entered the hall and breathed a weary sigh. After spending the entire afternoon at the castle's construction site and listening to the builders instruct him on how many more men they'd need come spring . . . and all the different supplies he'd need to order by then, Valteri wanted nothing more than to find his wife and enjoy a quiet evening in solitude.

Preferably naked.

God help Wace if he disturbed him for anything other than the donjon being on fire.

And that change wasn't lost on him. Never had he thought to crave the presence of any person as much as he craved Ariel's.

She was the air he breathed.

His bare sustenance.

He pushed open the door to their chambers and froze.

The tunic Ariel had been mending lay folded on his bed, but no other sign of her existed.

Cecile ran out from under the bed, collided with his legs, then proceeded to circle his feet.

Frowning, Valteri placed his helm and gloves on the table beside the bed and stooped over to gently rub the kitten's head.

"Where is our lady?" he asked, but his only answer came as a soft meow.

Where could Ariel have gone? It wasn't like her to venture far when she knew he was returning.

She must be researching in the chapel.

He looked there first, and found it empty.

A quick search of the hall and bailey yielded nothing, either. As he entered the stable, a disembodied voice stopped him. "If you seek my sister, then I fear you've again allowed her to escape."

Tired of hearing the demon in his ear, he turned toward Belial. "What say you?"

His expression grim, he stepped out of the shadows, his eyes hollow.

Valteri held the distinct impression the demon's anger had reached its shattering point.

Belial shook his head, disbelief flickering in his light gaze. "'Twould appear our little bird has lied to both of us. A new skill that, and I must say that I'm very impressed. She told you that she'd be by your side forever and me that she was riding out to join you. But if you're here seeking her . . . It can only mean that she's flown."

He shook his head as if he couldn't comprehend it. "An unbelievable action, really. I never thought her capable of such."

Valteri's blood ran cold. "Then how do you know she left?"

"Since she's been gone all afternoon . . . it's the only thing that makes sense, isn't it? She left the same time the Saxons did. You haven't seen her and she hasn't returned. What other deduction can be made than she ran off with them?"

The bastard was right, but he didn't want to admit that.

"Perhaps she's with Thorn or Shadow?"

Belial shook his head. "Already asked, and they appeared as baffled as you are."

Valteri bit back a curse. "Do you know which way they went?"

Belial snorted, his eyes bitterly amused. "They rode to the north when they left here, as if they were riding toward the castle, but they may have altered their direction once they were out of sight."

Wanting to punch the smug bastard in the face, Valteri grabbed a fresh horse and saddled it. With practiced ease, he worked the leather straps around the horse's belly and his thoughts focused on his wife.

Had Ethbert taken her, or had she left of her own accord?

I'm such a fool.

Ever since he'd almost been crushed, she'd been more and more panicked. He should have seen this coming.

She was trying to protect him, and while he appreciated the thought, he wanted to strangle her, too.

I should have eased her fears more.

This was all his fault. If something happened to her because of it, he'd never forgive himself.

Valteri tightened the cinch with one last tug then swung himself up on the horse.

"Do you not wish for supplies?" Belial asked, a strange glow in his eyes.

"Nay." All he wanted was for this bastard to get out of his way.

Literally and figuratively.

Ariel had already been gone most of the day.

Would he be able to find them?

If he rode through the night, he might be able to overtake them. Provided they stopped to sleep.

Surely they hadn't been traveling without stopping for breaks. If they'd done that, he should be able to catch up to them.

Well, there was only one way to find out.

Wheeling his horse about, he kicked it into a full run.

Ariel stared at the flames of the fire, her mind traveling back to the blizzard and how Valteri had found her in the storm.

How he'd made love to her in their damp little cottage.

The fire before her warmed her cheeks, but did nothing for the coldness inside her, the coldness that needed her husband's touch.

The empty ache inside her threatened to swallow her whole. God, if it hurt this much now, how was she supposed to live the rest of her life without him? This was excruciating.

Watching him die would be worse.

That was the only thing that kept her going.

This was to save him. Not only his life, but his soul.

And the world.

She had to do this.

Ariel closed her eyes against the agony that tightened her throat. Truthfully, all she wanted was to go back to him.

"Milady?"

She looked up at Ethbert, his face shadowed by the darkness. He extended a bowl of porridge toward her. "I thought you might be hungry."

"My thanks." She took it from his hands even though her cramped stomach protested the smell.

He squatted by her side and tossed more wood on the fire. Strange how that had seemed so incredibly sexy whenever Valteri did it and yet it left her completely unaffected now.

After a silent minute, he looked back at her. "He won't find us. You're safe now."

Safe.

That was the least of her concerns. The Saxon had no idea what she was really running from.

And her stomach clenched at the thought of Valteri.

Would he ever understand what she'd done and why?

Or would his pain be so great that he wouldn't even care about the reasons?

Pain squeezed her heart in a brutal grip that stole her breath. The last thing she'd ever wanted was to be another regret for him.

I'm so sorry, my love.

"Milady?" Ethbert's concerned tone did nothing to alleviate the misery inside her. He touched her arm and it took all her control not to flinch or flee. He'd been so very kind since they left, but he wasn't Valteri and she wanted no other man to touch her in any way.

"I am fine." Offering him a smile, she took a hesitant bite of porridge.

With a nod, he rose to his feet. She sensed he wanted to say something more.

The younger of his brothers—Arthur, if she remembered his name correctly—stepped forward with a blanket.

Ethbert took it, then wrapped it around her shoulders. "You should rest yourself and try not to worry overmuch. I'll not let anything harm you. I swear it."

Thanking him, Ariel set the porridge aside and settled down by the fire. She drew the blanket up to her chin, and wished to the gods that things had been different.

Damn you, fate and curses.

Ethbert and his brothers had dug through the snow to make her a pallet on the ground, but still the cold dampness seeped through her body.

Watching the flickering flames in front of her, she allowed her thoughts to drift.

For a while she remembered her real home, with her father and mother. While they'd seen her trained in her duties and had instilled in her an indelible sense of honor, they had basically been absentee parents.

Michael because he had other duties that kept him away, and her mother, Lailah, preferred fighting against Kadar and the rest.

Really, she barely knew her mother. As an Arel, she hadn't possessed enough curiosity to ever ask about either of them. How they'd come together to create her. Though to be honest, her father and his ilk were prone to leave children like her strewn about.

It was something they all accepted. Those like her who were Arelim did their duties and never questioned their births.

Those like Shadow, who were of mixed blood, hated their Arelim origins that had been used against them. At least all the ones she'd ever met.

Funny how she'd never given any thought to that before. It'd never mattered.

An Arel didn't question. They just obeyed.

Being human had changed that. Now she was curious and she wanted to know if her parents had ever cared for each other. Had her mother ever felt like this?

Or her father?

Sighing, she thought of her brethren and friends. She knew more about Wace and Mildred than she did those she'd fought beside for centuries.

And none of them filled her with the passion that Valteri did.

In truth, the Arelim were a bit stodgy. They were nothing like Shadow and Thorn.

Or Valteri.

All rules and decorum, her ilk were an extremely boring lot.

How weird that she had accepted their muted emotions as "normal."

But then, like Valteri with how others reacted to him, she'd never seen or experienced anything else.

Therefore, she'd never questioned it or thought about what she was missing out on.

While she'd been content, it was nothing like the happiness she felt in his arms.

"Ariel?"

Her blood ran cold at the last voice she expected to hear.

Belial.

Scanning the campsite, she tried her best to find a trace of the beast. All she saw was Ethbert and his brothers, talking on the other side of the fire.

Damn him for his tracking abilities. How could she ever avoid that beast?

"So, here you are," the disembodied voice said in her ear.

She turned to see the winged shadow beside her. "You wager much appearing this close to the humans."

He laughed, his voice ringing through the trees, but she knew its pitch was higher than that which the human ear could detect.

The night animals screeched and gave flight at the insidious sound.

In response to the animals, Ethbert and his brothers unsheathed their swords and looked about the forest.

"Milady? Fear not!" Ethbert returned to her side. "Hubert is going to check on the noise we heard."

She nodded.

His brother clapped him on the back before heading into the woods.

"Pathetic bastards." Belial laughed. "Do you think I should gather wolves to feast on his hide? Or maybe feed him to something worse?"

"Nay!" she gasped.

Ethbert looked at her with a frown. "You don't want him to go?"

Ariel cast a heated glare to Belial, then looked back at Ethbert, her temper carefully shielded. "It wasn't your brother's search that I spoke of. Rather a response to the sudden cold that bites my flesh."

He offered her a knowing smile. "I shall get you another blanket."

Belial brushed a cold, shadowy hand against her cheek. "What a liar you've become. I'm impressed by your abilities. What would your father say?"

"For me to gut you." Ariel slapped at his hand and a fierce jolt shot through her arm.

Belial tsked. "Now, now, little Ariel, you know better than that. You can't harm me when I'm in this form." He wrinkled his nose. "You're still mortal."

Ariel trembled. He was getting ever stronger. Soon she'd be no match for his powers, and he'd have the strength to brew whatever evil he wanted.

What would she do then?

Ethbert returned with the promised blanket. He offered her a timid smile as he draped it over her. "Rest easy, milady. I'm sure the noise was nothing serious."

"Thank you." She returned his smile.

When he'd left her once more to join his brothers, she turned toward Belial. "Why are you here?"

"I wanted to find you."

She glared at him. "Why?"

Before Belial could answer, she heard a horse approach. Dread took root in her heart.

"Nay," she whispered, knowing the rider even without seeing him. Panic consumed her.

Valteri stormed into the clearing, scattering Ethbert and his kin.

Ariel scrambled from her pallet to rush toward the demon. "You treacherous beast!" she snarled at Belial as he drifted away from her. "How could you?"

"'Tis what I do." He laughed.

Ariel wanted to tear him apart. If only she had her Arel powers, Belial would be in more misery than if he faced Kadar himself.

If she ever returned to her own body, she'd beat him worse than a Malachai.

Unsheathing his sword, Ethbert shouted at Valteri, "Nay, you evil bastard! You'll never take her."

Those words brought a whole new terror to her.

Don't you dare!

Ariel looked back toward her husband. The Saxons were no match for his skill. He would tear them apart.

Valteri had reined to a stop. His spine rigid, he stared down at the Saxons. A sudden gust of wind caressed the blond braid he wore draped over his right shoulder and billowed his cloak out behind him.

Even from her distance, she could see the malice shining in his mismatched eyes. "Don't make me kill you, Saxon. 'Tis my wife solely that I want. Give her over and you may leave in peace."

She held her breath as Ethbert charged forward.

Valteri's horse reared, dancing away from Ethbert's sword. "I'd rather send you to hell first!"

With expert skill, Valteri brought his horse under control, then slid from his saddle and unsheathed his sword. He headed for the Saxon, his eyes filled with bloodlust.

They couldn't fight! Not with the curse and not with her present to witness the event. 'Twould be Valteri's death!

Valteri and Ethbert doffed their cloaks.

"Nay!" She ran toward them and placed herself between them before they could engage each other.

She grabbed Valteri's brown woolen tunic and held tight. "Milord, please, for my sake do not do this."

He wrapped his arm about her and held her close to his chest. "Did they take you or did you leave?"

She choked on a sob, feeling his heartbeat race beneath her fingertips. The thought of touching his chest and not feeling that steady throb . . .

"There's no chance for us. You know that. I am your death."

His jaw tensed. "Don't you dare say that! 'Tis not so."

"Aye, Valteri, but it is, and I beseech you to leave while you still can. You must live for me."

"I'd rather die for you."

"That I can oblige!" Ethbert grabbed her and shoved her into his brother's arms. "Hold her, Arthur."

"Nay!" She tried to break free, but Arthur held fast.

"This is between us, Norman. 'Tis time for you to pay for the souls you've taken. The innocent lives you've destroyed."

They crossed swords.

Ethbert spat at him. "Give your hellish master my best!"

Metal clanked against metal, the sound blistering her soul.

"Please, God, no!" she cried, the words searing her throat.

She winced at the sight of them fighting and the memories she had of countless battles.

Only in the past, she didn't care who won or lost. Because her role had been simple.

Claim the soul of the loser and take him to her boss.

Now . . .

She cared about the outcome.

Most of all, she cared about Valteri, and she refused to watch him die.

Suddenly, a light broke over their heads.

Ariel looked up through her tears and gasped. Invisible to the men, Raziel descended.

His armor glistened as he glanced at the combatants then slung his hand out toward her.

The impact sent her reeling and knocked her from Arthur's grasp.

...sped as the cold seeped into her flesh.

...r released her just as Hubert returned to the clearing. Rebel-
...ed in both their eyes, but Valteri pressed his sword tip closer to
... throat. "Don't," he warned them, his tone most lethal. Hubert
...his sword and moved to stand beside Arthur.

...ed that the fight was over, she went to her husband.

...i wrapped a protective arm about her, then removed his sword
...bert's throat and sheathed it. "I suggest you be on your way, Saxon.
...ou nor your brothers are welcome on my lands ever again."

...y, Valteri set her up on his horse, then mounted behind her.

...rt didn't move from his place on the ground, but his glare was
... she almost expected him to rise and again attack Valteri.

...i ignored his hatred. Kicking his horse forward, her husband held
... as they left the Saxon camp.

...te of the fact that he said nothing, Ariel sensed the pain inside
... she longed to soothe it.

...es flew by before Ariel found the courage to speak. "I had to leave."

...ow."

...n why did you come for me?"

...r mixed with tenderness in his eyes and his arms tightened about
...t. "I will always come for you, Ariel. I can't live without you."

...gh his words brought a painful, warm rush to her heart, frustra-
...med her and she wanted to shout at him to see reason.

...ad, she bit her tongue.

...' could she argue when the love that made her leave was the same
...t made him come after her?

...s so cruel.

...tter.

... so incredibly precious and sweet.

...t were they going to do?

...rs was an impossible situation.

...l grimaced. Once more the internal pull tightened his gut. "Damn

...had to go. Whether he wanted to or not.

...sing his eyes, he surrendered to the bidding he hated most. Light
...ound him as he fell through the dimensions of time and space and
... pit of the Nether Realm that held his noose.

...body aching, he soon found himself in the deepest pit of Kadar's

... as he'd expected, he landed in the main throne room. Orange

Or so she thought.

Catching herself, she realized that they st

she stood outside herself, dressed in her Arel

Raziel tossed her battle sword to her. "Pro

Grateful beyond belief, she rushed forward

with her own and sent it flying.

So . . . Raziel was Valteri's guardian.

Her husband was wrong. He wasn't alone,

ziel had come to her before. Not because of he

Because of Valteri.

More grateful than she'd ever been, Ariel

kicked Ethbert back, away from Valteri, so th

his breath.

Belial flew forward with a snarl. "Nay! This

Raziel blasted Belial back with a power-bolt

"This isn't Valteri's time to die, demon. *You'd*

not to interfere! Nor are you to harm a hair on

Ariel almost dropped her sword as relief tore

This isn't Valteri's time. That single phrase

repeated it over and over, reveling in its sweet s

Her brethren would help her protect him.

Yet even so, Ethbert rushed toward Valteri

waist. Valteri tossed his own sword aside and

fists.

She stepped back and let them get their rage

Belial flew to her side. He started to reach for

sword and he knew better than to try. With *this* v

"Don't smile yet, Arel. You might have him

row . . ."

She glared at him. "Really, Belial? Must you b

can't you be something more than what Kadar b

He bared his fangs at her before he vanished.

The fistfight continued on for a few minutes m

Ethbert to the ground.

Retrieving his sword, he held it to Ethbert's thr

Saxon," he said, his breathing labored.

Ethbert leaned back against his elbows and gla

harsh and damning.

His sword never wavering, Valteri looked to he

She handed the sword back to Raziel. "Thank

He inclined his head to her. "Be careful."

"Always." And with that, Raziel reunited her w

She g

Arthu

lion glov

Ethbert'

dropped

Relie

Valte

from Et

Neither

Gent

Ethb

such tha

Valte

her close

In sp

him and

Leag

"I k

"The

Ang

her wai

Tho

tion cla

Inst

Hov

love tha

It w

So l

And

Wh

The

Beli

it!"

He

Clc

shot a

into th

Hi

prison

Jus

lights danced along the dark walls. Screams echoed around him and he looked up to his master's bone-encrusted throne.

To his shock, it wasn't Kadar or Azura.

Death sat on the throne.

Audacious and stupid. He'd give Grim that. Ballsy beyond ballsy. Although, if either god caught him, Grim wouldn't have his balls for long.

Even if he was Kadar's son-in-law.

Handsome and devious, Grim stared at him as if he'd like nothing better than to rip his demon flesh apart. He stroked the bleeding demon chained to the throne's arm and raked a hostile glare over Belial.

Granted, Belial had never cared for Grim even when they'd battled together, but still he had to admire his bravery right now.

"Greetings, Belial."

"Where's Kadar?"

Grim shrugged. "Amusing himself with some poor slug, no doubt."

"Then why was I summoned?"

An evil smile curved his lips and a tremor of fear chilled Belial's spine. "A little demon told me what you're up to."

"Six feet?"

Grim wasn't amused. "Your plan, nimrod."

Trying to remain nonchalant, he looked about, curious as to who had betrayed him. He knew it wouldn't be Thorn or Shadow. While they might not like him, they had even less love for Grim. Last time Shadow had been near him, he'd almost fed the bastard his own intestines.

As for Thorn, they had once been allies.

Now they were mortal enemies, and if Grim could deliver Thorn's head to Kadar, he'd gladly do so.

Nay, someone else had heard him.

Who?

In this place? There was no telling. Every corner had ears.

Or eyes.

"I don't know what you're talking about."

Grim laughed, balling his fist up in the demon's hair, causing it to hiss and bare its fangs. His hand froze and a delightful gleam lightened his red hue. "Don't play coy, brother. You want your freedom. We all do. Do you really have the soul of an Arel in your palm?"

Belial relaxed a degree as he realized that Grim had no knowledge of Valteri fitzJaden. "If I did, what's it to *you*?"

Grim left the throne and approached him slowly. "Have you given thought as to what would happen if you bypassed our master and gave her over to the Malachai instead?"

Not really.

Grim slapped him on the head. "Think, imbecile! The prophecy!"

Belial gasped as he remembered.

As it began, so it would end.

A child born of light and dark.

The final Malachai.

"But she's destined to die."

"Then you better protect her, little brother. We need that bitch to breed with Adarian Malachai. If she does . . ."

They could overthrow the dark powers.

Take the throne and the world themselves.

He grabbed him up by his neck and held Belial before him. "That was always your shortcoming, Belial. You never saw the bigger picture."

But he did now, and it was glorious. "What if the Malachai doesn't accept her?"

"Born. In. Violence." Grim growled each word. "To do violence and to die violently." That was the creed of the Malachai race. "The very nature of that beast is that he rapes the mother of his heir. Trust me. Put her with him and he will do what it is that he does. All we need is your little Arel and nature will take its course. He won't be able to help himself. She is a creature of light and he will attack her."

Why had he not thought of that?

Because unlike Grim, he wasn't a servant to the Malachai.

In fact, the Malachai tended to pull the wings off demons like him. Which caused him to avoid the Malachai as much as possible.

Just like any demon with a brain in their head would do. Unlike Grim, who'd once been a god.

"Are you sure this will work?"

Grim laughed. "I was there in the beginning when the Malachai race was cursed. The one thing I know is the Malachai bloodline. Bring me your Arel and I will give you your freedom."

In spite of the pain, he smiled. This was even better than the curse.

Fuck it! He didn't have to wait for anyone to die. All he had to do was get Ariel here.

"I'll have her back in no time."

"Don't fail me, Belial."

"I won't."

Suddenly, he found himself returned to the forest. He reached behind his back and touched his aching spine. When he pulled his hand away, he saw the blood.

You bastard. He'd always hated Grim.

Sadistic bitch.

Groaning, Belial stretched out on the ground, needing time to regain his strength.

Fine. New plan.

And this one was going to be so easy. . . .

CHAPTER 24

J ust as dawn broke, Valteri and Ariel entered the bailey.

Honestly, Ariel was happy to be back, even though she knew she should still be running.

Valteri slid to the ground with her in his arms. Embarrassed by his continued embrace, she tried to squirm from his hold, but he tightened his grip.

"I can walk, milord."

"Aye, and run as well."

She stopped moving and gave him a chiding grimace.

His gaze blank, he said nothing more as he carried her inside. The people were just waking and they paused in their morning routines to stare at them.

Ariel averted her gaze, embarrassed by the speculative gleam in their eyes. Heat crept up her cheeks, and despite the need to insist Valteri release her, she kept her silence.

At last Valteri entered their chambers and deposited her on the bed. "I should chain you," he said, his voice as empty as his eyes.

She swallowed, her heartbeat slowing in guilt. He would never do such to her, and she knew it. 'Twas only his pain that made him threaten it.

"I didn't mean to hurt you."

His gaze seared her. "Damn, Ariel, if you did this much harm to me unintentionally, then I'd hate to see what you could do if you actually applied yourself."

His sarcasm cut deeper than any sword stroke.

He had a right to be angry.

When he spoke again, his voice was barely more than a whisper in the quiet room. "You told me you wouldn't leave."

"That was before a chandelier had almost killed you." Why couldn't he be reasonable? "I was trying to find a way to break the curse, but when the chandelier fell, I realized I was tempting fate by staying here. I only wanted to protect you."

Valteri braced his hands against the back of the chair in front of him. Still facing the wall so that she couldn't see his expression, he sighed. "I don't want your protection. I only want you."

She closed her eyes against the warmth his words brought to her heart.

Don't let him weaken your resolve.

Whatever she did, she must keep her mind unclouded by those tender emotions. "Please, Valteri, understand that I cannot stay here and be responsible for your death. I just can't."

She crossed the room and placed a hand on his rigid shoulder. His muscles bunched beneath her fingertips, but he made no move to pull away. "How can you ask this of me?"

He turned about and held her by her arms. His pleading gaze searched hers. And beneath his rage, pain flickered in the odd-colored depths, stealing her breath, her will. Ariel swallowed, her chest tightening in fear and apprehension.

"I don't want you to die," she begged.

"And I don't want to live, unless I have you."

She closed her eyes, unable to face the sincerity of his gaze. Why was Valteri doing this? Why was he being so stubborn? "Are you willing to damn yourself for a moment's worth of pleasure?"

"For one sweet moment with you, aye! Point me to the road to hell and I'll gladly walk it. Never once in my life have I ever expected to grow old, and I would rather live one day held in your arms than to live out the rest of my life in the empty void that has followed me since my birth."

Ariel pulled away from him, his words branding her. It would be so easy to stay, so very easy to give her pledge that she'd remain with him for whatever time fate had set aside for them.

But the price was too high and she was unwilling to pay it.

Her thoughts whirled through her head as she sought some argument that would make him understand her side of the matter. If only he could see things as she did.

Aye, that was it. She must show him.

"And what if the curse said that I was the one destined to die in *your* arms, Valteri?" She touched his cheek, his whiskers gently scraping her palm. "Would you be willing to take your pleasure in the present if you knew that any day my life would end and that you might have to live out the whole of your life without me? Could you stay by my side knowing that was the price?"

Valteri opened his mouth to speak, then stopped. He'd never once thought of it that way.

"As I thought. You'd never take such a risk. Yet you expect me to."

Damn it, she was right. But still, he didn't want to admit it. "It's not the same."

"It is, and you know it."

Valteri clenched his teeth, the knot in his stomach tightening even more. Aye, he did know it. He knew it and cursed it. "Then what's left?"

"I don't know." She walked away from him, her shoulders slumping. Her obvious misery sliced through his conscience and brought a painful burning to his heart.

Indecision racked him. Life had never been more than a grueling burden for him that he'd gladly leave behind.

He'd resented every fucking breath he'd ever drawn.

Yet it would be selfish of him to ask her to live on with the guilt of knowing she'd caused his death.

How could I do that to her?

Valteri sighed, uncertain what to do. He clenched his teeth and cursed himself. He was a selfish bastard, but not so selfish that he would hurt her so needlessly.

So be it. He'd had his time with her. He wouldn't ask for more. Since death was his sentence, he would meet it bravely.

Away from his Ariel.

I came into this world alone and that's how I'll leave it.

Not exactly true. He'd had a twin brother, but even his own brother had abandoned him in infancy.

Because no one wants you.

It was time to let her go.

"Very well," Valteri said at last. "You stay here where you're safe and protected. I shall make terms with my brother for your welfare. I'm sure he'll appoint a steward loyal to him, but you will retain final say in all things. This will be your home and you will be the one in charge." Clearing his throat, he pulled his gloves from his hands. "I'll leave for London on the morrow."

Ariel gasped as she finally won her war.

'Twas what she'd wanted, so why did her heart ache to the point she feared she'd die from it?

"Come, milady. Neither of us has rested. I doubt I shall die in my sleep, so let us take our slumber."

Ariel nodded, her throat too tight for her to speak. Inside, her heart shriveled up. She bit her lip to keep her tears from falling.

It must be this way.

And yet she cursed their fate.

Fully dressed, she lay on the bed, her soul crying out for her to keep him near.

Don't let him go.

I can't ask him to stay!

Valteri pulled his tunic from his head and joined her. His strong arms reached around her and drew her closer to his warmth, his hard chest.

She shivered, wanting nothing more than to stay like this forever, but knowing how impossible a dream it was. His breath fell against her neck and she trembled. Was there truly no way to break this damnable curse?

Perhaps in his absence, she might find some way, then she could send for him.

Aye, that was what she'd do. 'Twas only a temporary separation. As soon as he was away and safe, she'd do whatever she must to dissolve the pact, and then they'd be together.

Forever.

I will find a way. So help me!

Valteri came awake to Wace's insistent shaking. "Milord, forgive me," he whispered, "but a sickness has come over your horse. The groom bade me to fetch you."

Valteri pushed himself up, careful not to wake Ariel. Retrieving his tunic, he frowned. What could have happened to Ganille?

He pulled his tunic on and excused Wace. His destrier had been fine this morning when they'd returned. What ailment could have come upon his horse so suddenly?

Narrowing his eyes, he knew the answer.

Belial. The beast had probably poisoned his horse to keep him here. His anger rising, he made his way out of the hall and to the stable.

As he pushed open the door, his anger dissipated.

How would Belial know he'd planned to leave? Ariel had said Belial couldn't read minds. Yet what else could have tainted the stallion if not Belial's mad schemes?

The avener met him in the stall, his face grim. "Must've been bad oats, milord."

Sweat covered Ganille's body, and the horse struggled for breath. Valteri stroked his velvet nose, wishing he could alleviate some of his old friend's obvious pain. "Will he be all right?"

"Hard to say." The avener wiped at his cheek with a grimy hand. "Don't know exactly what ails him."

Valteri let out a tired sigh. "Keep an eye on him and do your best."

"Aye, sir."

His heart heavy, Valteri stood. Ganille's illness wasn't enough to preclude him from leaving. He could easily use another horse to reach London, and once there buy another destrier.

But he'd been through much with the stallion and he hated to lose such a well-trained animal.

He's more than that to you and you know it.

Aye, he was. Ganille had been the best friend he'd ever had.

With one last pat to the horse's head, he started to leave the stall, but something solid struck him across the back of his head.

Pain exploded through his skull, and he stumbled to the ground. Shaking his aching head to clear it, he tried to rise, but a strong blow across his back knocked the air from his lungs.

What the hell?

Rough hands seized him and tied ropes to his wrists. Anger burning through him, Valteri struggled against his attacker. But he was too dazed by the blows.

"Hold him!"

Two large, burly Saxons pulled him against the front of the stall. There they tied his hands to the wooden posts and forced him to kneel before the friar.

Edred stepped forward with a vial of water and splashed his face and tunic with it. His voice rang out, the words of exorcism all too familiar even to Valteri's dazed senses.

"Saint Michael the Archangel, defend us in our battle against principalities and powers, against the rulers of this world of darkness, against the spirits of wickedness in the high places!"

Are you fucking kidding me?

"What do you think you're doing, Friar?" Valteri growled, his sight still hazy from the blows.

"Watch the door," Edred called to one of the men next to Valteri, ignoring the question. "He might summon one of his minions to save him."

Edred turned back to face him. "I saw you last night in my dreams and I know you for what you are!" Again he slung water across Valteri's face.

His breathing ragged, Valteri glared at him as they gagged him.

Whoever stood behind him slit his tunic, and exposed his back. Valteri clenched his teeth against the fury boiling inside his veins. Memories surged through him and without being told, he knew what would follow.

Damn them for it!

Valteri pulled against the ropes until his wrists burned. He lunged at the priest.

You better kill me, old man. When I get out of this, I'll feed your entrails to you!

Edred stumbled out of his reach and began reciting his call to God. "Behold the Cross of the Lord, flee bands of enemies. May Thy mercy, Lord, descend upon us. As great as our hope in Thee. We drive you from us, whoever you may be, unclean spirits, all satanic powers, all infernal invaders, all wicked legions, assemblies, and sects. In the Name and by the power of Our Lord Jesus Christ, may you be snatched away and driven

from the Church of God and from the souls made to the image and likeness of God and redeemed by the Precious Blood of the Divine Lamb.
Most cunning serpent, you shall no more dare to deceive the human race,
persecute the Church, torment God's elect and sift them as wheat. The
Most High God commands you, He with whom, in your great insolence,
you still claim to be equal. God the Father commands you. God the Son
commands you. God the Holy Ghost commands you. Begone, Satan, in-
ventor and master of all deceit, enemy of man's salvation!" He paused and
nodded to whomever stood behind Valteri.

Pain ripped through his back as he recognized the familiar burning of
a lash strike.

As hard as he could, Valteri pulled against the ropes, and once more they
held fast. Over and over, the whip crossed his back, pain exploding through
him until Edred's voice died out and all around him faded.

A riel stretched and yawned. She reached out for her husband, but met
only emptiness.

"Valteri?"

Had he left her without saying good-bye?

Nay . . . surely he wouldn't have done that.

Why not? You've done it to him enough.

Afraid that he might have gone, she stepped from the bed and opened
the shutters. Stunned, she realized it was late afternoon.

How had she slept so late?

People rushed about below, busy with their chores and duties. But there
was no sign of Valteri among them. She left her chambers and entered the
hall.

Wace sat in one corner, carefully wiping Valteri's armor with pumice.

That relieved her instantly. There was no way he'd have left his armor
or squire behind. And if anyone knew where Valteri had gone, 'twould be
Wace.

"Good day," she called, drawing near.

Wace looked up from his task with a smile. "Good day, milady. I trust
you slept well?"

She nodded, returning his smile. "Have you seen Lord Valteri?"

"I wouldn't seek him if I were you."

She stiffened at Belial's voice. How had she missed noticing his stench?
"And why not?"

Belial paused by her side, his hands held behind his back. "He was terribly angry at you when he found you gone. Wasn't he, good Wace?"

"Aye, milord." Wace paused in his task as he looked from her to Belial.

The demon gave a wistful sigh. "He even swore he'd beat you for your actions."

Ariel scoffed at him. "He didn't seem so angry when we went to bed."

A crude smile curved Belial's lips as he raked a snide glare over her body. "Few men hold their anger when a beautiful woman lies beneath them."

She wrinkled her nose in distaste, disgusted by his crudity. "Where is he?"

Belial shrugged. "How would I know?"

"Milady?"

She faced Wace.

"He went to the stable nigh on an hour ago to check on his horse. I haven't seen him since."

"Thank you, good Wace." Turning around, she found Belial blocking her path. "Excuse me." She tried to step past him, but he refused.

A tremor of fear shook her body.

What was the demon up to? Something must be amiss.

A knowing light glowed in his eyes. "Remember, he can't die unless he does so in your arms," he whispered.

How could she forget?

Suddenly, she caught his meaning. Valteri was in danger! Ariel started to leave, then paused. If she sought him, would that cause his death?

And yet she felt a pressing need to find him and make certain nothing had happened to him.

An entirely new fear seized her. Could Valteri die even without her present? What if he was merely injured?

By not going, would she cause his death?

Go to him.

There was no mistaking Raziel's voice. "Wace, come with me!" Lifting the hem of her kirtle, she ran for the stable.

As soon as she reached it, she pushed against the doors, but they held fast. Panic ripped through her.

Something was wrong, terribly, terribly wrong.

Wace joined her and he, too, tried to open the doors. "They're locked?"

"Is there another way inside?"

"Aye, milady. There's a small door in the rear."

Determined to find it, she hurried around to the back. Wace rushed ahead and had it opened by the time she got there.

He waited for her, and together they entered.

Ariel stopped dead in her tracks. Unable to believe the sight before her, she went numb for the flicker of a heartbeat, then anger pounded through her.

"Nay!" she roared.

"Holy Mother," Wace breathed, then crossed himself. "I shall get help!"

Ariel barely understood his words through the horror filling her.

Dazed, she raced toward her husband.

Brother Edred looked up and caught her before she reached Valteri's side.

"Milady, please!" He held her back. "You must not interfere. 'Tis God's business we're about. He must do penance for his evilness, if we're to save his soul."

Tempted to beat the imbecile, she twisted out of Edred's arms. "'Tis you who are evil! Move!" She fell to her knees and reached for Valteri.

He rested on his knees, his entire body soaked in blood. She cupped his face in her hands and raised his head.

His fevered skin burning her, she recoiled in horror. A filthy gag covered his lips.

"Milady, please do not interfere!"

The main doors burst open. She looked up to see Wace with Thorn and Shadow, leading a group of Valteri's men. They seized the three men with Brother Edred.

The friar was indignant as he fought against them. "You've damned his soul with your actions."

Shadow slapped him. "Just wait until you meet the friends I have waiting for you."

Ignoring the friar, Ariel pulled the gag from Valteri's lips. His breath fell in shallow, pain-filled gasps. "I'm so sorry."

Thorn came forward and sliced the ropes holding Valteri up. He fell into her arms and she held him close, her entire body shaking in fear of losing him.

"He's the son of Lucifer!" Brother Edred insisted. "I can prove it to you, milady."

She looked up at him, her rage dulling her sight. She wanted his heart for what he'd done. "You can't prove what isn't true!"

"Look beneath his hair and you'll see the devil's mark. Why do you think he wears it long while others of his kind wear it cropped?"

Her anger doubling, she grabbed the friar by his sleeve and forced him to kneel beside her. Cradling Valteri's head against her breast, she pulled his hair back and showed Edred what mark rested there. "'Tis the mark of a cross he bears, brother, not the devil's mark."

Brother Edred's jaw dropped, and shock darkened his eyes.

Thorn grabbed the friar by the scruff of his frock. "'Tis an innocent man you've punished, you old fool."

He exchanged a look with Shadow to let her know that the friar wouldn't get off so easily.

Her heart aching, Ariel reluctantly released her hold on Valteri and allowed his men to carry him out of the stable. Rising to her feet, she stood before the friar. "Were I you, brother, I'd worry about my own soul . . . and my hide."

She left him to Thorn and Shadow, and followed after Valteri.

Hours went by as Ariel tried to stanch the flow of blood and brewed poultices to fight infection.

Valteri remained unconscious. He couldn't die, not like this.

Long after the hall had settled down to sleep, Ariel left Wace to watch over Valteri, while she went to seek Belial.

During the last hour she'd tended her husband, a new way to break the curse had come to her.

One she'd never thought of.

Though the mere thought of it terrified her, she realized this price was one she could afford.

Ariel found Belial in the little garden outside the main hall. She drew her cloak tighter about her, amazed he could stand the coldness as yet another chill wind blew across her face and took her breath.

Without a cloak for warmth, he sat on a wooden bench, staring up at the sky. "'Tis a lovely view, isn't it?" he asked as she drew near.

Ariel glanced up, shocked he would even notice. "I couldn't care less for the view this night."

"Nay, I guess you couldn't." He looked at her, his red, glowing eyes unreadable. "How is he?"

She stiffened at his audacity. "Why do you even ask?"

He shrugged and looked back at the stars. "Valteri is an exceptional opponent."

"Is that all people are to you?"

He laughed, and tilted his head back. "Look who's accusing *me* of callousness. The little psychopomp?" Sitting up straight, he pierced her with a malicious glare. "At least I don't dump their miserable souls in the respective hells. I'm not the one they cling to and *beg* for forgiveness. How many souls have you left to final agony?"

She swallowed, his words hitting a little too close to home. "None. That's not my job."

"No. You hand them over to fight in an army where they're nothing but sacrificed pawns."

She winced at a truth she didn't want to face. "I have no choice."

"And neither do I."

Not wanting to think about that, Ariel approached him, and, in spite of the part of her that urged her to flee, she sat down beside him. "What is it like to be damned?"

He quirked an eyebrow at her question. "Well, it's not fun."

"I'm serious, Belial. What's it like in Azmodea?"

"You cannot imagine." The bitterness in his voice took her off guard.

"Why not?" she whispered, wondering what it was like in the place he and Thorn called home.

"Because there's nothing like it in this world or in yours. There's no place where you're safe. No one you can call friend."

She nodded, her heart pounding in fear and remorse. "Do you ever regret what you've done?"

Belial looked at her, his red eyes haunting in their pain. "I regret every decision I've ever made." He stiffened as if suddenly aware of her for the first time, and again he looked up. "So, what brings you out here?"

Ariel drew a deep breath for courage. "I have something to ask of you."

"Of me?" He laughed incredulously. "I find it hard to believe that you would deign to ask me for a favor."

"Believe what you will, but here I am."

"So you are, Arel." He chewed his lip and glanced her way. "What is it that you want?"

"A trade." Then she rushed on with her practiced words before she lost the courage to utter them. "If I willingly give you my soul, will you spare Valteri's life?"

CHAPTER 25

elial sat straight up, his attention finally on her. Could it really be *this* easy? "You jest."

"Nay," she breathed, her voice scant more than a whisper. "But you must never let Valteri know of this!"

Stunned, he stared at her. "Does he really mean so much to you?"

She didn't have to answer. He saw it clearly in her eyes.

Aye, he did.

What the hell?

"You are a fool, Arel."

No one and nothing was worth one minute in Azmodea. Especially given what Grim had in store for her.

Her cheeks brightened in the darkness. "Is it a deal?"

He nodded. "Of course."

She let out a relieved breath. "Thank you," she whispered, rubbing the chills on her arms.

Belial opened his mouth to respond, then shut it.

How the fuck could he answer that?

Thank you?

For what?

Destroying her? Feeding her to one of the greatest monsters ever created?

Why?

Because she *dared to love the unlovable*?

He was completely flummoxed. Who would hand themselves over to their enemies to be led into hell?

To be raped?

His memories surged through him.

As did his rage. *Better she suffer than you!*

No one would weep if he suffered. No one would care at all.

But they would if she did.

Because she's decent and doesn't prey on others.

Because she cares.

Damn it all to hell. . . .

He leaned his head back and roared in fury. "I can't do it!" Furious at all of them, he met her gaze. "You fucking little bitch! I have to tell you the truth."

"Pardon?"

Growling, he rose up and grimaced, wanting to cut her throat, and knowing that not even he was that evil. "If I take you to Azmodea, they plan to breed you with the Malachai."

Her jaw went slack. "Pardon?"

He paused to meet her astonished gaze. "You heard me, sunshine."

"But what about the curse?"

Belial snorted. Then, before she could move, he pulled out a dagger and sliced her throat. "Fuck that, too."

Ariel gasped and touched her stinging neck, but where blood should have been pouring, there was nothing save smooth skin.

She looked up at him in horror. "What is this?"

He replaced the dagger in his belt and shrugged nonchalantly.

Looking away as if the matter bored him, he sighed. "You're still immortal, babe. Something not even I thought about until I was having a conversation with Death in hell."

Flabbergasted, she gaped. "I don't understand. I have hurt myself since I've been here. I have—"

"But you've never once bled."

She opened her mouth to deny it, then clamped it shut. He was right. When her mare had thrown her in the snow, she'd only been bruised. No blood had fallen.

Why hadn't she thought of that?

Because she wasn't human.

Agony and hopelessness invaded her heart, her soul. Was there truly no way to save Valteri?

"You told me the curse could be broken."

Belial snorted. "I never said those words. You told yourself that. I merely offered to barter. You drew your own conclusions and I let you. Nearly every word out of my mouth has been a lie of some sort, and you fell for each and every one. You, my Arel, are far too naïve."

Stiffening at his insult, she narrowed her eyes. "Why are you telling me this *now*?"

Belial studied his hands. "I'm an evil bastard, but even I'm still capable of feelings. I've never minded claiming humans like Edred who bring their damnation on by their own actions, or even the ones who were stupid enough to fall to my temptations, but you . . ."

He ground his teeth and moved away.

She caught his hand and held him by her side. "What about me?"

Emotions played across his handsome face and she longed to call them by name, but their source eluded her.

Finally, he sighed again. "You're the only truly altruistic creature I've ever seen. No matter how much I would love to hand you over to that bastard and bitch I serve, I can't. Grim made me realize that. Even if it means my ass. I can't let them do to you what they did to Seth. What they've done to so many." He cursed himself under his breath. "I take back what I said. Valteri isn't the biggest idiot ever born. I am."

Stunned, she could do nothing save stare at him. Was this merely another of his lies to manipulate her? "And I'm supposed to believe you?"

He shrugged. "Believe what you will. Just leave me in peace." With a grimace, he twisted his arm from her grip. "Go back to your husband, Arel."

Disgusted with himself, Belial left her and walked to the other side of the keep.

How could he be so stupid? She'd handed herself over to him and he'd handed her right back.

I deserve what I get.

Sitting down on a fallen log, he leaned forward and hung his head in his hands. Perhaps it'd been the peaceful night that had weakened him. Ariel had caught him in a pensive mood and he'd confessed to her.

Damn him for his stupidity!

"You already are."

He looked up to find Grim standing over him. "I'm in no mood to deal with you this night."

Grim backhanded him.

Belial recoiled from the blow, his face burning. He changed to his demon form and lunged for Grim, but it did no good.

"I've always said that you were too tenderhearted for your missions. But Kadar wouldn't listen. He liked your pranks too much. Thank you for finally proving to him what you really are."

Belial tried to loosen the grip on his throat. "Release me!"

Grim tightened his hold even more. "I've come with a directive straight from your masters. Kill the Norman and bring them the Arel or you'll be enslaved to me, personally."

He dropped him.

Belial choked and coughed, his throat burning as if the very coals of Hephaestus's forge were wedged in the base of his esophagus.

"Personally, I don't care which you choose. Either way, I win. You were a fool, Belial. You had Kadar's favor and you traded it for the blood of Michael!"

Belial reached for him, but he vanished.

Of course he vanished.

Leaning his head back against the ground, he listened to the gentle sounds of the night, the breeze drifting through leaves. So much for compassion.

No good deed goes unpunished.

What now? He ran through his accomplices.

It really was their ass or his.

Ethbert was gone. Mildred had been converted, and Edred had failed. All his pawns had been effectively neutralized.

Where did that leave him?

Between Kadar's fist and Azura's backhand.

Sighing, he knew he had no choice.

Betrayal as always.

"Sorry, Ariel. That's life."

For three days, Ariel stayed with Valteri while his fever raged. Since his injuries covered his back, they'd been forced to lay him on his stomach, which made it almost impossible to feed him.

She prayed for his recovery before starvation took his life.

Mildred stood at the table, mixing herbs and uttering her own prayers. "Here, milady." She handed Ariel a goblet. "This should break the fever."

She hesitated.

Shame filled Mildred's gaze as she realized why. "I swear I didn't poison it." The old woman took a drink of it to prove it was untainted before she handed it back to her.

"Sorry."

Mildred patted her on the arm. "I understand your mistrust. I've earned it."

Grateful that Mildred was still trying to make up for what she'd done, Ariel gently guided the drink into Valteri as best she could. But so very little of it actually made it inside him from this position. "Oh, Mildred, what are we to do?"

Sighing, Mildred shook her head. "I know not, Lady Ariel. I've tried to find some way to break the curse and heal him, but nothing has worked."

A soft knock interrupted them.

"Enter," Ariel called.

The door opened and Brother Edred stepped in. The bitter taste of hatred scalded her throat. "What brings *you* here?"

He swallowed, his fat jowls flopping.

Clearing his throat, he gave her a baleful look. "I've come to make peace. For days, I've fasted and prayed until a voice told me to come and apologize."

She knew the source of that voice.

His conscience.

Or Belial playing some other game with all of them again.

"I made a mistake, milady. I falsely accused an innocent man and now he may die because of it."

Ariel opened her mouth to order him from the room, but she paused. Over Brother Edred's shoulder, she saw Thorn and Shadow. The smirk on Shadow's face said that he might have had something to do with this rather than Belial.

Edred took a step and gulped. "Can you ever forgive me for what I've done?"

"It's not me you need to win over, brother. It's Lord Valteri and a much higher power. But if you wish to offer a prayer for milord and his recovery, then I'll welcome it."

With a sad smile, he moved to the bed and sank down on his knees.

While he prayed, she stepped out into the hall so that she could visit with her "brothers" and still watch him.

She narrowed her gaze on Shadow. "What did you do?"

He flashed one of his cockier grins. "I find that when someone believes in demons, they should occasionally meet a real one."

Thorn rolled his eyes. "We've tried for centuries to do something with him. Believe it or not, this is him improved."

She laughed at them. "Well, I welcome the change you wrought in the man and his stupidity. If only you could do that with more people."

Shadow shrugged. "I do my best. Sadly, there's just so damn many of them who need attitude adjustments." He slid his gaze meaningfully over to Thorn.

"There's nothing wrong with my attitude. 'Tis my company that's insufferable most of the time."

"Ouch! You bastard."

Ariel shook her head at their bantering. She knew they were jesting, otherwise they'd be bleeding.

Letting out a sigh, she lowered her voice before she spoke again. "Have either of you seen Belial?"

They shook their heads.

"He . . . tried to cut my throat."

Shadow gaped while Thorn's gaze narrowed dangerously.

She held her hand up to calm them both. "It's not what you think. I offered him my soul and he did it to show me that I'm still immortal."

Thorn scowled. "What the bloody hell?"

"I know. Then he refused to take my soul. He said that he would rather face Kadar and Azura, and their wrath, than hand me over to them."

Shadow snorted. "He's an idiot. No offense, Ariel. You're sweet and all that, but my mother will tear him apart."

Thorn nodded in agreement. "My father isn't known for his forgiveness. Especially when he wants something."

"I know. That's why I'm telling you this."

Sighing, Shadow crossed his arms over his chest. "What was he thinking?"

"I don't know."

Suddenly, a deep, ragged breath drew Ariel's attention back to the room and the bed.

"Oh my God!" She left them and went rushing back inside, past the kneeling friar.

Valteri shifted slightly on the mattress, and slowly opened his eyes.

Relief poured through her as she fell to her knees next to the bed. The friar got up and moved away.

Her heart hammered as she reached a shaking hand to touch Valteri's fevered cheek.

"There you are, my precious." Nothing had ever been more beautiful than the sight of his open, dual-colored eyes, with their lucid intelligence staring back at her.

She heard the door close.

Looking over, she realized Brother Edred and Mildred had both made a discreet exit.

Shadow and Thorn must have remained in the hall, as well.

Valteri tried to push himself up, but Ariel stopped him. "Please, don't. You'll hurt yourself."

He dropped himself back to the mattress and released a weary sigh.

"How do you feel?"

He answered her with a pain-filled grimace. "Like my horse not only trampled me, but that he brought friends along this time to help."

Smiling, she brushed a lock of hair out of his eyes.

"So, what happened to the bastards?"

Anger mixed with pain. She didn't need Valteri to explain which bastards he asked about. "They were all beaten and banished, per your brother's laws. And Brother Edred . . ."

Ariel paused, unsure how to tell him.

"You released him." As a member of the clergy, he wasn't supposed to be harmed.

Ariel wrinkled her nose. She hadn't exactly followed King William's dictates. "I surrendered his punishment to Thorn and Shadow. I'm told he's had some rather unpleasant dreams and visitations from those he fears."

He snorted at that, then reached out a hand and took hers. His weak grip brought a wave of guilt to her that she hadn't done more.

"'Tis fine what you did, milady. My kingly brother would have been sorely vexed had you broken his law and harmed the friar—even for me. Never mind what my brother the bishop would have done."

"Then you're not angry?"

A light came to his eyes, and if Ariel didn't know better, she'd swear he smiled. "I'm not angry. At least not at you."

As Valteri returned to health, Ariel began to suspect that the curse was broken, as nothing else happened to him.

Nothing.

No more close calls. Not even a pimple.

Even Thorn and Shadow thought it odd that peace stayed with them.

If only they knew for certain.

Several times, she'd tried to consult Belial, but he refused to speak further on the matter. Which made her think that the curse must still be holding, otherwise he'd have left them.

Wouldn't he?

And because he stayed, Thorn and Shadow seldom left her side.

Valteri's back healed rather quickly, but even so he was in no condition for travel to London. And though she wished him far from her and any harm that her presence might incur, she also enjoyed their days together, grateful for every touch and glance he gave her.

Now Valteri sat before her in a large tub the servants had brought into their chambers and filled with steaming water.

As carefully as she could, she sponged his bruised back. Most of the cuts had healed, but fresh scars attested to the brutality of his attack.

Again, she found the incongruity so peculiar. "How is it that you bleed like this, but not in battle?"

He shrugged. "No idea. It's just always been so."

It made no sense to her that weapons couldn't harm him, but that other items could.

Ariel traced one of the scars with her fingertip, her heart aching at how many times he'd been so abused in his life. She'd give anything to remove every such vicious scar and memory from him.

Running her hand down his back, she marveled at the velvety smooth texture over his hardened muscles. Chills sprang up beneath her caress and she smiled at his reaction.

"Careful, Ariel." Valteri turned his head to look at her over his shoulder. "You're tempting me beyond my endurance."

Her smile widened. "You shouldn't make such empty threats."

"Empty threats?" He was aghast. "Madame, I assure you 'tis not empty."

She cocked an eyebrow at his double meaning, and pleasure rippled in her stomach. Before she could move, he ran his hand under her hair and pulled her forward until his lips claimed hers.

Ariel moaned with pleasure, delighting in the feel of his soft mouth. She opened her lips and drew him in. Nothing had ever tasted finer, ever felt better.

His kiss deepening, he again pulled on her, and before she could protest, he had her in his lap in the tub. She stiffened with a cry of protest. "You've soaked me!"

One corner of his mouth turned up. "I thought you'd gladly hurl yourself into a lake for my attentions?"

Ariel laughed at his memory and thought about the night she'd uttered that statement. Her blood warmed. He'd changed so much since then, as had she. But she decided she liked the difference in his personality.

"Mayhap I've changed my mind."

"Have you now?" His voice deepened with desire.

She opened her mouth to respond and once more he kissed her. Ariel wrapped her arms about his shoulders, sliding her hands down his spine. A thousand flames ignited in her stomach and her body throbbed. He felt so good in her arms.

With a tight groan, Valteri lifted the hem of her wet kirtle to remove it from her body and ran his hands over her bare buttocks and hips. Fire ran through her veins. His wet caresses sent shivers over her and her body demanded him.

Ariel gasped and adjusted her legs until she straddled him.

Her heart pounded in her ears as her lower body came into contact with his. Valteri sucked his breath between his teeth, and closed his eyes as he slid himself inside her.

Ariel smiled at his reaction, reveling in her power over him. She buried her lips in his neck, tasting the salty stubble of his throat, and pressed herself closer to him and rode him.

He dropped her kirtle to the floor, where it landed with a splat. Ariel laughed at the sound, but her humor fled as he touched her breast. Leaning her head back, she bit her lip as his mouth played upon her, and the throbbing increased. She held his head in her hands and moaned with pleasure.

Ariel gripped the sides of the tub, her body afire as he thrust against her. Her breathing labored, she looked into his eyes and the love that shone there sent another wave of chills over her.

He dipped his hands in the water and caressed her lower hips. "Stay with me, Ariel," he whispered, leaning forward until he kissed the flesh just below her ear. His warm breath on her neck sent shivers streaming down her arms. "I know I have no right to ask, but I can't let you go."

Ariel closed her eyes against the agony his plea brought.

He moved his hips against hers and she clenched her teeth at the searing pleasure that overshadowed her sadness. She wanted him, longed for his presence.

How could she deny his request when 'twas her own fondest desire that she stay by his side?

She couldn't. "I shall stay with you, milord. No matter what comes on the morrow, I will remain by your side and not force you to leave."

Valteri pulled back, his body rigid. "Ariel?" He blinked as if he couldn't believe he'd heard her correctly.

She laid her hand against his cheek. "You heard me, Lord Valteri fitz-Jaden."

Cocking his head, he gave her a suspicious look.

She smoothed his furrowed brow with her fingers. "But you must promise that you'll stay and never leave."

"On that, you have my word. Forever." He pulled her back into his arms and crushed her with a fierce hug until she was forced to cry out. "Milord, please!"

Suddenly, he rose from the tub.

Oblivious to the water dripping from them, he carried her to the bed and laid her on it. Ariel stared up at him, her heart pounding.

His hair cascading over her like a wet cloak, Valteri pulled her legs around his waist and again slid inside her.

She trembled, needing him, afraid that tomorrow would tear them apart.

But she'd given her pledge, and she intended to stand by it. She held him close to her heart.

All her worries fled and she concentrated on the smell of his sweet skin, the taste of his flesh.

Over and over, he thrust against her, and she raised her hips to meet him. Her body tingled and throbbed and before she could beg for more, she found her release.

Crying out, she tightened her hold on his arms.

With two more thrusts, he joined her. His breathing labored, he collapsed on top of her.

Ariel moaned in satisfaction, her body still pulsing. Running her hand over his back, she smiled.

Valteri nibbled her neck, his teeth raising chills along her body. "I love you, Ariel," he whispered, then nibbled her earlobe.

Cold terror seized her and Ariel stiffened at his words. He pulled back and stared down at her. "Does that displease you?"

Tears gathering in her eyes, she shook her head. "Nay."

How could it?

But why had he uttered those words out loud?

Inside, she had a bad feeling that by saying that to her, he'd just invoked the curse.

Invoked something evil to come for them both.

Ethbert reined his horse at the castle site, his anger charged by the half-finished wall before him. A wall that further reminded him of the Norman pestilence feeding on his people.

It was time they rid themselves of the rats.

He'd gathered Saxons all the way from his sister's home to Ravenswood. Good Saxon men chased from their lands and fields by the Norman filth.

While not as large an army as he'd have liked, they were still numerous enough to finish the task ahead of them.

To annihilate the filth entrenched here.

Ethbert scanned their dour faces and he thought of what the Normans had put them through.

What the Normans had robbed them of.

Safety. Home. Peace.

Loved ones.

Suddenly, an image of his sister's sweet, innocent face swept before his eyes. His stomach tightened in grief and rage. She'd died because of *them*.

Norman dogs had taken her home, killed her husband, then their leader had forced her to live as his concubine. Raped and degraded by her position, she'd severed the veins in her wrists.

Fucking bastards!

They'd taken everything from him.

Ethbert tightened his grip on his reins. He hadn't been able to rescue his sister, but he vowed to save Ariel.

He refused to see her meet his sister's fate.

Come the morrow, he'd take the Norman's head and use it to decorate his home just as his ancestors had done!

CHAPTER 26

Valteri watched his men training. He'd tried for a time to exercise himself, but his back was still too stiff. Too sore for him to do more than a few strokes of the sword.

A flutter of red caught in the corner of his eye. He turned his head and watched Ariel cross the yard.

She looked just as she had on the day they'd met. Like an angel. A group of children surrounded her and she laughed with them, her face more beauteous than any creature ever born.

Heat rushed through his body, inflaming his loins.

Without thinking, he took a step toward her, intending to seize her in his arms and carry her back to their chambers.

But before he could cross the distance, an unfamiliar rider came through the gate. Frowning, he stared at the serf astride a mule. He remembered seeing the boy tilling a field with his father, who lived not far from the castle site.

He paused as the boy stopped before one of his servants and leaned down to talk. The servant gestured toward him and the boy followed the line of his arm and nodded.

What the hell?

Valteri waited for his approach.

The boy rushed forward. "Lord Valteri?"

"Aye."

"My father bade me fetch you. There are men destroying the castle wall on the hill, and setting fire to our fields. My father begs you come quick, milord!"

His sight dimming in rage, Valteri called to his men to assemble.

He ran toward the stable, but before he could enter, Ariel caught up to him. "What is it?"

Valteri opened his mouth to speak, then paused.

Masking his emotions, he realized she'd only worry if she knew the truth. So he chose to keep her from needless stress. After all, he'd never been harmed in battle.

Weapons couldn't harm him.

He had more to fear walking across the hall than riding into battle.

His mind racing, he searched for a quick lie. What could he tell her . . . ?

An idea struck him. With any luck, she wouldn't know construction of the castle had stopped for the winter.

'Twas at least worth trying. "The builder needs assistance with his work. I'm taking some men to see if we can help."

"Should I wait supper on you?" Her ready acceptance of his lie brought guilt to his heart.

It was for her own good.

Valteri shook his head. "Nay. If I'm not back, eat without me."

She nodded. "Then take care, milord. I'll see you anon." She stood up on her tiptoes to kiss his cheek.

Valteri watched her walk away, his face tingling.

Damn it, he'd much rather take her to bed than deal with this. Clenching his teeth, he forced his mind to the coming task and promised himself that on his return, he'd carry out what he'd originally intended.

Bedding his wife.

After the midday meal and after Thorn and Shadow had ridden off to join her husband, Ariel decided to take the men a bite of food while they worked. She didn't know what kind of provisions they had up on the hill, but they probably were not enough for all the extra men Valteri had summoned.

Not to mention, Shadow, alone, could eat a horse.

The cook wrapped leftovers in plain pieces of cloth and packed her saddlebags, while the groom saddled a palfrey.

The groom helped her into her seat.

With a smile, she thanked him.

Whispering to the mare to take care and not frighten or throw her, Ariel urged the small horse across the yard and out the gate.

The weather was pleasant and crisp, and she decided she couldn't wait to see the coming spring and what new beauty it would bring to the land.

She hummed to herself as she rode toward the new site.

It didn't take long to reach the hill.

Yet as she drew closer, her stomach shrank at the last thing she expected.

The sounds of battle.

Of men dying in war.

The wind blew an acrid black smoke around her that choked her and burned her eyes. The scent of burning flesh was unmistakable and it brought tears to her eyes.

Just as the sound of clashing steel and moans of the dying.

Terrified and filled with disbelief, Ariel dismounted so that she could stare at the horror. 'Twas no honest work they were about!

Fierce battle raged all around her.

Though her mind screamed at her to run, she couldn't move, couldn't take her eyes off the horrifying sight before her as the men tried to kill each other.

"M ilady, why do you come?"

Valteri froze at the familiar voice, a voice he hadn't heard since the day his angel had been carried into his hall and laid at his feet.

His heart pounding, he turned in his saddle and saw Ariel rising out of the billowing smoke and standing in the center of the Saxon men. Wind whipped her cloak and pale hair around her body.

Just as it'd been in his dreams.

The Saxons rallied around her as if to protect her.

Without thinking, Valteri whirled his horse about, trying to reach her, but the men around him prevented it.

Thorn headed for him while Shadow dispatched the man he was fighting and started for Ariel.

A shadow passed over his body. Valteri turned in his saddle, expecting the sword to slice his thigh as it'd always done in his dream.

Only this time, it wasn't his thigh they aimed for. His stroke too low, his attacker's wooden pitchfork bounced off his blade and straight into his heart.

Valteri gasped at the sudden pain that seeped through his chest. His sight dulling, he fell from his saddle.

"T he Norman bastard is dead!"

Ariel flinched as that fetid cry went up among the Saxon men.

"Nay!" she screamed, knowing who must have fallen.

She picked up the hem of her kirtle and ran across the field. Men scattered from her path, staring at her as if her presence frightened them even more than the demons they feared.

"Ariel!"

She heard Shadow's call, but paid no heed as she continued to race across the fallen bodies, searching for the familiar form and colors of her husband.

Maybe he hadn't fallen.

Mayhap he was . . .

Then, she saw him.

And Thorn, who was holding him in his arms.

Valteri's light blond braid was coated with blood. His helm and sword were next to him where Thorn must have placed them.

Screaming out in denial, she ran to his side.

This isn't real.

Her mind refused to accept what her eyes saw.

But as she fell to her knees beside them, she knew it was no dream. Anguish twisted through her body. Tears filled her eyes and her heart shattered.

How? How could this have happened? He was never harmed in battle.

Thorn met her gaze and snarled. "A fucking pitchfork. Seriously?"

Shadow winced as he stood above them. "Why do we protect humans, again?"

"Ariel?" Valteri's hoarse voice was scarce more than a croak as he squeezed her hand.

"Shh." She used a corner of her cloak to wipe the red blood from his lips. From his pale cheeks. "You must save your strength."

"Nay, 'tis mortal." His accepting words ripped her soul asunder. He reached his hand up and touched her cheek. A slow smile spread across his face. "'Tis as wondrous as I thought."

She frowned at him and the misplaced happiness in his gaze. "What is?"

"Dying in your arms."

Closing her eyes against the sudden wave of agony, she held on to him, willing him to live. "You can't leave me," she whispered. "I won't let you."

Rage filled her as she grabbed Thorn's shoulder. "Do something! Heal him!"

"I don't have those powers. Conceived in deception. Born for destruction."

"Shadow?" Adidiron was his father. Surely, he could do something.

"I'll get Acheron. Hold on." Oblivious to the humans around them, he vanished.

Ariel bit her lip. "Did you hear that? Shadow has help coming. Just hold on, my love."

Valteri cupped her cheek and smiled. "I . . ."

The light faded from his eyes and his hand fell from her face.

"Nay!" she screamed.

This was not how he would end.

This was not how she'd let it end.

Suddenly, she felt a burning inside her as her powers returned.

All around her, psychopomps appeared, claiming souls.

She saw them so clearly.

Ariel looked up and met the sad eyes of Raziel, who'd come for Valteri's.

Hollow and aching, Ariel rose to her feet. She would not allow this to happen. With a courage she'd never had before, she faced her brother and willed Valteri's soul back into his body.

"You can't do this, Ariel." Raziel stood firm before her. "You know the rules and the limits of your power."

"You're not taking him. I will not allow this!"

"You can't stop it." Raziel held out his hand for Valteri.

With a confused expression, his soul rose up from his body and reached for Raziel.

Nay. Nay. Nay!

Desperation filled her. She would not allow them to steal the life and soul of an innocent man. He had suffered too much to have this be his ending.

"You're not taking him!" she repeated.

Before Raziel could move, she grabbed the one thing she knew would end this. . . .

The dagger from Thorn's side.

Without a second thought or hesitation, she plunged it deep into her own heart.

Pain spread through her like fire.

"No!" Raziel screamed.

Thorn cursed as he caught her in her arms. "What have you done!"

"I can't let him pay for my sins."

Thorn winced. "You have no idea what you're doing. You fucking idiot."

In spite of those harsh words, Thorn's hold was tender. His expression kind and pain-filled. He may have been demonspawn, but he was a gentle being.

"I know what I'm doing. I'm letting the better soul live." Feeling more at peace than she ever had, she felt the pain drain from her body.

And everything stopped.

Ariel floated up, and once again her wings flapped behind her.

With a deep breath, she stared down in amazement. Thorn still held her next to Valteri's body.

The sight of her husband's undeserved death filled her with an unexpected rage. Something that shouldn't have been possible while she was in her Arel form.

Yet she felt it now. It was raw and palpable, and made her want to rip apart everyone who had a hand in it.

For the first time, she understood Ethbert's fury.

And Mildred's.

Their need for vengeance and for justice. It flowed through her and it took everything she had not to lash out at those around her.

But she wouldn't be that person.

Valteri had taught her to be better than the abusers. He'd risen above, and she refused to dishonor so noble a heart.

So instead, she narrowed her gaze on Raziel.

"Don't interfere, Ariel."

Don't interfere. He was as crazy as they'd accused her if he thought for one second that she was going to allow him to complete this mission.

"Sorry, brother. I must."

Before Raziel could stop her, she broke his hold on Valteri.

Grabbing both of Valteri's wrists, she pulled him away and turned with him.

In these forms, Valteri should have no memory of her. He shouldn't be able to see anything more than where he was heading.

Yet he focused on her with utter clarity.

"Ariel?"

The tenderness in that one word wrung her heart and brought tears to her eyes.

She loved him more than she'd ever thought to love anyone. Touching his face, she grimaced at how cold his skin was. "I'm sorry, Valteri, but it's better this way. Please forgive me."

"Don't you do it, Ariel!" Raziel shouted.

Ignoring him, she kissed Valteri's lips one last time. "I love you, Valteri the Godless. Never forget me." Then, she shoved his soul back into his body.

Valteri jerked awake, his entire body aching.

"'Tis a miracle!" Wace shouted, his youthful face beaming. "I thought you were dead, milord."

Shaken and uncertain, Valteri ran his hand over his chest. It'd been a direct strike.

Straight through his heart. His mail was torn where the pitchfork had pierced his chest, but no other mark existed to prove he'd ever been wounded.

Looking around him, Valteri realized that his men had defeated the Saxons. And a few feet away, he spied the body of Ethbert. He shook his head and sighed. Though he held no great love for the Saxon, he regretted the end the poor man had come to.

Moans filled his ears as his men searched the bodies and gathered the wounded.

Then, his gaze fell to Thorn beside him. . . .

To the body Thorn held in his arms.

Nay . . .

Excruciating agony ripped through him, piercing his heart and scalding his soul.

Please, not this!

Anything but this.

He forgot everything else as he scrambled toward Ariel. With a trembling hand, he took his wife's body from Thorn and cradled her against his chest. Tears filled his eyes as he inhaled the sweet rose scent.

'Twas no dream.

Ariel had saved him. Her words circled his mind like beasts of prey seeking to bring him low.

And bring him low they did. Raw, brutal grief ripped through him as he realized the price she'd paid.

What she'd done for a worthless piece of shit.

"I love you, Valteri the Godless," her gentle words whispered in his mind, slicing his soul with agony.

Valteri clutched her body tight, willing her back to life as tears flowed down his cheeks. "Don't leave me, Ariel. Please."

His heart shattering, he glared at Thorn. "Do something!"

"There's nothing I can do. I can't interfere with free will."

"Then you're useless."

Thorn let out a bitter laugh. "More than you know." Rising to his feet, he sighed. "If you—"

"Just go! All of you have done enough."

They had done what no one had ever done. All those years the monks had tried so hard and failed.

Now . . .

He was finally broken.

A riel stood before her father and his council, her head sedately bowed. By the stern look on his face, she knew she'd long outworn his patience.

Even now, Kadar was demanding they hand her over since she'd broken countless rules. She was his prize and he wanted her.

"You know we're not to interfere with human life!" He circled around her with a glare that should have left her a smoldering pile on the floor.

"Aye."

"Then why did you push his soul back into his body?"

Ariel swallowed. One of the worst parts about having been human, she still had human emotions, and now it was hard to rein in her feelings. So while she felt a degree of remorse for breaking their strict rules, the moment she thought of Valteri, all guilt vanished.

For him, she'd do it again.

And that defiance was pissing off everyone around her.

Constantly.

"Ariel? You haven't answered me."

"What do you want me to say? I couldn't let him die. It wasn't right, and I loved him too much to stand by and do nothing."

Michael growled at her.

"I would apologize, but it wouldn't be sincere." Ariel moved forward and again bowed her head. "I'm ready for my punishment. I'm aware that Belial is supposed to take me to Azmodea for what I've done. Go ahead."

The look on her father's face had to be similar to the one on hers when Raziel had shown up for Valteri's soul.

Though to be honest, Belial didn't look as pleased about this as he should have. He and Thorn, along with Shadow, were off to the left, and they all had the same tired expression.

Sneering, Sraosha flicked his wings. "She has to go, Michael. We have to do our duty. No one can be immune. Not even your daughter."

"Wait!"

She frowned as Gabriel appeared and pulled her father aside, out of her hearing.

Nervous, she glanced over to Thorn and Belial, neither of whom would meet her gaze.

What were they talking about?

Obviously, it was her, as Gabriel kept gesturing in her direction.

Nervous and unsure, she wished she had some clue as to what was going on.

Could they be planning something worse than sending her to Azmodea?

Was there anything worse?

That very thought sent a shiver down her spine.

After several terrifying moments, they moved to stand in front of her.

Gabriel stepped forward and Ariel flinched, half expecting him to motion for Belial.

Instead, he inclined his head toward the Arel behind her.

Bracing herself for her trip to the worst of the hell realms, she drew a ragged breath.

"Come, Ariel." Raziel took her by the arm and her wings dissolved.

She was losing her wings? That wouldn't happen for a trip to Azmodea.

Confused, she looked at her father. "I'm being banished?"

Her father nodded. "For a time, or for eternity depending on the choices you make." He turned his back to her.

"I don't understand." But he refused to say anything more.

In fact, no one would say a word.

What the . . .

Ariel bit her lip to keep from pleading for mercy. She'd known the consequences for her actions, and the least she could do was meet them bravely.

Like Valteri would do.

For him, she'd condemned herself. Whatever her fate, she would face it with the same courage she'd learned from him. And regret nothing.

Not as long as he lived free.

But why wasn't Belial or Thorn escorting her?

This didn't make any sense.

"Where are you taking me?" she asked Raziel.

His eyes grim, Raziel pulled her from the room. "To a fate worse than death."

Valteri sat in his chair, holding Cecile in his lap. She purred contentedly and he wished he could be so easily soothed. Once again, pain was all he knew and he had no hope of anything better.

Over and over, he saw his Ariel in all her beauty and kindness reaching out to him.

Why had she forced him back into his body?

Why couldn't she have allowed him to die and be free from the misery of this life, once and for all?

"Valteri?"

He froze at the sound, his heart stilling. When he heard no more, he sighed. "Now I'm even hearing her voice."

"Can you feel my touch?"

A hand brushed his cheek.

Valteri sprang from his chair and he swung around with a gasp. Cecile let out an indignant yowl as she fell from his lap and landed on the cold floor.

His heart pounding, Valteri blinked, unable to believe his sight. "Ariel?"

A smile curved her lips and she reached for him. "Aye."

Seizing her in his arms, he held her tight. "Are you truly here?"

She laughed in his ear, the sound sending waves of joy through him. "Aye. My father returned me."

"But how? Why?"

Her smile melted his heart. "Thorn. He not only convinced his father to release me, but he worked out a deal for Belial. Since I'd broken so many rules, the others didn't know what to do with me and my defiant ways. It's hard to be an Arel once you've been corrupted by human emotions. So, here I am." She touched his cheek, and he marveled at the warmth of her flesh.

A sudden pain replaced his joy. "For how long?"

She sighed heavily. "Hard to say. The gods are cruel beasts."

"What do you mean?"

"My father, bastard that he is, thought the worst punishment imaginable would be to tie my life to yours." She smiled at him. "So take care, Valteri fitzJaden. You not only have my heart. You have my life in your hands, too."

"And I will spend eternity making sure no one ever again threatens either."

EPILOGUE

Ariel sat at banquet and held her daughter out toward her *god*father, the Dark-Hunter Acheron. Tall and lean, he had long dark hair and mercury eyes that swirled like a stormy sea.

The babe loved the Dark-Hunter leader. "Have you decided on a name yet?"

Looking up, she met Valteri's proud gaze. "Daciana."

The baby cried in protest and Acheron gently rocked her.

She wrinkled her nose. "She has her father's lungs."

Valteri smiled. "A good thing, that. Should anyone ever bother my girl, I want everyone to know and come running."

Laughing, Acheron soothed Daciana with an unnatural ease. "Maybe next time you'll have that son you wanted."

Valteri screwed his face up. "Bah, I have no complaints with what I have. Besides, I'll have my Alexander eventually."

Ariel laughed. "I'm sure you will."

He winked at her. "But 'tis a pity that you have no Arel powers left."

She raised a brow, curious about his words. "And why is that?"

"I've a feeling that our girl shall need more than one of us to watch over her."

Ariel laughed. "If she's anything like her father, 'twill take an army to guard her." She reached for her daughter.

"Which is why I'm here." Acheron surrendered her.

Shadow stopped beside them, then stepped back. "I think that kid has passed her expiration date."

She scowled. "Pardon?"

"She's rotten. What did you feed her to make her smell like that? Sheez! I've smelled two-year-old garbage that was less foul."

Mildred tsked as she stepped forward. "Here, milady. I'll change her." She skimmed a peeved grimace over Shadow. "And I don't want to be knowing how it is that you were sniffing around two-year-old garbage."

Acheron laughed.

Shadow was not so amused. "Go ahead and laugh, you Atlantean asshole. Have you checked *your* daughter lately?"

Acheron sobered. "Where's Simi?"

"Yeah . . . Valteri's probably missing some horses."

"Oh dear God." He went running for the doors.

Ariel shook her head at Shadow's play as she handed Daciana over. "You're terrible. Thank you, Mildred."

Mildred took the baby and headed off to change her swaddling.

Shadow passed a smirk toward Valteri. "You say that, but last I saw, Simi was getting ready to eat a couple of those, and this is a direct quote, 'yummy beasties that Akri didn't say weren't on Simi's no-eat list.'"

Valteri turned pale. "I best go check on Ganille."

"Yeah, big guy. You go do that. He was probably the first one she went for."

He rushed for the door.

Ariel shook her head. "You are such a beast, Shadow. Why do you love to rib people so?"

"I have no idea, but it's so much fun." His gaze went to an attractive maid who was eyeing him. "Speaking of . . ."

Ariel laughed as he made straight for the poor woman.

Thorn, who was off to the side of the room with Wace, exchanged an amused look with her.

Grateful for her family, Ariel saw a small shadow in the corner.

Cecile sat alone, bathing herself.

Making sure that no one was paying attention to her, Ariel went over to the cat. She picked the cat up and glanced around. Assured that the humans were occupied with other things, she placed her hand over the cat's eyes.

Her body warmed and her hand glowed.

Cecile hissed.

"Shh," Ariel soothed. Then, stroking the cat on the ears, she smiled down at the animal.

Cecile gave a yowl and her uncrossed eyes sparkled.

"There you go." She set the cat down, and watched her run across the floor in a straight line.

Someone tsked behind her.

Turning, she saw the tall, dark-haired version of Valteri standing there. He was the one who'd really worked the bargain to free her, but she wasn't allowed to tell a soul about it.

That had been part of the deal.

"You know you're not supposed to be doing that."

She smiled at her father-in-law. "I only interfered a little. Besides, 'tis not a *human* life."

Jaden shook his head. "I'm going to regret that I unbound your powers, aren't I?"

"Never." She patted his arm reassuringly. "But you should introduce yourself to your son."

"No. Trust me. It's better this way. I've too many enemies who would harm him if they knew he existed."

Which was why he'd unlocked her powers.

And Valteri's.

Her husband just hadn't learned about that yet, either.

"Besides, too many years separate us. Let him have his hatred of me and his love for you. I would rather be the bad guy." Jaden kissed her knuckles and stepped away. "Take good care of him, Ariel. Thank you for letting me know he was here."

"Don't be a stranger."

Jaden laughed. "You want me to be a stranger. Trust me. But don't worry. I'm never far away."

Good, because she had a feeling that trouble would be the same way.

But that was all right with her.

It was life, and she'd fought hard to have this one.

So she was going to savor every single moment of it. She had no idea what they'd be facing. No one ever did.

But whatever hell came for them, she'd be ready.

An Arel and a demigod.

And their daughter.

The world had no idea what it was in for.